Love & Other Lies

A Terrible Romance Novel By
M.J. Fifield

FAVORITE SPOON PUBLISHING

Printed in the United States of America
First Printing, 2020

ISBN: 978-0-9961074-6-4

Favorite Spoon Publishing, LLC
1720 Malabar Road #500509
Malabar, FL 32950

Cover Design by ebooklaunch.com

Also by M.J. Fifield

Effigy
Second Nature

For those who NaNoWriMo, we salute you.

And for Maddy, who wanted to read it first.

ACKNOWLEDGEMENTS

In November of 2009, I embarked on a two-pronged experiment: writing a romance novel during NaNoWriMo—a worldwide event where people attempt to create a 50,000-word novel in just thirty days. I had never done either of these things before and had no idea if I could.

By December 1st, I still didn't have an answer. I had written over 50,000 words, but there was neither an ending nor any romance in sight. The only thing it had going for it were two characters from whom I just couldn't walk away. Eleven short years later, I actually managed to complete their story.

Here are the amazing folks who helped me get over the finish line:

My writing community, whose comments such as "I don't want these two characters to spend any more time together" and "Are you going to put this poor character out of her misery at some point?" helped me decide where *not* to take this story.

Jacob Jordan, whose brainstorming prowess has no equal and who agreed to go on a three-hour road trip with me, even though he knew it would mean talking about the plot of this novel the entire way. Thank you for helping me figure out where *to* take this story.

Heidi and Madison Fox, whose feedback was invaluable and whose reactions to the story made my day. (I'd say I'm sorry for making you cry, but who am I kidding? I'm an author. I *live* for that response.) Thank you for your willingness to read whatever madness comes out of my head and for helping me make it better. This book would not exist without you.

And last, but certainly not least, I want to acknowledge the rest of my family and friends who continue to support this journey any way they can through every twist and turn and flight of fancy. Thank you for just going with it all these years.

I love you all.

No lie.

Love
&
OTHER
LIES

M.J. FIFIELD

1

THERE ARE FEW PLACES IN the world more miserable than the teachers' lounge at a public high school.

Logically, I know this is a gross exaggeration, but today does not feel like a day for logical thinking. Today is a day for flights of fancy and elaborate daydreams with an 'anywhere but here' theme.

Because this place is damn depressing.

The staff's private oasis is outfitted with a pair of low loveseats that are equal parts vinyl and duct tape, a selection of cafeteria tables deemed too damaged for the students' use, and the oldest appliances known to man—a refrigerator that barely deserves the name, a toaster with two settings: cold and burnt, a microwave that, on its best days, only can manage lukewarm, and an industrial coffee maker left over from the Cold War.

I'm sitting in a plastic chair with a broken back at a table in the corner—a prime spot to survey the wasteland—with a cooling mug of coffee sitting in front of me along with a stack of essays I just can't bring myself to read. Who wouldn't want to be elsewhere?

A white sand beach, sipping a cocktail adorned with a paper umbrella. At a café in Paris, enjoying a decadent dessert. On my couch with a bottle of domestic beer. The where or the what doesn't even matter. Just so long as it isn't here.

I need more coffee—hot coffee, all the coffee in the entire damn world—but our esteemed principal, John Tolliver, is blocking the way as he discusses God knows what with the World History instructor, Rex Talbot—a man so old, he probably has a first-hand account of half the events his curriculum covers. Why this particular conversation has to take place in the coffee maker's vicinity, I do not know nor appreciate, but I ogle the pot longingly until Susannah Price enters the room.

Blond and rail-thin, Susannah commands attention with her mere presence. John trails off mid-sentence, momentarily stunned by her arrival, but picks up where he left off as she makes a beeline for the coffee. She flashes me a quick smile before placing a hand on Rex's shoulder and turning on the charm. If she's not careful, she'll give the man a heart attack. I'm immediately jealous when she pours hot coffee into her mug. However, jealously gives way to revulsion when she reaches for the sugar. After living with her for the past three years, I know just how much she adds. Coffee deserves better.

Mug in hand, she heads to my table. John watches her ass as she walks away. Always keeping it classy, our principal. He doesn't notice me judging him. A not-uncommon occurrence when Susannah is your companion.

"Vinnie," she says in greeting as she sits across from me. She indicates the stack of essays. "Whatcha got there?"

If I had to hazard a guess, I would say I have a waste of paper sitting before me. Assigning an essay on the role of religion in *The Epic of Gilgamesh* seemed like a good idea at the time. Not so much anymore.

Because now I have to read each essay. Grade each essay. And not cry while doing it. It has become increasingly more difficult to achieve the last.

"Essays," I answer. "Terrible, terrible essays."

"I love your unfailingly positive outlook."

"They refuse to write a proper sentence." I pick up the essay on top of the stack. "I mean, look at this—I'm surprised it's not just one big emoji."

"The little poop one?"

I drop the essay. "I love your unfailing immaturity."

"Aww. You're so sweet."

"I am not. I'm a mean old lady."

"That's what the kids tell me."

"Why do they love you so much? You teach math, for crying out loud," I say. "Aren't kids supposed to hate math and those who teach it?"

"I guess I'm just that good."

I flick a paper clip at her. "Or that immature."

"You're right. It's probably the latter."

"Probably?"

"You know how math teachers feel about absolutes."

I really don't. Math isn't an area in which I excel. "I'm going to assume that was clever."

"I appreciate that," she says. "So, what's on the books for tonight?"

"Paper grading and lesson planning, I imagine."

"You should have been a math teacher. Far easier grading. Far less subjective."

"There's nothing subjective about good grammar."

Susannah laughs. "They should put that on a T-shirt."

I don't laugh. "Don't you have somewhere else to be?"

"Not for another"—she checks the clock on the wall behind her—"forty minutes."

I slide my mug across the table. "Then make yourself useful and get me a refill."

Susannah snorts and glances over her shoulder at John and Rex. "Are you really that afraid of small talk?"

"No talk I've ever had with John could be considered small."

"Well, maybe you should stop terrorizing the faculty."

"Well, maybe they should…" There is no way to complete that sentence. They aren't the problem. They never were. I sigh. "Please?"

Susannah reaches for the mug. "Okay. But only because you asked so nicely."

"Thank you," I call as she walks away.

I forego watching her flirt with the guys again and pick up my turquoise pen to start on my grading. I use turquoise ink because studies have shown that children are often demoralized by red ink splashed across a page. The fact that they can't construct a proper sentence means nothing. I read the first page, making corrections and notes in the margins. When I flip to the second page, it's more of the same. Suppressing a groan, I close the essay and write a big fat 'F' on the top of the page. I repeat the exercise with the next essay.

I'm on the third essay when Susannah returns. She sets my coffee in front of me and watches me issue another failing grade.

"Feel better?" Susannah asks.

"Not yet," I reply. "But I'm getting there."

2

ON FRIDAY, I SIT AT my desk as my third-period students meander into the classroom, faces glued to their phones. I hate those phones, and all the social media crap that comes with them. The argument could be made that there isn't much these days I don't hate, but I really despise those goddamn phones.

The bell rings to signify the start of class, but I don't move. Minute after minute ticks by. Five minutes, ten minutes. Twenty minutes. More. Class is half over and I have yet to utter a word. Most of the kids don't notice. I've gotten a few looks — no complaints — but mostly students talk and text amongst themselves, showing each other God knows what on their phones. They would do this the whole period, if I let them. Hell, some of them would do it anyway.

Time was, I would have requested they follow classroom rules and put their phones away. Time was, I would have started class. Time was, I would have cared.

That time is clearly over now.

I know I told Susannah I was getting there, but I am not getting there. I don't know where there even is, but wherever it is — whatever it is — I am not getting there.

In fact, I am getting nowhere.

I glance at the clock. Fifteen minutes left.

Opening the drawer to my right, I extract a stack of graded essays and drop them on the desk. The sound startles a few kids, but most merely glance at me before returning to their conversations.

"Let's chat," I say.

A few more students look at me. I stand and pick up the essays, then move around the room to distribute them to their authors.

"I know it's been a while since the start of the school year—like, three whole weeks, maybe—but I thought I was pretty clear when I said on that first day that I expect full and complete sentences in each and every assignment you hand in. You're not texting your assignments to me, and your work should not be written as though you were. So, please, consider this rather impressive collection of failing grades a life lesson—the first, I suspect, of many. Don't forget to post them on what-ever social media app you're all currently obsessed with."

They're paying attention now. All of them. Maybe I should take advantage of the situation and cram some litera-ture down their throats. I pass back the last essay and return to the front of the room.

"Bitch," one kid mutters.

I turn around. "You're right. I am. But here's the thing: you're going to come across the occasional bitch in your life, bitches who will expect you to do crazy things like write in complete emoji-free sentences because until we fully revert back to the glory days of hieroglyphics, complete sentences are how we communicate. You want to survive in the real world? You may need to know how to write a complete sentence. How to understand something you read. How to form a coherent argument without using a smiley face.

"And this isn't about the role of religion in *The Epic of Gilgamesh*. This may come as a surprise, but you don't need to know about the role of religion in *The Epic of Gilgamesh*. No one ever will need to know about the role of religion in *The Epic of*

Gilgamesh. Or *The Epic of Gilgamesh*. There is no real-world application for *The Epic of Gilgamesh*. It's not like math where the ability to add or divide or work out percentages can actually help you later on in life. *The Epic of Gilgamesh* will not help you. Hell, it probably wouldn't even help you on *Jeopardy!*

"You don't want to read it any more than I want to teach it. The person who originally wrote the damn thing a million years ago probably didn't want to read it, either, but I have to read it every year. Every time I teach this class, I have to start with the goddamn *Epic of Gilgamesh*. I don't want to, but I do it. Every single year, I do it—and do you know why I do it? Because it's my job. And this, children, this is important. This is why you need to care. This is why you need to put forth that extra iota of effort once in a while.

"Because do you know where not caring gets you? It gets you here. Stuck in a job for which you have no passion, just going through the motions, until one day you lose your mind and start yelling at a bunch of teenagers about *The Epic of Gilgamesh*."

The bell rings, and students bolt for the door.

I wave them off happily. "Thanks for playing, kids. Be sure to tune in next week when I rant about Shakespeare and semicolons."

As soon as the last kid is out the door, I drop back into my desk chair. Oh yeah. This will be bad for me. So very bad. Strangely, I do not care. For the first time in a long time, I feel good. I feel *great*. Perhaps I should have done this sooner.

I take my suddenly fantastic mood to the cafeteria for lunch duty. It's an hour of patrolling a cavernous space that is too loud, too hot, and too filled with overly strong smells. Normally, I despise having to watch out for inappropriate behaviors while the masses eat, but today, I am immune from it all. The Gilgamesh rant is a gift that just keeps on giving.

Some of the kids from my third-period class are here, stealing glances at me before whispering to their friends. As their friends then crane their necks to look at me, I imagine only the most flattering things are being said.

How long will it be before I'm suspended? Monday, probably. Tuesday or Wednesday at the latest. Well, who couldn't use a forced, unpaid vacation once in a while?

I am completing a circuit when Martha, John's secretary, enters through the double doors. She scans the room, but I wander her way. She's looking for me. No sense in avoiding it.

"John would like to see you in his office," Martha informs me.

I'm sure he would. "No problem," I say. "I'll stop in after lunch."

"No. He'd like to see you now."

Maybe it won't be Monday after all. Thanking Martha, I head for the office. I've never been in trouble with the principal before. Not even when I was a student. What will it be like?

The office staff stops to stare when I walk in. That's definitely a good sign. Tales of my exploits have apparently preceded me. I wave as I turn toward John's office. He sits behind his desk, frowning at his computer monitor. Angry emails about his crazy sophomore English teacher?

I knock on the door frame. "Martha said you wanted to see me?"

John looks up. "Have a seat. Close the door behind you."

I close the door and sink into a seat in front of the desk.

"I've had a few parental complaints," he says.

"Already?"

John cocks his head. Probably not my smartest response ever. Perhaps I should have started with surprise.

I mimic his head tilt. "About me?"

"Yes, about you. And this."

John turns the monitor toward me and hits the space bar on his keyboard. I hear my voice before the video catches up, but I'm soon watching an encore performance of my one-woman freak-out from this morning. Oh good. I was hoping someone would record it and post it online. You know, for posterity.

As soon as the video ends, John rights the monitor and looks at me expectantly. "Well?"

"Has it gone viral?" I ask. John becomes even less impressed with me. I fold my arms across my chest. "How long's the suspension?"

"I need you to resign."

"Resign?" I echo. How did I not see that coming?

"Yes. I can offer you severance, but I will need your resignation by the end of the day."

"Seriously?"

"Yes. You can't swear at students."

"You saw the video. I didn't swear *at* them. I swore…*near* them."

John sighs. "The end of the day, Lavinia. Please."

Lavinia? Really? He's going to use my full name like he's my mother? I don't think so. I look around his desk and grab a yellow legal pad that's sitting beneath his elbow.

"Why wait until the end of the day?" I ask. "Do you have a pen?"

John doesn't move. I snag a pen resting near the phone and write 'I QUIT' in big letters across the paper. I sign it, tear off the page, and drop it on the desk in front of him.

"Will that suffice?" I ask. "Or should I have it typed up for you?"

He looks at the paper for a moment, then lifts his head. "I think we're done here."

"I think so, too," I say.

I walk out. The staff gawks at me, as do a few lingering students. The rumor mills will be working overtime today. I leave the building next, not stopping until I reach Susannah's Prius in the faculty parking lot.

She has the keys, so I can't leave, but neither can I go back inside. There was something freeing—if fundamentally stupid—about my departure, so going back is definitely out.

9

Instead, I sit in the passenger's seat and wait. Just after three o'clock, Susannah appears.

She opens the driver's side door and peers inside. "So, uh…what's going on?"

"School's out for summer," I say.

"It's September."

"You noticed that, too?"

Susannah slides onto the seat. "How long have you been sitting here?"

"Since lunch."

"Why didn't you come get the keys?"

"Would've ruined my dramatic exit," I say. "Could you please go inside and get my bag?"

"Anything else?"

I shake my head. "My World's Greatest Teacher mug can stay."

Susannah puts her things on the back seat and returns to the school. Other faculty members are coming out now. Some are looking at me. Others are trying hard *not* to look at me. I consider flipping them off but ultimately slump lower in my seat until Susannah returns.

"What happened today?" she asks, handing over my bag. "The kids in my afternoon classes were all going on about how Miss Kelly lost her mind."

That is surprisingly accurate. I toss the bag in the back, my possessions spilling out in the process. "You didn't see the video?"

Susannah hesitates. "I may have seen the video."

"How many times?"

"Just once."

"Really?"

"Well, once in full. The rest of the day, I caught random snippets of it when telling students to turn it off."

Super. "And?"

"Shakespeare and semicolons?"

I shrug. "I do love alliteration."

"Yeah," Susannah says. "Did John fire you?"

"I think I technically resigned. But I did write 'I QUIT' on a piece of yellow legal pad paper, so it could go either way."

Susannah looks at me, her jaw working like she's trying to decide whether to say something I won't want to hear. Must be some serious disappointment. She's not exactly known for holding back.

She squares her shoulders and starts the car. "Maybe you could fight it. The teachers' union—"

"Will laugh in my face when they see the video."

"Well, maybe—"

"It doesn't matter. I don't want my job back."

"Okay. Here's your chance to finish your great American novel."

"I'm not writing a novel."

"Well, here's your chance to start one."

"I am not writing a novel," I say. "Great, American, or otherwise."

"I don't know what else former English teachers do."

Neither do I. "Work at Walmart, I guess."

Susannah backs out of the parking space. "Maybe this will be a good thing. I don't think you've been happy there for a while now. Not since—"

"Yeah," I say before she can finish the thought.

"This can be a fresh start," she says instead, forcing cheerfulness into her tone. "Fresh starts are good things."

"Yeah."

"At least you had the good sense to do this on a Friday."

"Good sense? I'm not sure anything I've done today could be considered sensible."

"That is true," Susannah says. "But because it's Friday, we can get super drunk together, and I'll have two days to recover from the hangover."

A two-day hangover. That sounds like a challenge. Besides, it's not like I have anything else to do.

"Sure," I say. "Why not?"

We don't talk on the ride home. I appreciate the silence, as the reality of what happened this afternoon keeps hitting me over and over again. I lost my job. I *quit* my job. Resignation came with some form of severance, but will my exit still be considered as such? I have to hope so; I need money. I don't have a mortgage—my house was left to me by my grandmother when she passed away—but there's still property tax and insurance and utility bills to pay. My German shepherd needs to eat—*I* need to eat. All these things require money, and right now, my only income is the rent Susannah gives me every month. That might be all right for a while, but I'll need something more eventually. I'm going to need a new job.

But what do former high school English teachers do? Teach adult ed classes? English as a second language? Museum docent? Not that I know anything about anything that would be in a museum. I'd have to work in the gift shop. Or I really will have to apply at Walmart.

When we arrive home, Susannah pulls into the driveway and cuts the engine but otherwise doesn't move. I get out of the car and start shoveling my belongings back into my bag.

"Are you coming?" I ask.

"Yes. Once you let your crazy German shepherd outside."

"Rufus isn't crazy," I say. "He's...spirited."

"Well, please go let your spirited dog outside so I can get in the house without being jumped on."

"Rufus does not jump on people."

"Not normally, no," Susannah says. "But today, he'll pick up on your weird I-got-fired vibes and spaz out like the anxiety-ridden freak he is."

Yes, that is probably true in a slightly less dramatic way. "I didn't get fired. I quit."

"Because you were being fired," Susannah returns. "Please, Vinnie?"

I close the car door. "Fine."

Rufus meets me at the front door. Dropping my bag in the living room, I go into the kitchen. He follows obediently, panting a little more than usual. Dogs always know when something's up, don't they? I rub his chest and tell him everything will be all right before shooing him into the backyard.

Returning to the front door, I wave Susannah inside. She goes upstairs to her bedroom. I go play with Rufus and wait for her to join us.

"Where do you want to go tonight?" she asks when she does. "There's a new place in the city we could try."

"I have zero interest in going into Boston," I reply. Doing that would mean a level of dressing up for which I have even less interest. I have no patience for makeup or short skirts tonight. Or ever, really. Throwing Rufus's ball to the far end of the yard, I join her on the porch. "Can't we just order in and drink at home?"

"You have the rest of your life to drink at home," she says. "Let's at least go to The Howling Sailor. You *love* The Howling Sailor."

Yes, I do love The Howling Sailor. One step up from a dimly lit dive, it's local, casual, and comes with a much more generous pour than any other place I know. That could just be because Susannah and I are well-established regulars there, but the reason why has never mattered. Not to me, anyway.

I sigh. "First round's on you."

3

THE FRIDAY NIGHT CROWD AT The Howling Sailor is a mix of off-duty cops and locals too lazy or poor to make the trek into the city. It's more crowded than usual tonight. The billiards tables have all been claimed, and even the dance floor is packed. It's enough to make me wish I had held firm with my drinking-at-home suggestion, but as there will be no convincing Susannah to leave until she's had multiple martinis, I head to the bar. Fortunately, Frank is tending bar tonight. He's my father's friend but serves us anyway.

"The usual, girls?" he asks.

Susannah flashes a brilliant smile. "Please."

Frank mixes her a very dry martini, adds two olives, then looks at me. "Nia?"

"Yes, please." I claim an empty seat at the end of the bar. "More Jack than Coke."

"You are so butch, Vinnie," Susannah says.

She sips her martini and flirts with the bar-backs. No one takes her seriously; they know better. I decline to flirt with anyone and concentrate on my drink.

"You okay, Nia?" Frank asks after Susannah hits the dance floor.

"Right as rain."

Frank nods and moves on to attend to another patron. After I finish my drink, I stare at the empty glass. Maybe I should have asked him to leave the bottle.

When he works his way back to my end of the bar, he brings me a second Jack and Coke. This one is even weaker than the first. I won't lie. There are occasionally drawbacks to your bartender being friends with your father.

A little later, someone sidles up to the bar on my left and asks for two pints before poking my arm.

"Hey, Nia."

I look up and smile at the guy standing there. "Craig Parker. What cat dragged you in?"

"It's Friday night, and I'm off duty. Where else would I be?"

"Aww. That's kind of pathetic," I say. "And you used to be so cool in high school."

"Need I point out that you're also here on a Friday night?"

"Which really just confirms the pathetic theory, if you think about it."

Craig gestures to my glass. "How many of those have you had?"

"Two." I look at the liquid inside. "Well, one and a half."

"Maybe you should slow down a little."

I snort. "That's rich coming from the king of the stoners and slackers."

Craig points at me. "Hey, that was high school, and you know it. I don't do that anymore."

I nod. "Police departments can be pretty strict about that kind of thing."

"Very much so."

"You don't have to worry about me, Officer Parker. The overprotective bartender has it covered. There's barely any Jack in this."

"I'm glad he's looking out for you," Craig says.

"Yeah, yeah, yeah." I twist around to scan the room for his girlfriend. I'm not particularly interested in conversation, but if she's here, I should at least wave hello. "Is Mandy with you?"

"Nah. She's out with the girls," Craig says. "I'm here with a friend tonight."

"Anyone I know?"

"Don't think so. Where's Susannah?"

I glance at the dance floor. "In the middle of that big throng of men over there."

Craig looks over his shoulder. "Isn't she dating your brother?"

"Last I checked." I shrug. "Susannah likes to flirt. You know that."

Craig laughs as he turns back to the bar. "It's too bad that girl's so shy."

"It's too bad she isn't," I say as Frank sets down two pints in front of Craig.

"Thanks, Frank. Put it on my tab?" Craig says, and Frank nods. Picking up the pints, Craig looks at me. "You're not driving home tonight, are you?"

I shake my head. "We'll be taking a cab."

He grins. "I'll leave you to it, then."

I toast him with my drink. "Cheers."

He returns to a table where a brown-haired guy is waiting. Craig's right—I don't know him. Whoever he is, he's far too preppy and well-dressed for this shitty dive, like he stepped straight out of a J. Crew catalog or something. The guy smiles at me as he leans in to say something to Craig. I salute them both before turning back to the bar and finishing my drink. Waving down Frank, I request another.

After confirming that I have no intention of driving home, he obliges, again adding more Coke than Jack. Worrywart. I nurse it, drawing patterns in the condensation on the bar to pass the time. How long before I can convince Susannah to go home?

"This seat taken?" a man asks.

For crying out loud. Am I wearing a sign saying 'please bother me'? I sigh. "Does it look like it's taken?"

"No, but I didn't know if maybe you had a boyfriend—"

"No."

"—or girlfriend—"

"Oh, how very progressive of you."

"—maybe using the facilities or something," he finishes.

I look at him. "No, that seat's not taken."

Holy shit. This guy is hot. Not that I have a thing for blue eyes, chiseled cheekbones, and some seriously sexy five o'clock shadow because I definitely…do not. He's wearing a T-shirt and jeans, both of which do a lot to promote his athletic build. As he slides onto the stool, he smiles, revealing very white and straight teeth.

Damn. Thank God Frank was stingy with the whiskey.

His Royal Hotness signals to Frank. "You're here on your own, then?"

"Just me and my friend, Jack."

Frank comes over, and my companion asks for a beer. Whatever's on tap. He's not picky. Frank pours a mug of a local craft brew. The man places some money on the counter and takes a swig of the beer.

Frank looks at me as he scoops up the money. It's an expression I've seen before. *Is this man bothering you?* I shake my head. He's nothing I can't handle. Frank nods and turns to the cash register.

The man sets down his beer. "Jack?"

Not too bright, this one. Probably gets by on his looks, making people everywhere crazy with those well-muscled arms of his. He then dazzles them with his easy grin and washboard abs so they don't notice his total lack of wit. Too bad for him I'm immune to such manipulation.

I glance at the abs again. Probably immune to such manipulation.

I indicate my glass. "Jack. As in 'Daniel's'."

"You want another?" Frank asks me.

I nod. Frank makes me another Jack and Coke that's barely deserving of the name. I do not put any money on the bar, and Frank walks away again.

"Come here often?" the man asks.

"Wanna know my sign next?" I say. "Look, if you're trying to pick me up, I'm not interested. Save us both some time and hassle, you know?"

"Who said I was trying to pick you up?"

"You certainly seem like you're trying to pick me up."

The man shakes his head. "Just making conversation."

"Just checking."

He laughs. "I think I may have stumbled onto why you're here alone."

"Oh, okay. Good work, Sherlock," I say. "But for your information, I may be sitting at this bar alone, but I am not alone in this establishment. I have a friend—"

"Besides Jack?"

"—who dances." I point in the general direction of the dance floor. "She's over there."

He glances that way. "You don't dance?"

"Haven't had enough to drink yet to consider it."

"Oh, so you're one of those."

"Whatever that means."

"Are you always like this?"

"Drunk?"

"Pleasant."

"Why do you care?"

"Are you new to the concept of conversation?"

"I didn't ask you to sit here."

"True."

"Nor did I invite you to converse with me," I say. "In fact, I think I've done quite a lot to discourage conversation."

"Also true."

"And yet," I say.

He grins. "Here I am."

"Yes, here you are." I study him. "Are you a glutton for punishment?"

"Not especially."

"Someone put you up to this?" I check to see if Susannah is having a good laugh at my expense. She isn't. She's thrown herself into an energetic and intoxicated version of the Robot.

"No." He laughs. "Can I ask your name?"

"I don't know. Can you?"

"If I asked you your name," he says then, "would you tell me?"

"Ah, now there's a valid question."

"And the answer?"

I consider his request as I sip my drink. "Nia. My name is Nia."

"Nia. That's nice."

"I'm so glad you think so," I say. "What's your name?"

"Lew."

"Like, short for Lewis?"

He glances over his shoulder again. "Like that, yeah."

"Am I keeping you from something? Someone?" I ask. "Wife? Girlfriend? Boyfriend? Your mother, maybe?"

He shakes his head. "I'm flying solo tonight."

"Left your entourage at home?"

"I don't know how much of an entourage it is," he says. "No wife, no girlfriend."

"Boyfriend, then."

"No, but that's very progressive of you."

"Well, I try to keep an open mind." I look him over. "So, what's wrong with you?"

"What do you mean?"

"You're good looking, kind of nice, entirely single, and apparently free of any emotional baggage. Yet here you are, sitting alone, talking to an overly hostile woman in some smoky dive on a Friday night," I say. "What's wrong with you?"

"What's wrong with you?"

"What makes you think something's wrong with me?"

"You're good looking, kind of nice—"

"Kind of nice?" I interrupt. "That's one hell of a curve you're grading on."

"—entirely single, but unfortunately broke from excess emotional baggage fees," Lew finishes.

"And you still have to wonder what's wrong."

"Maybe I'm just being polite."

"Are you?"

"Are *you*?"

"Who says I'm trying to be polite?"

Lew laughs. "No one within earshot. Another round?"

He doesn't wait for a response before signaling to Frank. Frank obliges and pours another pint. He serves me yet another Jack and Coke, and I toast him with the glass.

"Thanks, barkeep," I say, and Frank rolls his eyes as he walks away. I turn to Lew. "Tell me your story."

"What will you do if I tell you my story?"

"Unfairly judge and mock you."

"I like that you're honest." He drinks some beer. "How about this: I will tell you my story if you tell me what you're celebrating."

"What makes you think I'm celebrating anything? Maybe I do this every Friday night."

"Do you?"

I shrug. "Depends on the rest of the week."

"What happened this week?"

"I joined the ranks of the unemployed today."

"Your idea or your employer's?"

"Mutual, really, in the heat of the moment, but if the unemployment office asks, it was definitely theirs."

"Not budget cuts, then."

"More like insubordination."

Lew fakes surprise. "I'm shocked."

"Everyone is."

"What did you do before this insubordination got in the way?"

"Taught high school English to a group of adolescent ingrates."

"An insubordinate English teacher? Don't they usually make inspirational movies about you?"

"Not when you refer to your students as adolescent ingrates. Sends the wrong message."

Lew laughs again. "What are your plans now?"

"To get drunk. Very, very drunk." Or as drunk as one can get on watered-down Jack and Cokes.

"And then?"

"Sleep it off."

"I meant for work."

"I don't know. I'll find a paid position somewhere at some time. After all, it is what one does when one is not independently wealthy and has bills to pay. You understand, I'm sure."

"I don't, actually. I happen to be independently wealthy."

"Independently wealthy men do not spend their evenings talking to hostile women in smoky dives," I say as Frank passes by. "No offense, Frank."

Frank waves me off. No offense taken. He's cool like that.

"You know that for a fact?" Lew asks.

"I do. I read a lot, you know."

"I don't recall that lesson showing up in *The Wife of Bath's Tale*."

All right, so that reference is kind of impressive, but I work hard to keep from showing it.

"Maybe you weren't reading closely enough," I say. "Your turn now. What's your deal?"

Before Lew can say anything, Susannah bursts onto the scene, slamming into me hard enough to spill my drink down my front. I swear and reach for a napkin.

Susannah hangs off my shoulder. "You drunk enough yet to come dance with me, Vinnie?"

She's slurring her words. She must have found a sucker or two to buy her drinks. Better them than me.

"Not by a long shot," I say.

"Well, what have you been doing all this—?" Susannah notices Lew. She smiles as she looks him up and down. "Oh. So this is what you've been doing."

"No one is doing anyone," I say as Susannah pushes between us to belly up to the bar.

Lew leans to his right. "Vinnie?"

"It's a nickname," I say. "Don't your friends have a nickname for you?"

"Maybe."

"Is it embarrassing?" I ask, and he looks away. "What is it?"

"I'd rather not say."

"If you don't tell me, I'll just make one up for you."

Lew sighs. "They call me Ellen."

"Like the talk show host?"

"Yes."

"Because you're a lesbian?"

"No."

"Because you love to dance?"

"I love to dance!" Susannah proclaims, pulling back from the bar with a martini in hand. "Let's get to it, Vinnie. You can come, too, if you want, Ellie."

"Ellen," he corrects.

I grin. "Because that's *so* much better."

The opening chords of a disco classic blare from the speakers. ABBA. *Dancing Queen.* It's a sure sign that Susannah has been flirting wildly with the DJ. She squeals in delight, downs her drink, and puts the empty glass on the bar.

"Vinnie, come on!" she cries, rushing to the dance floor.

I slide off my stool. "Well, Ellie, it's been a blast, but I've gotta go. They're playing my song."

"Maybe I'll see you again sometime," Lew says.

I spread my hands as I walk away. "I should be so lucky."

4

THE NEXT MORNING, I WAKE when Rufus walks across my very full bladder. I swallow a groan and pull a pillow over my head. He doesn't settle down again—a sure sign that mine isn't the only full bladder—so I throw the covers back and attempt to get out of bed. My head feels as though it has doubled in size and my legs suddenly have fifty-pound weights attached to them, but I fumble my way downstairs to let Rufus into the backyard.

After using the bathroom, I collapse into a chair at the kitchen table. Coffee would be so great right now. If only the damn coffee maker wasn't on the other side of the room. What was I thinking? Laying my head on the table, I don't move again until Rufus barks to be let back into the house.

As he would not find my hangover an acceptable reason to delay his breakfast, I fill his bowls with kibble and water. The act is exhausting. I should go back to bed, but it's entirely too far away. As is the couch. Why didn't I ever put a couch in the kitchen? It seems like such an oversight now.

"We are stupid," Susannah says, slinking into a seat at the table.

I can't disagree. "We are that."

"You didn't make coffee?"

I sit down across from her. "Like my brain is that functional right now."

Bracing her hands against the table, she stands. "Maybe we shouldn't drink anymore."

Yeah. That will happen. Knowing us, we'll fall back into old habits by the end of the day. Maybe we should get a hobby—somewhere alcohol doesn't exist.

"Dare to dream," I respond.

When Susannah returns with her mug, she sets it down and lays her head on the table. Even though I know what she does to coffee, I am desperate enough to remove the mug from her hands. She makes sounds of protest but doesn't move.

I take a sip and make a face. "Jesus. Have some coffee with your sugar."

"No thanks," Susannah says, her voice muffled by tablecloth. "Completely ruins the taste."

I put down the cup. "Since when do you know anything about taste?"

Susannah sits up. "Whiskey makes you mean."

"Being awake makes me mean," I correct. "Whiskey makes me happy."

"And hungover."

"That, too."

Susannah sips her coffee. "So…Ellie was nice."

I get up to fetch my own coffee. "Who?"

"Ellie. You know, the guy from the bar last night?"

The guy from the—oh. Him. "You think so?"

I already know the answer. A good-looking guy who weathered the particular brand of bitchiness that is Hurricane Vinnie? She probably spent the night planning our wedding.

"I do," she says. "He likes you."

I pull a mug from the cupboard and fill it with coffee. "Well, let's rent a hall."

"Cut it out. I'm not saying you should marry him. I'm just saying…it's been a while."

I definitely don't need a reminder of how long it's been. "You're being unfair."

"I'm being a friend. One who doesn't want you to end up the lonely old maid with nothing but cats to keep her company."

"What's wrong with cats?" I ask as I return to the table. I know she thinks she's looking out for me or whatever, but the truth is I'm not interested. An image of Lew's abs enters my mind, and I bite my lip.

Probably not interested.

"Don't you want something more than that?" Susannah says. "Things with Brian—"

"Stop."

"—didn't work out—"

"Susannah," I warn. "Stop now."

She sighs. "You shouldn't let it define the rest of your life."

I have absolutely nothing to say to that, so we sit in silence and drink our coffee. Susannah keeps sneaking looks at me, trying to come off as though she's actually interested in other things. There's something else she wants to say, but I'll be damned if I ask what it is. She'll break eventually.

"Ellie is hot, okay?" she blurts. "Seriously hot—like, God's-gift-to-anyone-with-eyes hot—and he likes you, so bring him home, tie him to your bed, and have at it!"

That is not what I thought she'd say. The expression on her face is so damn desperate—she sincerely wants me to get laid—that I burst out laughing.

She rolls her eyes. "You are such a jerk."

"Oh, you know you love me."

"Yeah, I do. Lucky for you." She sighs again. "Just think about it, all right?"

"Why? It's not like I'll ever see him again."

"You might, if you text him."

"I don't have his number," I say as though that is the only thing preventing me from contacting him.

Susannah pats her robe. "Wait…what's this?" She pulls a crumpled napkin from the left pocket. "Oh, that's right. I have his number."

What? I snag the napkin from her and open it to see Lew's name and number scrawled in unfamiliar penmanship. "How did you get this?"

"I asked him for it. In case you wanted to call him."

"You're shameless."

"One of us should be."

I shake the napkin before dropping it on the table. "This is a little old-fashioned, isn't it?"

"Says the woman with a landline."

I guess she has a point there. "Fine. It's a little low tech for you, isn't it?"

"Well, if you had left your phone behind when you went to the bathroom, I wouldn't have had to resort to such primitive methods."

"My phone was locked."

"It's never locked." Susannah groans and puts her chin in her hand. "God, I need to go back to bed."

That's not a bad idea. I am contemplating doing the same thing when the landline rings. As Susannah covers her head with her arms, I locate the handset under a pile of magazines in the middle of the table.

"Yeah?" I say into the phone.

"Yeah?" my mother echoes. "That's how you answer the phone?"

"It is today. What can I do for you, Mom?"

"You can come to dinner tonight. Six o'clock. Both you and Susannah. I'm making pot roast."

"What about Rufus?"

"Can't you ever leave that dog at home?"

"He gets lonely."

"Well, we can't have that," my mother says. "Bring him, too."

I scan my mental database for any forgotten birthdays or anniversaries. Dad's birthday's coming up, but not for a couple of months. What else is there? "What's the occasion?"

"Your father has a new partner. A nice, young man," my mother says. "He's new in town and — "

"This isn't some kind of set-up, is it?" I ask.

"I wouldn't do that to him," Mom says. "Colin is coming, too."

A Saturday night with my parents, brother, roommate, and a perfect stranger. Sounds fun. Still, it's not like I have anything else to do. At least there will be pot roast.

"Rufus and I will be there," I say. "I'm sure Susannah will come if she's stopped seeing double by then."

Susannah laughs.

"Tell that girl she needs to stop drinking so much," my mother says.

"I will give her that message," I reply. "See you tonight."

As I put the phone back under the magazines, Susannah turns her head toward me. "What message?"

"You drink too much."

"So very true," Susannah says. "What's happening tonight?"

"We're invited to dinner. Dad has a new partner who doesn't know anyone in town."

"Isn't he getting a little old to be breaking in the new guys?"

"Try telling him that." I shrug. "He likes mentoring. Sharing his worldly wisdom and all that."

"We all have our quirks," Susannah says. "What time's dinner?"

"Six."

"Great. That gives me plenty of time to go back to bed."

"Be sure to shower at some point, too," I say. "I am not taking you anywhere smelling like a gin distillery the way you do."

Susannah leans back in her chair, head tipped toward the ceiling. "Your words cut me, Vinnie. They really do."

I grin. "No doubt."

5

As Susannah refuses to allow Rufus to ride in her Prius, we take my aging Jeep Cherokee to my parents' house. The front door is unlocked, so we let ourselves in and go into the living room where Colin is lounging in our father's recliner. Rufus leaps into his lap.

Colin scratches him between the ears. "If it isn't Rufus the Doofus."

I flop onto the couch. "Oh, Colin, you're killing me, you're so funny."

"Your dog did flunk out of obedience school."

"K-9 training, Mr. I-finger-paint-for-a-living."

"Not exclusively. Sometimes, I play with clay."

"And to think, you're the successful one," I say. "Where are Mom and Dad?"

"Kitchen. Dad will be back in a minute. Mom has yet to leave the stove but is currently refusing all offers of help."

Sounds about right. Of course, given how unskilled the rest of us are in a kitchen, it's probably easier if she does everything on her own.

Rufus jumps out of Colin's lap to run circles around the living room. Susannah takes his place, draping her arms around my brother's neck before kissing him.

"Hello, lover," she says.

He returns the greeting, then they kiss again. I make very mature gagging noises.

Colin looks at me. "Must you do that?"

I grin. "My question exactly."

Just as my brother flips me off, Dad comes out from the kitchen, a beer in each hand. Susannah and I dissolve into laughter. My father shakes his head as he hands Colin a bottle.

"I see and hear nothing." Dad kisses my cheek. "Girls. Thank you for coming."

Susannah moves over to the couch. "You know me. Anything for pot roast."

"Can I get either of you something to drink? Beer? Wine? Something stronger?"

"Wine, please," Susannah says. "Red, if you have it, but I'm not picky."

Dad looks at me, and I shake my head. He gives me possession of his beer and disappears back into the kitchen. When he returns with the wine, Mom comes out with him, staying only long enough to say hello.

The rest of us sit in the living room and make small talk. I conveniently forget to mention my new unemployed status. It definitely won't go over well—especially with my mother—and my father's new partner doesn't need to spend an evening with the Kelly family when they're at odds.

Ten minutes before six o'clock, there's a knock at the door. Rufus goes mad with excitement.

"Lavinia!" my mother yells from the kitchen. "Do something about your dog and answer the door!"

Leaving Rufus under Colin's command, I head for the front door. Lew waits on the other side, a daisy-laden bouquet in one hand and a bottle of wine in the other. We stand there, looking at one another in surprise.

I recover first. "Are you stalking me?"

"What are you doing here?" he asks.

"This is my parents' house. What are *you* doing here?" I say, just before realizing the answer. "You're my father's new partner."

Lew steps back. "Patrick Kelly is your father?"

"Yeah."

"So he's—"

"The man who provided half my chromosomes. You really need to catch up here, Ellie." I shake my head. "I should have pegged you for a cop. I'm surprised I didn't. It's so obvious. You have the look, the haircut—"

"I have a cop haircut?"

"That can't be news to you."

"Nia?" my father calls. "Are you going to let him in?"

"Still deciding, Dad," I shout back.

I move to allow Lew to enter but change my mind before he's all the way inside and step back in front of him.

"What are you—?" he starts.

"Ix-nay on the me losing my ob-jay," I say.

"Ob-jay?"

"Seriously, not a word, all right? I haven't told anyone I lost my job, and I don't want them to hear it from you."

"Okay," he says. "Is it all right for them to know we met last night at a bar?"

"Umm, The Howling Sailor isn't *a* bar. It's *the* bar. And yes, it's fine for them to know that because Susannah's here, and they'll know it just as soon as she sees you."

"You girls hang out at the bar a lot?"

"Small town." I step aside. "Come on in."

"Thank you."

I close the door. "Nice flowers."

"They're for your mother."

"I should hope so. My father's always been more a roses kind of guy."

"I'll make a note of that."

"I detect a hint of sarcasm in your tone."

Lew raises an eyebrow. "Only a hint? Where's your father? Is he home?"

I gesture down the hall. "The living room, Officer Eager Beaver. This way."

"Thank you."

As I walk into the living room, I hold out my hands as though I am showing off a fabulous prize on *The Price Is Right*. "Presenting Lew Judgey McJudgerson."

"It's Weiss, actually," Lew says.

Susannah squeals. "No way! Ellie!"

Mom chooses this moment to come out of the kitchen, wiping her hands on her apron. She looks at Susannah with an inkling of suspicion before focusing entirely upon her guest.

She smiles warmly. "Welcome. You must be Patrick's new partner."

Lew steps forward, evades the dog, and gives her the flowers. "Thank you for having me over, Mrs. Kelly."

Mom waves him off. "Oh, none of that. Call me Nancy."

Susannah plucks the bottle from his hand and reads the label. "You have excellent taste in wine, Ellie."

Lew shakes hands with Dad and Colin. "I have no taste in wine. That selection was pure luck of the draw."

"May I ask why Susannah keeps calling you 'Ellie'?" my mother says.

"We met last night, Mom," I explain. "At The Howling Sailor. Lew tried to pick me up."

Both my mother and Lew look horrified. She's probably gearing up to apologize for any obnoxious behavior on my part. Lew, I imagine, is preparing an apology for having hit on her daughter.

"I wasn't trying to pick you up." Lew looks at my parents. "In fact, when asked if that was my intention, I denied it. I was just making conversation."

"Trying to impress Nia?" my father asks.

"Trying and failing," Lew admits.

Dad nods. "Most men do."

Well, this has suddenly become mortifying. It's a relief when Mom tugs me toward the kitchen.

"Come help me finish dinner, Lavinia," she says.

"Lavinia?" Lew asks. "Another nickname?"

Of course he heard that. I scowl at my roommate's overly delighted expression. She's practically vibrating with excitement. "Susannah will fill you in."

Stealing the wine from her, I follow my mother into the kitchen.

"You didn't even tell him your name?" she asks when we're alone.

"I did tell him my name," I say. "My name is Nia."

"Your name is Lavinia." Mom hands me the flowers and a pair of scissors. "Snip the ends. At an angle, remember."

I put the wine on the counter and do as I'm told. My mother places a vase in front of me, and I drop flowers inside, making the bouquet look far worse than before. I can rule out flower arranging as a potential new career.

"You should stop giving him a hard time," my mother says.

"He makes it so easy, though. Like, he's begging me to give him a hard time."

"I don't care. Rise above the temptation."

"I'm not sure I have that sort of strength."

My mother takes my face between her hands, forcing me to meet her eyes. "You have that and more."

"Jeez, Mom. Way to make it weird. I was just being a jerk."

"I know."

She shoos me away to take over the arranging of the flowers. When she's finished, the bouquet looks lovely. She takes the vase over to the already set table and places it in the center.

"You left a spot open," I comment. "Did you know he would bring flowers?"

"I thought he might. His mother must have raised him right."

"Are you suggesting my mother didn't raise me right?"

She smiles. "Not for a lack of trying," she says. "Give Llewellyn a break, Lavinia. Show him you weren't raised by wolves."

"I'm sorry," I say. "*Llewellyn*?"

"He didn't tell you his name, either?"

"Would you, if your name was Llewellyn?"

"You will not give that young man a hard time about this."

"If I stop now, he'll know something's up."

My mother removes a tray of rolls from the oven. "You will be nice to him. It will not kill you to do so."

"Everyone keeps saying that. I don't know why."

Mom dumps the rolls into a basket and holds it out. "Put this on the table."

I do. When I come back, she hands me a corkscrew and Lew's wine. I open the bottle and set it in front of Susannah's usual seat. By then, the green beans are ready. A bowl of mashed potatoes and the roast follows.

"I think we're ready now," my mother says. "Go let everyone know, please."

Ever the obedient daughter, I do that, too. Everyone shuffles into the dining room and sits at the table. I end up next to Lew and across from Susannah. I make eye contact with her briefly; she waggles her eyebrows and grins. Jesus Christ. When did she fully revert to a teenager?

"You girls knock off your foolishness," my mother says as she takes her seat. She holds out her hands. "Shall we say Grace?"

It's well after eight when Susannah, Rufus, and I leave the house, loaded down with leftover-stuffed Tupperware. Lew left before us, but he didn't go home. Instead, he's leaning against my car, his arms folded across his chest, as he stares at the ground.

"This, I believe, does constitute as stalking," I say.

He looks up. "Be sure to make your report to the local police."

"Don't think I won't," I say. "You're the new guy. They'll be on my side."

Lew smiles. "So, Lavinia?"

"Llewellyn?"

He nods. "Your mother ratted out both of us."

"Nancy's fair like that," I say. "You told me Lew was short for Lewis."

"You asked if it was short for something like Lewis. Technically, it is." Lew shrugs. "Also, if I recall properly, you told me your name was Nia."

"Then your recall is excellent," I say. "Is Llewellyn a family name, or did your mother not like you very much?"

"Excuse me?"

"She named you Llewellyn. Does she not like you?"

"I think she liked Wales more."

"I think I like Wales more, too."

Susannah laughs and takes the Tupperware from my hands. "You two play nice now."

Bidding Lew adieu, she gets into the Jeep. I motion for him to move so I can let Rufus into the backseat. After closing the door behind the dog, I turn and look at Lew.

"It can't have been easy being the kid on the playground whose name was Llewellyn," I say. "I thought being the kid named Lavinia was bad, but I'm betting Llewellyn was worse."

"You put a lot of store in names," he says.

"Is that a bad thing?"

He leans into me, and I resist the urge to move. He smells good. Really good. As soon as the thought enters my mind, I do slide away. But just a little.

"I'm not sure," he says before walking away.

"Let me know what you decide," I call after him.

He holds up his hand in farewell but doesn't turn around. When he gets into a beat-up truck parked on the street, I get in the Jeep.

"Well," Susannah says. "*That* was interesting."

Maybe a little too interesting. I stick the key in the ignition. "Let's get drunk."

Susannah grins. "Excellent."

6

YEARS OF CONDITIONING MEANS THAT even though I no longer have anywhere to be, I am still awake at five on Monday morning. Unable to go back to sleep, I slump downstairs to watch Susannah get ready for her day.

"Have fun living your life of leisure," she says on her way out the door. "But I expect dinner to be on this table when I get home."

"Just call me Donna Reed. Or June Cleaver," I say. "Is one better than the other?"

"As if either of them could hold a candle to your mom," Susannah calls as the door closes behind her.

I stay at the table a while longer to finish my coffee. I forego any other form of breakfast in favor of lying on the couch underneath one of my grandmother's handmade quilts. Turning on the television, I catch the headlines on the local news before flipping down to the Game Show Network. It's an unexplainable guilty pleasure of mine.

Which is why I'm in the middle of an episode of *Match Game* when Susannah calls me at noon.

"Get your résumé together yet?" she asks.

I mute the television. "Putting the finishing touches on it now."

"Good," Susannah says. "The kids say hi."

"Oh, I'm sure they do."

"You really made an impression on them."

"Well, sure. It's not every day you see an authority figure go completely off the deep end."

"It's cute you think of yourself as an authority figure."

"Everyone needs delusions," I agree. "Anything else?"

"Got a hot date I don't know about?"

"You'd like that, wouldn't you?"

"Well, I don't like the me-not-knowing-about-it part, but yeah."

"Sorry, but no," I say. "I'm working on my résumé and reading job listings. It's a labor-intensive process."

"Don't you mean you're watching Bob Barker give away toaster ovens?"

She knows me too well. "Gene Rayburn," I correct. "And I think all the prizes on this show are cash."

"Stop watching *Match Game* and get to work," Susannah commands and hangs up.

Tossing the phone aside, I reach for the remote. Maybe there's a *M*A*S*H* marathon on.

The Soap Opera Network is playing when my phone rings again. Muting the volume, I accept the call.

"I'm not watching *Match Game* anymore," I say in greeting.

"Good?" my brother says.

I sigh. "What do you want?"

"Shouldn't you be at work? Are you sick or something?"

Or something. Why didn't I check the Caller ID before answering?

"Yeah." I cough. "Had to take a sick day."

"Is it that shitty flu that's been going around?"

"I think so. I'm doing the rest and plenty-of-fluids thing. I'm sure I'll be fine tomorrow."

"Want me to call Mom and have her bring you some chicken soup?"

"No. You don't have to bother her with that."

"Mom wouldn't think it's a bother."

"I don't need her to make me any damn soup. I'm not that sick."

There's a short pause before Colin speaks again. "You know, Susannah told me you were, uh…let go."

"So you were having a bit of fun just then."

"A little bit, yeah."

"Jerk."

"I couldn't help myself."

"It's a good thing Susannah's a math teacher and not a spy," I say. "The entire world would be doomed."

"And not just because she can't keep a secret."

"Did she tell Mom and Dad?"

"Not that I'm aware of."

"Did *you* tell Mom and Dad?"

"Not that I'm aware of."

"Thank you for that."

"Yeah. Anyway, I just called to see how you're doing."

"You've been unemployed before. You know how it goes."

"Have you started looking for anything new yet?"

"No. I'm still—I don't know—decompressing or something."

"With the Game Show Network?"

"And the Soap Opera Network."

"Oh? What show are you watching?"

"I have no idea. Does it matter? They're all pretty much the same."

"Shades of gray," Colin says.

"Don't use your artist jargon with me, young man. I won't stand for it."

"Yes, ma'am."

"Don't call me that," I say. "I flunk students for less than that."

"So Susannah tells me."

"I'm hanging up now."

"Okay," Colin says. "Call me if you need some company or whatever. I have a fairly light schedule this week."

"What a coincidence," I say. "So do I."

That afternoon, I move on to daytime talk shows, even though I hate them. Amidst the celebrity interviews, diet fads, and silly games are always those segments devoted to real people and their real problems. I hate them for making me all weepy and introspective. But it's nice, I guess. Even the shows where you get the feeling that these segments are nothing more than one gigantic publicity stunt, they're making a difference in someone's life. Not every talk show host gives me that feeling. Some of them seem like they legitimately care about people and using their platform to make the world a better place.

I don't think I've ever felt that strongly about anything.

That makes me sound like a bad person, and I don't think I am. But maybe all bad people think the same thing. I'm a lost, disillusioned, twenty-something who's closing in on being a lost, disillusioned thirty-something, with a sarcastic mean streak longer than the Mississippi. I've failed at my chosen profession. I'm a lapsed Catholic who will be sharing a lovely condo in hell with Susannah once our livers finally give out. But I'm not a bad person. At least I don't think so. I don't discriminate; I'm mean to one and all. I don't kill people; I can't even slay them with my oh-so funny jokes. I don't abuse children or animals. I don't steal. I've never embezzled money. Even if I understood how to embezzle money, I don't think I would do it. I occasionally speed but not excessively so. I throw my spare change into the Salvation Army collection buckets every holiday season. I donate food when the town has a food drive and help out with church fundraisers when my

mother asks. Whenever the Girl Scouts come by selling cookies, I buy some.

So maybe I'm not a bad person, but does any of that make
me a good person? I haven't built a house for the homeless. I
only occasionally work at the church soup kitchen. I used to
volunteer at an animal shelter, but I stopped. I stopped doing
everything. There were reasons for that, but maybe they
weren't good ones. Bad things happen all the time to people,
and they go on with their lives. They continue to do good
things for other people. Sometimes, they even do more.

But not me.

All I did was collapse in on myself like some kind of human black hole.

What is wrong with me?

Unable to divine an answer, I reach for the remote and
search for something less introspective to watch. There must
be some stupid sitcom on somewhere.

By the time Susannah comes home, I've switched to the
local news. She walks into the living room, looks at me in my
pajamas, and raises an eyebrow.

"How's that résumé coming?" she asks.

"It's a work in progress," I say.

She nods. "I'm sure it is."

7

MY COMPLETE LACK OF ACTIVITY continues on through the week, eventually inspiring Susannah to issue an ultimatum: either leave the house, or she tells my mother how I lost my job.

As I can't risk her following through on that threat, I shower, dress in something that cannot be counted as sleepwear, and go to the neighborhood gym.

Susannah's been a member there for a while now. She attempted to coax me into joining with her, but despite her excellent track record of talking me into doing stupid things, I decided to stick with couch surfing. But exercise is supposed to be good for you. Endorphins and whatnot. Given my current state of affairs, it couldn't hurt to find some. Or get some. However that works.

I pay for a day pass at the reception desk and turn down the offer of a free session with a personal trainer. After changing into never-before-worn workout clothes, I step into the world of chrome and sweat.

There's a row of treadmills lined up in front of a floor-to-ceiling mirror. Ugh. No. Isn't it bad enough that I intend to run—or at least briskly walk—on the damn thing? Do I really have to watch myself doing it? A trio of elliptical machines wait along an opposite wall. No lines, no waiting, no mirrors. Works for me. I choose the one on the end and put in my earbuds. Finding a playlist on my phone that might have something resembling a beat, I jab at buttons on the elliptical's control panel and begin my workout.

Approximately ten minutes later, I end my workout. Holy hell, I am out of shape. A sly glance toward the juice bar shows a pair of idle trainers laughing at something. Me? Probably. I must look pretty ridiculous. I'd laugh at myself if I could breathe.

Screw the endorphins. I'm done.

Limping and wheezing back to the locker room, I clean up and change into my street clothes. I keep my head down and my earbuds in as I make for the exit—better to discourage anyone from making any sort of conversation—but before I reach the promised land, I run head-on into something solid.

Some*one* solid, I realize, as hands wrap around my upper arms in an attempt to keep me upright. I appreciate the effort.

I pull my earbuds out. "Oh shit, I'm so sorry. I wasn't paying attention at all."

"It's fine," the guy says, still holding onto me. "You all right?"

"Yeah." I look up. "Oh hey—J. Crew Guy."

J. Crew Guy's face creases with confusion. He lets me go. "I'm sorry?"

"You were at The Howling Sailor the other night," I say. "With…uh, Craig. Parker."

Recognition flashes in his eyes. "Girl at the bar."

"My Native American name, I believe."

He smiles. "What do they call you when you're not on the reservation?"

"Nia."

"Josh." He shrugs. "Not as interesting as J. Crew Guy, I admit, but…"

"Sorry. You were a little out of place. The Howling Sailor tends to attract a blue-collar crowd, and you looked more like you should have been at a polo match, or on a yacht, or something."

"On a yacht?"

"Or something. I don't actually know what people wear on yachts. Or at polo matches, for that matter." Why can't I stop talking? "My world is very small."

"I doubt that," Josh says. "So, how do you know Craig?"

"We went to school together. Now he's on the force with my dad."

"Your dad's a cop? What's that like?"

"Let's just say I had a lot less fun in high school than Craig did."

Josh laughs. "That's true of most people."

"Well," I say, easing away, "sorry for that whole not-looking-where-I-was-going thing, but thanks for the assist. I'll try not to let it happen again."

I have a hand on the door when he calls out for me to wait. I look at him over my shoulder.

"Are you doing anything right now?" he asks. "Could I buy you some lunch, maybe?"

He wants to buy me lunch? Why would he want to do that? I turn around. "Uh…well…"

"Do you already have plans?"

"No, no plans." That is the magic of unemployment. I am decidedly free. However, I opt not to share this tidbit.

"Let's go, then. Anywhere you want," Josh says. "You can tell me what Craig was like in high school, and I can embarrass the hell out of him when I see him again."

I laugh. "Spoken like a true friend."

Josh shrugs. "What can I say?"

Lunch with a virtual stranger. He is a man, though, and a fairly good-looking one. Susannah would be so pleased. Me, moving on with my life and all.

"You understand I'm talking about some place public and well-lit, not the back of my windowless van," Josh says. "Is there a place nearby where all the cops have lunch? We could go there."

The cops like to have lunch at Dottie's Diner, but if I show up with a guy, my father will hear about it before our food arrives. I'm not all that interested in having an audience or a chaperone.

"Neither of us want to do that," I say. "But I appreciate the offer."

"Is that a no on lunch?"

"No, let's go to lunch. What the hell."

Josh nods. "There's the enthusiasm I was hoping for."

"Sorry." I wince inwardly. How many times have I apologized to him now? "It's been a while since I've done this."

"Had lunch?"

"Had lunch with...someone," I say. "You know, like a date. Not that I think this is a date, or I think that you think it's a date, or..." I sigh. What is wrong with me? "I'm going to melt into the floor now. It's been nice talking with you. Have a great life."

Josh smiles again. "You can relax, Nia. We don't have to call it anything but lunch."

"That may be safest."

"But if you wanted to call it a date," he continues, "I'd be okay with that."

"Well," I say, feeling a little flutter in my stomach, "why don't we see how lunch goes first?"

Susannah is already out of school when I arrive home. I park behind her car and go around back to find my dog frolicking in the yard. Susannah's sitting on the back steps, looking at her phone. Rufus drops a soggy tennis ball at her feet before bounding over to greet me.

"Something about this picture does not compute," I say, rubbing Rufus's belly when he flops onto his back.

"I think you meant to say 'thank you.'"

Susannah gingerly picks up the ball, capturing the dog's immediate attention. He's up and running the moment it leaves her hand.

"You're right. I did." I sit next to her. "Thank you."

"You're welcome," she says. "Where have you been?"

If I tell her where I was, an interrogation will be forthcoming. Is it better to just get it over with? I cringe. "I was having lunch."

Susannah's head tilts. "Alone?"

"No."

"With a guy?"

"Yes."

"Ellie?"

"No, not Ellie. I am not dating Ellie," I say. "Not only is he a cop—which would go against my strict no-dating-cops policy—he's my father's partner, okay? There will be no dating—or anything else—of Ellie. At least not by me."

"Well, who were you on a date with?"

"I don't even know if it *was* a date."

"You don't know if you were on a date?"

"He doesn't know, either."

"Who is he?"

"No one you know."

"What's his name? How did you meet him? *When* did you meet him?" Susannah asks. "You haven't been anywhere other than the living room and The Howling Sailor—and if it had been at The Howling Sailor, I would have been there, too. How did you meet a guy and I didn't notice?"

"I don't know. Could it be the fifth of gin you inhale every time we're there?" I say. "We didn't exactly meet at The Howling Sailor. It was more…our eyes met across a crowded, smoky room, and then we literally ran into each other at the gym today."

"Oh my God. You were at the gym? Were you lost?"

"I was trying to not become part of the couch, okay? Jesus Christ. I thought I would go do something healthy. Why are you mocking me for it?"

"You went to the *gym*. Did you put on workout clothes? Did you work out?"

"Yes. Well, kind of. An attempt was made."

"What did you do? Treadmill? Elliptical? One of those Zumba classes?"

I stand. "I'm leaving."

Susannah grabs my arm. "No, no, no, come on, I'm sorry. I won't tease you anymore. Stay and tell me about the guy."

"So you can tease me about him?"

"I won't say a word. I promise."

"You have never not said a word."

"You've never been to the gym," Susannah says. "It's a day for miracles, Vinnie. Let's celebrate together."

I sit. "You are a horrible human being."

"I know. Does the guy have a name?"

"Josh. He's friends with Craig Parker."

"You saw him at The Howling Sailor?"

"Yes. The night I was fired," I say. "You were dancing; I was sitting at the bar. Craig came over to get pints, and I saw Josh when Craig went back to their table."

"But you didn't talk to him until today."

"No. I ran into him on my way out of the gym. Like, literally ran into him because I wasn't watching where I was going. We recognized each other from the bar, started talking, and then he asked if he could take me to lunch."

"Where did you go?"

"A bistro in the city called Adele's. Would you like to know what we ate?"

"I'm good, thanks. Are you going to see him again?"

"Maybe. I gave him my number."

"Your actual number? Not a fake one?"

"Yes, I gave him my actual number."

Susannah sits back. "Oh, Vinnie. I'm so proud of you."

"You're making me regret telling you anything."

"When do I get to meet him?"

I stand, this time intending to leave regardless of what staying tactics she tries. "Never."

"What? Why?"

"Because you'll interrogate him! You'll embarrass me — and him — and this…thing we're doing here will be over before it starts."

"Would I do that to you?"

"Yes. Yes, you would absolutely do that to me. I know because you have a well-documented history of doing that to me."

I open the back door and walk into the house. Susannah follows me into the kitchen.

"That is categorically untrue," she says. "You've been living like a nun for the last three years. There's been no one to embarrass you in front of. No one to interrogate. You hang out with me, and you hang out with your family. That's it."

"Well, now I'm going to hang out with Josh."

"Good," Susannah says. "I still want to meet him, though. If for no other reason than if you go missing, I can tell the cops where to start looking."

"He's not a serial killer."

"Did he tell you that? Because all serial killers say that."

"See, I finally agree to go out with some guy, and now you won't stop bugging me because of it."

"Is it too much to ask that you be happy *and* safe?" Susannah says. "Look, I think it's great you found someone you may like to see again some time, or whatever it is you've decided to call it. Keep him to yourself if you want. I will stay out of it. But, if you do decide to bring him home, I promise I won't interrogate him or embarrass you."

"I'll believe it when I see it."

"I'll surprise you, Vinnie. I will."

"I can only hope."

"*Now* will you tell me about him? What is he like? Is he cute?"

"Yeah, he's cute. Kind of preppy," I say. "My first name for him was J. Crew Guy."

"Does he know that?"

"Yeah."

"He still took you to lunch?"

"He even paid."

Susannah grins. "I think we've found a winner."

"Boy, is our bar low."

When my cell phone rings, I pick it up to see Josh's name on the screen. I feel a smile coming on but hold it back.

"Is that him?" Susannah asks.

I shush her and answer. "Hello?"

"Nia? It's Josh."

"Hey." I turn my back to Susannah. "What's going on?"

"Just checking to see if you gave me a fake number."

"Did you really think I would do that?" I ask. "Lunch wasn't that bad."

"That bad? You didn't like lunch?"

"Lunch was fun. I was only teasing."

"Well, so was I," Josh says. "I was actually calling to see if you might be interested in going out Saturday night."

"With you?"

"That's the idea, yes."

"What did you have in mind?"

"Dinner? Maybe something in the way of a movie?"

"Pulling out all the stops," I say. "Are you trying to impress me?"

"Is it working?"

"Probably depends on the movie."

"What if I let you pick it?"

"Ah, now we're talking."

"Then it's a date?"

I smile. "Yeah, it's a date."

Susannah lets out a whoop loud enough to startle me. How did I forget she was there? Giving her a dirty look, I go back outside.

"If you text me your address, I can even come pick you up," Josh says. "All proper-like."

"If you come to the house, you'll have to come inside and meet my roommate," I warn. "Before you agree, you should know that she can be rather tenacious."

"Better or worse than meeting your parents? Not that I'm asking to meet them, mind you."

Thank God for that. "Well, she doesn't own a gun, but it might feel like she does."

"I look forward to the challenge," Josh says. "Pick you up at seven?"

"Yeah," I say. "Seven's great."

8

THE CLOSER I GET TO seven o'clock on Saturday night, the less great it becomes. It's been entirely too long since I've been on anything that could even remotely be considered a date, and I have forgotten how damn nerve-racking preparing for one can be.

I stand in front of my closet, surveying the options. All of my clothes are stupid. How is it that all of my clothes are stupid? I'm going to have to wear this robe out, aren't I? Because that won't be stupid at all.

"How's it going?" Susannah asks from the hall.

I look at her. "I'm canceling. I don't know what I was thinking when I said yes."

"You were thinking, 'boy, wouldn't it be nice if I had someone else to talk to for once besides my German shepherd,'" Susannah says. "Don't you dare cancel. I'll confiscate your phone if I have to."

I sit on the end of my bed. "I don't know what you're talking about. Rufus is a great conversationalist."

"Uh-huh. Would you like some help?"

"No." I sigh. "Yes."

Susannah walks over to the closet to flip through the options. "It's interesting to see you like this."

"Like what?"

"Nervous. Actually caring about what sort of impression you'll make."

"I don't care about…" I shrug when Susannah glances at me over her shoulder. "Fine. Whatever. Maybe I care a little."

"Which is interesting." She hands me a black button-down. "Try this."

I hold the shirt at arm's length. "This is too dressy. We're just going to dinner and a movie."

"It's fine. Put it on." She opens the bottom drawer of my dresser. "Do you have any jeans that shouldn't be in your mother's wardrobe instead?"

"Are you calling my mother unfashionable?" I ask, heading for the bathroom.

"I'm calling *you* unfashionable."

Fair enough. I make a face as I close the bathroom door. "Bottom left."

A moment later, Susannah cackles with glee. "Yes! This is what I'm talking about!"

Sliding off my robe, I put on the shirt, buttoning it slowly while looking at my reflection in the mirror. I can't believe I'm doing this. The door opens a crack, and my one pair of tight, low-rise jeans appear.

"Put these on, too," Susannah says, and I take them from her. "I'm getting you boots."

I shimmy into the jeans. "No boots. I'll wear my Chucks."

"No Chucks," she replies. "This is your first real date in three years, Vinnie. Make an effort."

I fasten the button on my jeans and open the bathroom door. "Boots will be uncomfortable."

Susannah walks out of her room, a pair of black boots dangling from her hand. "Beauty is pain."

I take the boots. "I hate that expression."

"We all do," Susannah says. "Put them on anyway. We need to do something about your hair."

It's quarter to seven when Susannah finishes fussing with my hair and makeup. I pretend to admire her work, but I don't want to see what she's done. I'm nervous enough as it is. I'll just have to trust that she hasn't made me look like I belong at Barnum and Bailey's.

Susannah grips my hands tightly. "Go forth, Vinnie. Interact with members of the opposite sex."

"Do I have to?"

"Yes."

As we head downstairs, there's a knock at the door. Rufus barks madly until Susannah traps him in the kitchen. She returns to the living room and perches on the arm of the couch.

"Why, that must be your gentleman caller," she says, affecting a southern accent. She smiles serenely and lays her hands primly in her lap. "Bring him hither so that I might inquire as to his intentions."

Bring him hither? How drunk is she right now? I shake my head. "Nope. Not if you're going to do this…whatever this is."

Susannah slides onto the seat. "You're no fun when you're nervous," she says in her normal voice. "Let him in, so I can meet him."

"If you start up with that accent again," I say, "I will freeze your bras when I get home."

"Noted."

When I open the door, a very preppy-looking Josh is standing on the front step, holding a bouquet of multi-colored carnations from the corner grocery store.

"Hey," he says. "You look great."

I indicate the flowers. "What are those?"

He nods. "Yeah, I figured you'd make that face, but I thought they might score me some points with your tenacious roommate."

"Good call. Would you like to come in, or should we make a break for it now?"

"If we do the latter, what are the odds of your roommate tracking us down wherever we go?"

I consider this. "Better than you'd think. Come on in."

He hands me the flowers, and we go into the living room where Susannah is, thankfully, still sitting on the couch like a normal human being.

She stands and holds out her hand. "You must be J. Crew Guy."

Josh looks at me as he shakes her hand. "You told her my secret identity?"

"Secret?" I look him up and down. "Do you own stock in the company or something?"

He smiles. "Is this how it's gonna be?"

"Very possibly," I say. "This is Susannah, by the way. Susannah, Josh."

"Tell me, Josh—if that is your real name," Susannah says. "What are your intentions for our girl here?"

I am going to kill her. Or at least smack her with this bouquet.

Josh smiles. "I intend to take her to dinner and then to the movie of her choice."

"What time do you intend to have her home by?"

"That would depend upon which movie she selects. Is there a particular time you would like her to be home by?"

"No," I interject, "there isn't."

"Midnight sounds good," Susannah says. "Not a minute after."

I roll my eyes. "Oh my God. If you two are finished."

"Midnight, it is." Josh looks at me, amusement written all over his face. "Are you ready to go?"

"Are you?" I ask. "Or would you two like to decide how many goats I'm worth first?"

"Oh, lighten up, Vinnie. We're just playing," Susannah says. "Run along and have a good time."

"I'll try." I hand her my flowers. "Put these in some water?"

Susannah holds the bouquet to her nose. "Have fun."

I collect my jacket and bag. Josh salutes Susannah, puts his hand on the small of my back, and ushers me out of the house.

"Vinnie?" Josh asks as we walk toward a dark-colored Toyota Camry.

"It's a nickname Susannah has for me," I say. "She's big into those, if you didn't notice."

Josh opens the passenger's door. "Does that mean she'll call me J. Crew Guy every time I see her?"

I slide inside. "And even when you don't."

"Good to know." Josh closes my door and walks around to get in on the other side. As he pulls onto the road, he asks, "Where did Vinnie come from?"

"Well, when a man and a woman love each other very much—"

"No, come on. How did Susannah come up with that nickname? You into Italian gangsters or something?"

"No, she got it from my name."

"Nia?"

"No, my…" I look at him. Have we never had this conversation before? "My real name."

Josh glances at me. "Nia's not your real name?"

"No, that's another nickname. My real name is exceedingly embarrassing, and I hate it, so I choose to go by Nia."

"What's your real name?"

"Will you promise not to make fun of me?"

"Is it really that bad?"

"I think so."

"What is it?" Josh asks. "I promise I won't make fun of you."

I sigh inwardly. "Lavinia."

"Lavinia? Like, from the Shakespeare play?"

I was not expecting that. "Yes, like from the Shakespeare play. You know Shakespeare?"

Josh shrugs. "Just what I was forced to read in school. I can't even remember which play it was from."

"*Titus Andronicus.*"

"The super violent one, right?"

"That's the one," I say. "You read that in school? What the hell kind of school did you go to?"

Josh laughs. "Your namesake doesn't fare too well in that play, if I recall correctly."

"No, she does not."

"Were you named after that character?"

"No. I was named after the heroine of some regency romance novel my mother was reading while pregnant with me."

Josh laughs again, and I lightly smack his chest. He laughs harder.

"You said you wouldn't make fun of me," I accuse.

"I'm not!"

"You're laughing."

"I was just imagining you in a regency romance novel," Josh says. "I'm not overly familiar with the genre, and I honestly have no idea what 'regency' means in this context, but—"

"It means it's set in Britain in the early 1800's."

Josh laughs more. "Yeah, I can't imagine you in the 1800's."

"Why? Because I'm not a prim and proper young lady?"

"Thank God for that," Josh says. "The idea is funny. That's all. Though the idea of you in a corset..." He glances at me again and winks. "That's hot."

"Well, don't get too attached to the idea because you'll never see me in one."

"We should never say never, Nia."

It's well past time to change the subject. "Where are we going anyway?"

"To dinner."

"Yes, but where will this dinner occur? A restaurant? This car?"

"Do you really think I would take you to a drive-thru on our first official date?"

"You might," I say. "I don't know you well enough to be sure."

"Then we'll have to change that."

Though his attention is on the road, he holds out his hand toward me. I look at it, then quickly look away as I remember the last time I held someone's hand. My hands clench and I squeeze my eyes shut to prevent any tears from escaping.

What is *wrong* with me? I can't fall apart over something so stupid. It's just a hand. It doesn't mean anything.

"Nia?" Josh asks. "You all right?"

"Yeah." Opening my eyes, I discreetly wipe away any trace of tears, then look at him and smile. "So, where are we going?"

It's a little after midnight when Josh pulls up in front of the house. Only the porch light is on. Did Susannah go to bed? I honestly thought she'd wait up to badger me for details. I don't know whether to be grateful or insulted.

Josh looks at the dark house. "Does this mean she decided to trust me?"

That, or she's planning to ambush me. "Could be."

"Walk you to your door?" he asks.

"Afraid I'll get lost?"

"No. Just thought I should offer."

I kiss him on the cheek. "Thank you for tonight. I had a good time."

"Good enough to, say…come out with me again some night?"

"That's a definite possibility." I open the car door. "See you around."

"At the gym?"

I laugh as I slide out. "That is definitely *not* a possibility. Good night."

Josh idles at the curb until I get inside the house. As I lock the door behind me, Rufus rushes over, whining in his relief at my return. I shush him—waking Susannah when her life isn't on the line is never a good idea—and go into the living room.

"You're late," she says.

Ambush it is, then. I switch on a table lamp. It takes me a minute to find her stretched out on the couch, covered by the duvet from her bed. Only her face is visible.

"Were you waiting up for me?" I ask.

"Yes, but not by choice," she says. "Your dog was concerned you were never coming home."

I look at Rufus, sitting at my feet. "Thank you for keeping him company."

Susannah sits up and stretches. "How was it?"

I slouch into an armchair. "Good. It was good."

"Your words say 'good.' Your face says 'not good.'"

"My face is tired. As is the rest of me." I lean over to remove the boots. "Particularly my feet. These things really are murder."

"But they look fantastic." Susannah studies me for a moment. "Are you sure you're all right?"

Probably depends on her definition of 'all right'. But I don't want to get into it. Not tonight. Possibly not ever.

"Yeah, it's just past my bedtime." I push out of the chair. "See you in the morning?"

"Yeah," she says as I climb the stairs. "See you then."

9

SUNDAY MORNING, I FIND MYSELF with an excess of nervous energy as well as a burning desire to avoid any conversation about Josh, our date, or the possibility of future dates. Before Susannah gets out of bed, I take Rufus for a jaunt in the park. It's colder today than it's been all month, drizzling and bordering on outright rain, but I don't care. Rufus doesn't care, either. He prances at my side as we leave the parking lot and head to the trails. We spend a few hours wandering around, only returning to the car when my shoes are too wet and my fingers are too cold to consider any other option.

My next stop is my parents' house. Rufus and I arrive in time for lunch. My mother's surprised, but happy, to see me. I suspect she's less enthusiastic about the very damp dog, but she hides it reasonably well.

"Where have you two been?" she asks.

"Oh, just out walking," I say.

"In this weather?"

I shrug. "Dogs have to walk."

She nods. "And you kids wondered why I never wanted one."

"We always thought you were mean."

"I suppose I was," she says. "Go dry off, then come have some lunch. I'm making tuna."

Rufus and I go to the bathroom to towel off. When we're dry — or at least drier — we return to the kitchen where my mother is assembling sandwiches at the counter. I sit at the table, Rufus at my feet. Mom serves me tuna on whole wheat bread, alongside a handful of potato chips. She gives me a glass of iced tea, then calls my father to come and join us.

He sits at the head of the table. "I didn't know you were coming over, Nia."

"Rufus and I thought we'd stop by," I say. "See if we could get Mom to feed us."

"I am not feeding that dog," she says, but it's a lie. She'll make Rufus his own sandwich. Though she won't admit to it, she keeps a jar of peanut butter in the cupboard just for him.

Dad chuckles. "Pretty safe bet."

"Yeah, I've never been much of a gambler," I say between bites. "You on shift today?"

"Going in this afternoon. Won't be home until late," Dad says. "I imagine you'll be tucked safe and sound in your own bed by then."

I nod. "Or passed out in a puddle of my own vomit."

"Lavinia," my mother admonishes.

"Just joking, Mom," I say. "Susannah and I do not drink on school nights."

"Well, I'm certainly glad to hear that," she responds, but the look on her face tells me this matter isn't yet closed. A follow-up scolding will be in my very near future. I hope I at least get dessert first.

After lunch, I help with the dishes, then join my mother in the living room. She sits in her recliner and pulls out a knitting project. Rufus curls up in front of the fireplace to nap. I settle on the couch and look at the Sunday edition of the *Boston Globe* scattered on the floor. My parents always read the entire paper from one end to the other. I tend to be more selective. I pick up the comics page and pretend to read the strips but keep glancing at the classified section. Probably wouldn't be a completely outlandish idea to at least *scan* the want ads.

When I think my mother might not be paying attention, I swap the comics for the classifieds.

"Are you reading the want ads?" Mom asks.

Of *course* Nancy's paying attention. She always pays attention. One would think I would have learned that lesson a million times over by now. "Yeah."

"Looking for a new job?"

"I don't know. Maybe. I was more curious what's out there."

She shakes her head. "Terrible time to be looking for work."

Tell me about it. "Yeah."

I watch her knit. It looks like the start of a mitten, which makes sense given the time of year. She makes hats and mittens for the local elementary school to have on hand for students who don't have them. She also makes blankets for the church and a million other things for a million other people. How could someone as miserable as me come from someone as good as her?

"Everything all right?" she asks.

Maybe I should tell her the truth about what's going on. About my fun new lack of direction and income. About Josh.

"Lavinia?"

A knock at the door keeps me from answering. Rufus lifts his head but flops over and goes back to sleep. My mother sets down her knitting and pats my knee on the way out of the living room. A moment later, she returns with Lew.

He nods at me. "Nia."

"Llewellyn," I say, then grin at the mildly dirty look he gives me in response.

"Could I get you some coffee, Llewellyn?" my mother asks. "Something to eat?"

"No, thank you, Nancy."

"All right, then," she says. "Make yourself comfortable, and I'll hurry Patrick along."

She leaves, but Lew doesn't move. Does that mean standing at an informal attention is comfortable for him, or is he just afraid to be in a room I'm already in?

"Looking for a new job?" he asks.

I look at the paper in my lap. "Considering a change."

"Change is good."

"Yeah," I say. "You can sit down, you know. I won't bite."

Lew smiles. "I didn't think you would. I just assumed I wouldn't be here long enough to make it worthwhile."

I lean toward him. "I don't know if you've realized this yet, but my father is quite possibly the slowest person on the face of the earth. Susannah gets ready faster than he does. Not only do you have time to sit, you have time to watch the director's cut of several cinematic classics."

Laughing, Lew sits at the opposite end of the couch. As he does so, Rufus pads over to the new arrival, not breaking eye contact until Lew pets his head.

I put the newspaper on the floor. "So, how are you liking Boston? Visit the Tea Party Museum yet?"

"Should I?"

"No. Well, unless you have a real hankering to throw tea into Boston Harbor."

"I don't, no," Lew says. "I haven't actually seen much of the city. Too busy getting settled in."

"If you'd like a tour guide, I'd be happy to show you around sometime."

Lew raises an eyebrow. "Really?"

"Why not? If you're going to live here, you should know all the places we avoid like the plague."

"Well, I may take you up on that."

"You should. I'm one hell of a tour guide."

"I'm sure that's true."

"I'm serious. When are you off this week?"

"My week's surprisingly packed, but your dad and I aren't on shift until Friday afternoon. I could squeeze in a tour that morning."

"Let's go then," I say.

"Okay. If you're sure you don't mind."

"I don't mind. You'll be saving me from a day alone with my thoughts."

"That scary, huh?"

"And then some," I say. "Really, you'll be doing me a favor."

"All right. Friday it is."

I hold out my hand. "Give me your phone. I'll put my number in it."

Lew doesn't move. "Um..."

My hand falls. "Unless Susannah already did that the night we met."

"She did."

Some people just can't stop meddling, can they? "Were you planning to use my number?"

"I had considered it," he admits. "But then I found out you're my partner's daughter. Some lines shouldn't be crossed, you know?"

I nod. Oh, I know.

As we hear my parents approaching, Lew stands. "I'll see you later, Nia."

I wave. "Bye."

After Lew and my father leave, Mom sits back down and takes up her knitting again, adding a few rows to whatever she's making.

"Maybe now you can tell me the truth," she says, switching from blue yarn to red.

Apparently, panic feels like a cold egg broken over my head. I look at my mother. "About?"

"Whatever's going on with you."

"Nothing's going on with me."

Mom nods. "What's his name?"

"Whose name?"

"Your new beau."

My new beau? "How the hell do you know about him?"

My mother looks at me over the top of her glasses. "Language, Lavinia."

"Sorry," I say. "How do you know about him? Did Susannah tell you?"

"I heard from Colin, who I imagine heard from Susannah." Mom squints at her knitting. "But I would have known there was someone new anyway."

"How?"

"I can always tell," she says. "What's his name?"

I make a mental note to kill both Susannah and Colin later. "His name is Josh. We've only been out a couple of times, and there probably won't be a third, so—"

"Why won't there be a third?"

Because I'm emotionally stunted and unavailable. "I'm not sure we're really clicking."

"Because of Brian?"

She hasn't mentioned Brian in a while. His name has been taboo for so long—at least in my presence—that it's shocking to hear it now, dropped in an almost casual manner. I need a moment to compose myself before I can respond.

"Brian is—was…" I sigh. "Whatever. It's over. It doesn't matter."

"Don't say that. What happened there was—"

"Mom," I plead, my eyes watering.

"Heartbreaking," she says. "It was not nothing. It does matter. You'll carry that for the rest of your life. It is a part of you—*he's* a part of you, and you do not dismiss that."

Now I'm crying. Not full-fledged, unstoppable sobs or anything, but fat, silent tears that roll down my cheeks. It's not much better than the unstoppable sobs.

I wipe them away. "I'm not."

"But you shouldn't let it control you, either. That, I'm afraid you're doing."

She's right. As much as I would like the opposite to be true, it's pretty damn hard to deny. "I don't mean to. I just…"

"I know, honey," she says. "Tell me you're trying. Tell me that, and I won't say another word about it."

"I am. I am trying."

She smiles. "All right, then. Is there anything else you want to talk about?"

Hell, I didn't even want to talk about *this*. "No."

She switches back to the blue yarn. "Martha Taylor called me the other day."

Busted. Somehow, I forgot the principal's secretary and my mother have been friends for a long time. Certainly long enough that one would call the other when one's daughter is fired in such a spectacular fashion.

"She did?" I ask.

"Yes. She wanted to know how you were doing."

"Well, that's nice of her."

There's a pause then. A long, weighted one.

"I was going to tell you," I say.

"Were you?"

"Yes. Eventually, anyway. I just wanted to have some good news to tell you at the same time. You know, like a new career or something. I just…I haven't found one yet. But I am looking. Or I will be soon. I promise."

Can my mother hear that lie, too? If she does, she doesn't comment on it.

"A lot of changes," she says instead.

"Susannah thinks a fresh start is good."

"Susannah is right."

I shake my head. "It was bound to happen eventually."

My mother laughs. "Don't tell her I said so. I wouldn't want it to go to her head."

I laugh as well. "Too late."

10

IN AN ATTEMPT TO KEEP my promise to my mother that I am, at least, trying, I call Josh to see if he might be interested in going out again. He invites me to a bar in Boston to check out a local band I've never heard of. It sounds like it will be loud, smoky, and crowded, but as there will be whiskey, I accept.

When I tell Susannah where we're going, she suggests a double date.

"With my *brother*?" I ask.

"I'm not dating anyone else."

"Ugh. You two will just make out the whole time."

"Not the whole time. I don't have the lung capacity."

I laugh. "What does Colin see in you?"

"The world may never know," Susannah says. "So? What do you say? Double date? Could be fun…"

I sigh. "I'll ask Josh."

For some unknown reason, he agrees, and on Wednesday night, I go on a double date with my roommate and brother. We meet Josh at a bar on Tremont Street called The Rebel Fly. The place is crowded — especially for a weekday night — but we find a curved booth along the wall and watch four guys in ripped jeans and graphic T-shirts move around the stage, setting up equipment and tuning guitars. The logo on the bass drum reads *Why Wolves Why*.

A waitress approaches our table. "What are we drinking tonight?"

After collecting our orders, she disappears. The band moves into position for a sound check, the crowd heckling the continued delay. We forego the taunting in favor of making stilted conversation amongst ourselves. It's nothing Josh and I didn't already cover the other night, but as Susannah and Colin weren't there, we go through it again. Josh is in sales. Colin is an artist. Susannah teaches math. I watch daytime television. Josh grew up a couple of towns over, and our high schools are long-time rivals. This prompts good-natured ribbing between the boys, which helps to alleviate any awkwardness. Still, it's a relief when the waitress returns with our drinks.

"Oh, thank God," Susannah says, "alcohol."

"See if you can sound more like you need to be at a meeting," I say, and she toasts me with her glass.

The band finally finishes their pre-show prep, and someone comes to the mic to introduce them as Boston's favorite band. I'm not sure about that, but the audience whoops and hollers as a loud, bass-heavy number I don't recognize begins. An original song, or just a really crappy cover? Susannah leans into Colin, head bobbing to the beat. Josh puts his arm around my shoulders. I will myself not to tense up. I can do this.

Josh looks at me. "Is this okay?"

I smile and lean forward to lay claim to my Jack and Coke. "Yeah," I say, settling back against him. "This is good."

The band has launched into its third raucous rock song when my phone lights up, vibrating across the table. I pick it up to find a text from Lew.

Are we still on for Friday morning?

We are, I text back. *Meet at the swan boats at 10am?*

"Lew?" Josh says in my ear. "Who's Lew?"

"A friend," I tell him. "My father's partner."

"Why are you meeting him on Friday?"

Swan boats? Lew texts.

In the Public Garden. Think you can find them on your own?

"He's new in town," I say. "I offered to show him around."

"Should I be jealous?"

I'm sure I can manage, Lew replies. *See you then.*

I put down the phone. "Why would you be jealous?"

"My girl going out with another guy? Why wouldn't I be jealous?"

"Huh." I sip my drink. "I'm not sure where to start."

"What are you—?"

"Two dates does not make me your girl."

"Three dates."

"Three dates? No, we're not counting lunch."

"No, *you're* not counting lunch."

"Whatever. Three dates doesn't make me your girl, either."

"How many dates does?"

I finish my drink. "I'll let you know."

Josh leans back. "You're really making me work for this, Vinnie."

"It'll take a whole lot more dates if you call me that."

"What if I get you a refill?"

I smile. "Certainly a good start."

Josh twists around, searching the room. After a moment, he gives up and brushes a kiss across my cheek. "I'll be right back." Pointing to Susannah and Colin, he asks, "Either of you want anything from the bar?"

"I'll go with you," Colin says. He looks at Susannah. "Another round?"

"Please," she says, and slides up next to me after the boys have gone. "Are you all right?"

"Why wouldn't I be all right?"

"You looked like you were going to jump out of your skin when Josh put his arm around you."

"I did not."

"You did. You came home weird after your first date, and you've been avoiding me ever since, and — "

"Is that why you're here, drinking on a school night? Because you think I need a chaperone?"

"No, I just…I wanted to make sure you're all right."

"Are you the happiness police?"

"Just a concerned citizen, ma'am," Susannah says. "Are you okay?"

I glance at the bar to make sure Josh and Colin are still there. "I promise I'm fine. I just…"

"What?"

I sigh and look back at Susannah. "It's harder than I thought it would be. You know, being close to someone again."

Susannah's face registers her surprise. She hadn't expected a serious answer. "Do you like Josh?"

"Yeah. He's nice. He…" I smile. "He banters."

"You do love to banter," Susannah acknowledges. "Okay, so maybe try to relax about the rest of it. If you like him, the intimacy will come. Don't put too much pressure on yourself."

"Thanks, Dr. Ruth."

"Jesus, how old are you? Can't you make a reference from this century?" Susannah smacks my arm. "And hey, next time just tell me this stuff, so I don't have to spend a school night drinking bad cocktails while listening to some shitty band."

"They're not that bad."

"Well, then, for once, you are the nice one," Susannah says, then moves over as the boys return.

Josh slides in next to me. "Everything okay?"

"Oh sure," I say. "We just had to talk about you behind your back."

Josh sets down a glass in front of me. "Should I be worried?"

I glance at Susannah, already nestled against Colin. "Nah. I think she likes you."

"What about you?" Josh drapes his arm around me again. "Do you like me?"

"You're not half bad." I attempt to relax against his chest. "You might even be kind of okay."

"High praise."

"Don't let it go to your head."

As the rest of the night passes, I relax more and more. I'm sure the whiskey has a hand in that, but maybe this thing isn't entirely impossible or crazy. When we're ready to leave, Josh offers me his hand and I take it.

This might be better than kind of okay.

"I'll be out of town for a few days," Josh says before we part ways, "but can I call you when I get back?"

I look at my hand in his. "Yeah. I'd like that."

11

FRIDAY MORNING, I TAKE RUFUS with me to meet Lew. When we arrive at the Public Garden, Lew is sitting on a bench, talking on his phone. It doesn't appear to be a particularly happy conversation. I slow as we get closer, not wanting to interrupt.

Lew eventually sees me and waves. "I gotta go," he says into the phone and ends the call. "Hey, Nia."

"Hey. Everything all right?" I ask.

Lew slips his phone into his jacket pocket. "Yeah." He crouches to greet Rufus. He doesn't seem to mind being coated in dog hair and slobber. That is an endearing quality. He glances at me. "Where to?"

"If you don't mind, I thought we might start with some coffee," I say. "Susannah and I ran out this morning, and I didn't have time to stop anywhere to get some."

"Sure." Lew stands and looks around. "Is there a coffee cart nearby?"

"Even better. On Newbury Street is a dog-friendly coffee place called Jitters, and Rufus just happens to be one of their favorite customers."

Lew smiles at the dog. "Of course he is. Lead the way."

It's quiet on Newbury Street—a rare mid-morning lull. Jitters is even emptier; we're the only customers in the place. The barista behind the counter—a woman named Lacey—calls out a greeting.

"What are you doing here, Nia?" she asks. "Isn't it a school day?"

"Playing hooky," I say. "Lacey, meet Lew."

"Well, hello." Lacey looks at Lew admiringly. "I'd play hooky, too."

Lew glances at me. His expression suggests he is wondering what is wrong with my friends. It's an excellent question for which I have no answer.

"What can I get for you three today?" Lacey asks.

I order the usual—a caramel latte for me and a lightly toasted bagel for Rufus. Lew requests a large coffee. Black.

After Lew pays, Lacey prepares our drinks and toasts a plain bagel for Rufus, spreading a little peanut butter on it when it's ready. Food and drink in hand, we sit at a corner table with a view of the street. Rufus lays at my feet, tail thumping in anticipation. I break off a piece of bagel for him.

"Thank you for the coffee," I say. "Rufus thanks you for the bagel."

Lew nods. "You're both welcome."

We sit for a few minutes, sipping coffee and not speaking. Lew alternates between looking out the window at the passers-by and watching Rufus inhale his bagel.

"So…where are you from?" I ask.

"Arizona."

"What brought you up north?"

"A little of this, a little of that," he answers. "Have you told your parents you've lost your job?"

Changing the subject. Interesting. Why doesn't he want to talk about why he's in Massachusetts? I lean back. "Well, my mother knows, which means she's probably told Dad, but neither of them heard it from me."

"Why didn't you tell them?"

"I don't know. I guess I wanted to be able to tell them I left teaching because I found an exciting new career as a…"

"As a…?" Lew prompts.

I sigh. "I don't know. I've got nothing."

"Perhaps you could parlay sarcasm into a career. You'd be a CEO in no time."

"I'm not sure that's a compliment."

"I'm not sure, either," Lew admits. "What made you want to be a teacher?"

"Isn't that a little deep for coffee talk?"

"You don't have to answer, if you don't want to."

"No, I'll answer. I just…I don't really know." I gaze out the window while I think about it. "My mother used to teach elementary school, so maybe it just seemed the thing to do. What about you? What made you want to be a cop?"

"Found a badge in my cereal box one morning and thought I'd go with it."

"Come on. I gave you a serious answer."

"I know. I'm still surprised by that."

I throw a crumpled napkin at him.

Lew laughs as he catches the napkin and sets it on the table. "Why does anyone become a cop?"

"According to every show and movie I've ever seen, it's because of the unsolved murder of at least one parent."

"Is that how your dad got started?"

"Nah. He just likes to help people, and being a cop was the best way he knew to do it."

Lew nods. "We have that in common."

"Or…" I point at him. "You're just trying to suck up."

"Well, I gotta get in good where and when I can. As soon as you realize I don't root for the Red Sox—"

"Oh God. Please tell me you're not a Yankees fan."

Lew shakes his head. "Diamondbacks. Will my Arizona loyalties be a problem?"

"Well, there are two religions in the Kelly household: Catholicism and Boston sports. Not necessarily in that order, either," I say. "But better Arizona than New York."

Lew toasts me with his coffee cup. "I'll drink to that."

"Did you move here to find out what it would be like to have teams that actually win championships?"

"Those sound like fightin' words."

"Oh, please. If you think those are fightin' words, the actual fightin' words will make you cry."

"I don't know about that. I don't cry easily."

"I suppose we'll find out."

"We'll be seeing each other again, then?"

"You're my father's partner," I say. "Seeing each other from time to time will be unavoidable. Especially because my mother will try to adopt you."

"Excuse me?"

"Not, like, legally, or anything," I say. "But because you're a handsome, single police officer and her husband's partner, her mothering instincts will kick in, if they haven't already."

"What will that mean for me?"

"Endless dinner invitations. A place to watch all the Boston sports you can handle. A seat at her world-renowned Thanksgiving dinner. Oh, and Dad's birthday party, of course."

"Your dad's birthday?"

I nod. "It's, like, the week before Thanksgiving. Mom goes all out, drives herself — and, by extension, all of us — crazy with planning, but it's ultimately fun. You should come."

"Should I?"

"It's better than hanging out by yourself in your swingin' bachelor pad. Besides, Nancy doesn't take no for an answer."

Lew smiles. "Sounds great."

"It will be. You'll see."

Lew has some more coffee, eyes dancing with amusement. I am immediately suspicious.

"What?" I ask.

He sets down the cup. "You think I'm handsome, huh?"

"So I said you were handsome. Are you twelve?"

Lew laughs. "You're the one who said I was handsome."

What an ass. "Well, don't get your hopes up, stud. I don't date cops."

"Really?"

"Yes, really."

Lew sits back, looking at me thoughtfully. "Did something happen to make you form such a policy?"

I force myself to stay relaxed. "What makes you think that?"

He shrugs. "You're a cop's daughter. The force seems to be a big part of who you are. I get that. You've been surrounded by it all your life. I also think it makes sense that, at some point, you could have ended up dating a member of that force."

I can't argue with his logic, mostly because he's right. Except it was more than dating. We hadn't made it official, but everyone was waiting for the big announcement. Brian and Lavinia were going to get married and have babies and live happily ever after.

And then we didn't.

I sigh. "I guess that just goes to show how much you know."

"I guess it does," Lew replies.

He's quiet, studying me as I studied him earlier. Did he see something in my face just then? God, I hope not.

I fiddle with the cardboard sleeve around my cup. "It doesn't matter anyway. I have a boyfriend."

"Do you?"

"Well, I might have a boyfriend. We haven't talked terminology or exclusivity or anything, but...yeah. There's a guy I'm seeing. Socially. I mean, we've gone out a few times."

"Sounds serious."

"It's new."

"You sound absolutely thrilled about it."

"It's new," I repeat. "It's always strange when it's new. Don't you think? Everyone being all…weird and fake, just trying to impress the other person."

"Have you been weird and fake with this guy?"

"Weird, definitely. I kind of have the market cornered on that."

"You'd be surprised," Lew says. "What about fake?"

I consider this. "I'm trying not to be."

"I guess that's all any of us can do."

"Some people don't have to try," I say. "Susannah, for example. I don't think I've ever seen her try to come off as someone she's not."

"I haven't seen you do that, either."

"Yeah, well, you never saw me in the classroom."

"No, but I hear there's a video I can watch."

Oh God. I don't even want to know how he heard about that. I drop my head in my hands. "I'm gonna be in the bad teacher hall of fame forever and ever, aren't I?"

"Maybe not forever."

I look at him. "Thanks. That's reassuring."

"I'm here to serve."

"I thought it was because you didn't know anyone else."

"That, too." Lew looks out the window. "Do you want to know why I'm here?"

"Here in Boston?"

"Here with you."

Yes. No. I sip my coffee. It's getting cold now. It's not as good when it's cold. "Okay. Why?"

"The night we met, I really wasn't hitting on you," Lew says. "I was just making conversation at first, but there was something about you. Something interesting. You seemed — I don't know — you seemed lost."

"That was interesting?"

"Seemed like something we had in common."

He sounds serious. He looks serious. I don't know what to do about that. I'm not even sure how I feel about being called lost, no matter how truthful a description it may be.

"Did you come to Boston because you were lost," I ask, "or are you lost because you came to Boston?"

"Neither."

"Why did you come to Boston? It couldn't be the job. There are a lot of places between Arizona and here where you could have been a cop. What was the draw? Snow and ice?"

Lew smiles. "No."

"Then what?"

"Why do you care?"

"I don't. I'm just curious."

The smile disappears, Lew's demeanor becoming less of an open book and more...me.

"You're pressing pretty hard for idle curiosity," he says.

I shrug. "You don't want to talk about it, and I want to know why. It's interesting."

"It really isn't."

"Your denial only makes me want to talk about it more," I say. "Come on. Tell me."

"No."

"Tell me."

"No."

"I'm unemployed and have no life, so I can literally do this all day," I say. "Tell me."

"No."

"Come on. What's the big deal? Just tell me."

"No," Lew says flatly. "Thanks for the coffee."

I start to remind him that he was the one who paid when he walks away. Rufus snaps to attention at the first sign of movement, and together we watch Lew disappear from view.

I look at Rufus. "Well, how about that."

12

ALL THE WAY HOME, I think about Lew.

Who knew — who would have even *guessed* — that he was the dramatic exit type? Especially when that exit was spurred by a question as innocuous as 'what brought you to Boston?'

What is he hiding? Or avoiding. I suppose he could be avoiding something. Either way, what could be so terrible that he wouldn't just tell me?

He didn't even try to lie or tell me to mind my own damn business. No, instead he just up and left like I said something unforgivably rude about his mother.

What's his deal? Something brought him here. Something led him to The Howling Sailor, and something caused him to sit next to me. All right, so that last one was probably just a lack of other available bar stools, but the rest is true enough.

How do I find out what that something is? It'll be a challenge. I can't imagine Lew will be interested in hanging out or talking to me at any point in the near future. Or possibly ever again.

But almost as soon as Rufus and I walk through the front door, my theory is disproved when I receive a text from the man of mystery.

Sorry I had to leave. Can we reschedule the tour for another day?

Huh. Maybe I was wrong. Perplexed, I look at the message for a moment before responding.

If you want. I'll even try not to be such a nosy pain in the ass next time.

You're many things, Nia, but not that.

So…we're OK?

We're OK.

I should feel better—relieved, maybe—but an odd sensation lingers in my chest. Why is Lew affecting me like this?

I don't know what to do about that, either, so I build a nest of blankets and pillows on the couch and hunker down with Rufus to watch the Lifetime Movie Network until it passes. Nothing like some mindless entertainment to keep one's mind blank.

A couple of hours later, Susannah comes through the front door, an L.L. Bean tote bag hanging off each arm. She drops the bags and sinks into a chair before releasing a sigh that screams exhaustion and frustration. Not her typical entrance. Interesting.

"Hi, honey. I'm home," she says.

I mute the television. "Where's the bacon?"

Susannah slips off her shoes. "Did you need bacon?"

What a waste of a perfectly clever joke. I turn my attention back to the movie. "No, I didn't."

"What are you watching?"

"Lifetime Movie Network."

"What's it about?"

I check the guide. "A nanny suspects her brother killed a member of the family she now works for."

"Feel the need to destroy some brain cells?"

"I wasn't using them anyway." I glance at her. "Something wrong, sunshine? You seem out of sorts."

Susannah slumps in her chair. "Colin and I had plans to go out tonight, but he canceled on me."

Sounds like a dodged bullet to me, but then again, I do like dogs more than most people. "Ah."

"Do you want to go into the city with me tonight?" she asks. "Booze, boys, and Boston? Sounds pretty great, doesn't it?"

"Not even a little bit," I say. "What are you even planning to do with these boys, given that you're in a committed relationship and all."

"I'm in a committed relationship, not dead," Susannah says. "What about going to The Howling Sailor?"

"I'm not in the mood."

"You're never in the mood, Vinnie. Let's go anyway. Come on—call your boy toy and get him to join us."

"Josh is not my boy toy. Also, he's away for work."

"Let's call Ellie, then. Of course, he might already be there."

I snort. "Lew's on duty tonight."

"Okay, so we'll go to The Howling Sailor and start a brawl. Then Ellie will have to come and break it up."

I envision that scenario with amusement. "Well, that would be special. My father would be particularly proud."

"Does that mean you're in?"

"No. Frank wouldn't even let it get that far. You'd just end up annoying him, and then he would never serve us alcohol again."

"Fine. We'll go celebrate the three-week anniversary of your firing."

"You're full of festive ideas, aren't you?"

"It would make me feel better."

Susannah sticks her bottom lip out in an exaggerated pout. I throw a pillow at her, and she bats it away.

"We have alcohol and disco music here," I say. "Let's stay home."

"Jesus Christ, grandma. You can stay home when you're dead."

Charming. I sigh. "Leave me alone, you lunatic. I'm tired."

"Oh yeah? Long day of lounging on the couch?"

"I haven't been here all day. I went into the city this morning and had coffee with Lew."

"You had coffee with Ellie?"

"Well, until he threw a hissy fit and stormed off."

"I can't imagine Ellie throwing a hissy fit."

"Okay, so it wasn't a literal hissy fit. But he did take off."

"Why? What did you do?"

"Nothing!"

"You must have done something."

"I didn't do anything. I asked him what brought him to Boston, which was apparently something he really didn't want to talk about—"

"So you harassed him."

"No. Well...maybe a little."

"Vinnie!"

"What? You wouldn't have let it go, either."

"Maybe not, but I'm guessing I would have been nicer about it."

"Like that's hard," I say. "But come on, why wouldn't he tell me? What's he hiding?"

"Maybe it's private. Sometimes, people keep secrets."

"Yeah, but Lew?"

"Did you tell him about Brian?"

"You know I didn't."

Susannah sits back, arms folded across her chest. "I rest my case."

"You'd be a terrible attorney."

"I'd be an *amazing* attorney," she says. "Why do you even care what Ellie did?"

I shrug. "I wasn't expecting it."

"I thought you would have appreciated that. A refusal to give in? A dramatic storming-off? You usually love that stuff."

"I do, but with Lew...I don't know. It just seemed so out of place."

Susannah looks at me intensely, as though searching for something. "Can I ask you a serious question?"

I'm immediately on the defensive. "If you think we're up for it."

"Do you like Lew?"

"Yeah. He's a nice guy."

"No, I mean, do you *like* Lew."

Do I like Lew? What the hell is that supposed to—oh. Do I *like* him. I shake my head. "No."

"Are you sure?" she asks. "You seem super invested in this. In him."

"I'm not—no. I'm not super invested in him. He's a friend. Not even my friend, really," I say. "He's this new person who's been shoved into my family, and I'm curious about him. Anyone would be."

"Okay. But if you did like him—"

"I don't."

"But if you did, it would be—"

"Hey," I say loudly, reaching for the remote, "let's go out."

13

AFTER A WEEKEND SPENT PLAYING with Rufus and watching *Law & Order* reruns, I am more than ready to leave the house on Monday morning. My first stop is the local animal shelter, Pine Knolls. Though I have driven past more times than I can count, I haven't been inside for a few years.

It hasn't changed. Warm and smelling like dog, it's instantly familiar and comforting. I shouldn't have stayed away for so long.

A woman I haven't seen before smiles at me from the receptionist's desk. "Hi! Welcome to Pine Knolls. How can we help you today?"

"Uh, yeah," I say. "I was wondering if—"

"Well," a new voice interrupts. "If it isn't Lavinia Kelly."

Glancing up, I see Gretchen Hamilton coming out of her office. She's been the shelter director for longer than I can remember. She doesn't appear to have changed, either.

"Hi Gretchen," I say.

"How are you, hon?"

"Surviving."

"Good. That's good," she says. "Though I never thought you wouldn't."

Glad someone did. I smile, the action strained.

"What brings you in today?" Gretchen asks. "Looking for a friend for that shepherd of yours?"

As much as I would enjoy the look on Susannah's face when she came home to find a second dog in the house, I shake my head. "No. Actually, I was hoping you could use a hand around here."

Gretchen smiles. "I think we can find a use for you."

I spend the next few hours scrubbing pens and cleaning litter boxes and small animal cages. I walk a few dogs, play with the cats, and help with a backlog of filing in between loads of laundry. When I finally head out, I am pleasantly sore and tired. It's a good feeling. I'll have to do this again.

My mother calls as I am getting into the car to leave. For a moment, I debate letting it go to voicemail, but as I'll just have to call her back, I answer.

"Hey, Mom," I say.

"Are you available for dinner Wednesday night?" she asks. "I'd like to have the whole family over."

"What's the occasion?"

"I need to have an occasion to have my children over for dinner?"

"No. Just asking if there is one. You know, like Dad got another partner, or—"

"There's no special occasion. Your father did not get another partner. He and Llewellyn are doing very well together."

"Well, good for them," I say. "Yes, I can come over for dinner Wednesday night."

"Thank you. Bring Rufus, if you find you cannot possibly part with him for a few hours."

"You know I can't."

"You can bring your new boyfriend, too. We'd love to meet him."

Yeah, like I'm going to do that. "I think he's working, but if he's free, I'll bring him along."

"You do that," my mother says.

Her tone suggests she knows I'm lying through my teeth. Which I am. I don't care if Josh is as free as a bird Wednesday night. No power in the universe will compel me to bring him to a family dinner. If the relationship continues, meeting my family will be inevitable, but it's best to do it one member at a time.

"I will," I say. "See you Wednesday."

"Six o'clock?"

"I'll be there."

Hanging up, I toss the phone on the passenger's seat and head home to rescue Rufus from his solitude. I'm nearly there when the short blare of a siren catches my attention. Glancing at the rearview mirror, I see a patrol car with its lights flashing behind me. Then I look down at the speedometer. I'm going forty. The speed limit is thirty-five.

I pull over. "You cannot be serious."

I lean over to find the registration and insurance card in the glove compartment, then pull out my license. When I have all three in hand, I roll down the window. Lew is standing there, smiling.

"License and registration, please," he says.

"I may be wrong, but this seems like a gross misuse of your authority."

"You were speeding. License and registration, please."

"I was not speeding. Much, anyway."

"This is a posted thirty-five zone. We clocked you exceeding that speed. License and registration, please."

"Who are you riding with today?" I look at the rearview mirror again to see if I can tell who's in the car. "It can't possibly be my father."

"No, Patrick was needed elsewhere. I'm riding with Parker."

"Parker? You mean Craig Parker?" I twist around to see. The figure in the passenger's seat waves. I think about flipping him off but refrain.

"Yes, Craig Parker. Nice guy," Lew says. "He thought you'd be mad."

"Why would he think that?"

"I have no idea. I've always found you to be delightfully accommodating. Now, license and registration, please."

I look at Lew. "Come on. You're not serious."

He points at me. "Law breaker." He points at himself. "Law enforcer."

"Guy who's pushing his luck," I say, but hand over my license and registration anyway.

Lew looks over my information. "Did you get an invite to dinner Wednesday?"

"If that's what you wanted to talk about, you could have just called me."

He shrugs. "This is more fun."

"For you, maybe. I'm the one being judged by every passer-by."

"Remember that shame the next time you feel the need for speed."

I laugh. "You are such an ass. Are you giving me a ticket or what?"

"I think I can let you off with a warning this time."

I snatch my cards from his hand and drop them next to my phone. "Am I free to go, Officer?"

He steps back. "Absolutely, ma'am. Enjoy the rest of your day."

I smile as I roll up the window. "May a belligerent drunk puke on your shoes."

"By the way," Lew says just before the window closes, "your license is expired."

14

As I have nothing better to do, I go to the DMV the next morning. By the time I arrive, the waiting room is packed. I'm issued number fifty-five, then make the mistake of checking to see what number they're currently helping. Four. Maybe I should go home and try again another day. On the other hand, what does it matter? The Game Show Network will still be there when I'm done.

Wedging myself into an open seat between two people, I pull out my phone to search through online job listings in my area. Might as well take advantage of my forced downtime. At least until the battery dies.

Medical training assistant? No. Dental training assistant? No. Network technology person? No. Process engineer? Since I don't know what that job entails, it probably means no. Software engineer. See above. Tax manager. Probably not. Taxes involve numbers and laws, neither of which is particularly my thing. Not that I know what my thing is.

Interior and furnishings designer. The ideal applicant must have knowledge of textiles and furniture construction. He or she must also have excellent customer service skills. They likely wouldn't be impressed with the reason I am currently seeking employment. They would be even less impressed with my complete lack of style.

I look at the number board. Still serving number four.

A cell phone rings, and the woman on my right digs through a flower-patterned bag to find it. She talks with someone named Steve about waiting in line at the DMV. I go back to the job listings.

I skip the education section. Been there, done that, got the pink slip. Next, I skip over the technology and engineering section. I can barely check my email. I also skip the medical portion. Other people's bodily functions are not something with which I want to deal. The process server ad catches my eye. Well, the 'up to $50 an hour' part catches my eye. I honestly have no idea what a process server is. What else is there?

Meanwhile, my neighbor receives another call. This time she talks to Bonnie about how she's in line at the DMV. I scroll through another screen.

Construction, construction, and more construction. Auto body technician, and an assistant wrestling coach. Truck drivers and flooring installers. Handyman and goldsmith.

Oh wait. People are needed to deliver newspapers. Great. I could be a twenty-something with a paper route. Wouldn't that be a dream come true. Next?

Am I a self-motivated, energetic go-getter with a background in sales and fitness? No. Not even a little bit.

Administrative assistant. Must have at least four years of experience and strong interpersonal skills.

When did I become so utterly unemployable?

The ads end then. I scroll back and forth a couple of times to make sure it isn't some kind of mistake.

"Are you expecting it to change?" the woman says. "Because it won't."

It takes me a minute to realize she's talking to me. I look at her, trying to think of something clever to say in response. Her phone rings again and she turns away before answering it. This time, it's Peter, and she describes for him in detail the extent of her nervous stomach problems.

I close the job listings and look at the board again. Now serving number six.

The man sitting on my left is reading a magazine. *Forbes.* That was smart, bringing a magazine. I should have brought something to read. But since I didn't, I read over his shoulder. I don't much care about finances or the stock market, but I also have nothing else to do.

We're in the middle of an article about how tax credits are hurting the middle class when he notices I'm reading along with him. He looks at me as though I have stolen his wallet and shifts so I can no longer see the magazine.

I look at the number board. Now serving seven.

When my phone rings, Chatty Cathy gives me a pointed look. I return it as I locate my phone. It's Josh. Smiling, I answer it.

"You came back," I say.

"I told you I would. How's it going?"

"I'm at the DMV."

"Starved for entertainment or applying for work?"

"Neither. My license expired. I thought I'd put my unemployment to good use and get it renewed."

"A worthy goal," Josh says. "How's the wait?"

The board flips to an eight. I sigh. "Oh, you know. I'm going to die here, but other than that, it's not too bad."

"Glad to hear it. Are you free for lunch?"

"I have no idea. For all I know, I'll be here until lunchtime *tomorrow.*"

"I could bring lunch to you."

"Oh yes, the DMV is such a popular lunching spot amongst young couples."

"I do believe I read that in a Zagat guide," Josh says. "What about dinner? If you're not free tonight, we could do it another night."

What would he say if I told him about tomorrow night's family dinner? Do I really want to find out? Ugh. No. What if he said yes? "I don't know. Can I check my calendar and get back to you?"

"Sure. Call me later?"

"Will do."

I end the call and drop the phone in my bag. Seeing that they are still serving number eight, I slouch in my seat, tilt my head back, and count the holes in the ceiling tiles.

"Lavinia Kelly?"

I lift my head and scan the room.

"Is Lavinia Kelly here?" a woman standing in front of a door marked 'Employees Only' calls.

I raise my hand. "Uh…yeah?"

The woman beckons to me. "Come with me, please."

Why? What did I do? Exchanging suspicious looks with my neighbors, I gather my belongings and make my way over to the woman. She leads me through the 'Employees Only' door and down a corridor, turning into a small room filled with four monitors showing the waiting room from different angles. Someone's sitting at a desk in front of them, his back to me.

"I just need to get my license renewed," I say. "I don't—"

"We'll take care of that in a minute," the woman says.

"In a minute? I'm number fifty-five, and you're currently serving number eight," I say. "Maybe a minute in DMV time is different than a minute anywhere else, but—"

The man watching the monitors laughs. I narrow my eyes at the familiar sound.

"Lew?" I say, and he turns around. "What are you doing here?"

"Turns out, I have a friend at the DMV."

I nod. "Of course you do. Why didn't you mention that yesterday?"

"Where would be the fun in that?" Lew gestures to the woman. "Get your license taken care of, and we'll go do that tour."

I smile. "Fine. But you're buying lunch."

15

I AM THE LAST PERSON to arrive at my parents' house for dinner on Wednesday. Even Lew's already here. Which surprises me. The man spent an entire day with me, wandering around Boston, and still came back for more. That's some serious staying power. Or resilience or something. Stupidity, maybe.

I park in the driveway behind Colin's sedan and smile at the rusty pickup on the street before letting Rufus out of the car and heading inside.

Susannah meets me at the door, bouncing with such energy, I have to question what possibly illegal substance she's on. She waves me off and drags me into the living room. Colin's talking to Dad on one side of the room. Lew is sitting alone on the couch, a bottle of beer in hand. He looks as wary as I'm feeling. When Susannah releases me, I sit next to him. Strength in numbers.

"Nia," he says. "No boyfriend tonight?"

"I'm not ready to subject him to a family dinner."

Lew smiles. "They're a good bunch. Trust me—you lucked out in the family department."

"Strange, but loveable," I agree. "Thanks for coming. I have a feeling I'll need the back-up."

"For what?"

I study the group on the other side of the room. "I'm not sure yet. There's just a weird vibe in the air, you know?"

"I know."

"You feel it?"

Lew nods. "I feel it."

"Any idea what's happening here?"

"I have my suspicions."

"Do tell."

He hands me his beer. "Let me get you a drink first."

"Why? What do you think is happening?"

Lew leaves me alone on the couch. Susannah looks over, still smiling like a maniac, and I beckon to her.

She settles at my side. "What's up?"

"What's going on here?"

"What makes you think something's going on here?"

I gesture to the rest of the room. "Everyone's being all weird."

"How can you tell in this family?"

"I can tell. There's something weird happening here."

"No, there isn't."

"Yes, there is. What are you not telling me? What does everyone else in this room know that I—oh my God. Are you pregnant?"

Susannah rolls her eyes. "I am not pregnant."

"Are you sure?"

Looking exasperated, she snatches the beer from my hands, guzzles the liquid inside, then shakes the bottle at me. "Happy?"

"Like that proves anything."

"I am not pregnant," she says. "Now behave yourself."

She disappears into the kitchen with the empty bottle. Lew reappears a moment later, a new beer in one hand and a glass of amber liquid in the other. He smiles at Dad and Colin, then comes over to me.

"Here." He holds out the glass. "I think you'll need this."

Why does he think that? Taking the glass, I survey the room again. Colin has the same damn look on his face that Susannah's been wearing all night. My father seems pretty pleased, but I don't put it all together until Susannah and my mother emerge from the kitchen, holding hands.

Oh God. I look at Lew, who nods.

"You should have made it a double," I mutter, raising the glass to my lips.

"I did," Lew responds.

Colin moves to the center of the room. "All right, I think everyone already knows what I'm going to say, but let's make it official."

I gulp whiskey. Lew should have made it a triple. Or just brought the whole damn bottle.

Colin's grin grows. "I asked Susannah to marry me, and she said yes."

There's not much in the way of big shock or celebration — like Colin said, we pretty much knew what he would say before it was said — but my parents immediately hug the happy couple. Lew gets up to shake Colin's hand and kisses Susannah on the cheek. I lag behind to finish my whiskey.

"Vinnie! Get over here!" Susannah says.

Setting my glass on the side table, I join the big group hug that has formed in the living room. Lew opts out, standing awkwardly to the side, as I am embraced by the rest of the family. Our eyes meet, and he smiles. I offer him a slight eye roll. It's nice to have someone to share this with.

Eventually, we make it to the table for dinner. Lew and I sit across from the newly engaged couple and watch them be sickeningly adorable together. We exchange the occasional meaningful glance but say nothing. I don't know about Lew, but I'm torn between vomiting or starting a food fight. It's only fear of my mother's wrath that keeps me from doing either.

As dinner draws to a close, Susannah decides to ride home with me. The four of us leave at the same time, but Susannah and Colin stop by his car to say their goodbyes. Not needing or wanting to bear witness to that, Lew, Rufus, and I keep walking.

"Here's my stop," I say as we reach my car.

Lew gestures to Susannah and Colin. "Have fun with this tonight."

I open the car door for Rufus. "Right? She's gonna make me stay up all night, talking about wedding stuff."

"She's excited."

"It would be pretty bad if she wasn't," I say. "Still, I value my sleep."

"Who doesn't?" Lew waves and walks away. "See you around."

I watch him leave, then get in the car to wait for Susannah. She's giddy when she finally climbs into the Jeep. As soon as she fastens her seatbelt, I pull out of the driveway.

"Thanks for giving me a ride home," she says.

"Thanks for taking my brother off my hands," I reply.

"I thought you'd be thanking him for taking me off your hands."

"How do you know I haven't already?" I say. "Do you realize I am the one person who has lived with the both of you?"

"Yes, we've talked about that."

"That's unusual, isn't it? I mean, you two have spent nights and weekends together, but you've never *lived* together. The maid of honor, however, has lived with both of you."

"To be fair, Colin was an adolescent when you two lived together."

"To be fair, he still is."

"To be fair, so are you."

I grin. "It's always good to be fair."

"A lot of couples don't live together before they're married," Susannah says.

"Is that still true? Seems old-fashioned to me."

"So what if it is? Is there something wrong with being old-fashioned?"

"No."

"You're saying it like there's something wrong with it."

"I don't mean to. I was just teasing."

"It's okay if you're serious once in a while."

I nod. "I'm sure I've heard that said."

"You know," Susannah says then, "I haven't actually asked you to be my maid of honor."

"I assumed you would. It's not like you have any other friends."

"True. You have scared them all away."

I smile as I turn onto our street. "My evil plan worked."

Susannah snorts. "What, exactly, were you hoping to gain from this evil plan?"

"Your undivided attention," I say. "Which was working great until you started dating my brother."

"Well, I'm sorry if I caused you any inconvenience."

I pull into the driveway. "You sound sorry."

"Hey." Susannah's tone shifts from amusement to seriousness. "Are you going to be okay? With this?"

I put the car in park. "Why wouldn't I be okay with this?"

Susannah shrugs. "I'll be moving out, and you'll be..."

"I have successfully lived on my own before."

"Yes, but—"

"I need you to stop." I turn toward her. "I was a mess for a long time, I know, and in a lot of ways, I still am a mess. That probably won't change anytime soon. But in spite of that, I am a semi-functional adult. It's not your job to babysit me."

"I wouldn't call it babysitting."

"Then what would you call it?"

"I don't know. Worrying?"

A smile tugs at the corner of my mouth. "Not that I don't appreciate it, but maybe you could worry about your wedding instead. I hear planning one of those things can be time-consuming."

"I've heard that, too."

"It'll be good for you to have a hobby."

"You're making me regret asking you to be my maid of honor."

I get out of the car. "You haven't actually asked me to be your maid of honor yet."

Letting Rufus out, I walk to the front door.

"Hey!" Susannah calls, and I look back at her. "Wanna be my maid of honor, you big pain in my ass?"

I smile. "More than anything."

16

BEING SUSANNAH'S MAID OF HONOR is exhausting. More accurately, dealing with her *mother* is exhausting. Jacqueline Price is a walking, talking etiquette guide for the upper class. I'm pretty sure she's the reason why Susannah and Colin don't already live together. Such things are not done in polite society, and Jacqueline is all about being polite and proper. Which is, I suspect, the only reason why she tolerates me as well as she does. I've always been a little too middle class and unconcerned with polite society for her tastes.

But the fact remains that I am her daughter's best friend and maid of honor, so she is obliged to include me in the planning of the engagement party. Sadly, because I am Susannah's best friend and maid of honor, I am forced to slap a fake smile on my face and participate.

Thus begins a month of increasingly mind-numbing decisions about the venue (an upscale art gallery in South Boston), music (the Great American Songbook, naturally), hors d'oeuvres (bacon-wrapped scallops and a bunch of other things I can't pronounce), alcohol selection (at least there will be quality whiskey), and a host of other things I didn't even realize I didn't care about until Jacqueline brought them up.

And this is only the beginning. Susannah and Colin have set a date for the end of June—sending Jacqueline into a tizzy over only having seven months to plan and execute the perfect wedding—which means I have seven more months of dress shopping and flower arrangements, band auditions and cake tastings. I won't mind the last one too much, but it's love for the happy couple that'll keep me going through it all. They are incandescently blissful. I'm certainly not going to ruin that by being me.

Which is why, the night of the engagement party, I allow Susannah to do my hair and makeup, then dig my one and only little black dress out of the back of my closet. I can't remember the last time I wore this dress. It's a relief that it still fits and looks reasonably decent. Sliding my feet into my one and only pair of dress shoes, I teeter my way downstairs.

"Josh won't be able to keep his hands off you," Susannah says when I walk into the living room.

I put my phone in my clutch. "Josh will have to keep his hands on me. I can't walk in these things."

"Well, I appreciate you making the very awkward effort," she says. "Are you ready? The cab's waiting."

"I can't believe your parents didn't send a limo."

"They offered. Repeatedly."

"You turned them down?"

"Repeatedly."

"But you know how much I love traveling in style."

Susannah rolls her eyes. "Yeah, that's so well-documented. Just get your stubborn ass to the curb, okay?"

I pick up my wrap. "Now say that like you're not my pimp."

"Go!"

We ride into the city in unexpected silence. From the corner of my eye, I watch Susannah fidget with her hair, jewelry, and the hem of her dress. She checks her phone repeatedly, glances out the window, and taps her fingers erratically on her thighs.

"Nervous?" I ask as the cab pulls up in front of the gallery.

Susannah hands the driver some folded bills. "Worlds are colliding tonight. Wouldn't you be nervous?"

Definitely. But I'm me. Susannah has never been prone to nervousness. It's unsettling to see it now. I shrug. "It'll be fine. It's not like this is the first time everyone's meeting."

"It's the first time with an open bar."

"What do you think will happen?"

She sighs and opens her door. "Probably nothing. But I hear Saturday night's all right for fighting."

I grin as I slide across the seat. "Well, let's go get a little action in."

The gallery's event space has been totally transformed from the exposed brick box it was when I saw it last—and not just because of the addition of the bar and the DJ working his way through the carefully selected playlist. Strings of clear lights are draped around the room and on the branches of young birch trees. Paintings adorn the walls. Multiple days were spent discussing which to feature. Well, Jacqueline spent days discussing it. I spent days pretending I gave a shit. I don't even know upon which ones she decided. Even looking at them doesn't tell me anything. Maybe Colin will explain them to me.

He's standing with two other people, gesturing to a painting on the wall and probably talking about technique or the symbolism behind the colors the artist used. When he sees us, he waves us over. At least he waves Susannah over. As I have nothing else to do, or anyone else to talk to, I tag along. Colin introduces me to his friends—colleagues of his—and we shake hands. Susannah already knows them and kisses them on the cheek. After thanking them for coming, she and my brother exchange a kiss that has the rest of us looking away.

"Hi," she says afterward.

"Hi," he says. "You look fantastic."

"It's the ring." Susannah holds up her left hand and wiggles her fingers. The light catches the diamond just right. "Makes everything look good."

"I do have excellent taste," Colin says.

I open my mouth to say something snarky, but Susannah points at me.

"Behave," she says, then looks at my brother. "I'm going to make the rounds. Don't hide in the corner all night."

He smiles. "I won't."

Susannah walks away and Colin's friends excuse themselves to go to the bar. I allow Colin to pull me in for a hug but push him away before he can mess up my hair or makeup.

"Thank you for coming," he says. "And for dressing appropriately."

"I can take instruction, you know."

"I also know Jacqueline has been a real pain in the ass the last couple of weeks, so I appreciate you not showing up in ripped jeans and some profane T-shirt just to spite her."

"Would I do that?" I ask. When Colin raises an eyebrow, I clarify, "Would I do that to you or Susannah?"

"Probably depends on how annoying you find us in the moment."

"Probably." I look around the room. I have to admit it's rather pretty and elegant. It looks like Susannah. How did she ever end up slumming it with us slackers? I shake my head. "I can't believe you pulled it off."

"Pulled what off?"

"Convincing Susannah's parents that their daughter marrying a penniless artist was a good idea."

"I'm hardly penniless."

"We're all penniless compared to them."

"True, but it doesn't matter. I'm marrying Susannah. Not them."

"Marry a girl, marry her family."

"Well, she's been married to you for years, and you seem to have survived them."

"This conversation is going to an uncomfortable place for me."

"Yeah, me too." Colin removes two champagne flutes from a passing waiter's tray. He hands one to me. "To uncomfortable places."

I clink glasses with him. "What an amazingly weird toast. If you have to make one at the wedding, get someone else to write it."

"Sounds like a plan," he says. "Hey, the in-laws are waving me down. Talk later?"

I nod. "Happy ass-kissing."

He grins. "Thanks."

As Colin walks away, I catch sight of Lew coming through the double doors. Clean-shaven and wearing a suit that fits pretty damn perfectly, he looks so different that I stop to stare. Who knew he could get any hotter? I put my empty glass on a tray and head over to him, wolf-whistling as soon as I'm within earshot. He turns toward me.

"Damn, Officer Weiss. You clean up good," I say. "I didn't even know you owned a suit. Or a razor."

"You own a dress." Lew glances down. "One that shows off your legs."

"Bet you didn't know I had those."

He smiles. "I assumed they were under all those layers of denim somewhere, but it's nice to have confirmation."

"You're just lucky I found a razor under the bathroom sink."

"Well, you look nice."

"Thank you. As do you."

Lew looks around. "Are you here alone tonight? Or is the guy who may or may not be your boyfriend coming?"

"Josh is coming. He had to work, but he'll be here soon," I say. "Are you here with someone?"

"No."

"My mother didn't try to set you up with anyone?"

"Oh, she tried, but I assured her it wasn't necessary."

"Well, I guarantee she'll try anyway," I say. "She'll find you at some point, link her arm with yours, and ask if you've met so-and-so."

"She wouldn't."

"She would." I move to his side as I scan the room for likely candidates. "Who will it be?"

Lew laughs. "Blond by the bar?"

I scope out the bar. The blond is wearing ridiculously high heels and a short cocktail dress. Her hair is twisted up in a complicated knot. Pretty, but not someone I imagine my mother thinking worthy of Lew.

I shake my head. "Nah, too fake. Nancy's all about authenticity."

"Okay. You tell me. Who's the lucky girl?"

An excellent question. My parents are talking to a drop-dead gorgeous redhead. Judging by my mother's body language, she isn't the one, but I point her out anyway.

"How about her? The redhead with my parents."

"Not my type."

"Like that matters."

"Why wouldn't it matter? It is my life we're talking about."

I grin. "Fine. We'll consider taking your opinion into account."

"Generous of you."

"I know." I sigh dramatically. "Well, if it's so important to you, you better tell me your type before I change my mind."

Before Lew can answer, my phone buzzes. I remove it from my clutch to find a text from Josh waiting.

Problem at work. Be there ASAP.

"Something wrong?" Lew asks.

I hit reply. "No. Josh is running late. Work emergency."

OK, I text back, *but you're missing out. The bacon-wrapped scallops are almost gone…*

"Work emergency, huh?"

"What? They happen."

Lew nods. "That they do."

My phone buzzes with another message.

Save me some?

I snort and type out a reply. *Not bloody likely.*

"Something funny?" Lew asks.

"Just Josh thinking I'll save him some scallops."

"As if you'd be able to. They seem to be pretty popular."

"You know how New Englanders get around seafood." I drop the phone back into my bag. "Well, it looks like you'll have to entertain me until he gets here."

"Lucky me."

"Once more with feeling, maybe."

"I'm going to get a drink," Lew says. "May I bring you something from the bar?"

"Please," I say. "Whiskey. Neat."

"Coming right up."

He heads for the bar, pulling out his own phone as he does so. The blond is still there, and she sidles up to him. He smiles at her and slides his phone into his jacket pocket. He pointed her out. Does that mean she's his type? As she puts her hand on his arm, a flare of jealousy propels me toward them.

What am I doing? Why do I care who he talks to?

When I arrive, the blond is laughing at something Lew said. It makes me want to push my way in between them, but that's probably too aggressive for someone who doesn't care who he talks to, so I stand on his other side. He doesn't notice me.

"Hey," I say.

He turns. "Oh, hey, Nia. This is…" He looks at the blond. "I'm sorry, what did you say your name is?"

"Julia," she says.

"Julia." Lew looks back at me. "Do you know Julia?"

Julia and I exchange glances. She's sizing up the competition. I'm definitely not doing that.

"Nope," I say. "Haven't had the pleasure."

"Nia's the maid of honor," Lew tells Julia.

"How do you know Susannah?" I ask.

"We're sorority sisters," she answers.

Of course Julia's a sorority girl. She definitely wouldn't be my mother's pick.

"Super," I say.

The bartender sets two glasses in front of Lew. Lew thanks him and holds out one of the glasses to me.

"Your whiskey, my lady," he says.

My lady? I take the glass. "Thank you."

Lew takes my free hand. "It's been nice talking to you, Julia, but I promised my girl here a dance."

Julia looks me over again as she sips her red wine. "Enjoy."

"We will. Thanks," I say. When Julia flounces away, I look at Lew. "Not your type, either?"

Lew lets go of my hand. "I'm all about authenticity, too."

"Nancy will be glad to hear it."

"What about you?"

I have some whiskey while I consider it. "Well, it doesn't make me unhappy. But it's not up to me who you date."

"Just your mother."

"Nancy sets up because Nancy cares," I say. "But she'd be cool with whatever. She just wants you to be happy."

"Your family's good like that," Lew says, eyes focusing on something behind me.

I glance over my shoulder but see nothing out of place. What's he looking at? "Pushy and overbearing?"

"Just the opposite."

"What's your family like?" I ask. "Are they all down in Arizona?"

"Just my dad," Lew says. "My mom passed away when I was young."

My heart drops. I honestly can't imagine losing my mother. "Oh, I'm so sorry."

"It was a long time ago, but it was just my dad and me after that. He's a good guy, a really good guy, but..." Lew shrugs. "Not everyone gets what you have. I hope you know how lucky you are to have each other."

I nod. "I do. I joke a lot, but I do."

"I wasn't expecting to find a family when I moved here, and I wasn't expecting to be so welcomed so quickly into one, but the Kellys—for all your claims to the opposite—are an effusive group."

"Or we're just lonely and bored."

"I suppose it could be that, too." He finishes his drink and sets the empty glass on the bar. "Care to dance?"

"I have a boyfriend, you know."

"So you keep saying."

"Don't believe me?"

"Just making an observation here, but he never seems to be around."

"He'll be here later," I say. "He's not imaginary or anything. He's real."

"Did you really feel the need to add the last part?"

"A little bit, yeah."

"Finish your drink, Nia," he says. "Let's dance."

"Well," I say, obliging his request. "If you insist."

Lew leads me to the dance floor. Some Frank Sinatra song is playing. It's a nice middle-of-the-road song—not so fast that I'll break my neck trying to keep up, but not so slow as to require Lew and I to stand too close together for too long. For some reason, that part seems super important.

"Would you like to lead," he asks, "or shall I?"

"By all means," I say, "lead away."

Lew, as it turns out, is a surprisingly good dancer. I stumble at first, requiring him to adjust his grip, but we muddle through it. I'm laughing and apologizing for having stepped on his feet so many times when a new song starts. A slow song.

Lew wraps his arm around my waist. "Maybe this will be more your speed."

"I think sitting down is more my speed."

He pulls back. "Do you want to stop?"

"Uh…no," I say. "I'm willing to risk it, if you are."

"What's life without risk?"

"That's always been my motto."

"Really?"

"No."

Lew draws me closer. "What is your motto?"

"I don't have one. You?"

"No."

"Do you suppose that means something?"

"We have better things to do?"

"Maybe you do. All that protecting and serving."

Lew shakes his head. "I'm just in it for the money."

I laugh. "Because nothing says 'lifestyle of the rich and famous' more than a civil servant's salary."

Lew smiles. "You get me."

I smile, too. "Yeah. I think I do."

"There you are," a new voice says.

It takes me a moment to recognize Josh's voice. I find him on my right and step out of the dance. "Hey, you made it."

"I told you I would." He leans in to kiss my cheek. "Who's this?"

"Oh, this is, uh…Lew," I say. "He's my father's partner. Lew, this is Josh."

"Nice to meet you," Lew says, his tone suddenly very formal.

"Yeah, you, too." Josh offers Lew his hand. "Thanks for keeping Nia company."

Lew takes the proffered hand, shaking it efficiently. "The pleasure's mine. Enjoy the rest of the party."

"Yeah," I say as he walks away. "You, too."

Josh puts his arm around my waist. "You look amazing. Do you know that?"

I look at him. "You think flattery will get you out of trouble?"

"I'm in trouble?"

He isn't, but I say, "You *are* exceptionally late."

"Couldn't be helped. I had an angry client to appease," Josh says. "They don't tend to care about your weekend plans."

"A likely story."

"A true story. Promise." Josh kisses his way along my neck. "Wanna dance?"

"With you?"

He kisses my shoulder. "That's the idea."

"Can you dance?"

"I can do the Robot," he says. "Running Man, of course."

"Oh, of course."

"The Electric Slide," he continues. "The Time Warp, the Hokey Pokey."

I laugh. "That's what it's all about."

Josh slides closer. "I also slow dance."

"Well, aren't you a man of hidden talents."

"You have no idea," he says. "So? Can I interest you in a dance?"

"Only if it's the Hokey Pokey."

He smiles. "Deal."

17

FOLLOWING THE ENGAGEMENT PARTY, I spend so much time volunteering at the animal shelter that Gretchen eventually offers me an actual job with an actual salary—assistant director. It doesn't pay a lot, but neither did my old career. Still, as my roommate will be moving out in the not-so-distant future, I accept because I would be stupid to turn it down. The work is good—clearly, I am much more suited to working with animals than people—and it's starting to feel like maybe—just maybe—life is on an upswing.

A few weeks later, I come home from an especially exhausting shift, wanting nothing more than a long, hot shower and some ice cream with a side of Jack Daniel's. Susannah's Prius is already in the driveway. She's home early. Maybe she was fired, too. I park behind her and go into the house. Rufus meets me at the door, sniffing my legs with intensity as he attempts to determine with whom I spent my afternoon.

I make it as far as the living room when Susannah comes downstairs, dressed in a black silk robe and not much else.

As soon as she sees me, she stops short and ties the robe closed. "What are you doing here?"

"I live here." I gesture to her outfit. "If you're trying to seduce me, you could have just met me at the door with a pint of Ben & Jerry's."

"Funny. Colin didn't call you, did he?"

I remove my phone from my pocket. No missed calls, texts, or voicemails. "No."

"Okay, so I'm going to kill your brother," Susannah says. "But first, I need to kick you and Rufus out of the house."

"My house?"

"Our house."

"Are you serious?"

"Please? Just for a night? It's our anniversary."

My shoulders sag. "But I'm so tired."

"Well, maybe just this once, you can be tired somewhere else."

"Like where?" I ask. "My standing reservation at the Four Seasons?"

"Or your parents' house," Susannah suggests.

I close my eyes and pinch the bridge of my nose. "You want me to spend the night with my parents so you can have sex with my brother?"

"What about Josh? Maybe you can stay with him tonight."

Stay with Josh? I can't do that, can I? We're not ready for that step. At least I don't think so. Is there a way to know for sure without actually doing it?

"Did I mention it's our anniversary?" Susannah says.

I look at her. "Don't you usually do this sort of thing at his place? You know, so you don't have to kick me out of my house?"

"Our house. There was some problem with the electricity or wiring or whatever at the loft, so we had to make a last-minute change," Susannah says. "I'm sorry, Vinnie. Okay? I know this sucks, and if I had found a decent hotel with an available room, we would be there. This will never happen again, but will you *please* go somewhere else tonight?"

I sigh and reach for Rufus's leash. "You owe me."

Susannah nods vigorously. "I do. The next time we go out, drinks are on me."

"The next two times."

"At least."

Clipping the leash to Rufus's collar, I turn toward the door. "Make good choices."

"Thank you, Vinnie!" Susannah calls. "I love you!"

Rufus and I get in the car and drive away. We're halfway to my parents' house when I pull into a convenience store parking lot to consider my options.

An evening with my parents means either answering or avoiding Mom's endless questions about my new boyfriend. An evening with Josh would mean something different. Fewer questions about my love life, at any rate.

I glance at Rufus in the backseat, then locate my phone to call Josh.

"I've been kicked out of my house," I say when he answers.

"What? Why?"

"Colin and Susannah wanted to have some special alone time together, and apparently, they had to do it in my house."

"Her house, too, isn't it?"

"Sure, if you want to be all reasonable about things."

"Which you don't."

"Maybe not so much at the moment."

Josh laughs. "Understood. Do you need a place to stay tonight?"

"Maybe."

"Maybe?"

"It depends on how you feel about dogs."

"Rufus can come, too," Josh says. "Hey, hold on a second."

As he shifts the phone to talk to someone else, I look at Rufus. "This is a good idea, right?" I ask, and he licks my face.

"Okay, I'm back," Josh says a moment later. "I'm being pulled into a meeting, but go on over to my place whenever you want. There's a key under the mat."

"You hid a key under your doormat?"

"Well, I would have put it in a fake rock in my garden, but I don't have a garden. I do, however, have a doormat."

"Clever. Will you be at the office much longer?"

"Shouldn't be too long. If you don't mind waiting a little on dinner, I'll bring Chinese home with me."

"I'm not sure Rufus would care for Chinese."

"I'll bring him a cheeseburger. Will he care for that?"

"I think he could be persuaded," I say. "Have a good meeting."

"Yeah. See you soon."

When we hang up, I text Susannah to let her know where I'll be. *Make poor choices*, she texts back. Laughing, I toss the phone onto the passenger's seat and head to Josh's townhouse to search for the skillfully concealed key.

We haven't spent much time here, in the course of our still-young relationship. It hasn't been anything more than a pitstop on our way to some other destination. I haven't even made it up to the second floor, but the first floor looks like he copied a spread in *Bachelor's Pad Monthly*. It's all black leather, chrome, and stainless steel. Whatever he sells, it must come with a generous commission. I'd ask him for a job, if I didn't already know I would be terrible at it.

While Rufus sniffs and explores the new space, I wander through the living room and into the kitchen. The top-of-the-line appliances would be completely wasted in my house. Upstairs, there are three closed doors. The first leads to the bathroom. The second looks like his bedroom. The furniture — a queen-sized bed, a chair, and a dresser upon which a flat-screen television sits — is more minimal, but still nice. It puts my entire house to shame.

The last room is set up as an office and workout space, equipped with free weights, treadmill, and one of those Bowflex things. How the hell did I end up meeting this guy at a gym when he has all this right at home? Some people are too damn devoted to exercise for their own good.

My tour complete, I use the shower to wash off the smell of the shelter, then change into a pair of Josh's boxers and one of his T-shirts. Josh still hasn't come home, so Rufus and I return to the living room to wait.

I'm watching television when Josh finally comes through the door, loaded down with brown paper bags. The smell of Chinese food wafts through the room. Rufus carefully sniffs his way over.

I mute the volume. "Crab rangoons?"

Josh shakes the bags. "A double order, just for you."

"Oh, good boy."

"Are you talking to me or Rufus?"

"Both." I stand. "Let me help you with those."

A few minutes later, dinner is spread out on the coffee table, and Rufus is enjoying a cheeseburger at my feet. I give Josh control of the remote, a gesture I soon regret when he settles on *The Wolf of Wall Street*. It's a relief when his phone rings halfway through.

He glances at the screen and pauses the movie. "Sorry. I have to take this."

I reach for the lo mein. "Okay."

Josh heads upstairs and closes a door. When he finally comes back, he doesn't look happy.

"I'm really sorry," he says, "but I have to go."

"Everything all right?" I ask.

"There's a problem with a system at work. The on-call people can't figure out how to fix it, so I have to go in to do it."

"The sales guy has to help out tech support?"

"It's a topsy-turvy world."

"I guess so." I watch him put on his shoes and jacket. "How long do you think you'll be?"

"I don't know. It could be a while." He looks genuinely sorry. "But don't go anywhere. I'll come home as soon as I can, and we'll get back to the original plan."

"The original plan was for me to fall asleep on my own couch."

"Okay." Josh puts his car keys and phone in his jacket pocket. "I'll come home as soon as I can, and we'll get back to Plan B. How's that sound?"

"Like a perfectly acceptable Plan C," I say. "Drive safe."

"Will do." Josh nods at the television. "You gonna finish watching the movie after I leave?"

I reach for the remote. "Not a chance."

I sit up and wait for Josh until I can't keep my eyes open any longer. It's almost midnight when Rufus and I make ourselves comfortable in Josh's bed. I fall asleep quickly, not waking up again until Rufus walks over me to jump off the bed.

Groggy, I lift my head to check the clock. It's after 2 a.m. I look next to me. No Josh. Is he still out?

Rufus returns and joins me in bed, facing the open door. A moment later, I hear someone moving around downstairs. Josh, I assume, but when he fails to appear in the bedroom, I go downstairs to investigate. Rufus follows.

The only light in the kitchen is coming from over the stove. Josh sits on a stool at the island, lazily swirling a glass of amber liquid in one hand while scrolling through something on his phone with the other. A bottle of Macallan 12-Year is open in front of him. Damn. I did not see that when I was looking around earlier. Maybe he brought it home with him.

"Hey," I say from the doorway. Rufus sits on my left.

Josh glances over his shoulder. "Nia." He puts down his glass and rotates to face me. "Did I wake you?"

"No, Rufus did. He must have heard you come in." I step into the kitchen. Rufus stays at my side. "Did you get every-thing straightened out at work?"

"For the time being."

"Sounds ominous."

He turns back to his phone. "Does it?"

"Maybe they should have called a tech person to deal with the tech problem."

"It wasn't a tech problem."

I lean against the counter. "Then why did you say it was?"

His head comes up. "When did I say that?"

The irritation in his voice makes my hackles rise. Where the hell is this coming from? "Before you left. You said there was a problem with the system the on-call guys couldn't han-dle, so you had to do it. Topsy-turvy world. Remember?"

"Not as well as you do, apparently."

"It was six hours ago."

"Well, it was a long six hours."

"Why? What happened?"

"Nothing happened. Everything's fine."

"Sure. Because nothing sells 'everything's fine' quite like sitting in the dark, drinking scotch."

"You have something against drinking scotch?"

"No. Not at all. In fact, if I had known you had Macallan in the house, I would have had some."

"Then what's the problem?"

"You tell me. What happened at work?"

"Nothing happened at work."

"Where *did* the something happen? Where were you?"

"You know where I was."

"Do I?"

"Jesus." Josh sits back. "Are we really doing this?"

"Seems that way."

"Could we possibly do this later? After I get some sleep, maybe?"

"Long night, huh?"

He tosses back the remainder of his drink. "And getting longer."

I nod. "Working late has that effect."

"As does fighting with my girlfriend over stupid shit. Yet, here we are."

I am so not in the mood for this. I push off the counter and walk back toward the stairs. "No, here I was."

"What are you doing?"

"Going upstairs to change."

"Why?"

"Because I'm not wearing your boxers home."

He sighs. Loudly. Like I'm irritating him. "You don't have to leave, Nia."

I start up the steps. "You're right—I don't. But I'm going to."

He mumbles something under his breath.

I stop and turn around, hands going to my hips. "You got something to say? Don't be shy."

He grins. "Anyone ever tell you you're sexy when you're angry?"

Is he kidding me with this? Am I supposed to find that charming? I call Rufus to me before realizing he's already glued to my side. Together, we go upstairs where I change and gather my things. When we come back down, Josh is still seated at the island.

He shakes his head. "You're really leaving."

"What gave it away?"

"Being a little overdramatic, don't you think?"

I smile. "Hey, do you always become a major asshole after midnight, or am I just lucky?"

He reaches for the Macallan. "Come around tomorrow night. Maybe we'll find out."

"Maybe not." I walk away. "Enjoy the scotch."

18

I DRIVE HOME ON NEARLY empty streets, but it's the last place I want to be right now — and not just because of whatever Colin and Susannah may be in the middle of doing. Stopping at a red light, I spot Dottie's Diner up ahead. It's as good a place as any to hide out. Dottie's pancakes can't be beat.

I pull into the parking lot and look inside the diner before reaching for my phone and calling Lew. He answers on the second ring.

"Nia?"

He sounds like I have woken him up. I glance at the clock on the dashboard and cringe. I forgot how late it was. "What are you doing right now?"

"It's this newfangled thing called 'sleep.' You should try it sometime."

"I should. I've heard wonderful things about it."

"Nia," he says, emphasizing my name. "Are you hurt?"

"No."

"Are you in danger?"

"No."

"Is Susannah hurt or in danger?"

"No."

"Your parents or brother?"

"No."

"Rufus?"

"No."

"Is your car broken down on the side of the road or in a ditch somewhere?"

"No."

"Then why, for the love of God, are you calling me at...three in the morning?"

"Never mind. I'm sorry I—"

"What do you need, Nia?"

I hesitate. What possessed me to call him in the first place? "I wanted some company."

"Company?"

"And pancakes."

"Pancakes?"

"I was going to ask you to meet me at Dottie's Diner," I say. "Do you know it?"

"Yeah."

"Well, I was going to ask you to meet me there."

"For pancakes."

"And conversation," I say. There's nothing but silence on the other end. Has he fallen back to sleep? "Lew?"

"Are you okay?" he asks.

Now I hesitate for different reasons. "Physically, yes."

He sighs. "Give me twenty minutes."

"Thank you," I say, but he's already ended the call.

I'm sitting in a corner booth, Rufus on the floor at my feet and a cup of coffee in front of me, when Lew comes through the door and makes his way toward us. Rufus bolts upright and prances in place until Lew has greeted him.

Lew slides onto the bench across from me. "Is there anywhere in Massachusetts Rufus isn't allowed to go?"

"If there is, I haven't yet found it." I shrug. "Dottie's friends with my dad. She lets Rufus come in when it's slow."

LOVE & OTHER LIES

"Of course she does," Lew says as Dottie shuffles over to our booth.

"Hi, sugar," she says, putting her hand on Lew's shoulder. "You two ready to order?"

Lew looks at me. "Nia?"

"Pancake platter, please," I say. "Scrambled eggs, bacon, and wheat toast."

Dottie nods. "For you, Llewellyn?"

"Same."

"Coffee?"

"Sure."

Dottie bends down to scratch between Rufus's ears, then heads behind the counter. Lew leans back, resting his arm across the booth. When Dottie returns with his coffee, he thanks her, and she pats his shoulder before moving away.

"So," Lew says, "why are we here?"

"Haven't you had Dottie's pancakes before? They're really good. They may even be better than my mother's."

"Nia."

"Not that you heard that from me because you did not. And if you make any claim to the opposite, I will vehemently deny it."

Lew picks up his mug to take a sip of coffee. "Why are we here?"

"I was lonely."

"Yeah? Where's Susannah? Where's your boyfriend?"

I roll my eyes. "He's not my boyfriend."

"Trouble in paradise?" he asks in an overly innocent tone.

I snort. "You sound absolutely heartbroken."

"I don't like your boyfriend."

"Good thing he's not my boyfriend, then."

"Did you two have a fight?"

"I don't know what we had. Whatever it was, it was stupid."

"What happened?"

"I don't even know. One minute, everything was fine, and the next…" I sigh. "I don't know."

Dottie returns with our order. After placing pancake platters on the table, she sets down a third plate—this one holding a single, oversized pancake already cut into smaller pieces—in front of Rufus.

"You two need anything else?" Dottie asks.

I glance at Lew, who shakes his head. "I think we're good. Thanks."

Dottie walks away. "Holler if that changes."

Lew leans to the left to watch Rufus inhale his food. "That must be the most spoiled German shepherd I have ever seen."

I drown my pancakes in syrup. "I wouldn't have it any other way."

"Neither would I." Lew puts far less syrup on his pancakes. "Are you going to tell me about the fight?"

"Brief and bizarre." I poke at my eggs with a fork. "Maybe we were just tired."

"It *is* late."

"Or early."

Lew cuts his pancakes with precise, even strokes. "You and your glass-half-full outlook on life."

"Oh yeah, that's me all right."

Lew smiles. "You like this guy."

"Yeah. Well, usually, anyway. Maybe not so much right now."

"Must have been one hell of a fight."

"But it wasn't, though. It was…one hell of a *weird* fight," I say. "He invites me to stay over, and then…Never mind."

"And then what?"

I spear a piece of pancake. "It's stupid."

"What's stupid is you waking me at three in the morning and then refusing to tell me what's wrong."

I make a face. "I view it as more stubborn than stupid."

"I'm sure you do. Tell me."

I put down my fork. "He got a call saying there was a problem at the office and they needed him to come in to help fix it."

"Work emergencies happen. I remember you telling me so at the engagement party."

"Yeah, but he works in sales or whatever. What kind of work emergency do sales people have at eight o'clock at night?"

"I don't know. The kind stirred up by clients in different time zones?" Lew shrugs. "Did you ask Josh about it?"

"I asked how things went. If they got the problem fixed."

"And?"

"And he didn't seem to want to talk about it."

"Maybe he couldn't talk about it. Some kind of company privacy policy."

"Then why not tell me that? Why choose to be a giant dick about it?" I sigh. "I don't know where he went, I don't know what happened, but…"

"But what?"

I study Lew for a moment. "It felt like a completely different guy came back tonight. One I didn't like very much."

"And now you're not sure which one is the real Josh."

I nod. "Yeah. But maybe that's not fair. Maybe I was being oversensitive, and he was overtired. Maybe we both were. I mean, it was two in the morning, after all, and people do get tired and cranky."

"Sure," Lew says.

Two guys walk through the door and take seats at the counter. Dottie hands them menus. She glances over at us, eyebrow raised, and I lift my mug slightly.

"Do you want my advice?" Lew asks.

I look at him and smile. "Probably depends on the advice."

"He'll call you tomorrow—later today, maybe—and want to talk, patch things up, whatever," Lew says. "Tell him no. Tell him you're out."

"You want me to dump him for being tired and cranky?"

"I want you to dump him because you can do better. A lot better."

What the hell is that supposed to mean? I hold off on finding out until Dottie has been by to refill our mugs.

"What do you have against Josh?" I ask then. "You don't even know him."

"I know enough."

"Like what? His name?"

"I can do a lot with just a name, you know."

I sit back. "Did you run a background check on him?"

"No."

"Did you have someone else run a background check on him?"

"No."

"Then what did that mean?" I ask. "'I can do a lot with just a name, you know'? What did you mean by that?"

"That I *could* look him up. I *could* run a background check on that weasel if I wanted, but I don't have to," Lew says. "Because even though I don't know him, I know him. I know the kind of man he is."

"What kind is that?"

"The kind that will get you hurt."

"That's not an opinion for you to have."

"It's not your place to tell me what kind of opinions I can and cannot have."

"It is when it involves my love life."

"You told me—at Jitters, remember?—that me being your father's partner made me family," Lew says. "Did you mean that?"

"Yes."

"Then that makes you *my* family. And as my family, you getting hurt worries me," Lew says. "Josh isn't a good guy, Nia. If you stay with him, you'll get hurt. I don't want to see that happen."

"What makes you think he's not a good guy?"

Lew shakes his head. "I just know."

"Don't give me that," I say. "Tell me something concrete. Give me some evidence that your blind hatred of him is justified."

"It's not blind hatred."

"Prove it."

"Can't you just trust me?"

"That's not my style," I say. "You've exchanged a total of…what? Five words? What exactly in those five words made you believe he's not a good guy."

"It wasn't anything he said."

"Then what was it? The handshake? Was he too aggressive? Did he threaten your masculinity?"

The look on Lew's face telegraphs his feelings on that. "No."

"Then what?"

"I need you to trust me on this, Nia."

"Well, I can't do that."

"Well, maybe I can't stand around and watch you get hurt."

"Don't recall asking you to."

Lew looks at me. For a while, I stare back, but the unflinching scrutiny on the other side of the table soon becomes too much. I study my plate, completely uninterested in the food upon it.

"Okay, then," he says.

Lew moves out of my peripheral vision, and something hits the table. I lift my eyes just enough to see a twenty-dollar bill.

"Lew, wait," I say, but when I look up, he's already gone.

19

IT'S TOO LATE TO GO to my parents' house, so I go home. Colin and Susannah have to sleep sometime, right? Colin's car is parked on the street, but the house is dark and quiet. Going upstairs feels like tempting fate, so Rufus and I crash on the couch. He falls asleep. I stare at the ceiling.

How the hell did I end up in this mess? What the hell is wrong with me?

My phone chimes, and I look at it. I've missed a few calls—all from Josh. He's now moved on to texting. I scroll through his messages.

Where are you?

Are you home?

Are you OK?

Will you answer your damn phone? I want to talk to you.

I know you're mad, but at least let me know if you're OK.

I hit reply, but my fingers hover over the phone, refusing to type a single letter.

Tell him no, I hear Lew say. *Tell him you're out.*

Muting the volume, I drop the phone on the coffee table and go back to staring at the ceiling. I don't move again until I hear people walking around upstairs. When the shower starts,

I sit up and reach for my phone. It fails to respond to anything I do. Dead battery, then. Well, that's one way to get people to stop trying to contact you.

I take the phone into the kitchen and plug it into the charger on the counter. Letting Rufus into the backyard, I start a pot of coffee. I'm sitting at the table when Susannah comes in, looking entirely too happy. Even though I'm not supposed to be there, she smiles at me, humming as she gets her mug from the cupboard.

"You and my brother done defiling each other?" I ask.

"For the time being," she answers, unperturbed by my shitty mood. She definitely got laid. "What's the matter with you?"

"I had a fight."

"With Josh?"

"Him, too."

"Who else are you fighting with?"

"Lew."

Susannah shakes her head as she pours herself some coffee. "You have more fights before noon than most people have all day."

I shrug. "It's a gift."

"Which fight would you like to discuss first?"

"How about neither? Does neither sound good to you?"

She sits across from me. "If you didn't want to discuss them, you shouldn't have told me about them."

True. A rookie mistake on my part. I sigh. I really don't want to go through all this again. "As you know, after I was unceremoniously kicked out of my house last night—"

"Ha!"

"—I went to Josh's place. Everything was fine until he got called into work to deal with some emergency. He went, I stayed, but when he came back...I don't know. There was something off about him. I asked if everything was all right, and he...There's something he's not telling me."

"Maybe he can't talk about it. Like, a confidential work thing."

"Maybe, but I just asked if everything was all right. I certainly didn't ask for details. And so what if I had? I mean, we're sleeping together," I say. "Or I'm sure we would be if we could only manage to spend a night together."

Susannah leans in. "Some people do it during the day. With the lights on."

I smile. "The hell you say."

"It's true."

"Fine, but we're in a relationship. Or we're supposed to be in a relationship, anyway. Inviting someone to spend the night in your bed with you does indicate a certain amount of something, doesn't it?" I say. "I don't expect him to tell me his deepest, darkest secrets right away, but I think I deserved more than open hostility."

"Are you sure it was open hostility? I love you, Vinnie, but you kind of suck at picking up on things like that."

"I do not."

"You do when you're mad." Susannah looks at my phone as it rings again. "Maybe you should give the poor guy another chance. At least let him explain his side of things without immediately jumping down his throat."

I let the call go to voicemail. "I'll consider it."

"Good enough. Now for Lew," Susannah says. "It's six in the morning. How did you manage to get into a fight with Lew?"

I rub a spot on the table. "After I left Josh's, I didn't want to go home, so I called Lew to see if he would meet me for pancakes at Dottie's."

Susannah sits back. "You called *Lew* to meet you for pancakes?"

"Well, you were busy, weren't you?"

"You called Lew."

"Yes."

"What time was this?"

"I dunno. Around three, I think."

"Three in the morning?"

"Yes."

"Did he come?"

"Yes," I say, and Susannah makes a face. "What? What's that look for?"

"Nothing."

"Oh no. That's a something face. Why are you looking at me like that?"

"You called Lew."

"And?"

"You have a boyfriend."

"So I'm not allowed to have male friends? What century is this?"

"Lew likes you, Vinnie."

"Well, sure, we're friends," I say. "Or at least we were. I am pretty pissed at him still, and I'm thinking that feeling's mutual."

"No, he *likes* you. In the way that Josh likes you?"

"Because he met me for pancakes? Come on."

"No, you come on," Susannah says. "He met you for pancakes at three in the morning. Yeah, they are really good pancakes, but they're just as good at normal hours. He dragged his ass out of bed in the middle of the night because you called and asked him to."

"He dragged his ass out of bed in the middle of the night because he's my father's partner and felt obligated to," I correct. "He does not like me in any romantic kind of way."

"No? What did you fight about?"

I hesitate. "Josh."

Susannah raises an eyebrow. "What about Josh?"

"Lew doesn't like him."

"Imagine that."

"Lew seems to think dating Josh will get me hurt," I say. "But that does not mean he has any romantic feelings for me. If anything, he thinks of me like an annoying little sister."

Susannah snorts. "Unless you're those twins on *Game of Thrones*, Lew does not think of you like a sister."

"Well, he's not thinking of me as anything else, either."

"He is. He does. You're kidding yourself if you don't see it."

I shake my head. "I don't see it. Mostly because there's nothing to see. I am nothing to Lew but a gigantic pain in his ass."

"Oh, you're a pain in the ass all right."

I smile. "I love these little talks of ours. They always make me feel so warm and fuzzy inside."

"I do have that effect on people." Susannah glances at my phone as another call goes unanswered. "Now, will you please talk to your boyfriend? Try not to be so damn defensive about every little thing?"

I suppose I should talk to him. If for no other reason than I may need to use my phone again someday in the future. After checking that the battery is charged enough to make a call, I go outside, sit on the back porch, and watch Rufus try and fail to catch the leaves falling from the trees.

The phone rings again, and I look at Josh's picture on the screen.

Tell him no. Tell him you're out.

Stupid Lew. With a fresh rush of irritation, I answer the phone. "What?"

"You *are* alive. Good," Josh says. "I've been calling and texting you for hours now."

"I saw."

"Well, thanks for finally answering."

"What do you want?"

"To talk about what happened?"

"What's there to talk about?"

"Are you serious?" he says. "Where are you? Are you home? Can I please talk to you face-to-face and not over the phone?"

"Has it occurred to you that I might not want to talk to you?"

"Yeah, after I left about my twentieth message."

"One message would have been sufficient."

"Are you still pissed at me?"

"Yes. Yes, I am," I say.

"At least let me come over so we can fight in person."

Rufus drops a worn tennis ball at my feet. I obediently pick it up and throw it. "That doesn't sound like something I'd be interested in."

"That's it? You're just going to give up on this?"

Tell him no. Tell him you're out. I shake my head to clear it. "I don't know. Maybe."

"Look, I was a real asshole last night, and —"

"I know. I'm the one who pointed that out to you."

"I'm sorry," Josh says. "It's a shitty excuse, but I was tired and frustrated with work, and I was an asshole because of it. I shouldn't have taken it out on you, and if you'll let me, I would really like to make it up to you."

Should I let him? He's certainly not the first person to be tired, cranky, and drunk. God knows I've been all three of those things from time to time. Is it wildly unfair if I punish him for it?

"Nia?" Josh asks.

"I'm thinking."

"What if, while you were thinking, I brought you donuts or the breakfast pastry of your choice? Or I could meet you somewhere for breakfast, if you prefer," he says. "I just…I'd like to see you and talk about this in person."

I pull the phone away from my ear to check the time. "No. Not now, anyway. I have to go to the shelter."

"Tonight, then. Let me come over after I'm done at work, and we can talk. Or you can yell at me. Whatever you want."

"I don't want to yell at you."

"Okay. We'll just talk, then," Josh says. "Is that all right?"

Is it? I think of Lew, of what he said—*tell him no*—of Susannah's claim that Lew has feelings for me. *You're kidding yourself if you don't see it.* Is she right?

"Nia?" Josh says. "Is that all right?"

Finding Rufus's ball at my side, I throw it again. "Yeah. I'll be here."

20

JOSH ARRIVES AT THE HOUSE late. I would think he wasn't coming at all, if not for the series of text messages I received promising otherwise. I don't mind the delay, though. By the time his car pulls up to the curb, Susannah is long asleep. Talking to Josh will be much easier without her. I watch him approach the house, then open the front door before he has a chance to knock.

"Hey," he says.

"Susannah's asleep," I say. "So we need to—"

"Fight quietly?"

I smile. "Yeah."

"May I come in?"

I step aside to allow him to enter. Closing the door behind him, I slide the chain in place and follow Josh into the living room.

"Do you want something to drink?" I ask. "We have coffee, water, whiskey, and…Well, that's about it. There might be some wine or gin. I could check."

"No, thanks."

"Okay. How was work?"

Josh sits on the couch. "Uneventful. Where's Rufus?"

"Asleep on my bed, last I looked."

I settle in a chair. We fall into a silence that stretches on so long, I have to wonder why he bothered coming at all.

"Are you still mad at me?" he asks finally.

I glance at the clock on the wall. Nearly midnight. "Dunno. You gonna be an asshole tonight, too?"

"Not intentionally."

"Did you intend to be one last night?"

"Of course not." He sighs. "Look, there's a lot of confidential shit at work I'm not allowed to talk about. With anyone."

"Then tell me that next time. Because that vague, evasive jerk I found in your kitchen last night is not a guy I'm interested in being with. Or near."

"I apologized for that."

"Pro tip: when your girlfriend's mad at you, it is often best to apologize more than once. Profusely, even, some would say."

"You have no idea how sorry I am about how I acted last night."

"How could I? You only apologized once."

"Well, twice now."

"A few more times, and maybe I'll think about forgiving you."

Josh smiles and slides onto his knees on the floor. "I'm sorry, I'm sorry, I am deeply and truly sorry."

I throw a pillow at him. "Get up, you lunatic."

"Does that mean you'll give me a second chance?"

"Fine. But if you pull that Jekyll and Hyde crap with me again, there won't be a third chance."

"Understood."

"Okay, then. You're forgiven."

"Thank you." Josh moves back to the couch. "Do you mind if I ask you a question?"

"Probably depends on the question."

"Where did you go last night?" he asks. "After you left."

I shrug. "Home."

"You didn't. At least not right away."

"How do you know that?"

"You weren't answering your phone, so I drove here to apologize. Where'd you go?"

"I wasn't in the mood to go home right away, so I went to Dottie's Diner with a friend."

"What friend? Susannah?"

"Lew."

"Lew? You went out with fucking *Lew*?"

"Fucking Lew?" I laugh. "No need to be so formal."

"What the hell are you doing going out with another guy in the middle of the night?"

"It's not another guy. It's Lew," I say. "Also, I can go out with whomever I like whenever I like."

"No, you can't. Not with him."

I fold my arms across my chest. "You laying down the law, there, Joshua?"

He swears under his breath. "Go out with whoever you want. Just not him."

"Why not him?"

"Lew isn't who you think he is."

I laugh again. "That's what he told me about you."

"You and Lew talk about me?"

"We did last night. I was pretty pissed off, after all."

"What did Lew say about me?"

"He doesn't think you're a good guy. He thinks you'll hurt me."

"Of course he thinks that. He's jealous."

"Of what? Your amazing wardrobe?"

"Of you being with me. He's jealous," Josh says. "Not that I blame him. I'd be the same way if the tables were turned."

"Oh yeah, because I'm Helen of Troy."

"Pretty damn near."

"Save the flattery for someone else."

"It's not flattery if it's true."

"Do you find that line works on a lot of women? Or any woman?" I ask. "Lew is my friend. He's my father's partner, and that makes him family. If that's not something you can deal with, you know where the door is."

"Laying down the law, there, Lavinia?"

"You bet your ass I am."

Josh shakes his head. "I'm never going to like him."

"I didn't ask you to like him. Just accept him."

"Because you would be so accepting of a gorgeous female family friend of mine?"

"I don't know. I don't know any of your family friends. Or your friends. Or your family."

Josh stands and walks toward the kitchen. When he reaches the end of the room, he turns and looks at me. "Who hurt you?"

I stand. "What makes you think someone hurt me?"

"Pretty much everything about you? You're jumpy, you're uncomfortable. I put my arm around you, and you stiffen up. You don't want it there. You don't want me to touch you."

"That's not true."

"You stormed out in the middle of the night after a really stupid argument," he says. "It's like you were just waiting for me to screw up."

"You *did* screw up."

"Do you even like me?"

"I do. And I wasn't waiting for you to screw up." I step toward him. "Last night wasn't my fault. I was there. I was in your bed—*waiting* for you to touch me—and you couldn't have cared less."

"I wouldn't say that."

"What would you say?" I continue to close the distance. "You know my friends. You've met my family. You were at my brother and best friend's engagement party. You've been to my place of employment, and I don't even really know what you do for work! I know that you smile and banter and flirt, but I don't know you."

"Well, you're not much better," Josh says as Rufus comes thundering down the stairs.

I glance at the dog, seeing his raised hackles. "*Hier.*"

Rufus freezes. He looks at me, ears flattened. I repeat the command, and he slowly slinks to my side.

"*Platz,*" I say, and he lays down on my left.

Josh watches Rufus warily. "What was that?"

"Apparently, we weren't fighting quietly enough," I answer. "What do you mean I'm not much better?"

Josh gestures to the dog. "Is he going to do anything?"

"Nothing I don't tell him to do."

"What does that mean?"

"You first."

He leans against the wall. "You're complaining that you don't know me, right? Well, I don't know you. I know your best friend, your brother, your parents, your co-workers, but not you."

"Well, between them and my love of sarcasm, there's not much else to know."

"You're selling yourself short, Nia."

"I'm really not."

Josh pushes off the wall. "Who was he? What did he do?"

"He didn't do anything. It wasn't his fault."

"It's always someone's fault."

"Not this time," I say. Which isn't strictly true. It was someone's fault. Just not mine. Not Brian's, either. I look at the floor. "I don't want to talk about this. I don't want to talk about him."

"Okay. If you can't tell me about it yet, that's all right. I can wait."

"Generous of you."

"Will you ever stop being annoyed with me?"

Though my anger is starting to ebb, I say, "Not so far."

"Fair enough." Josh walks toward me and sits on the arm of the couch. "What happens now?"

Good question. I glance at the stairs, thankful we haven't woken Susannah. Next, I look at Rufus, still lying at my side.

"*Frei*," I say. Rufus stands and walks away, settling on the other end of the couch.

"Does this mean I'm no longer in trouble?" Josh asks.

I return to my chair. "Too soon to tell."

Josh slips onto the couch and slides to the edge. He leans forward until we're close enough to touch. "Hey, I really am sorry."

I nod. "I guess I'm maybe a little sorry, too."

Josh raises an eyebrow. "You guess?"

"Don't push your luck." Sighing, I check the clock on the wall. "It's late."

"It is."

"You must be exhausted," I say, and Josh shrugs. "You can stay here tonight, if you're too tired to drive home or whatever."

"Where would I sleep?"

"The couch is pretty comfortable."

"The couch? I thought we worked through the fight."

"We have. I just don't think you'll have any luck convincing Rufus to give up his side of the bed."

Josh smiles. "I don't know about that. I can be very persuasive when I need to be."

I roll my eyes. "Tell me about it."

21

FOR THE FIRST TIME SINCE losing my job, I stay in bed past 5 a.m. I haven't slept much, instead spending most of the night either staring at the ceiling or the guy sleeping on my left. Every time I look at him, I'm almost amazed — or surprised, maybe — that he's there. That I invited him to stay. That it's now the next morning and he doesn't show any signs of leaving. Or waking up.

It's been a while since any of those things have happened. I'm not quite sure how to feel about it.

Shortly before seven, Susannah knocks on the bedroom door and walks in. "Vinnie? Are you all right?"

Rufus rouses himself off the seldom-used dog bed to greet her. She shoos him away to keep her dress as free of dog hair as possible. Josh doesn't move.

I lift my head. "Please go."

Susannah looks at the bed. "Oh. *Oh.*"

Josh stirs, kissing my shoulder before looking at Susannah. "Barbie," he yawns. "How are you?"

"Oh," she repeats. "I'll, uh, I'll…leave you to it. See you later."

She backs out of the room and closes the door behind her. Out in the hall, she makes a strangled sound that might be a cheer. Embarrassing, yes, but much better than what it could have been.

I smile at Josh. "You should stay here more often."

"Maybe I should," he says. "What time is it?"

He leans over me to check the clock on my nightstand. I take advantage of the opportunity to run my hands over his chest. All that workout equipment certainly isn't going to waste.

Josh looks at me. "I'd love to—I really would, but I'm late."

"Be later."

He kisses my forehead and rolls out of bed. "I can't. Not today."

Pulling on his boxer briefs and jeans, he cracks open the door to peek into the hallway before leaving the room. I linger in bed until Rufus's whining convinces me I would be better served letting him outside. Getting dressed, I go downstairs, Rufus following happily.

I let him out the back door before starting a fresh pot of coffee. Upstairs, the shower is running. I sincerely hope Susannah didn't leave the bathroom too much of a disaster.

Josh appears in the kitchen twenty minutes later, shaved, showered, and dressed. Rufus is napping on the floor, and I'm at the table, working on my second cup of caffeinated goodness. Smelling like my body wash, Josh kisses me on the cheek.

"You shaved," I say. "How did you—?"

"There was a disposable razor under the sink."

He opens and closes cupboard doors until he finds the coffee mugs. He removes one with a German shepherd on it and pours himself some coffee. I open my mouth, but no sound comes out.

"Nia? You okay?"

I blink and shake my head to clear it. "You looked under the sink? I'm not sure I'm ready for you to be poking around my bathroom."

"I know girls use tampons, if that's what you're worried about."

"Yes, that is what I'm worried about."

He smiles. "Is there anything to eat?"

"Somewhere in the world, yes."

"And in this house?"

"Would you like some more coffee?"

Josh sighs. "I should take you grocery shopping."

"I can take myself grocery shopping, thank you very much."

He looks around. "I see absolutely no evidence of that."

I hold up my coffee. "Where do you think this came from?"

"Does it ever occur to you to get anything else while you're getting coffee?"

"Every time."

Josh finishes his coffee and puts the mug in the sink. "I really do have to go, but can I call you later?"

I look from the sink to him. "Yeah. You better."

After Josh leaves, I wash and dry the dishes, then put them away, carefully tucking the German shepherd mug in the very back of the cupboard.

A check of the time shows that I'm now running late, so I hurry through my shower. As I comb out my wet hair, I scroll through a series of texts Susannah sent. She's overjoyed that Josh spent the night. Apparently, it's a step in the right direction. I'm texting her back a line of middle finger emojis when someone knocks on the front door. Rufus loses his mind, and I send my message before heading downstairs.

When I open the front door, two tall, slender men in ill-fitting dark suits are standing there.

"Lavinia Kelly?" the man on the right says.

"You selling vacuums or religion?" I ask.

"No, ma'am."

"Well, what's left?"

The man flips open a black leather billfold to reveal a set of credentials proclaiming him to be an FBI agent. His shadow does the same.

FBI agents. Huh.

"I'm Agent Walker, and this is Agent Washington," the first guy continues. "We'd like to ask you a few questions."

"About what?"

"A person of interest in an ongoing investigation."

"Am I that person of interest?"

"No, ma'am."

"Who is?"

"May we come in?"

I don't move. "Who do you want to talk about?"

"Joshua Murray," Agent Washington says, his deep voice startling me. "I believe you know him?"

He holds out a photo. It's definitely Josh. I put my hand on Rufus's head. What the hell?

"Why do you want to ask me questions about Josh?" I ask. "What investigation is he involved in?"

Agent Walker gestures to the house. "Please?"

"Uh…sure. Come in," I say.

Rufus and I back away just enough to allow the two men inside. Closing the door behind them, I lead the way into the living room. Rufus stays close to my side.

"Is this okay?" I ask. "Or would you prefer the kitchen?"

"This is fine," Agent Walker says. Both men settle on the couch. "Would you care to sit?"

"Haven't decided yet," I say. "But thanks for inviting me to sit down in my own house."

Agent Washington smiles. "You can relax, Miss Kelly. We just want to ask you some questions."

"About Josh."

"About Josh," he confirms.

My heart is pounding so hard I'm certain they can hear it. The neighbors can probably hear it. "What kind of questions?"

"How long have you known him?"

"A couple of months, maybe. Not quite that." I think about it. The task requires an extraordinary amount of effort. Maybe I should sit. "We met in September."

"You started dating around that time?"

"Is that a problem?"

"We're just looking to establish your relationship."

"Heavy on the banter," I say. "Light on everything else."

"Excuse me?" Agent Washington asks.

"My relationship with Josh," I explain. "Heavy on the banter, light on everything else."

"Would you care to elaborate on that?"

"Nope." My legs are feeling numb so I sit. Rufus lays down in front of me. "What investigation?"

Agent Walker shakes his head. "We're not at liberty to say. It's an active investigation."

"Yeah, you've mentioned that. Doesn't change my question, though."

"You've been recently unemployed," Agent Washington says. "Is that correct?"

"Maybe," I say.

"You were fired?"

I tilt my head. "I believe I resigned, but you'll have to ask my former employer for the official story."

"How are you making ends meet? Are you collecting unemployment?"

"Is this part of your investigation, too?" I ask. They, of course, do not answer. "I was recently employed by a local animal shelter, and I have a roommate who pays rent. I can make ends meet because my grandmother willed her mortgage-free house to me when she passed away, my car is paid off, and I keep my expenses low. What investigation?"

"You're not under investigation," Agent Washington says.

"Well, that explains why I'm being interrogated by two government drones who shop the clearance rack at the Men's Warehouse."

Agent Washington smiles. Agent Walker does not.

"Government salaries," Agent Washington says. "You understand."

"I used to teach at a public high school," I respond. "What do you think?"

"What does Joshua do for work?"

"Have you asked him these questions?"

"Does that mean you don't know?"

I shrug. "Sales in some office in the city. You know, it's too bad there's no government agency that could tell you all about a person of interest's employment history and their annual income."

"You assume that's what we're after."

"I'm not assuming anything except that you have to be smarter than you're currently coming across." I wince internally. Can someone be arrested for being super rude to FBI agents during questioning? How close am I to finding out? "Now, you do work for a government agency, so I could be giving you entirely too much credit, but I have to assume there are at least a few brain cells rattling around up there."

"Maybe a few." Agent Washington slides forward. "Are you all right?"

Nope. "Never better," I snap. "Look, I'm late for work, so I need to wrap this up. Is there anything else I can not help you with?"

"Is there a better time for us to talk?"

"I'll have my people call your people," I say. "We'll get something on the books."

"Why don't we—?"

"Why don't you talk to my lawyer?"

Agent Washington smiles. "There's no need for that. You're not under investigation."

"Says the FBI agent asking me questions in my living room."

Agent Washington removes a white business card from his jacket pocket and tosses it on the coffee table. "Have your lawyer call me. We'll get something on the books."

I nod. "I'll do that."

I don't move as the two men leave. As soon as I hear an engine coming to life, I move to the window to watch a black sedan drive away. When the feds have disappeared from view, I find my phone and call Josh.

"Where are you right now?" I ask as soon as he answers.

"At work. Why?"

"I have to talk to you."

"Right now?"

"Yes, right now, but I don't want to do it over the phone. Can I meet you somewhere?"

"Right now?"

"Yes, right now. Am I speaking a different language?"

"No, it's just…you sound more agitated than usual. Are you all right?"

Excellent question. I'm not sure of the answer. "Can I meet you? Please?"

Josh is quiet for a moment. "Uh, yeah. Where are you?"

"At the house."

"Can you get into the city?"

"Yes."

"How about Adele's? Text me when you're close, and I'll meet you there?"

"I can do that. Yeah."

"Okay," Josh says. "Are you sure you're all right?"

"Yeah. Just…meet me."

After we hang up, I text Gretchen to tell her I'm sick and won't be coming in today, then rush to catch a train into the city. When I get off at the stop nearest Adele's, I text Josh and walk to the restaurant. He's already there, so I wave off the hostess and cross the room to join him.

He stands and kisses my cheek. "You okay? What's going on?"

"Thanks for coming," I say, sliding into the open seat.

Josh sits. "Do you want anything? Coffee, water?"

I shake my head. "No."

"You look wild," he says, face full of concern. "What happened?"

"I, uh, I had a visitor this morning. Two visitors, to be specific."

Josh nods again, looking unsure. "Anyone I know?"

"I don't—I don't know. They were FBI agents, with the bad suits and badges and everything."

"FBI agents?"

"Yeah. Two FBI agents, looking to chat," I say. "Do you know what they wanted to talk about?"

Josh shakes his head. He's coming across as wary, but that makes sense. I am bordering on maniacal right now.

"You. They wanted to talk about you."

Josh's eyes widen. "Me?"

"Yes, you. They wanted to talk about you. It was definitely you, too. They showed me a picture of you and everything. So, here's my question," I say. "Are you somehow involved in some sort of…criminal something?"

"No," Josh says. "Jesus, no!"

"Why do they think otherwise?"

"I don't know!"

"They claim you're involved in an active investigation."

"Well, I'm not!"

"What do you do for work?"

"Sales. I'm in sales. I've told you that."

"What kind of sales?"

Josh gapes at me. "Are we seriously doing this?"

"Two FBI agents came to my door today, asking questions about you, so yes, we're doing this," I say. "You're going to tell me what kind of sales you're in, and then you're going to take me to your office and introduce me to your co-workers."

Josh looks around the restaurant, then leans toward me. "I don't know why two agents came to your house today. I don't know why they wanted to ask you about me. I'm not involved in any sort of criminal investigation. Or any criminal anything, for that matter. Whatever it is, it must be some kind of mistake—a misunderstanding."

"A misunderstanding? Like what?"

"I don't know. Maybe I have an evil twin running around the city."

"An evil twin? Really?"

"I don't know, Nia! I don't. I am as surprised by this as you are, and to me, evil twin makes about as much sense as anything else."

"What kind of sales are you in?"

Josh blows out an exasperated breath. "Pharmaceuticals."

I sit back, folding my arms across my chest. "Really? Pharmaceuticals?"

"Not the illegal kind. I'm not a drug dealer. Jesus, Nia!"

"What am I supposed to think?"

"That I'm not a drug dealer," Josh says. "Okay? I don't know why they were there. I'm not involved in anything that would warrant an investigation. I don't even have any unpaid parking tickets. I can think of absolutely no reason why any federal agents would need to ask questions about me."

I look toward the back of the restaurant. A couple at another table is staring at us. How loud are we being? Perhaps I should have told Josh to meet me at his townhouse instead. Yelling at him about federal investigations in a public place was possibly not the smartest decision ever.

"What did they want to know?" Josh asks.

"Stuff. About you. About how long we've been dating. What you do for work. That kind of thing."

"What did you tell them?"

"That they were idiots. Poorly dressed ones."

"Of course you did." Josh reaches across the table to hold my hand. "It was a mistake. I don't know who I have to talk to in order to correct it, but I'll talk to that person. No more poorly dressed federal agents will come to your door. I promise."

Is that true? Are his promises worthwhile? Removing my hand from his, I search his face. How is it he looks so very different to me now? "Okay."

"Okay? Are we okay?"

No. I don't know. I sigh. "Yeah."

"You're sure?"

No. "Yeah."

His phone buzzes, and he glances at it. Is he trying to hide the screen from me, or am I being paranoid and suspicious?

"Shit." He looks at me. "I have to get back to work, but I don't…Nia, are you sure we're okay?"

I'm really not. "Yeah, it's fine. Go. Call me later, if you want."

Josh slides out of his seat. Stopping at my side, he tilts my head toward him. "It's a mistake. Some crazy misunderstanding about which we will laugh our asses off one day."

I hope so. I nod again and attempt to smile. Josh kisses my forehead before leaving. As soon as he exits the restaurant, I grab my bag and follow him.

He's walking away from the T station. Not ideal, but I can make it work. If he sees me, I'll tell him I have something else to do in the city while I'm here. What something, though? It probably won't matter. He's too busy texting while walking to notice me. Which is good, because I have completely lost my mind. That's the only explanation for the fact that I am trying to stealthily stalk my boyfriend through Boston. Where do I think he's going to lead me? His evil lair? Shit—what if there is an evil lair? What if he really is involved in some kind of criminal organization?

No, he isn't. That's ridiculous. Like he said, there's some misunderstanding. A case of mistaken identity. An evil twin running around the city. That's all. I have to stop being so goddamn crazy.

I slow as he enters a building on the corner. Doesn't look very much like an evil lair. As I pass, I steal a glance at it. An office building, home to multiple businesses, from the looks of the directory. Dare I go and take a closer look? Maybe I should knock on every door in the place until I find him.

Except if following him down the street was crazy, what would knocking on every door of a Boston high-rise be?

Maybe I should go home. I can always Google the address later. And then obsess over all the no answers that'll give me.

Lacking any sane options, I return home. As soon as I walk into the living room, my eyes go to the white card upon the coffee table. I pick it up and run my fingers over the raised lettering and FBI seal. Agent Jeremiah Washington.

"What do you know, Agent Washington?" I say.

Not that he would tell me anything, either. Goddamn men with their goddamn secrets.

I am so sick of it. Of everything. I don't know anything; I don't know anyone. There's just all these men hanging around, telling me that the other men hanging around aren't who I think they are. Who are they? Who do they think I am? *What* do they think I am? What the hell am I going to do about it?

When Josh calls my cell later, I don't answer. He calls the landline next. I don't answer that, either.

"Hey, Nia, it's Josh," he says after the beep. "I called your cell and left a message, but I'm trying to cover my bases."

"I bet you are," I yell.

"This is terrible timing, but I have to go out of town for work, and—"

I snort. "Well, that's not suspicious at all!"

"—I know how that looks, given everything that happened this morning, but—"

"But I promise that I am not a criminal," I finish.

Josh keeps talking, but I pick up Jeremiah Washington's card. What if I called him? Could I make a deal? I'll tell you everything I don't know about this guy I'm dating, and you tell me why you're interested?

"I should only be gone a couple of days—three at the most," Josh says now. "If I don't hear from you, I'll call you when I get back. Okay?"

"Oh, you bet."

"Just...please call me, Nia."

After he hangs up, I shove Agent Washington's card into my pocket and go to the kitchen to delete the message. The last thing I need is for Susannah to hear it. Returning to the living room, I flop onto the couch and turn on the Game Show Network. Time for Operation Distraction.

But even though there's a *Family Feud* marathon on, it doesn't alter my mood. In fact, it only makes me more frustrated. I'm going to need a new plan. A more active plan. Possibly one involving alcohol. Lots of alcohol. I bet I could get Susannah on board with that.

She walks through the front door a little after four o'clock and joins me in the living room.

"I'm surprised you're home already," she says. "Did you get fired again?"

"Hilarious."

"Everything all right?"

Nope. "What are you doing tonight?" I ask.

"Perusing wedding invitation samples while drowning my boredom in the world's largest tumbler of gin. Why?"

"I'm going to The Howling Sailor to get the drunkest that any human in all of history has ever gotten. Care to join me?"

"Oh, God, yes," Susannah says. "Let's go."

22

THE MOMENT WE WALK INSIDE The Howling Sailor, Susannah spots a few of her favorite fellow barflies in a corner booth. They wave us over. Grabbing my arm, she drags me in their direction, but I extract myself and tell her I'll meet her later. She gives me a disapproving look but lets me go to the bar without comment.

I slide onto a vacant stool. "What's happening, Frank?"

Frank puts a napkin in front of me. "The usual?"

"Hold the Coke," I say, and Frank raises an eyebrow. "Fine. Just a splash of Coke."

"Everything all right?"

"Peachy keen." I watch him add a lot more than just a splash of Coke. "You better not be charging me for that weak-ass drink."

Frank sets down the glass but doesn't remove his hand from it. "What's going on, Nia?"

"Just waiting for my drink, Frank."

"What's going on?"

"Nothing much. I'm in the market for a new bar with a less nosy bartender, though. Know of any?"

Frank sighs. "I'll be watching."

"I'll be here," I say as he moves on to another customer.

As soon as his back is turned, I lean over the bar, locate the Jack Daniel's, and fix the ratio of my drink more to my liking. When Frank glances at me over his shoulder, the bottle is back in place, and I toast him with my glass.

After a few doctored drinks, I feel better. I feel so good that I beat Susannah to the dance floor and flirt with the DJ until he agrees to play *Dancing Queen*. Susannah squeals so loudly, I'm pretty sure she can be heard for miles around.

"Who the hell are you, and what have you done with Vinnie?" she exclaims as she joins me.

"I drowned that bitch in Jack Daniel's," I answer, and Susannah laughs.

We dance and we drink. The barflies place orders for me, as Frank is less invested in their blood alcohol levels. It becomes a game for the group, of which I am the winner. I dance some more. I am the living embodiment of a dancing queen, and I am having the time of my life.

Until Lew walks through the door.

I see him immediately—as though we're the only two people in the room—and stop dancing. He makes his way to the bar, claiming an empty stool, and I stare at his back.

Susannah drapes herself over my shoulder. "Vinnie? You okay?"

I don't answer as I stalk to the bar and shove his shoulder. "You!"

Lew pitches forward. Straightening, he turns to look at me. "Jesus, Nia. What the hell?"

I point at him. "You ruined everything."

His face changes. "What's wrong? What happened?"

"You. You…happened." I push against his chest. This time, he doesn't move. It's like trying to move a wall. A rock-hard wall that smells *really* good. I shake my head. "You ruined everything."

"You mentioned that." Lew looks around and slides off the stool. "Come on, let's go."

He takes my arm, but I pull free, stumbling back. "I'm not going anywhere with you."

"Look in the corner," Lew says, pointing. "See that empty booth? We're going to sit there, and you're going to tell me how I ruined everything."

"What—do you see the future now?" I jab a finger into his chest. Is there any body fat anywhere on him? I poke a couple of other spots to find out. "Should I start calling you…" Are there any well-known future-seeing guys? Why can't I think of one?

"Come on, Nia. Let's talk."

I look at the empty booth. "If you wanna talk, you gotta buy me a drink first."

"I think you've had enough to drink."

"Oh, okay. If you say so." I turn toward the dance floor. "I'll just find someone else to buy me a drink. Talk to them instead."

Lew catches me around the waist. "Go sit. I will bring you a drink."

"It better have alcohol in it. Alcohol I can taste. Like, a Jack and Coke. Emphasis on the Jack. No emphasis on the Coke."

"I will bring you a Jack and Coke. But only if you go sit now."

I make a face and salute him. "Sir, yes, sir."

Lew rolls his eyes. "Can you walk over there, or do you need help?"

"I ain't so very drunk, Melly," I say in my best southern accent. It's pretty damn good, if I do say so myself.

"I have no idea what that means."

"It means I'm fine," I say, walking away.

Goddamn men with their goddamn judgment. I'm totally fine. I could have ten more drinks if I wanted. Twenty. I could have all the drinks in all the world. I don't need Llewellyn Weiss to babysit me. If he wanted to do other things to me, that might be—no. No, no, no. I don't need him or his abs. I bet they're not even all that great. Those tight T-shirts just make them look great. It's an illusion. He just walks around all the time, sucking in his gut, so no one will know he really has a beer belly the size of…something really big.

I am off my game tonight.

I flop into the booth and put my back against the wall to watch Lew at the bar. He's on his phone again. Why is it, every time I see him, he's on his phone? Who does he even have to talk to? I've never seen him with anyone other than my dad. My dad? Wait…he wouldn't call my dad, would he? That would be such a dick move.

Putting the phone in his pocket, Lew leans in to talk to Frank. Blah, blah, blah, Nia's drunk. Blah, blah, blah, how did that happen? Blah, blah, blah, it's a bar, dumbass. Blah, blah, blah, getting drunk's the point. Lew gestures in my direction and Frank glances over. I shoot him with my fingers and look at the dance floor. Why am I sitting here when I could be out there? Here is boring. There is fun.

I slide across the seat, but Lew sits next to me and blocks my escape. I poke his arm in retaliation. No body fat there, either.

Lew sets a mug of coffee in front of me. My arm drops as I peer into it.

"If that's supposed to be a Jack and Coke, I can tell you right now it's the worst one I've ever had."

"It's coffee."

"No shit. Where's my whiskey?"

Lew sets his phone on the table. "Sorry. Frank says you're cut off."

"You told him to say that."

"Your finger guns told him to say that."

"Whatever. Did you call my dad?"

"What? No."

I reach for the phone. "Who did you call?"

Lew nudges the phone out of my reach. "What are you doing?"

"Trying to look at your phone to see who you called."

"Why?"

"Because I have…" What's the word? I squint at the table. "Iz-use. Iz-shoes."

"Issues?" Lew asks.

I point to him. "Yeah. Those. I have those, and it's your fault."

"Because I ruined everything."

"So you already know."

Lew laughs and pushes the phone toward me. "Knock yourself out."

I snatch it to keep him from changing his mind and prod the dark screen. It doesn't change until Lew taps a button on the side. I concentrate on the geometric background. Where's the phone thingy? How do I see who he called?

"It's down in the—"

I hold up my hand. "I can do it. I'm not drunk."

"Clearly."

"Clearly," I mock, then spot the little blue phone icon in the bottom corner. I tap it, and a list of names and numbers appear on the screen. I don't see my dad anywhere.

"How's it going?" Lew asks.

"Who's…Ryan?" I say, reading the first name.

"A friend."

"You have friends?"

"Shocking, I know."

I smile. "Not shocking. Just…unexpected. I never see you with anyone."

"There are entire days when you don't see me at all," Lew says. "Are you satisfied?"

"In life?"

"With my phone."

His phone? I look around, finding it in my hand. Why do I have his phone? I pass it over. "Uh, yeah. Sure."

"So, are you ignoring the question, or did you forget it?"

Question? What question? "I did *not* forget the question. I think *you* forgot the question."

"I didn't forget."

"Then prove it. Tell me the question."

Lew laughs. "Drink some coffee, Nia."

I push the mug away. "I don't need any coffee. I'm not drunk."

"No, I think you might be slightly past that point," Lew says. "Let me take you home."

"I don't wanna go home."

"Where do you want to go?"

I point to the dance floor. "Back out there."

"You can't go back out there. You've been cut off from that, too."

I look at Lew. Why can't he stop moving? "Listen, bucko." I grab his arm to hold him still. It's a good arm. A Captain America arm. "I don't need a man to tell me where I can go and what I can do. I can go wherever I want and do whatever I want."

"Except drive a car or walk in a straight line." Lew sighs. "I'll take you to my apartment. How about that?"

"How 'bout that." I draw a line from his bicep to his shoulder. "Why would I want to go to your apartment?"

"I have Jack Daniel's."

I stop drawing and look at him. "No lie?"

"No lie."

"Okay." I push against him to get him to move. "Let's go to your place."

23

LEW'S TRUCK IS AN EVEN bigger piece of shit up close. Nothing but rust held together by dirt particles and probably some duct tape. He helps me into the cab and then buckles my seat belt because I am apparently a toddler incapable of doing things for myself. When I tell him this, he smiles.

"The last thing I think you are is incapable," he says. "Now watch your fingers."

He closes my door and walks around to the driver's seat. Starting the engine, he checks the mirrors before pulling into traffic.

"Why are you doing this?" I ask.

"You're my partner's daughter."

"Susannah says you like me. Like, like me, like me."

"Is it different when you say it three times?"

"Do you?"

"What? Like you?"

"Yeah."

He smiles again. "You're all right."

"I'm fucked up. I'm so fucking fucked up."

"That's what happens when you drink a fifth of whiskey."

"I didn't mean the whiskey. And I didn't drink the whole thing. Did I?"

"No," Lew says. "You're not alone, Nia. We're all pretty fucked up."

"Not you." My head drops back against the seat. "You're Mr. Clean-cut Good Guy —"

"Sexy."

" — with…morality and superhero arms."

"Superhero arms?"

I reach out to touch his arm. "Have you seen them?"

"My arms? Yes, I have seen my arms."

"They're good arms."

Lew makes a right turn. "If you say so."

"I do say so."

Stopping for a red light, he looks at me. "What happened today, Nia?"

"I drank my weight in Jack Daniel's."

"Yeah, I got that part. *Why* did you drink your weight in Jack Daniel's?"

"We were out of rum."

The light changes, and Lew eases off the brake. "You don't drink rum."

"I could drink rum. You don't know."

"Do you drink rum?"

"No."

Lew slows again, this time pulling into an open spot in front of a large Victorian. Even in the streetlight, I can see its run-down condition.

"This is it, huh?" I say.

"Home sweet home." He looks at me. "Let me help you out."

Stupid men and their stupid hero complexes. I do not need help getting out of a goddamn car. I unbuckle my own seat belt and run my hand along the door, looking for the handle. It must be here somewhere. It's not like they can have those things removed. The door opens before I find it, and Lew stands there with his hand outstretched.

"Really?" I say, and he shrugs. Rolling my eyes, I allow him to help me out. "Are you happy now?"

Lew closes the door. "Ecstatic. Come on."

I follow him inside and stand behind him as he unlocks a door on the first floor. There doesn't seem to be any body fat there, either. Maybe he just doesn't have any.

Pushing the door open, he leans inside and turns on a light. "After you."

The apartment opens into a small living room. The walls are white and bare, the carpet is beige, and the only furniture is a faded blue futon against one wall and a television sitting on its sagging stand in the corner. Two old lamps sit on milk crates on either side of the futon. It barely looks like anyone lives here.

"Love what you've done with the place," I say. "Very junkyard chic."

Lew laughs as he closes the door. "I owe it all to my decorator. Have a seat. I'll be right back."

The futon doesn't seem like something I'd want to sit on, so I trail behind him into the equally small and shabby kitchen where he lifts the tail of his shirt and removes a gun from his waistband.

"Do you always carry your weapon when you're off duty?" I ask.

He puts the gun into a drawer and slides it closed. "Not always."

"Why tonight?"

"Thought I might be seeing you. Figured it could come in handy."

I grin. "You sure do know how to charm a young lady."

"Well, I try." Lew leans against the counter. "You still want that drink?"

"Only if you expect me to talk," I say. This earns me a serious look from Lew. Groaning, I sit at the tiny table. "Are you going to lecture me now? Tell me again that I've had enough to drink? Whiskey isn't the answer, Nia. Try the power of prayer instead."

Lew sets a glass on the table, and I scrutinize the liquid inside. Three fingers. Okay.

"Talk or don't talk," he says, sitting across from me. "It's up to you."

"Now it's up to me?"

"It always was."

"Then what was that performance at The Howling Sailor? You were all 'we're talking whether you want to or not.'"

"I did not say that. You, however, claimed repeatedly that I ruined everything. Can't blame a guy for having a few follow-up questions," Lew says. "For example, what did I do? How did I ruin everything?"

I trace the rim of my glass with my finger. "You don't trust Josh."

"Last I checked, you didn't care what I thought about Josh."

"I don't. Didn't. I don't know." I look at Lew. "You made me doubt him."

"I can't apologize for that."

"Sure. Because you don't like him."

"No."

"Right. Because he's a bad guy. With the…black hat and the…twirly mustache."

"Twirly mustache?"

"You know, because they have the…the thing." I twirl an imaginary mustache.

"Uh-huh. What changed? How did you get from telling me to piss off to doubting your boyfriend? What did he do that led to the great Jack Daniel's consumption of Friday night?"

I wish I knew. I drag my finger along a scratch in the table. "How often does the FBI go around asking questions about innocent people?"

"Probably more often than you think. What does—?"

"The FBI came to my house today. Not all of them. Just two of them." I reach into my pocket for the crumpled card and hold it out to Lew. "They wanted to talk about Josh."

Lew takes the card. "What did they ask?"

"Stupid stuff. Like, what he does for work, what I do for work. That kind of thing."

"What did you tell them?"

"To talk to my lawyer."

Lew sets the card on the table. "You have a lawyer?"

"No. I just wanted them to go away. I was freaking out," I say. "I mean, first you're all, 'hey, your boyfriend's not a good guy' and then the next thing I know, the feds show up and are all, 'hey, your boyfriend's not a good guy,' and that has to mean something, right? I mean, otherwise it's a really big…something."

"Coincidence?"

I nod. "Yes. That is it. That is the word. It's a…What was the word?"

"Coincidence."

"Yeah."

I squint at the wallpaper. It looks like something that used to be in my grandmother's house before she got addicted to HGTV. How old is this place?

"Did you talk to Josh?" Lew asks.

"Yeah. Apparently, his evil twin is in town." I laugh and lean back. "And that's someone else he didn't introduce me to."

I laugh some more. It's funny. So…stupid funny. My boyfriend has an evil twin. I wonder what his name is. Maybe they rhyme. Bosh. Tosh. Posh. Nosh.

Lew says nothing, but his super serious face speaks volumes. This isn't funny at all.

I sigh. "Josh probably doesn't have an evil twin, does he?"

"Probably not."

"He's not a good guy, is he?"

"No."

I pick up my glass and take a gulp. Upon swallowing, I frown and look at the liquid inside. "This is iced tea."

"It is."

"You promised me Jack Daniel's."

"No, I said I had Jack Daniel's. Not that I intended to serve you any."

I put the glass on the table. "You're an asshole."

"I know. You'll thank me in the morning."

"That's what you think." I pick up the glass again, then remember Lew's betrayal, and set it down. Putting my elbow on the table, I rest my chin in my hand. "This sucks. I didn't think Josh was gonna be the forever guy, but he was supposed to be a good guy, not this…under-federal-investigation guy. I mean, what the hell is that about? The feds never showed up to talk about Brian."

"Who's Brian?"

I straighten and pull away. "Who said anything about Brian?"

"You just did. You said the feds never showed up to talk about him," Lew says. "Who is he?"

"No one. He's no one." Tears are rising fast, filling me the way the whiskey was supposed to, and coming up the same way. I stand quickly, the kitchen tilting. God, his floors suck. I grab the table to keep from falling. "This dump got a bathroom, or do you just piss in the sink?"

Lew points. "Down the hall on the left. You need help?"

"Not since I was three."

I stumble in the direction he indicated, using the wall to stay upright. Lew follows, asking if I'm all right, turning on another light. Finding the bathroom, I go inside and close the door before Lew can come in. I don't know where the light is, but I don't care.

I slide against the door to the tile floor and cry.

24

DAMN, MY HEAD HURTS.

Groaning, I pull a pillow over my face. Awake is the last thing I want to be right now. But while I am conscious, I should let the dog out. That would be the responsible thing to do, and judging by the intensity of my headache, I could do with a dose of responsibility. And aspirin. So much aspirin.

I sit up and look around for Rufus. Where did he go? Wait—where's my stuff? What happened to—holy shit. This is not my house.

Where am I?

I fumble with the covers and nearly fall on my face as I get out of bed. The shirt I'm wearing doesn't belong to me. It's too big—a man's shirt—with some logo I don't recognize across the front. Where the hell are my pants? I was wearing pants last night, wasn't I?

I glance at the empty bed. It doesn't appear more than one person slept in it, but that doesn't necessarily mean anything. What did I do last night?

Somewhere, a door opens and closes. Footsteps cross a squeaky floor. Shit, shit, shit. Where are my pants? I look around the sparse room again, spotting my clothing draped over the back of a chair. Oh, thank God. Crossing the room, I snatch up my jeans and pull them on. I'm reaching for my shirt when the bedroom door slowly opens. Lew's face appears, but I don't relax. Snippets of last night come racing back. Superhero arms. Evil twins.

Fuck. Fucking fuckity fuck. Just...*fuck*.

Lew opens the door all the way. "You're awake. How's your head?"

Lew. Why did it have to be him? I point to the bed. "We didn't...did we?"

He shakes his head. "I spent the night on the couch."

Thank *God*. Now I indicate the shirt. "And this?"

"My shirt, but you undressed and dressed yourself." Lew's eyes slide down. "I see you mostly managed it."

Mostly? I look down.

"It's on backwards."

Of course it is. Tugging on the neckline, I see the tag. Fan-fucking-tastic. I would hate to get out of this experience with even a single shred of dignity.

Lew gestures out to the hallway. "I don't know if you're up for it, but I bought some potential hangover helpers."

I look at him with suspicion. "Hangover helpers?"

"You know—coffee, donuts, pancakes?"

"Donuts and pancakes?"

"Would you prefer something else?"

My preference would have been to wake up alone in my own bed in my own house, but I guess that's off the table. I need to get out of here.

I shake my head. "Thanks, but I should go. Susannah—"

"Is fine," Lew says. "Colin picked her up and brought her home."

Colin? Who called Colin? "Rufus—"

"Is also fine. Colin stayed at your place last night so he could take care of the dog this morning."

"Morning. Work. I have to go to work," I say, and Lew shakes his head. "I don't have to go to work?"

"I talked to Gretchen and told her you weren't feeling well. She says to take care of yourself, and she'll see you Monday morning."

I feel like my balance is lost all over again. "How did you—?"

Lew pulls my phone from his back pocket. "You left this at the bar last night. Frank requested I keep it safe for you. I figured you wouldn't mind if I used it to call Colin and Gretchen."

I am fully off my guard now. He did all of that. For me? I don't...Why?

"Nia?" he asks. "You all right?"

Of course he asks that. Because he is absolutely perfect. I walk toward him to claim my phone.

"Why?" I squeak as a rush of tears pushes its way forward. "Why did you do all that?"

Lew shrugs. "Maybe I like you."

I nod. It's unfair that his face is so goddamn flawless. It's unfair that he is who he is, and I am who I am. I put my hand on his chest and rise up on my toes.

He stiffens. "Nia—"

I kiss his cheek. "Thank you."

Lew visibly relaxes. "Any time."

My hand drops. "That horrifying, huh?"

"What?"

"Me touching you, kissing you."

Understanding crosses his face. "No, not horrifying at all. It's just...We should talk."

No. Hell, no. God, no. "What's there to talk about?"

"Josh? Brian?" Lew suggests. "The breakdown you had on my bathroom floor?"

The breakdown I had on his...I look past him to the bathroom. What is he oh fucking hell. I had a breakdown on his bathroom floor. I am never drinking again.

Looking back at him, I shrug. "You know how much whiskey I consumed last night. A breakdown was inevitable. Let's just be grateful it came in the form of tears and not…other things."

"What about Brian, then?" Lew asks. "Who is he? How did he evoke such a strong reaction in you?"

How much did I say last night? How did Brian ever come up at all? I spend so much time carefully *not* talking about him. I shrug again. "He's an old boyfriend. It's funny I brought him up. I haven't thought about him for years now."

It's not my best lie ever, and I'm pretty sure Lew knows it. If my mother were here, she'd be smacking me with whatever was handy. *He's a part of you, and you do not dismiss that.*

I don't want to dismiss it. But…

If things had been a little different. Just a little different, and I'd be married. Just a little different, and I'd probably have a snot-nosed brat or two. Isn't that always the way? Just a little different, an inch here, an inch there, a little to the left, slightly to the right, a deep breath, a moment's hesitation, and everything would be different.

It's not, though.

It never is.

"Nia?"

"Mind if I use your bathroom?" I ask, easing my way around him. "I promise not to have a breakdown in it this time."

"Sure," Lew says. "All yours."

After pulling myself together, I wander into the kitchen. On the table sits four coffee cups alongside a box of donuts, a glass of water, and a bottle of aspirin. Smiling, I glance at Lew to see him pulling something out of the oven.

"You bake?" I ask as I sit.

Lew sets down a plate of oversized pancakes that look like they've come from Dottie's. "Just keeping them warm."

I help myself to the aspirin. "Four coffees?"

"In case one wasn't enough."

Good call. I reach for a cup. "Do you have any cream or milk?"

Lew sets a small carton of store-brand half-and-half on the table before sitting down across from me.

I pour an unhealthy amount of cream inside my coffee cup. "Thank you, by the way, for all of this. Last night, this morning. I know when you went to The Howling Sailor last night to pick up chicks, you didn't plan on taking home the ultra-drunk, unavailable one."

Lew laughs. "Yes, that was a deviation from the plan. It's all right, though. I don't mind."

Of course he doesn't. I tear off a small piece of pancake. "What are you doing today? Are you on shift later?"

He helps himself to a plain donut. "Meeting up with some friends."

"Friends. Right," I say, remembering another snippet of conversation. "You have some of those."

"A few."

"What are you and your friends doing?"

"We haven't decided yet, but I imagine it'll involve drinking beer while watching some kind of sporting event."

I grunt. "Man stuff."

"Always. What's on your agenda?"

"Well, I thought I'd go home and die of shame. If there's time after that, I'll probably get some laundry done."

"There's no reason to die of shame."

"Oh, but there is," I say. "So, as much as I do appreciate everything you've done, I think I'll head home and get started on that."

"You want a ride?"

I shake my head. "I can get myself home."

"Do you even know where you are?"

"I've lived in this town my whole life. I'll figure it out." I stand, taking the coffee with me. "Have fun with your friends today."

"Thanks. I will," Lew says as I walk away.

25

COLIN'S CAR IS PARKED ON the street when I arrive home. I let myself in through the back door, and Rufus promptly meets me in the kitchen. I sit on the floor to greet him, and he ends up sprawled on his back with his head in my lap while I rub his belly. A moment later, my brother appears.

He stops when he sees me. "How's your head?"

"Still attached, surprisingly enough. How's Susannah?"

"She feels about as good as you look."

I wince. "I feel like I should be insulted by that, but my head hurts too much to be certain."

"I'm sure it does." Starting the coffee maker, Colin leans against the counter. "Your boyfriend called this morning."

I rest my head against the wall. "Josh called?"

"Yeah."

"Did you tell him where I was?"

"I told him you were sleeping."

"Did you tell him where I was sleeping?"

The coffee maker finishes brewing, and Colin pours some coffee into a mug. "No."

"Thank you."

Colin sits at the table. "He said you won't return his calls."

Did he happen to mention *why* I won't return his calls? I use the counter to pull myself up. "You two bosom buddies now?"

"What's going on, Nia?"

"Nothing that concerns you."

"Which is why I received a call last night to drive out here to pick up my intoxicated fiancée and spend the night with my intoxicated sister's crazy dog."

Our family really is too sarcastic for our own good. I sit across from Colin. "Rufus is not crazy."

"You're avoiding your boyfriend and spending nights with other men. What's going on?"

"Okay, it was one night and one man, and he slept on his crappy couch. I was there for whiskey, not sex."

"Lew gave you whiskey?"

"No, he gave me iced tea, but would this be a good time to remind you that I am well past my twenty-first birthday?"

"This isn't like you."

"You're right. I usually screw up way worse than this."

Colin sighs and drinks some coffee. It's amazing how well he can channel our mother. Especially when it comes to being disappointed in me. Having an older sibling is great.

"Why are you avoiding Josh?" he asks, setting down his mug.

"Lovers' quarrel," I say. "Some couples have those, you know. It's just a sign that we're human and not whatever you and Susannah are."

"You think I'm not human?"

"You're my brother. I've always thought that."

Colin rolls his eyes. "Brat."

"Comes naturally."

"You're my little sister. I've always known that."

I smile as I push off the table. "On that note, I'm going to bed. You and Susannah have fun doing whatever you're doing today."

"Wedding planning with Jacqueline."

"Sounds fun."

"You could come, too, maid of honor. Spend the night in the city with us."

I laugh. "Yeah…no. I'm way too hung over for a day with Jacqueline."

"You won't be able to avoid it forever."

"True. But I can avoid it today, so I'm going to bed," I say, walking away. "Thank you for taking care of my intoxicated roommate and not-at-all crazy dog. I will try not to require your services in the future."

"Hey," Colin says, and I look back at him. "Don't freeze out Josh too long, okay? He's a good guy."

At least someone thinks so. I glance at my phone. The voicemail icon is in the upper left corner of the screen. Can't wait to hear what excuses he has for me this time.

"I'll think about it," I say. "See you later."

Rufus and I retreat to my bedroom. I close the door to keep from crossing paths with Susannah, then collapse on the bed. Rufus joins me, and I rest my head against him as I access my voicemail.

Hey, Nia, Josh says. *I just wanted to…I don't like the way we left things, and…I don't know. Will you call me? Text me? Something? Please?*

I delete the message and let the phone fall from my hand. Downstairs, Susannah and Colin are talking. I can't make out the words, but they don't matter. They never do. There's never any suspicion, only trust. Why shouldn't there be? No one's ever knocked on Susannah's door to tell her that her boyfriend is a bad guy.

After the happy couple leaves, the house settles into silence. I wait a little longer to make sure they're not coming back, then drag myself into the bathroom for a shower.

The FBI could be wrong about Josh. They have a long and storied history of being wrong. There could very well be a misunderstanding at work here. Not an evil twin—that's just stupid—but something else. A case of mistaken identity. Someone who was in the wrong place at the wrong time.

Or it could be true. The FBI could be right. Lew could be right. Joshua Murray could be a bad guy worthy of being investigated by federal agencies.

But how am I supposed to know which is right? Who do I believe?

Myself. I believe myself. I trust myself. I find out for myself what's true and what's not. Which means finding out what the FBI knows—or at least suspects. How the hell do I do that?

Maybe I should call that agent who left me his card. Washington or Worthington, or whatever his name was. Could I make some kind of deal? I mean, it's not like I know anything. I followed Josh to an office building that one time, but if I could do it, the feds could do it, too. They probably did it first.

Okay, so I can't make a deal with what I know. Could I make a deal based on what I could potentially find out? I'm Josh's girlfriend. In theory, I could use that position to discover what he's hiding. I could be some kind of double agent or asset or informant or something. Well, maybe not any of those, but there must be something I can do that will lead to the truth.

Starting with a call to the FBI.

Getting out of the shower, I wrap myself in a towel and return to my room. I pick up my jeans from the floor and check the pockets for the agent's card. When the initial search yields nothing, I check again. What did I do with it?

I showed it to Lew at his kitchen table. I took it out of my pocket and gave it to him. Did he give it back? Is it still in his apartment?

I look at my phone. I could call Lew to ask, but something tells me he might counter with a few follow-up questions. Neither can I imagine he would be pleased to hear that not only am I not planning to dump my possible-criminal boyfriend but that I am instead considering running my own investigation into the situation.

So I won't call Lew.

But that doesn't mean I can't go over there to find the card. He's meeting friends at some point. I'll wait until he leaves, then go inside and have a look around.

Because breaking into a cop's apartment is a perfectly valid and sane option.

It is neither of those things, but I'm going to do it anyway.

I rush to get dressed, then return to the bathroom for a handful of Susannah's bobby pins and another dose of aspirin. Heading downstairs, I go to grab my keys from the bowl near the front door, but stop to look at the Prius key fob sitting next to them.

Lew knows my car. He may not know hers.

"Hey, Susannah, can I borrow your car?" I say to the empty house. Then, doing a slightly unflattering impression of her, I continue. "Of course you can, Vinnie! You're the best roommate ever!"

Swapping out my keys for hers, I go out to the Prius and drive to Lew's.

26

I PARK ON THE STREET a few houses down from Lew's building. His truck is still sitting at the curb. He never did mention when he was meeting his friends. For all I know, they could be getting together at his shithole of an apartment. Probably not, though. If their plan really is to drink beer and watch sports, they'd be doing it on a better TV.

When he emerges from the building, I slouch in my seat, not sitting up until the truck has disappeared from view. Then I slide out of the car and head inside.

Unsurprisingly, Lew's door is locked. I run my hand along the top of the door frame, in case he has a spare lying around. He doesn't. There are no doormats or fake rocks to look under, so I reach into my pocket for the bobby pins.

My lock-picking skills are rusty, so it takes me a little longer than I care to admit to gain entrance. As soon as the lock gives way, I go inside and close the door. Stuffing the bobby pins back into my pocket, I begin my search. The kitchen is spotless, the table bare. Why can't Lew be a lazy slacker like everyone else?

Leaving the keys on the counter, I look under the table and chairs. Nothing. Where could that card have gone? I open and close drawers and cabinets, not finding much of anything. Even the drawer where I hazily remember him stashing his gun is empty. Why would that be empty? Does he really need his weapon for an afternoon with the boys?

"Nia?" Lew says. "What are you doing here?"

I jump, slamming the drawer closed as I spin around. Lew's leaning against the wall next to the table. How long has he been standing there?

"What are you doing here?" I say.

"Oh, this? This is my apartment." He straightens. "Speaking of which...how did you get in?"

"The front door was unlocked."

"No, it wasn't."

"The back door was unlocked."

"No, it wasn't." Lew glances toward the front door. He laughs, but it lacks amusement. "You can pick locks."

"No." I shrug. "A little."

Lew shakes his head, appearing irritated. Understandable, I suppose. I did break into his apartment to rifle through his belongings. The question now is what he'll do about it.

"I thought you'd be gone longer," I say.

"Obviously. What are you doing here, Nia?"

"Looking for a business card."

"A business card? What, for that agent?"

"Yeah. Have you seen it?"

Lew doesn't move. "Why are you looking for it?"

"I have a wobbly table at home."

"What do you want with the FBI?"

"Fashion tips."

"Nia."

I resume my search, opening the doors under the sink to reveal a trash can. Would he have thrown the card away? "I want to know what they know, all right? About Josh."

"The FBI isn't in the business of sharing information," Lew says. "You can't just call them up and ask what they know."

I open the trash can and peer inside. Empty. "Well, not until I find that card."

"Card or not, they won't tell you anything."

I hesitate. Where else would it have gone? The bedroom? I did take off my pants there. "They might, if I have something to give them in return."

I try to pass Lew, but he blocks the way.

"You know something about Josh?"

"Just how he takes his coffee."

"They won't care about that."

"Then I'll find them something else," I say. "Are you going to move?"

For a moment, Lew looks as though he's going to say no, that instead of moving, he's planning to keep me hostage in his kitchen. Then he steps aside and follows me to the bedroom.

"You have to stay out of it," he says as I enter the room. "Whatever Josh is involved in is too dangerous for you to be poking around."

I check the floor around the chair where I found my jeans. Nothing. "I must have missed the meeting where you were elected the boss of me."

"I'm trying to protect you."

Getting on my knees, I look under the bed. Nothing. "Big, strong man, shielding the helpless little girl."

"Oh, Jesus Christ, Nia. I'm not fighting with you about this."

I stand. "Not very well, anyway."

"Not at all," he says firmly. "I can't even believe we're having this conversation. Not deliberately putting yourself in danger should really be one of those common-sense things."

"I have always found common sense to be highly overrated."

Lew snorts. "I don't doubt that."

"You know what, Howard Cosell, you can save the commentary. I didn't come to hear your opinion on anything." I close the distance between us. "I'm just here for a card. Do you know where it is?"

Lew looks at me as we stand toe-to-toe. "I want you to stay out of this."

I smile and put my hands on his chest. "Right back at you."

I give him a useless little shove, but he rocks back and I walk away. I don't make it two steps before he grabs my arm and pulls me back. Crashing into him, my fingers automatically tangle in his shirt.

I look at him. "What are you—?"

He presses his lips to mine and I forget my question. I forget everything as the kiss deepens and his arm wraps around my waist, urging me even closer. God, he feels good. Right. Parts of me are sitting up and taking notice in a way they haven't in a long, long time.

Those parts are in control now. Those parts are hauling up his shirt, but I have to stop this. We have to stop. This is crazy— I can't do this.

Lew strips off his shirt, and my eyes widen at the sight of what lay underneath. Nope. Definitely no body fat.

Oh, I'm doing this.

"Nia?" he says.

I kiss him before he can say anything else, ask anything else, think anything else. Nothing good will come from any of that, and this—whatever this is—is good.

Lew's hands slip beneath my shirt, fingers roaming freely. His touch is doing something to me, and can't he just rip my damn shirt off already? What the hell is he waiting for? An engraved invitation?

This time, I end the kiss. We're both breathing heavily now, and I look into his eyes as I remove my shirt. Letting it fall to the floor, I walk into the bedroom. I'm still wearing too many clothes. Goddamn Boston in goddamn November. Why does it have to be all long sleeves and layers? There is no graceful way to do this. I try to kick off my shoes and socks and end up stumbling as though I'm still drunk. I just might be, though. Punch drunk, drunk on the smell of him—does he bathe in pheromones? I think he must. That's the only reasonable explanation for why I'm doing this.

Laughing softly, Lew catches me around the waist and pulls me back against him. His lips work their way down my neck and across my shoulder. My head falls against him. What the hell is happening to me? I can't think straight, but that's probably for the better. I think too much—I'm doing it right now—and holy shit, this man really is God's gift to anyone attracted to men, and for some reason, he won't stop touching me.

He pushes the bra strap from one shoulder, then the other. Hands sliding to the front, he cups my breasts before locating the front clasp and releasing it.

As soon as my bra is off, I turn to kiss him again. My fingers run down his chest and over his abs—seriously, how does anyone have abs like this?—to his belt. I have to concentrate entirely too hard on the task—how the hell do belts work, anyway?—because the intensity of his stare is doing things to me. How does he expect me to focus when he's looking at me like that?

Lew picks me up and carries me to the bed—which does *not* help my concentration—laying me down gently before stepping away to unbuckle the belt himself. He undresses slowly, sensuously—or maybe he isn't. Maybe it just feels that way in my lust-drugged head. But that's all right. I'm not in any hurry for this moment to end.

When Lew is gloriously naked, he kisses his way down my body to my jeans. I raise my hips to allow him to ease them and my panties off. The touching, teasing, stroking continues. I am burning up. How much more can I take?

"Nia," he says, nearly breathless, "do you want—?"

"I want you inside me," I answer. "Don't make me wait anymore."

Lew rolls away, and I hear a drawer open, followed by the crinkling of a condom wrapper.

I laugh as he settles back between my legs. "God, you're such a boy scout."

"Eagle scout, actually."

"Of course you are."

He smiles. "You don't know what you do to me, Nia."

I run my hands along his back. "Oh, I think I have a pretty good—"

And then Lew slides inside and I forget what I was going to say.

27

MY BODY'S HUMMING. IS THAT possible? Do bodies do that—hum after really amazing sex—or am I just insane? Oh, I'm insane all right because I am in bed with Lew. I am naked and in bed with naked Lew, and we...

Oh my God. What have I done? Oh, I know what I've done; I can't stop thinking about what I've done. Why would I want to? That was seriously...I mean, there's a reason I can't catch my breath.

Lew shifts to kiss my shoulder. "Where did you learn to pick locks?"

That's what he wants to know? That's what he chooses to say first? What is wrong with him?

I look at him. "Who's asking?"

"That would be me. Remember me? The only other person in this room?"

"Yes, but is this your really weird version of pillow talk, or are you asking as the cop whose apartment I allegedly broke into?"

Lew smiles. "Allegedly?"

I say nothing. He laughs, but it quickly turns into a sigh. He's going to ruin the moment. I don't know what kind of moment this is exactly, but he's about to ruin it. He's going to open his big, fat beautiful mouth and fuck it all up.

Lew rolls onto his side. "We should talk."

And there it is. I get out of bed. Where's my underwear?

"What are you doing?" he says.

"Getting dressed. It's a little cold, after all, to be walking naked down the street."

Lew collapses onto his back. "We have to talk about this, Nia."

"No, we don't."

I pick up my pants. Forget the underwear. Who needs underwear? Going commando never hurt anyone.

As I shimmy into my jeans, Lew sits up and gestures toward the nightstand. "Your panties are over there."

I glance at the floor in front of the nightstand as I zip and button my jeans. Yep, there they are.

"Keep 'em," I say. "It'll be a little souvenir for you because we're never gonna do this again."

Lew snorts, but I'm not sure if it's laughter or derision or some kind of combination of the two.

I snatch my bra off the floor. "I have a boyfriend, Lew!"

"You have a boyfriend?" He leans toward me. "You mean the guy under federal investigation?"

Okay—pants, bra, shirt. I still need a shirt. "That's the one."

"Why are you still with him, Nia?"

I head for the hall. "It'll be pretty hard to figure out what he's under federal investigation for if I break up with him now."

"What? No. Nia, no. Do you hear me?"

I turn around. "Do I *hear* you?"

Lew climbs out of bed. "You're not doing this. I won't let you."

"You won't *let* me?" I walk back toward him. "What makes you think you're in a position to *let* me do anything? You think because you're James fucking Bond or whatever, I've been made powerless by your sexual prowess?"

"What are you talking about?"

"I'm talking about you thinking that because you flashed your magical abs at me—"

"I did not flash my magical abs at you."

"—that I'm suddenly going to be this docile, obedient...*whatever*, and   "

"I'm pretty sure those are two words no one will ever use to describe you."

In the absence of any heavier options, I pick up his jeans and throw them at him. Something thuds on the floor at my feet and I pick it up to throw that, too. A black leather rectangle—his wallet, I think, until it falls open in my hands.

Credentials. It's a set of credentials with a photo of Lew and a big, shiny badge with the words 'Federal Bureau of Investigation' written across it.

Oh my God.

"What is this?" I look up. Lew's standing on the other side of the bed, zipping his jeans. I hold out the credentials. "What is this?"

Lew leans against the wall, looking just...so damn sad. This makes it worse. This makes it true.

"You know what that is," he says, sounding even more miserable than he looks.

The shock's wearing off, and I nod. "Yeah, you're right, I do. Why do you have one?"

"Let's sit down."

"No. Who are you?"

"You know who I am."

"I know who Llewellyn Weiss is. I have no idea who"—I read the name on the badge—"Llewellyn Morgan is."

"Sit down. I can explain."

I don't sit. "Let's hear it."

He doesn't say anything. He doesn't do anything but stare at the floor.

"Well, when you put it like that," I say, "how could I possibly stay mad?"

Lew looks up. "I'm an agent for—"

"No shit." I throw the badge at him. It bounces off his stomach and lands at his feet.

"I'm undercover—"

"You're an undercover cop going undercover as a cop?"

"Yes."

"How dumb do you think I am?"

"Not dumb at all. The exact opposite of dumb," Lew says. "That's why I'm telling you the truth."

"Why are you undercover as a cop?"

"Corruption."

I shake my head. "That's an IA thing."

"Not when you can't trust IA," Lew says. "There's something wrong in that precinct, and I'm here to find out what it is and how deep it goes."

"You think my father's corrupt?"

Lew pushes off the wall. "No, Nia, no. I don't think he's corrupt. I think he may be just about the only honest one in the whole damn precinct."

"But you think Josh is involved?"

"I know Josh is involved."

My brain is firing in so many directions, I can't keep up with it and blurt out the first question that makes it to my mouth. "Were you behind Agents Dumb and Dumber coming to my house?"

"I knew they intended to interview you."

"Because you sent them?"

"I wasn't the only one who thought—"

"You sent them to my house?"

"You're involved with a person of interest, Nia."

"What did Josh do? What do you think he's doing?"

"You know I can't talk about that."

I put my hands on my hips. "What's your cover? Can you talk about that?"

"A cop with money problems. Someone who might be open to bribes."

"Is it working? Have you been offered bribes? Has Josh offered you a bribe?"

Lew shakes his head. "He's keeping me on the outside."

"You must not be very good at your job."

"I'm *very* good at my job, but these things take time. Your boyfriend's good at keeping his secrets."

"He's not my boyfriend."

"That's not what you said five minutes ago."

"Shut up!" I exclaim. "Don't change the subject."

"He is the subject."

I take an angry step forward. "No, he isn't! You lying to me is the subject. You sending men to my house to interrogate me is the subject."

"That was hardly an interrogation."

"Why would you even do that?" I continue. "Didn't you know the first thing I would do after they left would be to tell Josh…" The expression on Lew's face registers with me, and I nod. "You did know. You were counting on it."

"Yes."

I look at the floor. "You wanted to know what he would do. How he would react. You were trying to—I don't know—smoke him out, or spook him, or something."

"Yes."

"And I did that. I ran right to him, told him the feds were asking questions about him." I lift my head. "Am I bugged?"

"Your phone."

Disbelief swallows me whole all over again. "My phone? You bugged my phone? *You* bugged my phone?" I say, and Lew nods. "When did you do that?"

"The day you showed me around Boston. At lunch. You went to the bathroom and left your bag behind."

That was…When was that? A month ago? Longer? "So…what? There's some guy in some office somewhere listening to every conversation I have?"

"Yes."

"Every conversation?"

"Yes."

"Even the ones with you?"

"Yes."

"Stop saying that! Stop saying it so matter-of-factly, like it doesn't matter."

"It does matter, Nia."

"I know it matters!" I shake my head. "Nope. I can't—I can't do this."

Lew rounds the bed. "Nia? Are you—?"

I hold up my hand. "Don't you dare come any closer to me."

He stops but doesn't back away. We're too close now, but my feet refuse to move.

I stare at his stupid face. "All this time you've been spying on me?"

"Not the whole time. Just since The Rebel Fly."

The Rebel Fly? What the hell is—The Rebel Fly. That crappy bar with the crappy band and crappier drinks. I went to a bar with Josh one night, and two days later, the FBI put a bug in my phone. I think I might vomit. Or cry. Or both.

I gesture to the bed. "What about…What about that? Was that part of the job, too?"

Lew's face softens. "No, Nia, no. That wasn't part of the job. That was…" He sighs. "That was a mistake."

Just when I thought I couldn't feel any worse. "A mistake."

"I crossed a line, I broke a rule. I put the investigation at risk—not to mention my entire career. It was a mistake, but I don't care. I don't."

"Well, don't you think you should?" I ask. "It's not just your life you're screwing with here."

"I know. God, I know. But I don't care. I jeopardized everything because I wanted to." Lew steps forward. "Because I wanted *you*."

I can't seem to close my jaw. It's just broken by shock. What is happening? Why am I still standing here, watching Lew get closer? I should be running away. Or walking briskly away, at any rate. I should not be standing here, waiting to see if my heart will actually burst out of my chest or if it just feels that way. I should be—

He cups my face and kisses me hard. My traitorous knees go weak, and I grab his arms to keep from sliding to the floor. He interprets this as an invitation to deepen the kiss, and for a moment, I let him.

I hate him. I hate who he is, what he is, what he's done. I hate that his body pressed against mine feels so good—so *right*. It shouldn't. It's wrong. He lied to me, to my family. I shouldn't want him anywhere near me. I shouldn't want *him*.

I push him back. "I can't be here right now. Or ever again. I have to…I have to go."

"Nia," Lew says. "Wait."

I leave the bedroom, scooping up my shirt as I pass. Sliding it on, I work the buttons with trembling fingers and return to the kitchen to collect Susannah's keys. Lew follows me, but for once, he stays quiet. It isn't until I reach his front door that he speaks.

"Nia," he says. "Please."

I open the door. "Stay away from me."

28

WHAT'S THE BEST WAY TO destroy a cell phone?

Sure, I could turn the damn thing off, but destroying it feels like the way to go. More active, anyway — and I want to be active. I want to be destructive. I want to be someone who doesn't end up in these kind of situations, but that doesn't seem like it'll be happening anytime soon.

No, because I'm the fucking genius who dates criminals under federal investigation and then sleeps with the undercover FBI agents trying to catch them.

Which brings me back to the problem at hand. How do I destroy my phone?

I'm sure there are a lot of ways to destroy a phone, but what's the best way? How can I ensure there will be no saving it? Smash it with a hammer? Throw it in Boston Harbor? Drill it full of holes? Microwave it. No, that's probably a bad idea. I want to destroy a phone, not burn down my house. Maybe I could take it to the shooting range and use it as target practice. Drop it in a vat of acid? I'm not sure where I'd get acid. Do they sell that kind of thing at the hardware store, or do I need to ask Josh where he gets his supervillain supplies? Bleach. I have bleach at the house. Would that work? Maybe I could run the phone through the laundry a few dozen times. Run over it with my car? A semi? Train tracks! I could put it on some train tracks. Boston does not lack for train tracks. How hard would it be to do that? People flatten pennies on tracks all the time. A phone's just a bigger, thicker, squarer penny, right?

On the passenger's seat, my phone rings, and Lew's name flashes on the screen. Some people really can't take a hint, can they? Forget the train. I'll throw the damn phone out the window.

But I don't. I don't even reach for it. Throwing it out the window feels like leaving too much to chance. One would assume the endless line of traffic behind me would be enough to crush my phone into unrepairable little pieces, but it would be just my luck that I would throw the phone onto the one spot where no car would ever drive. No, it's better that the phone stays with me and dies its horrible death at my hands.

When I get home, I take the phone into the garage and drop it on the concrete floor. I root through my grandfather's toolbox, selecting both a ball-peen and claw hammer. Removing a pair of clear plastic safety glasses from the same shelf, I blow on the lenses to clear away some of the dust, then wipe them on my shirt. Good enough.

Kneeling next to my phone, I set the glasses in place and look over the hammers. Is one better than the other? Does it matter? Selecting the ball-peen, I hold it loosely in my hand as I put the phone on speaker and call Lew.

He picks up on the second ring. "Nia?"

I bring the hammer down on the phone, repeating the action until my arm aches. Then I hold the hammer with both hands to continue the assault. The phone bounces around and I chase it, playing the worst game of Whack-A-Mole ever, only stopping when the back pops off and a small metal disc slides onto the concrete.

That's it. That's the bug.

Removing my safety glasses, I stare at it. Has it already stopped working? Does the guy on the other end know what's happening? Have I affected anything at all?

Smash it. I need to smash the ever-living hell out of it, but I drop the hammer, pick up the bug, and head for the house. Rufus greets me at the door and I direct him into the backyard. Safety first. Always safety first. When it comes to my dog, anyway.

Stopping at the kitchen sink, I drop the disc into the disposal and turn on the water before leaning over to flip the switch.

The grating sound of Lew's bug and my garbage disposal dying is immensely satisfying.

However, my pleasure fades quickly. Just because I destroyed one bug does not mean there aren't more to be found. For all I know, my house is infested with them. Disconnecting the landline, I let Rufus inside and he follows me as I move from room to room, hunting for anything that could be construed as a surveillance device.

My search turns up nothing. Does that mean the FBI didn't bother to bug anything else, or are they just hidden really well? Is there any way I could find out without asking Lew?

Because I am done talking to Lew.

I'm surprised he hasn't shown up here. I would have thought he'd follow me home, worried about protecting his cover. Worried I would announce the truth all over social media. Worried I would tell Josh. Worried I would tell my dad.

I should tell Dad. I should drive over to the house right now and tell him the truth about his wonderful new partner. I should tell my mother the truth about that nice, young man she's so fond of. He's a liar, a goddamn liar, and I should tell them that.

I can't do that. Can I? I mean, sure, I can absolutely tell my parents the truth. I can announce it to all twelve of my social media followers. I could have a banner printed up, then hire one of those little planes to fly it over the city. But that doesn't mean I should. Undercover cops conceal their identities for a reason. As pissed off as I am, would I actively seek to put Lew in danger?

No. No, I wouldn't.

I move through the house, pulling drapes and shades tight and double checking that the doors are locked and bolted. For good measure, I slide dining room chairs beneath the knobs. Let's see the FBI get inside now.

Shit. The FBI. Lew, the fucking fed. What the hell was he thinking? What the hell was *I* thinking? Well, I know the answer to that. I wasn't thinking. I had, in fact, stopped thinking the moment his lips touched mine, and…Nope. Not going there. Not again.

I will stay far away from that. And him. I don't care what it takes, what I have to do. Move. Change my name. I'll do it. Sorry, family and friends, we had a good run, but Lavinia Kelly no longer exists.

I'll need a new name. Do you get to choose your own name when you're on the run? Is that one of the perks? What name would I pick? Something normal. Hell, it could be worth running away just for the opportunity to have a normal name. Jennifer. Jenny. Amy. There's no real nickname for Amy, is there? Not that I need a nickname; I don't. Jessica. Or Samantha. Sam. I could be a Sam. Sam Jones. No—Sam Smith. I like the alliteration.

That does it. My new name: Sam Smith.

Unless the alliteration makes it stick out too much.

Sam Jones. Just to be safe.

I make some popcorn—thank *God* I didn't damage the microwave—and take it and a bottle of Jack Daniel's into the living room. Building a nest out of blankets on the couch, I sit and stare at the television I am now too chicken to turn on. As Rufus naps at my side, I drink and snack and brood.

The Rebel Fly. The FBI has been watching me ever since The Rebel Fly. Every time I saw Lew, the FBI was looking back.

Every time I talked to Lew, the FBI was talking back. Every time. Every goddamn time.

Was any of it real? Is Lew really from Arizona? Did he really lose his mother? Did he really want me, or was it just another line, another lie, in the pursuit of justice?

It didn't feel fake. Which is probably the point. He said he was good at his job. I guess I now know how true a statement that is. But he didn't…Did it feel right to him? Did I feel right? How did I get things so wrong?

How do I always get everything just so goddamn wrong?

The anger is gone now, tears taking its place. They roll, unchecked, down my cheeks. It's stupid to cry over this, over him, but that doesn't stop my entire body from shaking with silent sobs. Rufus stirs and whimpers along with me, licking my cheeks until I wrap my arms around him and cry into his fur.

I wake to a frantically barking dog and slowly push myself up. What time is it? I reach for my phone to check, then remember why I can't do that. The sunlight peeking around the living room curtains suggests that it's a new day. So I spent the night on the couch. At least it was my couch.

Rufus is still barking, running between me and the front door. That can only mean someone is…Then I hear it.

Someone knocking on the door.

"Nia!" Lew shouts. "Nia, let me in!"

Oh, hell, no. I don't move.

"Come on, Nia, I know you're in there. Please. I just want to talk to you."

How does he know I'm in here? Is there a hidden camera somewhere? Can the government watch you through your TV, even if it's not on?

"Your car's in the driveway, Nia. I know you're home. Please, just…open the door."

My car. Right. I give the TV the finger anyway before sliding off the couch. The knocking loses some of its vigor but persists. Rufus stops barking and returns to my side.

"Nia," Lew calls, "I'm not leaving until you open the door."

There's a theory that's just begging to be tested. Nothing would bring me more pleasure than making that jackass stand out in the cold all damn day. Of course, that means I run the risk of Lew standing on my front step until Susannah comes home. I really don't want that to happen.

I'll have to get rid of him.

Swallowing a sigh, I go to the door. Rufus waits patiently as I move the chair and undo the locks. The knocking stops. I take a deep breath before yanking open the door.

My eyes immediately find Lew's. "There. I opened the door. Now you can leave."

I go to slam it shut, but he blocks it with his arm. It doesn't look as though he slept. Not that it makes him any less gorgeous. Which is incredibly unfair. He doesn't sleep, and he still looks like a goddamn Adonis. I probably look like I went twelve rounds with a tornado and lost.

"I need to talk to you," he says.

"I bet you do."

"May I come in?"

"No."

"Let me in, Nia."

"You got a warrant?"

"Of course I don't."

"Then piss off before I call the cops."

"I am the cops."

"No, you're a fucking fed."

Lew glances from side to side. "Say that a little louder next time."

"Don't tempt me," I say. "Is that why you're here? You're afraid I'll blow your cover?"

"That's part of it."

"What's the other part?"

"You know what the other part is."

My stomach clenches as though I've taken a punch. "We're not talking about that. There's no need to discuss the first part, either, because I've already told everyone I know. Starting with my dad."

"No, you haven't."

"How do you know that? You have cameras in my house? People tailing me?"

Lew drags his hand over his face. "I know because you're not stupid. If you say anything to your father, you could put him at risk."

"*I* could put him at risk? What about you?"

"Patrick's safer if he doesn't know."

"According to you."

"Yes, according to me. I think you know that, too," Lew says. "So, no, I don't think you'll blow my cover. You may hate me, but you still like him."

"I *may* hate you?" I ask. "Ever the optimist, aren't you?"

"Better than being whatever you are."

I nod. "I'm sure it is."

"Nia—"

"I want you to leave. Stop showing up wherever I am. Stop pretending you're some kind of good guy when you're really..." I shake my head. "Stay away from me. Stay away from my family."

"Your father's my partner. I can't—"

"Find a new partner."

"I can't do that."

"You mean you won't do that."

"I mean I can't. I'll keep him safe, Nia. I promise."

"Yeah. Because the word of a liar means so much."

"Nia—"

"Fine. Keep using my dad, if it makes you feel good. But that's as far as it goes. You work together, and that's it. No more family dinners. No more family anything," I say. "You're not family."

He straightens as though he has sustained an electrical shock, and I close and lock the door. After putting the chair back in place, I sink to the floor, pull my knees to my chest, and cry. Rufus lays down, resting his head on my feet. There's a moment of silence before I hear Lew walk away.

"Think he'll stay gone this time?" I ask Rufus, and he wags his tail in response. "Yeah. Me neither."

I clean up the living room and head for the kitchen to un barricade the door. I let Rufus into the backyard, then pick up his water dish to refill it, but end up standing at the sink, looking down the drain.

That seemed like such a good idea at the time.

Before I realize it, I'm crying again. Not body-racking sobs, just big, fat tears that serve no purpose except pissing me off. Setting the bowl on the counter, I scrub at my cheeks. I will not cry over this. Over him. It was a mistake—he was right about that—and it's over now. I will not cry. He—this—is not worth it.

A knock on the front door interrupts my misery, and I look over my shoulder. Is he back already? What part of 'stay away from me' doesn't he understand? Irritated anew, I march into the living room.

"Vinnie?" Susannah bangs on the door. "Vinnie, are you in there? Why can't I get in?"

"Hang on." I jog the rest of the way. Wiping my face quickly, I let her into the house. "Sorry about that. You're home sooner than I expected."

Susannah comes inside and looks around. "Colin had to cover a class. What's going on?"

"Nothing."

"Doesn't seem like nothing. What happened?"

"Nothing."

"Are you sure? Because it looks like you were preparing for a massive invasion. Are the Huns coming to town?"

"Nice topical reference."

"What can I say? I've lived with you for too long." Susannah returns the chair to the table. "What happened?"

Absolutely nothing I intend to tell her about. Where would I even start? I go to the kitchen to let Rufus back into the house. "I had a horror movie marathon last night with a bottle of whiskey and may have freaked myself out a little bit."

Susannah sits at the kitchen table, eyeing me with suspicion. "You watched horror movies all night? By yourself?"

I fill the water dish and set it on the floor. "Well, Rufus was there, but I did that, yes."

"Uh-huh. What really happened?"

"Nothing I want to talk about."

"Boy troubles?"

"Yes, because when I said I don't want to talk about it, I actually meant I wanted to talk about it."

Susannah nods. "I suspected as much."

I sigh as I give Rufus his breakfast. "I'm not in the mood, so I'm going to take a shower. Do us both a favor, and don't let anyone in the house. And for the love of whatever celebrity you currently worship, don't talk to Lew."

"Ha!" Susannah exclaims as I shuffle out of the kitchen. "I knew it was boy troubles!"

29

I STAY IN THE SHOWER until I'm certain Susannah will be engrossed in an activity other than questioning me and my questionable life choices. I already know how screwed up everything is. I don't need it pointed out to me.

When I finally return downstairs, Susannah's on the couch, watching television and grading homework. I say nothing as I return to the garage to hide any remaining evidence of my freak-out. Everything is where I left it. I pick up the hammers and safety glasses first.

"Vinnie?" Susannah enters the garage. "Are you in here?"

So much for that plan. I look at the hammers in my hand, then at her. She's holding out her phone, but her attention is on the mess on the floor.

"Is that your phone?" she asks. "What happened?"

I tuck the hammers and glasses back in their box. "I dropped it."

Susannah sighs, exasperation overflowing. "You're a liar, Lavinia Kelly, and if your mother wasn't waiting to talk to you, I'd make you tell me what the hell is going on right now." She thrusts the phone toward me. "So, talk to her, then come inside and talk to me. And if you try to disappear in any way, shape, or form, I will track you down wherever you hide and make you tell me there."

Though I have no intention of telling Susannah anything, I nod and take the phone. She plies me with a look that probably inspires fear only in her most timid students and backs out of the garage.

I bring the phone to my ear. "Mom?"

"What is wrong with your phone? Phones!" my mother exclaims. "I've been calling both your numbers and haven't been able to get you on either one."

I kick at the pieces. "Yeah. I, uh…I lost my cell yesterday. I didn't know anything was wrong with the landline, though. I'll check it."

I hate lying to my mother. It doesn't matter if it's a tiny, white lie or a big, whopping fat one, I hate it. And this is only the start because she has no idea about Lew. That's a real lie, not something stupid that doesn't matter. The pit in my stomach is enough to make me confess everything, yet I can't. Why am I so reluctant to spill Lew's secret?

"What's going on?" I ask. "Is something wrong?"

"Yes, something's wrong. It's a complete disaster."

There are entirely too many things that can currently fall under that category. "What's a disaster, Mom?"

"The party, Lavinia! The party!"

Party? What party is she—shit. I cringe. "Dad's birthday."

"Yes, Dad's birthday. Don't tell me you forgot."

"Okay, I won't tell you that."

"Lavinia, this party is happening on Friday night, and I do not have time for your jokes."

Certainly not when she's in the throes of her annual pre-party meltdown. "I'm sorry," I say. "How can I help?"

"You can come over. You, and Susannah, too, if she's not busy. I know she's planning a wedding, and—"

"Sure. I'll have to check with the bride, but your spinster daughter will be right over to help."

"Lavinia—"

"Gotta go, Mom. See you soon."

Ending the call, I put the phone in my back pocket. I scoop up the remains of my own phone, dump them in the utility sink, and turn on the water. Susannah reappears a moment later.

"Did you really think I would blow you off?" I ask as though that hadn't been my plan.

"Yes." She looks into the sink. "That had better not be my phone."

I hand it over. "Nancy's having a pre-party breakdown and would like us to come over and help."

"Sure. Just as soon as we talk about what's going on."

Oh good. She didn't forget. I suppose I have to tell her something. Not the truth, obviously, but there must be something I can say. A lower-calorie version of the truth, maybe?

I turn off the water. "Lew and I had a fight. A bad one."

"The fight to end all fights?"

I roll my eyes. "Can you just—?"

"Sorry. What did you fight about?"

"Nothing." I wince. Why does that have to be my Pavlovian response to everything?

Susannah raises an eyebrow. "The fight to end all fights was about nothing? Maybe you're not doing it right."

"Maybe you're not helping."

"Maybe that's because you're still lying to me. What did you fight about?"

"Josh."

"Okay, but you've fought about Josh before and you didn't resort to property damage then."

"Property damage?"

"I saw the garbage disposal and, you know, your phone in the sink here." She leans against the wall. "What was different about this fight?"

Let me count the ways I don't want to tell her this. I bite my lower lip. "I may have accidentally slept with Lew."

Susannah straightens. "You...what?"

"Slept with Lew."

"You slept with *Ellie*?"

"Accidentally."

"Accidentally? How do you accidentally sleep with some-one? Is there tripping involved?"

"Come on, you know what I mean."

"I don't know what you mean. I don't know—I mean, oh my God, Vinnie. You slept with Ellie. You actually slept with Ellie, and what about Josh? Did you break up with Josh?"

"No."

"Are you going to break up with Josh?"

I swallow. "I...I don't know."

Susannah's mouth drops. "Holy shit, Vinnie."

"Well said."

"I don't...I can't..." She shakes her head. "I don't even know what to say. When did this happen?"

"Yesterday. At Lew's."

"Before you came home?"

"No. I went back there after you and Colin left."

"You went back for sex?"

"No! I left something at his apartment so I went back to get it, and the sex just kind of...happened."

"Accidentally."

"It wasn't planned, okay? One minute we were fighting, and then all of a sudden, we were...not fighting." My face goes scarlet, and I cover my cheeks with my hands.

Susannah lets out a choked little squeal. "It was that good, huh?"

"I'm not telling you that."

"Oh, honey. Yeah, that blush already told me everything."

"It did not!"

"It did, too." Susannah laughs. "Of all the places I imag-ined we might have this conversation, never once did I think it would be in this garage."

My hands drop to my hips. "What conversation? You mean the one we're literally having at this moment where I just told you I had sex with Lew?"

"That's the one."

"How long have you been imagining us having this conversation at all?"

"Do you remember that night when Nancy had us over for dinner to introduce everyone to Ellie?" Susannah asks, and I nod. "Since then. Right around the moment when you were saying goodbye at the Jeep, and he leaned in and you didn't move away."

"That was in September."

"I remember."

"You've been imagining me telling you I had sex with Lew since September?"

"Not exclusively. I have indulged in a daydream or two about my wedding."

I shake my head. "I can't believe this."

"I'm hardly the first person in the world to daydream about her wedding."

"Stop trying to be cute. I'm pissed at you."

"You're pissed at me? I'm pissed at you!"

"Why would you be pissed at me?"

"Because you don't tell me anything!" Susannah exclaims. "We're supposed to be friends—best friends, sisters, even, but the kind of sisters who tell each other everything and can tolerate being in the same room together—but you stopped doing that. You stopped talking to me, Vinnie. I know something's going on with you—and I knew that before you destroyed your phone and garbage disposal and God only knows what else you've done—but like the big, stupid person I am, I've been waiting for you to tell me what it is, but all you've done is lie and blow me off."

"I haven't—"

"Yeah, you have. And yeah, I've been waiting for you to tell me you slept with Ellie because you two clearly have a thing for each other. I thought, hey, maybe Vinnie needs time to work that out on her own, or maybe you were just way more into Josh than you seemed, but now you're standing here, telling me—and only because I cornered and threatened you, by the way—that you slept with Ellie—sorry, *accidentally* slept with Ellie—which led to a fight over the boyfriend you're not sure you want to break up with, which, for some reason inspired you to go on an appliance killing spree—"

"It was one appliance. That hardly qualifies as a spree."

Susannah throws her arms in the air. "You're doing it again!"

I can't tell her the truth. Lew's right—it's safer if she doesn't know. It's safer if none of them know. Folding my arms across my chest, I blink back tears. "I'm mad at both of them, okay? I got sick of the phone calls and text messages, so I destroyed my phone to make them stop."

"Why didn't you just turn it off?"

"I was mad, I wasn't thinking, and I wanted to smash something."

"Okay, She-Hulk. Why? What did they do?"

"They just…" I sigh, causing tears to spill out. I can't tell her the truth. I can't. "Nobody ever is who they're supposed to be."

"Who are they supposed to be? Brian?"

The question robs me of breath. More tears escape. "Don't bring him into this."

"Why not? You bring him into everything you do, everything you don't do. Why shouldn't we talk about him?"

"Because I'm saying no."

"Well, I don't care. For three years, I let you decide—we all let you decide because no one wanted to say or do anything to upset you—but that's over now. I'm done with it. We're going to talk about this, and we're going to do it now."

"No, we're not. I don't care how upset you get. I don't have to say one word to you or Lew or Josh, or anyone else. Not about Brian. Not about anything."

"Why are you so afraid to talk about him, Vinnie? Every time his name comes up, you shut down faster than—"

"I don't want to talk about him!"

"Brian wouldn't want—"

"You never even met him," I seethe. "Don't you dare try to tell me what he would or wouldn't want."

"You're right—I never met him. I only got to see what losing him did to you, and—"

"That wasn't his fault."

"It wasn't your fault, either," Susannah says. "Stop punishing yourself for it."

"I'm not doing that."

She nods. "I know you like to think so, but as the person who has spent three years watching you do exactly that, I have to call bullshit."

"You don't have to do anything. I am not your responsibility; I have never been your responsibility."

"That's not what it feels like." Susannah's posture changes. "Do you know why Colin and I have never lived together? Do you know why we've never spent more than a long weekend on our own?"

"You're not putting that on me."

"Because we were too scared to leave you alone for too long."

I shake my head. "Stop it. Just stop it. You're making me out to be some woman who fell apart because she lost some guy, and—"

"Not some guy. *Brian*," Susannah says. "And you did fall apart. Anyone would have."

"I did not—"

"You were drowning, Vinnie. Everyone could see it. You were drowning, and everyone was terrified about what that would mean and what would happen to you."

"I never asked—"

"You didn't have to ask! We love you—me, your brother, Patrick, Nancy—we love you, you idiot, and we would do anything to make sure you're okay."

"I am okay! I'm fine!"

Susannah gestures to the utility sink. "That's fine?" She jerks her thumb toward the house. "That's fine? You're not fine."

"Yeah, I am. You don't get to decide what makes me okay. You don't get to decide how I live my life, who I sleep with, who I don't sleep with—"

"I don't care who you sleep with. Sleep with the entire city if you want! If you want to be with Ellie, be with Ellie. If you want to be with Josh, be with Josh. If you want to be the spinster daughter with a thousand cats, let's go to the shelter and get you started."

"Spinster daughter?"

"Yeah, I heard that."

"I can't believe you were eavesdropping on me."

"It's not like you've left me with much choice."

We stare at one another until her phone rings. She glances at the screen, then holds it out. I take it, seeing my mother's name before accepting the call.

"Mom, hi." I struggle to make my voice sound normal. "I'm walking out the door right now."

"You are? Now? Right now?"

"Yes, right now."

"What about Susannah?"

"Susannah's not coming. She has wedding stuff to do." Susannah shakes her head and walks out of the garage.

"But you're coming?" my mother asks.

"As soon as we end this call."

"Good."

She hangs up. I go inside the house to collect my keys and my dog. Susannah's sitting at the kitchen table, but she doesn't look at me as I return her phone. Moving to the living room, I pick up my keys and a leash before calling Rufus. He hurries down the stairs, grabs the leash in his mouth, and we play a relaxed game of tug-of-war to the front door.

"I won't be here when you get back," Susannah says. "I'm going to stay with Colin for a while."

Letting go of the leash, I look at her, now standing at the entrance to the kitchen, and nod. "I think you should."

It'll be easier if she's not here. I won't have to keep lying to her face. I won't have to…It'll be easier. Safer.

We share another long, silent stare, then I open the door and walk out.

30

AS THE DETAILS OF MY father's birthday party have changed very little since its conception, the planning is not difficult. Mostly, it's just calling Mom's friends to confirm who's bringing what for food and drink, and to find out what time the fellowship hall will be unlocked so we can get inside to decorate. I could do it in my sleep, but I dutifully work my way through the call sheet and jot down the answers. Each completed call, each noted response, is a weight off my mother's shoulders.

Though I don't enjoy the stress she inflicts upon herself, I love that she does this for Dad every year. I love my dad all the more, too, because I know he doesn't care about the party as much as he does seeing his wife happy. He'd be content with nothing but a terrible store-bought cake, just so long as he got to spend an evening surrounded by his loving wife and pain-in-the-ass children.

My parents are too damn adorable sometimes.

To thank me for my efforts, Mom feeds me dinner, then sends me home with all the leftovers I can carry. When I pull into the driveway, Josh is sitting on the front steps. I park the car and stare at him until Rufus whines and nudges me with his nose. I'd really like to drive away, but I suppose I can't avoid Josh forever—no matter how much I may want to. Breathing deep, I get out of the car.

Josh stands. "Hey."

I open the door for Rufus. He doesn't rush our visitor, instead staying at my side, hackles raised. He reads me so well. I scratch his head between his ears in an attempt to reassure him. "What are you doing here?"

"I just got back into town and thought I'd stop by to see how you are. You know, because you haven't returned any of my calls or texts."

"I lost my phone. Haven't had a chance to replace it yet."

"What about your landline? You lose that, too?" he asks. When I decline to comment, he continues. "I talked to your brother."

"He told me."

"But you still didn't call me back."

"I've been busy."

"Doing what?"

Lew. I motion for Josh to move so I can get to the front door. "You first. Where have you been?"

"I had to go out of town for work. I told you that," he says. "Is this about the FBI? I thought we—"

"Out of town where?"

"New York City. Midtown. Do you want to see my expense report?"

I unlock the door and push it open. "Yes."

"Then I'll email you a copy as soon as I fill it out." Josh gestures toward the house. "Can I come in?"

Moment of truth time. Or maybe it's the point of no return. How badly do I want to do this?

"Sure," I say. "Come in."

He follows me inside and stands awkwardly in the kitchen as I put away leftovers and give Rufus his dinner. When I run out of things to do, I lean against the counter.

"Do you want something?" I ask. "Like, something to eat or drink?"

Josh shakes his head. "Maybe you'll let me take you out."

"Why would I do that?"

He sits at the table. "You're still mad."

"I don't know what I am."

"But you don't trust me."

Nope. I sit across from him. "I don't know."

"I told you they had it wrong." Josh leans toward me. "Have they been back? Are they harassing you?"

Not as such. "No. It's just…"

"What?"

I shrug. "I have a hard enough time trusting people when the FBI *doesn't* show up on my doorstep to ask questions about them."

Josh nods. "What can I do? How can I make it better?"

"I don't know."

Why did I think I could do this? I have no poker face whatsoever. How will I bluff him well enough to find out what's going on? Maybe I shouldn't try. Maybe I should stay out of it. Break up with Josh here and now, and be done with the whole situation.

But I won't really be done with it, will I?

My father's still on the force. He's devoted the majority of his life to that badge. If Lew is right, there are people serving alongside him who are perverting everything he believes in. People who could—*would*—put my dad in danger if it meant protecting their secret.

Can I really stay out of that?

"Nia?"

I look at Josh. "What? Sorry, did you say something?"

He smiles. "What are you thinking about?"

"If I can be around you anymore."

"No, Nia, come on. I didn't do this—I am not the guy they're looking for."

Lew says otherwise. My gut says otherwise.

"Tell me what to do. I want you to be able to trust me," Josh says. "I don't want this—*us*—to get screwed up over some stupid misunderstanding."

Why is he trying so damn hard? We've only been dating for a couple of months—and I'm pretty sure we've spent most of that time fighting. It's not like we have some deep, meaningful history together. Why does he keep coming back? What's in it for him? Is he trying to use me to get to something? No, that's stupid. What could I possibly have that he would...

Dad. Is Josh trying to get to my dad? Maybe he views it as a challenge—Patrick Kelly, the incorruptible officer, the holy grail to a guy seeking to possess a complete set of crooked cops.

The thought pushes me out of my chair, and I stare at Rufus for a moment before moving to the pantry to get some cookies for him. The air seems to have thinned considerably. I need to calm down, but how the hell am I supposed to do that?

"Nia? You okay?"

Obviously not, but it doesn't matter. I have to figure this out. I can't leave it to Lew. It's not personal to him. My father is just a means to an end.

I return to the table. "Sorry, it's been a long, strange weekend."

"I'm sorry. I know I was a big part of that." Josh reaches across the table. "You're sure I can't take you out tonight to make it up to you? Anywhere you want to go. Or we could order in and watch Netflix. Anything you want."

"Not tonight. I'm way too tired. Maybe another night."

"Any night you want. Name it."

I look him over and sigh. I am really doing this. "What are you doing Friday night?"

31

MY FATHER — PILLAR OF THE community that he is — commands a large turnout for his birthday party. Mom is in her element, greeting each arrival with genuine delight and enthusiasm, whereas I hide behind the beverage table, pretending that adding scoops of rainbow sherbet to the punch is very delicate rocket science that requires my complete concentration. How did I come from these people? Did my mother have a one-night stand with a surly, sarcastic, whiskey-swilling milkman? I mean, I know she didn't, but there are days when that feels like the only explanation.

"Spiking the punch?" Josh asks.

I look up, the scoop of sherbet dropping into the bowl with a splash that leaves my cream-colored blouse spattered with red. Setting down the spoon, I grab a napkin from the table and dab at the spots, grateful to have something to do that doesn't require making eye contact with the man on the other side of the table.

"Sorry," he says. "I didn't mean to startle you."

"Doesn't matter." I nod at the bag in his hand. "What's that?"

"A gift for your dad."

"You brought a present? What did you get him?"

"A bottle of Jameson Black Barrel."

I peek into the bag, but the tissue paper obscures what's inside. "Really?"

"That's okay, right? He's not—"

"A prohibitionist? No. Whiskey's perfect." I move the paper just enough to see the bottle. "Though I may be tempted to dump it in the punch bowl before we get to presents."

"You want to spike the punch bowl at your dad's party?"

I look around. "Don't you?"

Josh smiles. "Anything to make my girl happy."

"I'm not your girl," I say automatically.

"Still not there yet. Got it."

Was he this annoying before the FBI got involved? I stick the cover back on the sherbet and pick it up, only to set it down again when Susannah and Colin enter the hall. I haven't seen her since our stupid fight in the garage, and apparently, I am not prepared to see her now. When Susannah spots me and her smile disappears, I know the feeling is mutual.

Josh looks between Susannah and me. "That's not a good face. What's going on there? You two fighting or something?"

Or something. "Susannah's mad at me."

"Why?"

"I told her I didn't like the bridesmaids' dresses."

"Seemed like a pretty intense glare for something so minor."

"All right, fine. I may have said I would rather walk naked down the aisle than in that dress."

Josh nods. "Okay. I can see how she maybe took some offense at that. What are you going to do about it?"

"Nothing."

"Nia, come on. She's your best friend. You have to do something."

The fact that she's my best friend is precisely why I can't do anything. I pick up the sherbet. "Well, right now, I'm going to put this in the freezer and get some club soda on my shirt. Don't spike the punch bowl until I get back."

Josh salutes me. "Yes, ma'am."

I head for the kitchen, walking a little faster than a relaxed partygoer should walk. Just before I can escape to the promised land, my mother intercepts me.

"I forgot a knife for the cake," she says. "Will you—?"

"On it."

She lets me go, and I push through the swinging door into the empty, quiet kitchen. I stand still for a moment to gather myself before returning the sherbet to the freezer and searching drawers for a cake knife.

"What is he doing here?" Lew says.

Startled, I jump and turn around. "Jesus Christ. Is that the only way you know how to enter a room?"

"What the hell is Josh doing here?"

"It's my father's birthday, and he's my very serious boyfriend. Where else would he be?"

"Your very serious boyfriend." Lew shakes his head. "Are you trying to get yourself killed?"

"Yes, I am. That is exactly what I'm trying to do. How clever of you to see it," I snap. "What the hell are you doing here? I told you—"

"Your father's still my partner. It would be unrealistic—"

"Right. I forgot how concerned you are with being real."

"Nia—"

"Susannah's pissed at me. Colin, too."

If the change of topic throws him at all, Lew doesn't show it. "Why?"

"Because I'm a shitty liar and shittier friend."

"Do they know?"

"No." I shrug. "Well, not from me, anyway."

"I'm sorry," Lew says. "I never wanted to involve you—any of you—in any of this."

"But you did."

"I'm sorry."

"A fat lot of good that does me."

"Would it help if I apologized again?"

I smile and look at the floor. "I don't know how you do this, live like this, with all these lies."

"I don't, either, anymore. I used to be…It used to come easy. I was good at it."

"You still are." I lift my head. "Was any of it real?"

"Probably too much."

"Like what?"

"My parents. Where I'm from. I didn't lie about that."

"Just who you are."

"That's the job."

Resuming my search, I open the next drawer. "Pretty stupid job."

"I didn't lie about how I feel. About you."

Mistake. That's the only thing I remember him saying about me. Though the drawer contains what I need, I slam it shut and whirl around. He's closer now. Close enough to lean in to, and…I want to. I want to melt against that wall of muscle. If I stood on my toes, I could…

Grabbing his tie, I tug him closer and kiss him. He responds immediately, hands going to my hips. He moves forward, pushing me back against the counter, then lifts me onto the Formica.

For a moment—one magnificent moment—it doesn't matter that we're in a fellowship hall kitchen at a party for my father at which my sort-of boyfriend is in attendance. It doesn't matter that my mother could walk in on us in search of that knife she sent me to get. Nothing matters except getting as close to Lew as possible. As much as I hate him, he's the only one who knows the truth, and I don't know how to be around anyone else. As fucked up as it may be, I need him. I need *this*.

Then he pulls back. He doesn't move far away—our foreheads are nearly touching—but now the Grand Canyon sits between us. My hand hovers over my mouth as I fight to keep tears at bay. What the hell was I thinking? What is it about Lew that makes my brain cease to function properly? A mistake—a goddamn mistake. That's what I am to him. That's all I'll ever be.

"Nia."

His fingers graze my cheek and I jerk back, hitting my head against the cabinets behind me. As I wince, Lew tries again to touch me, but I shove him away and slide off the counter.

"Are you all right?" he asks.

I straighten my skirt. "What do you care? I'm just a mistake."

"Not you. *This*. We can't keep doing this, Nia. Especially not at your father's birthday party with your very serious boyfriend in the next room."

"Jesus, Lew. You know I said that just to piss you off."

"Well, it did."

"Good. It was supposed to." I run a hand through my hair to restore some sense of order to it. "I wasn't really looking for a lecture on virtue, Sir Lies-a-lot. You're the one who followed me. I was just looking for a knife."

Now Lew's pissed, which is so damn satisfying to see, and he cages me against the counter. Our eyes lock, but we don't touch. His right arm moves and the drawer to my left opens. He glances away, then straightens.

He offers me a knife. "Here. Your mother's waiting."

I don't move. "What happens when your case is closed? Will you leave Boston? Is that how it works?"

"Why?"

"Is that how it works?" I repeat, and he nods. "Okay, then. I'll help you."

Lew steps back. "Help me."

"I need you out of my city, out of my life, and if that won't happen until your case is closed, I will help you close this case."

"Nia—"

"No." I walk to the other end of the room where I left my things upon arrival and fish my new phone out of my bag. Returning to Lew, I hold it out to him. "Here. Put a bug in it. Put whatever you want in it. I'll get you what you need."

Lew doesn't move. Fortunately, neither does he ask how I intend to make good on my claim because I have no idea.

"Do it. Take it!" I shake the phone. "You need my help. You won't get anywhere near Josh on your own—he knows who you are."

"Did he tell you that?"

"Not that exactly, but he said once—a while ago—that you weren't who I thought you were. It makes sense that—"

"Yeah." Lew glances toward the door. He takes the phone from my hand and leaves the knife in its place. "Your mom's still waiting."

I nod and walk away.

"I wish you wouldn't do this," he says before I reach the door.

I shrug. "I wish you'd never come to Boston. Guess we're both out of luck."

32

THE PARTY'S IN FULL SWING when I emerge from the kitchen. The energy stops me in my tracks for a moment, but I push on and deliver the knife to my mother. Afterward, I stand awkwardly behind her, hoping she'll have another task for me so I don't have to return to Josh and pretend all is well and I wasn't just making out with Lew in the kitchen as though my life depended upon it.

My knees buckle at the thought. Pressing my hand to my stomach to contain the sudden fluttering, I walk out of the hall and lock myself in the bathroom. Bracing my hands on the sink, I look in the mirror. My cheeks are flushed but not too badly. It could easily be explained away by the number of people in attendance and the underperforming air conditioning. It has absolutely nothing to do with a handsome, brooding, undercover FBI agent who shall remain nameless.

I have to get a grip. Lew cannot—*will* not—affect me in any way, shape, or form. I am not a silly school girl who has no control over her faculties because some mildly good-looking guy with a decent set of abs smiled at her. No, I am a woman who needs a man like a fish needs a bicycle, and Lew certainly has no effect on me.

I am a big, fat liar, but I nod at my reflection, make sure my appearance is in order, and return to the party. Inside the hall, Susannah and Colin are laughing about something with my dad, but joining them is still not an option. Josh is talking to Craig and Mandy near the beverage table. The gift bag is gone, and as I head over to them, I can only pray its contents are now in the punch bowl.

"Hey," Josh says when I reach them. His eyes drop down. "Didn't come out, huh?"

"What?" I look down, the red spatters catching my eye. Right. I was supposed to treat that stain in the kitchen, wasn't I? "Oh. No."

"Is it ruined?"

Lifting my head, I catch a glimpse of Lew working his way through the crowd. "Yeah. It's ruined."

"Let me get you a drink," Josh says. "Punch?"

"Did you spike it?"

"You told me to wait for you."

"Well, let's get on that, then."

Josh steps over to the beverage table, leaving me alone with Craig and Mandy. Mandy says something to me, but my focus is exclusively on Craig. Craig the cop. What does he know? Is he involved? If Josh is on a cop-corrupting mission, it would make sense to start with his own friend. Or maybe that's why they're friends in the first place.

"You seem tense," Craig says. "You okay?"

Josh returns and offers me a plastic cup. "She and Susannah are fighting."

"So?" Craig asks. "You two fight all the time, like some old married couple."

It would be wrong to kick a police officer in the shins, right? I sigh. "No, we bicker. We don't fight. Usually."

Craig laughs. "I stand corrected. What are you fighting about?"

"A dress," Josh supplies.

Roomful of cops or not, I'm going to kill them both. Fortunately, my mother interrupts with an announcement that it's time to cut the cake. Josh slips his arm around my waist and the fingers of my free hand clench into a tight fist. I can do this. I have to let him touch me. At least until I get the evidence Lew needs to prove…whatever he's trying to prove. I should probably find that out at some point.

We join the group in the center of the room, and I half-heartedly participate in a horribly off-key rendition of 'Happy Birthday'. Toward the end, Lew slips out of the kitchen and rejoins the festivities, smiling at fellow cops and their families as they welcome him into the fold.

He fits in so well here, in this life. I know his job is to fit in, regardless of where he is, who he's supposed to be, so maybe I would feel the same if I saw him somewhere else, being someone else. But I'll never do that, will I? Once he wraps up this case, he'll leave Boston and everyone in it behind.

Which is what I want. I want him to go, to leave us all behind. I do.

At the end of the song, I hand Josh my cup to help my mother pass out cake. I force myself to smile at the people who serve alongside my father, some for as long as I can remember. They've been to our house for dinner. We've celebrated holidays and birthdays together. How many of them are involved in this, too?

Lew comes to the table last, and my smile becomes nonexistent. I stare at him momentarily before checking to see where Josh is. He's not paying any attention, chatting with Craig, Mandy, and a couple of the youngest members of the force.

"Nia," Lew says under his breath.

"Cake?"

I hold up a plate, silently pleading with him to leave me alone. He can't keep staring at me like this. Someone will notice. Everyone will notice.

"Please, Lew," I mutter. "Just take the damn cake and walk away."

He takes the plate. "Check your voicemail."

My mother swoops in then, peppering Lew with questions about where he's been hiding the whole night. I take advantage of the interruption to gather up the unused plates and utensils and escape back into the kitchen. Dumping everything onto the counter, I move to the other end of the room and open my bag.

My phone sits on top and, with slightly shaking fingers, I pull it out. The voicemail icon waits in the upper left-hand corner. Glancing over my shoulder to ensure I'm still alone, I listen to the message.

Nia. If you are determined to do this, then this is how it will work, Lew says. *Before you see Josh, you will call this number and leave a message, telling us where you are going and how long you expect to be there. When you are home again, and alone, call this number to check in, and I will come to you for a debriefing. Memorize this number; don't write it down anywhere. Don't lose this phone, don't destroy this phone, and don't lend it to anyone. Please...be careful. I don't want to have to tell your parents something's happened to you.*

I erase the message and sit on the counter, staring at the phone in my hands.

"Hey, sweetheart," my father says. "You hiding back here?"

I watch him walk toward me. "Just taking a break," I lie. "What are you doing? Hiding from your adoring fans?"

Dad waves toward the party. "Your mother's doing."

I smirk. "You love it, and you know it."

"I love *her*." He pulls up a stool and sits in front of me. "Love you, too."

"Yeah, well, you have to do that."

Dad smiles. "Tell me something."

"It's said that banging your head against the wall can burn 150 calories per hour."

"Tell me something about *you*."

"Dad, you already know everything there is to know about me."

"Do I?"

"Are you finally going senile?"

"Funny. Come on, talk to me."

"About what? There really isn't anything—"

"What's going on between you and Lew?"

Where's an asteroid when you need one to fall on your head? "What makes you think there's anything going on between us?"

"I am a very wise man, Lavinia. Also, I have eyes."

"Oh. Those."

"Yeah. Those. What's going on?"

"A whole lot of nothing."

Dad nods. "Somehow, I can't quite bring myself to believe you."

"Well, you are a very wise man."

He leans forward. "I worry about you, hon. I want you to be happy."

"I am."

"Are you?"

Nope. "I'm fine, Dad."

"Being fine isn't the same as being happy."

"Sounds like someone's been watching too much daytime television."

"I'm just saying"—Dad straightens—"Josh may be your boyfriend, but Lew is the man who makes you smile."

Lew makes me do more than that. My face flushes, and the fact that my father is seeing it only makes it worse. My kingdom for a distraction. An earthquake. A fire. An alien attack. Godzilla crashing through the fellowship hall. *Anything.*

"Are you encouraging me to date your partner?" I ask once I've gotten the blushing under control.

"I'm encouraging you to be happy. I don't want you to be alone."

I groan. "Oh God. Did Mom tell you about the spinster daughter thing?"

"What spinster daughter thing? Did someone call you a spinster?"

"I called me a spinster. And I wasn't being serious." I sigh. "It doesn't matter how I feel about Lew—not that I have any feelings whatsoever for him or about him because I don't. He'll be gone before long, and I—"

"What makes you say that?"

Shit. Shit, shit, shit. Why can't I ever think before I speak? I shrug. "Everyone leaves eventually."

Dad puts his hand on my knee. "We don't all leave, Lavinia. I know you had your heart broken—"

Christ, he thinks I'm talking about Brian. Of course he thinks that. They all think that. Everything I do at any time is all about Brian. Everything I don't do is all about him, too. Brian, Brian, Brian. That's probably my fault, but I don't even know if that's fair. Do I sabotage everything because he's gone?

I shake my head. It doesn't matter. Brian doesn't have anything to do with this.

"Dad, I promise nothing is going on. Lew and I are…" Doomed. "Oil and water, or whatever. Just two things that won't mix together, no matter how long or hard you try."

Dad nods. "I worry about you, kid."

I nod, too. "Going soft in your old age."

He winks at me and jerks his head toward the party. "Don't tell the others. I have a reputation to uphold."

Oh, I am well aware of his reputation and his big, soft heart and his propensity for giving a damn about every person he encounters. More evidence that I'm some kind of change-ling or foundling or something. The number of people I'd go to bat for can be counted on one hand—and that includes my German shepherd.

But my dad is one of those people. He'd do anything for me. I'd do anything for him. I would.

I *will*.

"Your secret is safe with me," I say.

"I know it is." Dad stands. "I'm going back before your mother sends out a search party. You coming?"

I glance at my phone. "Yeah. In a minute."

He kisses my forehead and makes his way out of the kitchen. As soon as he's gone, I call the number from which the voicemail came.

"I'm in," I say when prompted to leave a message.

Ending the call, I put the phone away and walk out of the kitchen, damned and determined.

Time to be the best goddamn spy this world has ever seen.

33

I AM A *TERRIBLE* SPY.

That's probably one of those things that goes without saying, but the fact remains that I am, without doubt, a terrible spy. Or maybe one step up from a terrible spy because, for some reason, Josh has yet to figure out what I'm doing.

Of course, it's entirely possible he does know what I'm doing. Maybe my espionage attempts are so laughable, they don't warrant a response. Maybe he and his evil henchmen make popcorn and sit in front of some giant monitor in their secret lair, watching me fumble around. The Lavinia Kelly Amateur Hour, starring Lavinia Kelly.

But I still have to do it.

Even though I find Josh increasingly smarmy, I say yes every time he asks me to come out with him, making careful note of anyone he interacts with. Any time I'm alone in his place, I snoop through his belongings. Not that there's anything to find. I suppose he's too smart to leave a pile of incriminating evidence lying around where just anyone can find it. Really, the most suspicious thing is the exercise equipment in his office.

It bothers me more each day that he has all this at his disposal, yet I met him at the gym. It could mean nothing — maybe he was there simply to ogle women in spandex — but on my time off from both Josh and the shelter, I go to the gym and run on a treadmill, using the mirrors to watch for familiar faces. It isn't nearly enough, but I don't know what else to do. I don't know how to trip Josh up, how to convince him to let me in on his secrets.

Through it all, I follow the rules Lew set in place, calling the now-memorized number to report on my Josh-related activities. Late at night, when I'm alone in the house, Lew slips in through the back door, and we sit at the kitchen table while I go over what I've seen and heard. It never amounts to much, but Lew nods, takes notes, and asks follow-up questions.

Sometimes, he has to repeat the question over and over again because I struggle to concentrate when we're in the same room together. He doesn't seem to be affected the same way. Or at all. Whereas I can't stop thinking, remembering, *feeling*. My stomach is one giant knot, twisting and untwisting, only to twist again. I hate that he does this to me. I hate that I let him. I hate that he doesn't touch me or barely makes eye contact as he slides photos across the table for me to examine.

Do you recognize anyone, he asks in a monotone. *Where have you seen them? How often? Do they interact with Josh? Describe their interactions, please.* Everything, every request, spoken in that same flat voice. Llewellyn Morgan, serious FBI agent.

But it's better this way. It is. He'll get what he needs, he'll leave, and I will go back to whatever is left of my life.

Which is currently my parents, my job, and my dog. Three things I certainly wouldn't want to be without, but I miss Susannah. I miss my brother. She apparently got sole custody of him in the divorce. Not unexpected, but it still hurts. That's for the better, too. I can't let them get involved with this.

However, it turns out that when one isn't speaking with one's roommate, one's brother, or one's father's partner,

Thanksgiving is a thoroughly awkward affair. Thank God Josh is spending the holiday elsewhere.

The rest of us sit around the table in stony silence, carefully not looking at one another, while my parents watch in bewilderment. Later, while I'm helping with the dishes, my mother corners me, demanding an explanation. I offer her the ugly bridesmaid dress story. Unsurprisingly, it goes over even more poorly as it has with everyone else, and suddenly, there's one more person who's mad at me.

My mother's irritation leads her to kick everyone out early. Colin and Susannah walk to the Prius without acknowledging me. I let Rufus into the back of the Jeep, then lean against the car to watch them drive away.

"You okay?" Lew asks.

I laugh. "Oh yeah. I'm fantastic." I look at him. "Don't you dare apologize to me again."

The corner of his mouth twitches in an almost smile. How can I hate someone this much and yet still want him this badly?

"Is there anything I can do?" he asks.

God, I'm so tired of being alone. I sigh. Screw it. "Come home with me."

"Nia, I…" Lew shakes his head. "That would be—"

"What? A mistake?"

He flinches. "Wouldn't it?"

Yes. But that doesn't stop me from wanting him. I hate people every goddamn day and don't want to get naked with any of them. Why does Lew have to be different?

I shrug. "What's one more mistake between…whatever we are?"

Lew steps closer. "What are we?"

Besides royally fucked? "I don't know. I'm just tired of being alone," I say. "Aren't you?"

Another step. "Yes."

My fingers ache to find their way beneath his clothes, but I stuff them in my coat pockets to keep from acting on that impulse. "So come home with me. Unless you don't like me."

That crooked smile again. "I like you."

"Like me, like me?"

"Like you, like you."

"I only ask because you've been treating me rather formally lately, and—"

"I'm trying to do what you want, Nia. You said you wanted me out of your city, out of your life, and—"

"I did. I *do*."

His fingers brush my cheek before sliding around to the back of my neck and tangling in my hair. "Then I shouldn't go home with you."

"Do it anyway."

"I don't want you to get hurt."

"I'm already hurt." I put my hand on his chest. His heart is pounding. That has to mean something, doesn't it? "Stop trying to be a good guy for just one night and be the guy who wants to go home with me."

"Just one night?"

"I don't want anything more."

Lew nods. "Okay, then. Let's go."

I don't know what to call what we do that night. It lacks the frantic energy of our earlier encounters, but it's not any sort of languid lovemaking, either. It feels a little like solace, a consolation prize, a glimpse of what life could be like, if only things were different.

Afterward, we don't talk—which is probably for the best. I lie in his arms, my back pressed to his chest, trying not to think about how good it feels to be there. One night—that's all this is, just one night to keep me slightly sane, to stave off the loneliness for a little while.

It's not like either of us are capable of anything more.

Judging by his breathing, he falls asleep first, but I soon follow. When I wake, I'm alone in bed. According to the clock, it's not quite six. The bathroom light is on, illuminating the bedroom enough for me to see a fully dressed Lew sitting in a chair and putting on his shoes.

I sit up, wrapping the sheet around my body, and switch on the bedside lamp. "Were you going to tell me you were leaving?"

Lew looks up. "Hadn't decided yet."

"Well, let me know when you do."

"I didn't want to wake you. I'm guessing you haven't been sleeping well lately."

"What makes you say that?"

"Experience."

"Sleep with a lot of your informants, do you?"

Lew smiles, then sits on the edge of the bed. "You know I can't stay."

"Yeah. I know."

He puts his hand on my face, and I lean into it before I can stop myself.

"I wish things were different," he says. "I wish I met you under different circumstances."

I pull away. "They're not different."

"Nia...end things with Josh."

The pleading in his voice tugs at my stomach like some kind of hook has embedded itself there. "I...I can't. Not yet. You need—"

"I need you to be safe. I need you to be as far away from this as possible," Lew says, the begging now bordering on desperation. "I can't think straight when I know you're with him, and—"

"He's not interested in hurting me."

"He doesn't care if you get hurt, either. There's a difference." Lew shakes his head. "I shouldn't have let you get involved with this."

I laugh. "There you go again, thinking you get to let me do anything. I don't know how many times I have to say this, Lew, but what I do is not up to you. There's no way in hell I wasn't getting involved in this. This is my family, my *dad*. This is personal for me, and—"

"It's personal for me, too."

"Not like this."

Lew slides closer. "I will take care of your dad. I promise I will, Nia. But I could do an even better job if I didn't have to worry about you at the same time."

"I didn't ask you to worry about me."

"You didn't have to." Sighing, Lew kisses me, then presses his forehead to mine. "Just think about it. Please."

"Okay."

"Okay, you'll end things, or—?"

"Okay, I'll think about it." I shove him away. "Do you ever stop pushing your luck?"

"Not when it comes to the people I care about."

The hook tugs again, but I put more distance between us. Seems safer suddenly. "I'm on that list?"

Lew smiles. "Pretty sure you are the list."

What is wrong with him? Did he not understand the one-night-only concept? He can't go around saying things like that. What does he think will happen? How am I supposed to respond?

I look at the bed. "Are you on shift today, or are you doing mysterious FBI stuff?"

"Your dad and I are on shift," Lew answers stiffly as he stands.

"Well…" I glance up. His face matches his tone. Lew is gone. Agent Morgan is back. "Be careful out there."

He nods. "Are you seeing Josh today?"

I shake my head. "I'm going to the shelter."

"If your plans change—"

"I'll call. I always do." I expect Lew to leave then, but he just stares at me. "Is there something else?"

"I guess not," he says after a moment. "See you around."

He walks out. I stay put until the front door closes. Then I slide out of bed and begin my day.

The nice thing about being employed by an animal shelter is the never-ending work that comes with it. There's always a reason to go in early, stay late, or give up a day off when one can't stand sitting home alone anymore — a fact of which I have taken advantage more than once since the FBI first showed up on my doorstep. Gretchen has tried repeatedly to get me to talk about whatever is inspiring my extra-special work ethic, but I blow her off every time. I can't talk to her about what's going on any more than I can talk to anyone else. I can't talk to anyone — except Lew.

That's the damn problem.

Today, Gretchen asks roundabout questions about Thanksgiving and Susannah's wedding. I alternate between answering in noncommittal grunts and flat-out ignoring her. Eventually, she gives up and retreats to her office while I sit at the reception desk to fill out paperwork.

After a while, the front door opens. I keep my head down but issue a greeting when I hear someone approaching.

"Welcome to Pine—"

"Nia," Susannah interrupts.

I lift my head. She crosses the lobby and places her palms flat on the desk. She doesn't look at me. Something's wrong.

I put down my pen. "What happened?"

"Colin called me," she says.

She sounds shaken in a way I have never heard before, leaving me feeling as though a bucket of ice water has been dumped on my head. Behind me, Gretchen comes out from the office.

"Why did Colin call you?" My heart is pounding. Please let it be something stupid. Please just let them have broken up. "What happened?"

Susannah looks at me. She's been crying. "I-I don't know exactly; Colin wasn't sure. He said…We have to go."

I close my eyes. "Who was it?"

"Your dad."

34

SUSANNAH WEAVES IN AND OUT of traffic with the precision of a professional stunt driver. As she flirts with the breaking point of a Prius's maneuverability, I grip the Oh Shit handle and silently urge her to go faster. But the truth is she could be going twice as fast, or we could have one of those teleportation devices or whatever, and it would still be too slow.

I know because I have been here before.

Three years ago.

I was talking about the eyes of Doctor T.J. Eckleburg when Martha came into my classroom to tell me Brian had been in an accident.

What she didn't know was how it hadn't been an accident at all. When that many bullets are emptied into a single person, it ceases to be an accident and becomes something else entirely. Neither did Martha know that his mother, Joyce, was a nurse working the ER when they brought him in. Or that Joyce was covered in his blood before she realized who it was. They pulled her, screaming, from the room, but Martha didn't know that, either.

There's been an accident, was all she knew to tell me. *You have to go to the hospital.*

So I did.

I don't remember the drive itself or how many traffic laws I may have broken. None of them. All of them. It didn't matter. Upon reaching the hospital, I parked in the first open space, not knowing, not caring, if it was legal, and ran to the emergency room. It was crawling with Brian's fellow officers. Their anger and fear had burned up all the oxygen. I couldn't breathe.

When Brian's partner, Noah, came toward me, I threw myself at him.

"Tell me what happened," I begged. "Please, Noah, tell me Brian's all right."

"Come on," he said.

We took the elevator to the surgery ward and were met by two uniforms whose job it was to keep non-family members and non-hospital personnel from going any farther. They knew Noah, so they let us pass. Noah led me to the waiting room where Brian's parents were sitting. Joyce was still wearing her blood-stained apricot scrubs when she engulfed me in a hug.

"Oh, Lavinia," she sobbed. "Lavinia, Lavinia, Lavinia."

"He'll be all right," I sobbed. "Tell me he'll be all right."

No one told me he would be all right.

The chairs were uncomfortable and the sofa even more so, but we sat anyway, waiting to learn the fate of that beautiful green-eyed boy we loved. My parents arrived. Colin, too. I don't know who called them. The McFaddens' priest came and said his prayers. I didn't pray. Not to God, not to the eyes of Doctor T.J. Eckleburg, not to anyone. Instead, I stared at a lone staple in the wall no one had bothered to remove. At the one cracked tile in the floor. At the water stain in the corner of the ceiling that looked a little bit like a map of Brazil.

I don't know for how long I sat. Hours, minutes, days. Time didn't mean anything. In the waiting room, Brian was alive. In the waiting room, he was dead. He was Schrödinger's

Cat, and I held my vigil, wishing, praying, hoping the vial wouldn't break.

But it did.

He died.

I died, too.

I shut down.

I went away.

I returned to my empty, little house and slept heavily, like the dead, thanks to the sedatives they thought I needed because screaming like a banshee suggested one was disturbed.

Or so they tell me.

I don't remember screaming. I remember quiet. Shadows and ghosts. I remember stumbling downstairs to find my living room had been replaced with an ocean of flowers and my father asleep on my couch in its center, an odd lifeboat in a swell of loss.

The dining room table was covered with casseroles. Casseroles were the community's panacea because macaroni and cheese coated with saltine crackers would cure your ails. Tuna and egg noodles would make everything better. Shepherd's pie, lasagna and baked ziti, bread, cookies, cakes, and more. There was enough food to feed an army, but I couldn't eat. None of us could.

Even at the thought, my stomach lurches.

"Pull over," I say to Susannah. "Pull over, pull over, pull over."

She yanks the steering wheel to the right. Cars honk and tires squeal. I undo my seat belt and open the door to vomit before the car has completely stopped. I vomit a second time, the sour acidic taste of bile overwhelming my senses.

When I sit up, I am crying. Susannah rubs my back and holds out a bottle of water. I take a sip, swish to rinse my mouth, and spit it onto the pavement.

"I can't..." I shake my head. "I can't—I can't do this. Not again."

"You can," Susannah says. "It'll be all right. He'll be all right. You'll see. It'll be all right."

She can't make promises like that. It's a jinx—worse than a jinx—it's a curse. She doesn't know. She hasn't been through this before. She has no idea how bad it can get.

Will get.

I thought the funeral would be the worst part. I thought sitting next to a still-sobbing Joyce in that damn cathedral, surrounded by forlorn bagpipes and a nosy media would be the worst. Then I thought standing grave-side, listening to a gunfire salute and seeing only bullets tear through the body I had loved and touched and kissed would be the worst. I thought watching my future sink into the earth, wrapped in a black steel casket, and wanting only to crawl into that box with him, would be the worst part.

But it wasn't. It was the wake.

Gretchen helped my mother set it up at the McFaddens' home. Joyce disappeared early on, clutching the folded flag they had presented her with at the cemetery. She returned a few moments later, still holding her flag, but also holding something else.

A box.

A black velvet ring box.

"We found this in some of Brian's things," she told me. "I know he'd want you to have it."

Most of Brian's stuff was in my house, but of course he wouldn't have kept that there. I didn't open it. How could I? It wasn't for me. It was for Lavinia. It was for a woman lost, a woman who was no longer me.

But I sat on that sofa, clutching that box, and received condolences. *We're so sorry for your loss*, people would say. Everyone was sorry. Then it was a clasped hand, a kiss on the cheek, maybe a full hug. That, and a bowl of fruit salad for the buffet was all they had to offer.

I didn't blame them. I didn't know what they were supposed to say or do, either.

The rest of the time, I was what people called catatonic. But it wasn't that. Catatonic is a state. Catatonic is something.

And I wasn't anything.

Susannah was there. We didn't know each other well then, but we were friendly because we were the youngest members of the teaching staff, building a bond over the generation gap between us and the rest of our departments. But we weren't friends. Not then. We were acquaintances at best, which is why I was so surprised when she took advantage of Joyce's departure from the couch to sit next to me.

"Do you want to get out of here?" she asked.

I looked at her, amazed she hadn't tried to touch me, hadn't told me how sorry she was, hadn't, to my knowledge, brought a casserole.

"This is killing you," she said, not realizing her mistake in verb tense. "Let's get out of here."

Susannah handed the ring box to my mother before leading me out of the house. She put me in her car, and we drove to the movies and sat in the front row. I don't remember what was playing. It must have been a comedy, though, because people were laughing. I cried silent tears. Susannah had bought a box of gummy bears, and she systematically would lick one and throw it at the screen, trying to get it to stick.

I didn't laugh, not once, but I did stop crying before the end.

When she took me home, it was empty, except for Brian's ring, which had been left on the coffee table. Susannah tucked the box away in one of my dresser drawers.

Later, we drank a vodka toast to Brian, and I cried some more. Susannah touched me then, just a long, wordless hug. I lay on the couch, my head in her lap, and she stroked my hair. She sat up with me all night and the night after that. And a few nights after that.

She never once told me it would be all right. She never once asked me if I was all right.

She moved in with me the next month.

I never did open that damn box.

35

WHEN WE ARRIVE AT THE hospital, Susannah parks illegally near the emergency room entrance. She's on my side and opening the door faster than I would have thought possible.

"They'll tow you," I say.

She shrugs. "Let them."

The emergency room is a madhouse. It's nearly identical to the scene I witnessed three years earlier. Cops mill around, angry, confused, and concerned. Some of them nod in my direction. I nod back, but I don't bother asking any of them what happened. They won't know. Lew is the only one to whom I want to talk, but he's nowhere to be found. He must be upstairs.

"Lavinia!" Joyce McFadden calls. She comes straight toward us. "I've been looking out for you, hon. Your dad's in surgery."

I want to ask what she knows, if my father will be all right, but I can't form the words.

"Okay, then," Susannah says. "We'll go there."

"I'm sorry, Susannah," Joyce says, her words clipped. "Family only. You'll have to wait here."

I don't think Joyce has ever forgiven me for leaving Brian's wake, or Susannah for leading me out the door. I don't know that I've ever forgiven myself. Wasn't I supposed to be dead? Wasn't I supposed to be in that casket, too, rotting away a little at a time?

And yet, here I am.

"She is family, Joyce," I say. "She's coming."

Susannah links her arm with mine. "You heard the woman. Lead the way."

Joyce brings us to the surgery ward. Mom and Colin are sitting in the waiting room, her arm around his shoulders. She looks up when she hears us approach and beckons to me with her free arm. I go to her side and let her comfort me like I'm a six-year-old with a scraped knee. Colin squeezes my hand.

"He'll be all right," my mother whispers in my ear. "Do you hear me? He'll be okay."

"What happened?" I ask. "Do you know?"

"He took a bullet in the shoulder and another in the chest. He said Llewellyn knocked him—"

"He said? You talked to him? You talked to Dad?"

"I did. Before they took him to surgery, I talked to him. He will be all right. You know I wouldn't say that if I didn't believe it."

I look around for Susannah. She's sitting in a chair across from us. Eyes watering, she smiles and mouths *told you so*.

I nod and turn back to my mother. "Lew got him out of the way? Where is he now? We should—we should thank him."

When no one responds, I know. Lew was hit, too.

"How bad?" I ask.

"We don't know yet," Mom answers. "Your father said...He said it didn't look good."

"What happened?" Susannah asks, her voice wavering.

It's hard to be on this side. To sit in these chairs in this room. To stare at the walls and floors, and wait, wait, wait. She didn't understand before, but she will now.

Welcome to the family.

"They're still trying to figure that out," my mother says. "No one knows much yet, but they'll tell us when something changes."

I know what happened. It's Lew's case. He dragged my father into it and put him in the middle of a damn firefight. Momentarily forgetting I hate Lew for that, if he was right about the precinct, it means we can't trust anyone on the force. We can't trust anything they tell us.

A moment later, Craig Parker enters my eye line. *Craig Parker*, Lew said once. *Good guy.*

Maybe we can trust one.

Unless we can't. He's still friends with Josh. I may not have discovered any undeniable proof, but I can't believe he doesn't know *something*. Is he here because my father was shot, or is he here because Josh sent him to find out how the hit went?

My mother stands. "Craig."

"Any news yet?" he asks.

"No," she says. "What about on your end?"

Craig shakes his head. His eyes fall on me, and his head tilts slightly to the left. He shakes hands with Colin and kisses my mother on the cheek. After hugging Susannah, he promises to return when he knows more and walks away.

Craig Parker. Good guy.

Unless he isn't.

I chew my lip. Does it matter whose side he's on? I still want to know what angle he's running. My mother's just sitting down again when I rise. Everyone looks at me.

"Bathroom," I say. Susannah stands, and I shake my head. "I just need a minute to...I need a minute. Alone."

Susannah sits back down. "Don't get lost."

I assure her I won't and go after Craig.

I find him standing by the elevators. When he sees me coming, he steps back and props open the door to the ladies' restroom. I go inside, and he follows me.

"Lock the door," he says, opening each stall.

I do, then move over to the row of sinks. Craig completes his search and looks at me.

"The night you and Morgan met, he told you his nick-name was Ellen, and—"

"What? Why are you telling me—?" I stop. "You said 'Morgan.'"

"Yeah, I did."

"How do you know—?"

"He told me, Nia. I know his name, who he is. He told me about the night you met so I'd have a way to prove—"

"That you're one of the good guys."

"Yeah."

That can't be true. Why wouldn't Lew tell me that? Why would he be all cloak-and-dagger about it?

"He didn't want to tell you I was involved," Craig continues. "He wanted to keep you out of this as much as possible."

That part sounds right. I can't deny that. "So...you know, then," I say carefully. "You know who he's investigating?"

Craig nods. "Josh. Yeah, I know. I couldn't believe it at first. We're supposed to be friends."

"You seemed pretty friendly at the party."

"I was pretending at the party," Craig says. "Inside, I wanted to punch him, or strangle him, or...arrest him or some-thing. I don't even know what."

That makes two of us. "What happened today?" I ask. "Do you know?"

"I don't know all the details," he says. "Hell, I don't even know half the details, but a complaint was called in about tres-passers in an old warehouse. Your father and Morgan were the closest, so they responded. They went in expecting to run off some kids, but got shot at instead. I think they were set up."

"By Josh. You think they were set up by Josh."

"By him, or whoever's above him."

"Why? Why now? Lew's been here for months."

"I don't know. Maybe Morgan was getting too close to something."

I grip the sink behind me to stay upright. I am going to be sick. Just vomit continuously from now until the end of time. If Lew was getting close to anything these days, it was only because I led him to it. Does my father have a bullet in his chest because of me? Is Lew dying because of me?

"If this operation is even half as big as they think it is," Craig says, "there's got to be a lot of money tied up in it."

"Money."

Craig shrugs. "People have been killed for a lot less. You would know that."

Yes, I would know that, wouldn't I? There's nothing like being the town's poster child of misery. I wrap my arms around myself. "What happens now?"

"I'm working with Morgan's team. They're highly motivated to end this thing."

Could that be true? It's such a bold lie otherwise. Way too easy to confirm. Well, provided Lew's team does, in fact, exist, and that I could, in fact, find them. Are those the friends he claimed to have? How can I track them down? Maybe they'll find me. They'll show up here eventually, right?

"How much do you know about this whole thing?" Craig asks. "How much did Morgan tell you?"

Morgan. It sounds so wrong to hear him referred to like that. I shake my head. I certainly can't tell Craig the truth. Not until I know for sure what's going on.

"I don't know anything. I don't even know what Josh is suspected of doing. Like you said, Lew didn't want me involved."

"You're sure?"

"Yeah."

Craig nods. "Okay. Stick around here, and you'll be safe."

I tilt my head. "Why wouldn't I be safe?"

"The people running this thing — "

"You mean Josh."

" — know you're connected to Lew."

My arms fall to my sides. "I'm not connected to Lew. Yeah, he's my father's partner, but I'm way more connected to Josh."

"Josh may not be the only one you have to worry about. Whoever's above him is gonna wonder what you know," Craig says. "And then there's the rest of your family."

"What do they have to do with this?"

"Morgan is connected to all of you."

"Well, I don't know anything, and my family knows even less. I alienated them pretty thoroughly to keep it that way."

"Good. Make sure that doesn't change." Craig heads for the door. "I gotta go. You gonna be all right?"

Well, I have absolutely no idea who I can trust or what's going on, but I currently have no holes in my chest, or any other part of me, so I suppose I stand a better chance at survival than some. "I'll be fine."

"I'll let you know if I learn anything. Keep me posted on how things are going here."

"Yeah."

When he's gone, I collapse to the floor and put my back against the wall. My arms hang limp as numbness rapidly spreads through the rest of my body.

This is a mess — a goddamn *nightmare* — but it doesn't matter. I cannot fall apart. Not again. I have to find a way to hold it together because I will *not* be that useless lump my family had to shape their lives around for three years. No, this time I will be strong.

Just as soon as I can feel my extremities again.

The door opens and Susannah walks in. She looks at me for a moment, then sits next to me.

"I don't want to ask if you're okay because that's a stupid thing to ask, but..." She hesitates. "Are you okay?"

I rest my head against the wall. "You're right. That is a stupid thing to ask."

"Which is why I stated that upfront. So…are you? Okay, I mean."

I would shrug if I still had that ability. "How do I tell?"

"Well, you're talking. That's a good sign."

"Good for me," I say. "Have there been any updates?"

"Not yet. Are you coming back?"

I check to see if my legs work. They don't. "Not yet."

Susannah nods. "Are you…Is there maybe something else going on?"

Because there's not enough going on as it is? "There's nothing, okay? My father and my" — my *what*, exactly? — "my father's partner were shot. They're in surgery, and they may not survive, and I can't sit in that room and wait. Not in that room."

"Okay," Susannah says. "We'll wait here, then."

36

I DON'T KNOW FOR HOW long we sit on the bathroom floor. Mostly, we're alone because the few women who have come in slowly back out again when they see us beneath the hand dryer. It's some time later when Joyce enters. She does not leave.

"Your mother asked me to look for you," she says. "What are you doing in here?"

Susannah takes my hand. "Waiting. Is there news?"

Joyce ignores her. "Your father's out of surgery."

I hold my breath. Susannah's squeezing my hand so tightly, I may need an x-ray later to check for broken bones.

"He's doing well. He's in recovery now," Joyce continues. "As soon as they move him to his room, you can see him."

Susannah lets out a happy, little squeak and hugs me. I take my first real breath since she walked into the shelter.

"What about Patrick's partner?" Susannah asks. "Officer Weiss."

Joyce looks at me, her expression unreadable. "He's still in surgery. He'll be there a while yet."

Susannah embraces me again, but this time there's no joy in it. Only comfort. "Thanks for letting us know."

Joyce nods and leaves. I don't move.

Susannah stands and holds out her hand. "Let's go see your dad."

I don't know if I can. My arms and legs are so heavy, I honestly don't know if I can lift them.

"Lavinia," she says, using her teacher's voice, "let's go."

I smile and put my hand in hers. "It's cute you think you're an authority figure."

She pulls me up. "I know."

My father is unconscious when they wheel him into his room. We gather inside, my mother and me on one side, Colin and Susannah on the other. We don't talk much, just listen to the beeping of the heart monitor.

Hours pass before Joyce comes in to report that Lew is out of surgery. Critical, but stable condition. Mom thanks her, but I can't do anything other than barely breathe.

The vial is still intact.

It's after midnight when my father wakes up. We crowd around the bed to see him.

He coughs. "Who died?"

"That's not funny, Patrick," my mother scolds, sounding choked up.

"Sorry, Nan." He reaches for Colin. "Did the kid make it?"

Mom kisses his forehead. "So far."

"He saved me, you know."

"We know."

"Knocked me out of the way, got me down. Damn that kid," Dad says as he falls back to sleep.

We all stand there for another moment, staring at Dad like he might be faking it or something.

"All right," Mom says. "Colin, you and Susannah go back to your apartment and get some sleep. You can take over for Lavinia and me in the morning."

"Mom," Colin says, "we can—"

"Go." She points to the door. "Your father will be fine, and I'm sure Llewellyn will be as well. If anything changes, we'll call you. This will be a long process, and we can't do anything for them if we can't keep our eyes open. We will do this in shifts, and we will take care of ourselves. That's how we get through this."

Colin, unhappy with her decree, attempts to stare her down, but Susannah gathers her belongings. If there is one thing she's learned in her three years with the Kelly clan, it's not to argue with Nancy.

"We'll bring back breakfast," she says.

"That sounds fine, Susannah," Mom replies. "Thank you."

"Are you sure?" Colin asks.

Mom rounds the bed and hugs them tightly. "I'm sure. I love you both. Now get out of here."

I sit as Colin and Susannah leave. Mom fusses with Dad's bedding before joining me.

"I'm not leaving," I say. I will never learn not to argue with Nancy. "Not in the morning. Not until…I'm not leaving."

"I know, sweetheart." Mom pats my hand. "Who's taking care of Rufus?"

"Gretchen."

"He'll miss you."

"I know, but…it's Dad."

And Lew, who knocked him down and got him out of the way. Who took the worst of the ambush, at least in part because he promised me he would.

Mom nods. "Your father's not going anywhere. It's all right if you want to sit with Llewellyn for a while."

I rest my head on her shoulder. "I'd rather stay here for now."

"Whatever you want, honey," my mother says. "Whatever you want."

When my father wakes up a couple of hours later, she jumps from her chair. He's thirsty and in pain. She helps him sip some water, then argues with him about the pain. In the grand Kelly tradition, he claims he's fine. No need to bother anyone.

"I'm going to find a nurse," Mom says finally. "I'll be right back."

After she leaves, I stand, leaning in to hug my father as best I can. He groans a little, and I back off.

"Your mother's fussing," he says.

"Let her."

He nods, but there's barely any strength to the motion. "You didn't get to do this part last time."

No, I didn't. The last time I saw Brian alive, he was standing at the kitchen counter, drinking coffee from a German shepherd mug. I was rushed, trying to get to school on time, and called a hasty goodbye as I ran out the door.

The last time I saw him, and I missed it.

After that, he was nothing but a wax figure, a hollow, empty shell.

If only I had known.

"What are you doing here?" my father asks, pulling me from my memories.

"You got shot," I say. "Where did you think I'd be?"

"I'm fine. Go be with that young man of yours."

"Dad, Lew's not my young man. He's not my anything."

"Whether you wanted him or not, he's yours. I've seen it. And I wouldn't be talking to you now without him."

I duck my head to keep Dad from seeing me cry, but he knows I'm doing it anyway.

"Sweetheart," he pleads.

He moves his good hand in my direction, and I grasp it tightly. Oddly enough, my tears do not lessen.

"Go take care of him," my father says.

"I can't do anything for him."

"Then just sit with him. That'll be enough."

"He won't know I'm there."

"He'll know. Trust me, he'll know."

I nod, unable to form words, and continue to hold on to my dad.

When my mother returns, I leave. One of the nurses tells me where to find Lew. His door is open, and I lean against the wall outside of the room for a moment before going in.

The room is dark, lit only by a fluorescent strip over the head of the bed. A nurse is fiddling with one of the many machines. The respirator is hissing, and the heart monitor is beeping steadily. Screens display his vitals. I don't know what any of it means, but it's reassuring to know he does, in fact, have vitals.

Shit. If he dies, I'll never forgive him.

Damn him. Damn him for making me care.

The nurse turns and sees me. She opens her mouth, perhaps to tell me that visiting hours are over, but says nothing.

"How is he?" I ask.

"Stable. Critical, but stable."

"Can I...Can I sit with him for a while?"

She smiles. "Stay as long as you'd like."

As she leaves, I move to Lew's bedside. He doesn't look anything like himself with bandages and tubes everywhere. I carefully touch his cheek.

"Don't you die on me. Don't you dare do that," I whisper. "I won't survive it if you do."

I drop my hand and sit in a recliner-like chair to wait.

37

I WAKE TO THE SOUND of voices, low murmurings of people trying not to be heard, and open my eyes. How long have I been
asleep? Someone at some point covered me with a blanket, but
that could have been two minutes ago, for all I know. The room
is still dark, the only light coming from the hall and the little
fluorescent strip above the bed. There doesn't seem to be any
sunlight peeking around the curtains, so I can't have been out
for too long.

I look at Lew next. Does he still have vitals?

"Miss Kelly?"

Startled, I look at the man crouched in front of me. Where
the hell did he come from? A second man stands at the end of
the bed.

"Lavinia Kelly?" the first man says. "Nia?"

"Who are you?" I ask.

He flips open a billfold like Lew's. It's too dark to read his
name, but the badge itself is visible. FBI.

"I'm Ryan. The guy behind me is Jonas." The man—
Ryan—tucks his badge into the back pocket of his jeans.
"You're Nia, right? Nia Kelly?"

There's no point in lying. Lew would have made sure they knew who I was. I nod.

"What happened? What really happened?" I ask. "Tell me the truth, not whatever bullshit story they're trying to sell."

"I can only speculate," Ryan says.

"Well, speculate away, then."

Ryan adjusts his position and looks at Jonas. Jonas shakes his head.

"Look," I say, "my father got shot because of your little operation here, so I want to know what happened — what *really* happened — and I want to know now. You start talking, or I'll go see how much havoc I can wreak for you. Before you decide, though, you should know I have excellent lungs and an incredibly vindictive mean streak."

Ryan smiles. Asshole. I don't need him to be amused by me.

"We'll talk," he says, "but not in here."

"Afraid of the dark?" I ask.

"Not afraid. I'd just like to be able to see you better. Let's go to the cafeteria, get some coffee."

"The hall is as far as I go."

"Llewellyn's not going anywhere, Nia. He's tough."

"I'm not."

Ryan nods. "I think you're selling yourself short. But if it's the hall you want, that's fine. We'll go out in the hall."

Jonas leaves first. Ryan stands and offers me his hand. I shake my head and look at Lew again. After confirming he does, in fact, still have vitals, I join the feds out in the hall.

The corridor is empty of people. Did Jonas have anything to do with that? I lean against the wall and take my first good look at Lew's partners.

Jonas is unmistakably a cop. The taller and more rotund of the two, he must sit in the van, eating donuts and drinking coffee while watching Lew do all the heavy lifting because there's no way he wouldn't instantly be made. His suit jacket is ill-fitting, and I can see the bulge of a gun on his hip. Ryan is far younger and in better shape than his partner. He's dressed in jeans and a blue flannel shirt over a gray T-shirt, but seems to be sporting a gun in a shoulder holster. Is he undercover, too, or is this some kind of casual Friday thing?

"How much did Llewellyn tell you about the investigation?" Ryan asks.

I am so sick of that question. "That there was one."

"I need you to be more specific."

Because they don't intend to tell me anything I don't already know. I fucking hate this. I fold my arms across my chest. "I know you guys think all the cops in town are on the take or whatever, and that my...Joshua Murray is the man in charge. Or *a* man in charge. There could be people above him. Multiple people, maybe. You're here — the FBI, I mean — so this operation probably isn't limited to Boston. Or maybe it is, and we're all in that *Departed* movie, but with authentic Boston accents," I say. "Not that I know what the hell was going on in that movie, or not that the movie even matters because it doesn't. I just...Didn't Lew tell you I was helping out, that I was — "

"You weren't," Ryan says.

That's rude. "I'm not saying I delivered a smoking gun or anything, but — "

"No, Nia. You weren't helping," Ryan says. "Llewellyn didn't want you anywhere near this case, so he set it up to make you think you were helping."

I shake my head. "That's not right. There were pictures. He showed me pictures of people and — "

"We already know who they are and how they're connected. Llewellyn showed you pictures of people he knew you would see to keep you from getting suspicious and looking for another way to get involved."

Huh. I don't know whether to be impressed by Lew's duplicity or to go smother his comatose face with a pillow. "He lied to me."

"To keep you safe."

I laugh. "Amazing how that doesn't make it feel better."

"I'm sorry," Ryan says. "I —"

"What does your family know?" Jonas interrupts. "What have you told them?"

I shrug. "A bunch of big, fat lies. They don't know anything about who Lew really is, or why he's here. They don't even know there's a case."

"It's important that it stays that way."

"You think I want any of them involved in this mess?" I ask. "But come on, how much longer do you think you'll be able to keep this a secret? It's not like Lew can just walk this off and bounce right back into the field, so I'm thinking you're gonna need a new plan."

"The plan is to close our case," Ryan says. "That hasn't changed."

"Okay, but how are you going to do that?"

"We're not at liberty to discuss it with you," Jonas says.

I can't recall the last time I took such an instant dislike to a person. I give him my best intimidating stare. If he's afraid, he hides it well. "You're kind of a prick, aren't you?"

"Well, you're not wrong," Ryan says.

"About him being a prick?" I ask. "I didn't think so."

"There are crooked cops in your father's precinct, and we are having trouble getting what we need to close this case," Ryan says.

"Do you know who these cops are?" I ask.

"We're pretty sure," Ryan says.

"I need you to be more specific."

Jonas sighs in exasperation and walks away. As he disappears around a corner, I indulge in a small smile. Amateur.

"What about Craig Parker?" I ask Ryan.

He tilts his head. "What about him?"

"He claims he's working with you on closing this case. Is he?"

Ryan's jaw works, but he doesn't offer me an answer. Is he trying to decide which lie to tell?

"No," he says finally. "When did he tell you this?"

"Yesterday," I say. At least I think it was yesterday. I really have no idea how long I was asleep. "The day of the shooting. He came by the hospital to talk."

"Did he ask you about the case?"

"He wanted to know what I knew, and I told him I didn't know anything. Then he suggested I stick around the hospital because I'd be safe here," I say. "Apparently, my association with Lew — by the way, he knows Lew's secret identity — has put me in danger."

"We'll keep you safe."

"You mean like how you kept my dad safe?" I push off the wall. "I'm done here."

"Nia," Ryan says as I head back into Lew's room. "Take care of our boy."

"Better me than you," I reply.

I stop just inside the room, all my anger and bravado draining out of me as I look at Lew. God, I'm tired. Who knew exhaustion could be so damn heavy? I shuffle over to the bed and pick up Lew's hand.

"I need you to wake up now," I whisper, rubbing my thumb over his skin. "I don't know what to do, and I need you to tell me, okay? I need you to wake up and tell me what to do. I know I said you didn't get to do that, but you can now. This is your chance. All you have to do is wake up. Just wake up and tell me. Please, Lew. Please, wake up. Wake up, and —"

My plea is cut off by a rush of emotion. I close my eyes to hold back tears and bring his hand to my lips, not moving until someone enters the room. Lowering Lew's hand, I look over my shoulder, expecting Ryan and Jonas, but see a pair of nurses instead.

"We just need to take care of some things," one of them says. "It shouldn't take too long."

I back out of the room, not looking away until I have to. Neither Ryan nor Jonas are lurking in the hallway. Did they disappear back into the void? I walk to my father's room and hover in the doorway. My parents are asleep—Dad in the bed, Mom in the recliner, holding his hand. Unwilling to wake either of them, I retreat to the empty waiting room and flop down on the sofa. My eyes immediately find that lone staple in the wall. Muscle memory, I suppose, from having spent so long staring at it in the past.

Why is it still there? How, in three goddamn years, has no one taken the time to remove it? They hung a framed print of Boston Harbor on the wall but couldn't be bothered to yank out a staple that's serving no purpose whatsoever? It's not like it's a load-bearing staple holding up the entire hospital. No, it's just a stupid sliver of metal stuck where it's not needed and doesn't belong.

Pushing off the couch, I cross the room and wedge a fingernail between the staple and the wall. When that nail breaks, I tear it off, drop it in a nearby trash can, and start over. The staple is pretty determined to stay where it is—probably why it's been there for as long as it has. What does a goddamn staple matter in the grand scheme of things?—but I have nine other nails and nowhere else to be.

Five broken nails later, the staple is in the palm of my hand. The wall doesn't look right without it.

"We're all set in there, if you want to go back."

I look at the nurse on my left. How long has she been standing there? Has she called the nice men with the butterfly nets to come and take me away?

"Thank you," I say.

She nods and walks away. I dump the staple in the trash and return to Lew.

38

THOUGH LEW SURVIVES THE NIGHT, the official word on him remains the same. Critical, but stable. Whatever that means. All I know is that his heart is beating with encouraging regularity. A machine may be helping him breathe, but it's better than him not breathing at all. I will take what I can get.

Susannah shows up mid-morning, walking into the room with a coffee cup in each hand. She looks at Lew as she hands me a cup. "How is he?"

"Critical, but stable. Where's Colin?"

"With your parents. I'm here to relieve you."

I straighten. "Yeah, I'm not leaving."

"Yeah, I figured. Hence the coffee." She shakes her cup. "You know, it wouldn't be the craziest idea ever if you did decide to get some sleep."

"Which is why you brought me coffee."

"Maybe I dosed it with sleeping pills."

"That sounds likely."

Susannah shrugs. "Fine. Maybe it's decaf."

That may be worse. I set the cup aside. "Thanks for thinking of me."

"It was the least I could—"

"Lavinia?" Joyce interrupts.

Both Susannah and I look at her, standing in the doorway.

"Is my dad okay?" I ask.

Joyce nods. "He's doing real well, honey. You just have a visitor downstairs. His name is Josh—"

Josh. "Oh."

He's here. Josh is here. What the hell is he doing here? I may be a little fuzzy on the rules of polite society, but I'm pretty sure after one arranges for one's girlfriend's father to be shot that one doesn't then show up at the hospital.

Except…of course he came. He had to. It's all part of his game.

Which means I have to keep playing, too.

"They can't let him up," Joyce continues, "but—"

"No," I say, shedding my blanket. "It's all right. I'll go down."

How am I going to face him? How am I going to look at him and not murder him where he stands? If I knew how to get into contact with Ryan or Jonas, I could make Josh their problem, but that wouldn't work, would it? If they could arrest him, they would have done it already.

I'll have to do it. Somehow. I'll have to squash down my feelings. Shouldn't be that hard, right? I've been doing it for years.

"Do you want me to go with you?" Susannah asks after Joyce walks away.

I forgot Susannah knows more than most about my miserable little triangle. Maybe I should let her come. Maybe it would help to have someone else around. Maybe I'll be less apt to commit a brutal homicide that way.

"I can ask him to leave, if you want," she says.

"Why would I want—?"

"You spent the night in Lew's room."

I look at him. "You know he's in a coma, right? It's not like we—"

"I know. But you still spent the night here."

"That doesn't mean anything."

"Yeah, Vinnie. It does."

If she's reading that much into me sitting in a chair in a comatose guy's room, then I'm super fortunate she didn't witness that whole me-begging-him-to-wake-up thing.

Susannah shakes her head. "Look, I don't want to fight again — or ever, really — but I think you're lying to yourself and everyone else."

That's only because I am lying to myself and everyone else. But I can't tell her that. I stand. "Noted. I'll see you later."

After checking in on my parents, I take the elevator to the lobby. Josh waits across the room, his phone up to his ear. Another rush of emotion pushes through me. Again, there are tears, but this time only anger is driving them.

Thank God Josh is distracted. I'm going to need a minute.

"Hey," he says when he sees me. He puts his phone in his back pocket and rushes over. "Are you okay? I mean, of course you're not okay, but…how's your dad?"

How dare he ask about my dad? I put my hands in my pockets to keep from throttling him. "What are you doing here?"

"Craig told me what happened," Josh says. "I came as soon as I could. I'm so sorry, Nia. Is he okay?"

Play the game. I have to play the game. "They think he will be. I'm sorry I didn't call you. I didn't…"

"That's all right. Don't even worry about that. You had other things on your mind."

That is true. "Yeah."

Josh looks at me in concern. "When's the last time you ate?"

Thanksgiving dinner, I think. Was there anything after that? I honestly don't remember. I shake my head. "I don't know."

"Why don't we go to the cafeteria? Get some coffee in you, at least. Maybe some food, if there's something that doesn't look too terrible?"

I should go back upstairs. I should be as far away from him as possible. I should have told Susannah the truth so I'd have someone to help me hide his bloody corpse. I glance at the elevator.

"They'll come find you if something happens," Josh says, misinterpreting the look. "You have to take care of yourself, too, Nia."

His false worrying makes me want to beat the ever-living shit out of him. If only I knew how to beat the ever-living shit out of someone.

But I can't do that. I have to make him think everything's fine, that no one suspects him of anything. For my dad.

For Lew.

God, this sucks. I nod. "Okay."

We walk to the cafeteria, and Josh directs me to wait at an empty table while he peruses the options. He returns with two coffee cups and a selection of muffins and pastries. None of it appeals to me, but that's probably because of the creep who bought them.

Josh takes the top off his cup to add sugar. "How's the other guy? Your dad's partner."

Like he doesn't know Lew's name. I reach for the second cup. "Critical, but stable."

"What does that mean?"

I shrug. "I don't know. He's unconscious but not dead?"

"Well...that's good, isn't it?"

"I suppose."

"Have they told you anything about what happened, who's responsible?"

Like he doesn't know that, either. I have to count to ten before answering. "No. No one's saying anything yet."

"Yeah, Craig didn't know anything, either. I'm sure they'll have some answers soon."

I'm sure they already have answers. Lots and lots of answers. Josh has even more answers, but not me. I have no answers. I have nothing but a shaky tower of lies that will collapse if anyone so much as breathes on it.

I hate being so powerless. There's nothing I can do for my dad. There's nothing I can do for Lew. Even when I thought I was helping, I wasn't doing one goddamn thing that made any difference. I can't even hurt the asshole sitting across from me.

Or maybe I can.

Just a little.

Josh pushes the tray closer. "You should eat something. If you don't like any of this, I can —"

"I cheated on you," I blurt. "With Lew. I cheated on you with Lew."

"You...what?"

"Cheated on you. With Lew. It was terrible. Horrible. Not the sex. The sex was...good. Really good. Mind-blowing, even. I had forgotten it could be like that, you know? Not that you're bad at sex or anything — because you're not — but it's just..." I shake my head. "I'm not someone who cheats. I mean, I am because I did, but it was never the intention. I just...I didn't know."

Josh nods slowly, as though still processing everything I've said. "What didn't you know?"

"That I love him. *I* love him. I love *him*." I laugh. I fucking *love* him. "Which is a problem, you know, because he's upstairs, unconscious, in a hospital bed, and no one seems to know when he'll wake up again. *If* he'll wake up again.

"And I can't believe that I'm here again, doing this again. It's not exactly the same; Brian never made it to this point, but still...I was careful — so goddamn careful — with the policy and the not-caring, but here I am. In love with another cop who was shot in the line of duty."

"Nia," Josh says.

"I hate the line of duty. I hate it so fucking much because the people I love keep dying for it and because of it — not that Lew's dead. He's not dead. But he still could die. We're all going to die someday, but he could be dying right now, for all I know. He could be dying right now, and I could be missing it. Again. I could be missing it again. I missed it with Brian. I was here, sitting in that room, waiting, waiting, waiting, and I-I don't know when he died. On the table? In recovery? Somewhere in between? I don't know. I just…They came out to that room and told us, and…and that's it. He was gone. He was just gone, and I missed it."

"Nia."

"I can't do that again."

"Nia, I —"

"You should go." I laugh. "*I* should go. I don't know why I'm still sitting here. Hey — enjoy the baked goods."

I push off from the table and leave the cafeteria. When I get back upstairs, Susannah is alone in the waiting room, flipping through the pages of a magazine she's obviously not reading.

I sit next to her. "I think I'm in love with Lew."

"You think?"

"I know. I know I'm in love with Lew."

Susannah nods and turns another page. I see I have shocked her greatly.

"What about Josh?" she asks.

"I broke up with him," I say. "I didn't actually say the words 'I am breaking up with you', but I did tell him how I cheated on him with Lew, and how I was in love with Lew, and then I left him sitting alone in the cafeteria to go back to Lew, so I'm assuming the message got across."

Susannah closes the magazine and sets it aside. "I think that was the right thing to do."

I stare at the opposite wall. I hope she's right, but there's so much more she doesn't know. That I can't tell her.

"Lew's going to come through this," she says. "You'll see."

I nod. We will see. That much is true.

"What about the other thing?" she asks.

I look at her. "What other thing?"

"I know there's something you're not telling me. You can keep denying it, if you want—I really don't want to fight again—but I know there's something."

I can't tell her the truth. I can't. This case landed both Lew and my dad in the hospital. Craig came by with a warning for a reason. I could be in danger. My family could be in danger. He could have been lying, but can I take that chance?

"There is something. I just...I can't tell you." I wish I could. As useless as wishing is, as much as I hate the very idea of it, I wish I could tell her everything. Just lay it all out there so someone I trusted would be on my side. I drop my head back against the sofa. "I want to tell you—I really do—but I can't. Not yet."

Susannah leans back, eyes narrowing. "Are you okay? *Really* okay?"

I hate this goddamn ceiling. If I never see this ceiling again, it will still be too soon. I sigh. "Yeah. I'm fine."

"Liar."

In spite of everything, I laugh. "Yeah. I know."

39

MY FATHER IS RECOVERING NICELY. All things considered, his wounds were relatively minor. He's looking good—so good, in fact, that the doctors are starting to use phrases such as 'ahead of schedule' and 'going home' when they talk about him.

They are not using those phrases with Lew.

The first day, they wouldn't tell me anything about his condition because I wasn't family. I was someone allowed to sit in his room at all hours of the day and night, but not someone to whom they could release detailed medical information.

Then, on the second day, in a suspiciously altruistic gesture, Ryan spoke to the staff—or maybe flashed his badge—and requested I be included in discussions concerning Lew's health. These conversations are filled with a barrage of medical jargon I can't wrap my brain around. Apparently, I should have spent less time watching the Game Show Network and more time watching *Grey's Anatomy*.

But perhaps it doesn't matter. My concerns really only boil down to one thing: will Lew wake up?

"Give it time," the doctors answer.

And I have nothing but time because living in a hospital waiting for someone to regain consciousness is incredibly dull. Even so, I can't bring myself to leave. Not when I don't know what's going to happen.

I'm not going to miss it. Not again.

Fortunately, my complete shambles of a life offers me the flexibility to do this, so I join my mother in establishing a temporary residence in the hospital. Colin and Susannah, subject to their jobs, go back and forth, bringing us non-cafeteria food and changes of clothing, and Gretchen calls daily to provide me with updates on Rufus's well-being. I haven't heard anything from Josh—not that I expected to—but Craig stops in once a day, under the pretense of checking on his fellow officers.

My only other regular visitors are Jonas and Ryan, but I suspect that's only because I am, more often than not, camped out in Lew's room. They usually come after midnight and are long gone by dawn. I figure they're either vampires or trying to avoid being seen as much as possible. Jonas mostly ignores me, leaving Ryan to inquire about my interactions with Craig. When did I see him last? What did we talk about? The answers always are *yesterday* and *he asked about my dad and whether Lew has woken up.*

Which is true. With the exception of the first post-breakup visit, Josh's name hasn't come up once. I suppose these days I am little more than a way to keep a pulse on what's happening with Lew. If he knew something when they shot him, they need to know when he wakes up.

If he wakes up.

The possibility remains that he won't.

On the fourth day, they remove his breathing tube. That, they tell me, is a good sign. I would think an even better sign would be his eyes opening and his mouth moving, but that has yet to happen. I spend a lot of time at his side, holding his hand, and talking to him about whatever random subject pops into my head. I don't know if he can hear me—some people seem to think so—but if there's a chance he's still in there, I want him to know he's not alone. I want him to hear my voice and follow it back to me. But I don't say that out loud.

Often, anyway.

I've been living in the hospital for about a week when I come back from the bathroom late one night to the sound of men's voices coming from Lew's room. Ryan and Jonas are back. I stop in the hallway. Maybe I should go to my dad's room until they're gone. I'm not in the mood to deal with them tonight.

"We're running out of time," Jonas says.

"I know, but we have nothing," Ryan replies. "We know what Murray's doing, but we can't prove it."

Murray. He means Josh. Maybe I won't go to my dad's room. I silently creep closer, standing to the right of the door to avoid being seen.

"We could arrest him anyway," Jonas says. "Try to get a confession out of him in the room."

"He knows we don't have it. He'll lawyer up and bide his time until we have to release him."

"Well, he must think we have something. Why else would he go after Morgan now, two months after he first appears on the scene?" Jonas says.

"I don't know. That's been bothering me, too."

"Are we certain Murray knew who Morgan was from the beginning?"

Was. Past tense. My hand clenches into a fist. God, I hate that guy.

"According to Nia," Ryan says, "Murray's known about Ellen for a while now."

Ellen. The corner of my mouth curls into a smile. He told the truth.

Jonas scoffs. "She's a glorified dog walker. What does she know?"

I roll my eyes. Prick.

"You should give her more credit," Ryan says. "She's handled all this really well."

"She could be in on it, for all we know."

"Ellen says otherwise. Are you telling me you don't trust him or his gut?"

It takes entirely too long for Jonas to respond. If he doesn't say something soon, I'm going in there and punching him on Lew's behalf.

"Of course I trust him," he answers finally. "Both him and his gut."

"Okay, then."

They fall silent. Is that it? Is that all they're going to discuss? No wonder they don't have enough to take Josh down. If this is how they work, it's amazing they know anything.

"Maybe we should use her," Jonas says next.

"Her?" Ryan asks. "Nia?"

Me?

"Sure. Why not?"

"She's a civilian."

"We've used civilians before."

"Ellen wouldn't like it."

"Then *Ellen* can wake up and tell us so." Jonas sighs. "She's our only play. She has a connection to Murray—"

"She ended things with him."

My eyes narrow. How the hell does Ryan know that?

"It's still more of an in than any of us have," Jonas says. "Plus, that damn Parker kid keeps coming around to talk to her. He wouldn't be doing it unless Murray was sending him."

That damn Parker kid. Jesus, how old is this guy that he's calling a police officer a kid?

"We could exploit that connection. She could wear a wire, and—"

"No," Ryan says.

Fuck this. I step inside the room. "I'll do it."

Both men look at me.

"How long were you listening?" Ryan demands.

I focus on Jonas. "I'll be the bait, wear a wire, whatever. Tell me what you need, and I'll get it for you."

Ryan shakes his head. "You don't have the training."

"Well, you supposedly do, and it doesn't seem to be doing you any good." I walk to Lew's side and take his hand. "If you need bait, I'll be bait. If it wraps up this goddamn thing already, this glorified dog walker will be whatever you want."

"No," Ryan says. "It's too dangerous. Your boyfriend—"

"Ex-boyfriend," I correct. "As you apparently already know."

Ryan stands. All the better to confront me, I suppose. Jonas doesn't move.

"Your *ex*-boyfriend," Ryan says, coming toward me, "put your father in the hospital. He put a field agent in the hospital."

"Gee, thanks for the recap. I had no idea what I've been doing here for the past week."

"Two experienced law enforcement officers ended up with life-threatening injuries because of this guy," Ryan says. "I'm not letting you—"

"Letting me?" I meet him at the foot of the bed, hands on my hips.

He sighs. "Goddammit, Nia. Don't start with this. You can't get involved."

"No? How do you propose to stop me? Because if you think you get to *let* me do anything—"

Something sounding like laughter comes from the bed, quickly turning into coughing and groaning. My head snaps to the right. Lew's awake and looking at me.

Lew.

Awake.

Oh, thank God.

Ryan clears his throat. "We'll, uh…We'll go get a nurse."

As soon as they're gone, I carefully climb up on the edge of the bed and even more carefully place my hands on either side of Lew's face.

"Thank you," I whisper, trying not to burst into tears.

"For…your dad," he says.
I kiss his forehead. "That, too."

40

LEW'S ROOM IS SOON TAKEN over by hospital staff, leaving me to wait in the hall with Ryan and Jonas. Still numb from shock, I stand stupidly, staring at his door, for a moment before turning away.

"I have to tell my parents," I say. Why didn't I think of that before?

Jonas blocks my path. "No. You can't."

"Of course I can."

"No," he repeats. "You can't."

"Nia," Ryan says. "You can't."

I look at him. "I can, and I will. It's not like you'll be able to keep it a secret. People are in and out of this room all damn day. Eventually someone's gonna notice he's awake."

Ryan and Jonas exchange glances. I roll my eyes and try to leave, but Jonas prevents me from getting too far.

"Keep doing that, and you'll be in the hospital next," I warn.

"Are you threatening a federal agent?" he asks.

"Educating an asshole," I reply. "Now get out of my way."

Ryan joins his partner, forming a two-man wall. "Nia, we need to talk about this."

I hate their goddamn good-cop-bad-cop approach to dealing with me. "We really don't."

I move forward, and Ryan holds out his hand to stop me. I wish I knew jiu-jitsu so I could jiu-jitsu their asses. Or whatever one does with jiu-jitsu.

"We really do," he says. "Craig Parker comes here every day to ask you if Llewellyn's woken up yet. We can't let him find out the truth."

"Well, obviously, I won't tell him. Jesus, how stupid do you guys think I am?"

They look at each other again. Forget jiu-jitsu. I'll just straight up kick them in the balls.

"What about your family?" Ryan asks. "What would they tell him?"

They'd have no reason not to tell him everything. They'd seek him out, wanting to share the happy news, because they don't know that they shouldn't.

Because I haven't told them otherwise.

Which means…Which means if I tell my family about Lew, then I have to tell them *everything* about Lew.

I step back.

"There it is," Jonas mutters.

"I'll tell them," I say. "About Craig. About Lew. Everything. They'll understand. They won't let anything slip."

This is not the response for which Jonas was hoping. He gives Ryan a pointed sidelong look and walks away. I am Ryan's problem now.

"You really want to involve them in this?" he asks.

"No, of course not, but…" I sigh. "Lew is family. To my parents, my brother, my roommate. He's family—and he was family even before he almost got himself killed to save my dad. We've all been living and dying with every beep of that goddamn heart monitor. They need to know he's awake, and if that means they have to know other things, too, then I will tell them. Because they need to know."

Ryan looks at me for a long time. Then his gaze is drawn to something behind me. I don't look, but I imagine it's Jonas, shaking his head while holding up a big sign reading 'NO.'

Finally, Ryan sighs. "Do you think they can handle it?"

"Yes. Probably a lot better than I have."

Ryan's kind enough not to offer an opinion on that. "Okay. We'll tell them together."

I make a face. "Yeah, thanks for the offer, but I can tell them on my own."

"This is non-negotiable, Nia. If you want to tell them, I'm going to be in the room when you do."

How non-negotiable is this? Is there a way I can do it without him? Send out a group text, maybe? But no, that's not the way they should find out. I suppose I should let him tag along. They'll have questions I won't be able to answer—especially my dad. Ryan may lie to me, but would he do the same to a fellow law enforcement officer?

"Whatever. Come, if it means that much to you," I say. "But I do the talking. You stand in the corner and be quiet."

"Happily. Just so long as you make them understand they can't tell anyone."

"Happily." I glance at the clock on the wall. "It's almost five now. Colin and Susannah will be here in a couple of hours to check in on their way to work. We can meet them in my father's room and tell everyone at the same time. I know you're usually gone before the sun comes up, but will that work for you?"

Ryan nods. "Yeah."

"Great." I turn back to Lew's room. "See you there."

Lew's still surrounded by nurses and doctors, but I slip inside anyway and wait in the corner. He's the only one who notices, offering me a little wink. At least I think it's a wink. It could have been involuntary. Some kind of trauma-related something instead. God, he looks awful. Pale and tired, and…hurt. Which makes sense, given his condition, but it's hard to see. Finally, everyone withdraws, leaving us alone, and I drag a chair to his bedside.

Lew reaches for me. "You okay?"

He sounds even more exhausted than he looks. I smile as I take his hand. "You're the one in the hospital bed."

"How's Patrick?"

Tears prick at my eyes. I look at our entwined fingers and rub my thumb over his skin. "Alive, thanks to you."

"Hey, hey." He frees his hand and lifts it but doesn't seem to have the strength to do anything more. "Don't cry."

I laugh and lower his hand to the bed. "Don't tell me what to do."

"Nia—"

"Dad's okay. They're talking about sending him home soon, and they're able to do that because of you."

Lew closes his eyes. "All part of the service, ma'am."

"Don't do that. Don't make jokes, okay? I'm trying to thank you."

"You already thanked me."

"I'm sure I'll do it again in the future. That's what you get for saving my dad's life, you know—an endless amount of gratitude from the entire Kelly clan. You're gonna be so sick of us."

Lew manages a weak smile, but his eyes stay closed. "Doubt…that."

When I'm certain he's fallen back to sleep, I lean in to kiss his hand. A moment later, he wakes, something like panic in his eyes.

I cup his cheek. "Hey. You all right?"

He focuses on me and visibly relaxes. "You gonna…be here when I wake up?"

I nod. "You can't get rid of me that easily."

His eyes close again. "Good. That's…good."

This time, he stays asleep. I sit at his side, holding his hand and listening to the heart monitor's steady beeping. He's still out by the time I'm supposed to meet Ryan. I don't want to leave him, but neither do I have much choice. I started this. Now I need to finish it.

"I'll be right back." I stand and kiss Lew's forehead. "Don't go anywhere."

It's after seven by the time I reach my father's room. Ryan is leaning against the wall outside of it. He looks bored, but if I had to guess, I'd say he was just masking some good old-fashioned fear of what I might do next.

He straightens. "You're late."

"And you're annoying. Yet, we soldier on." I jerk my head toward the room. "Are they in there?"

"Yeah."

I walk inside, stopping short when I see my family sitting around the bed. I know I have to do this—they deserve to know the truth—but, God, what if one of them—all of them— gets hurt because of it?

Dad smiles at me. "There you are."

Mom looks up from her knitting. Her eyes gloss over me as she focuses on the man who followed me in. "Who's this, Lavinia?"

Now everyone looks at me. When Ryan closes the door, their expressions change. They know something's going on. Susannah stares, eyes wide. I nod. Yep. Gather 'round, children. It's secret story time.

"Lavinia?" my mother says. "What's wrong? Is Llewellyn all right?"

I glance at Ryan, who lifts an eyebrow in response. The message is clear: this is my last chance to change my mind.

I turn back to my family.

"I have to tell you something," I say. "About Lew."

41

I'M NOT SURE I CAN say my family deals with the news well, but they're at least dealing with it quietly. My revelations about Lew and what's really going on are met with a bunch of bewildered stares…except for my mother.

My mother has a look on her face that I have seen exactly twice in my life. It's a look that inspired a younger, slightly stupider Lavinia to research how to join the witness protection program because staying in her mother's vicinity would only lead to certain death. This is the look Nancy breaks out only when someone has unequivocally fucked up.

I should have seen that coming. Her daughter's boyfriend and her husband's longtime mentee—two men warmly welcomed into her home, into her family—are now suspected of shooting her husband and surrogate son. Where Nancy Kelly is concerned, there is possibly no greater betrayal on this earth than spurning that welcome.

And Josh and Craig think the FBI will be their big problem. Nope. Instead, it will be my mother, lying in wait in some dark alley, armed with nothing but a pair of knitting needles.

Nancy Kelly, vigilante at large.

It's a surprisingly satisfying image, but I'm guessing Ryan would not be so amused. I sit next to my mother and hold her hand as he assures everyone this case will be wrapped up before they know it. When he's finished, everyone looks at me. I'd like to call him out for his lie—they had jack shit two hours ago. I doubt very much anything changed so dramatically in so little time—but I nod.

"It's true," I say. "We just have to let this thing play out and do what we can to keep Craig in the dark. He can't know Lew's awake, or that any of us knows anything."

My dad and Colin nod. They may not have fully processed what's going on, but that request still makes sense. Mom only looks more murderous. Susannah gapes at me, probably wondering how a roommate who never goes anywhere or does anything ends up in this situation.

"Okay," Ryan says then. "I know this is a lot, so I'll give you time to work through it together. We appreciate your cooperation."

He walks out of the room. Wait…that's it? That's all he's going to say? I shoot out of my chair and head for the door.

"Vinnie?" Susannah says. "Where are you—?"

"Be right back," I say. "Promise."

Ryan is already halfway down the hall. I quicken my pace.

"Hey!" I call, and he turns around. Closing the distance between us, I glance over my shoulder to make sure no one followed me. "The point was to tell my family the truth. Not to keep lying to them."

"I didn't lie."

"Really? So, in the last two hours the FBI found a magical cache of evidence proving how Josh is doing whatever he's doing?" Off Ryan's look, I add, "Yeah. I know you can't tie Josh to a crime, and I know you're running out of time to change that."

"If this is about what Jonas said—"

"This is about making sure my dad and Lew didn't get shot for nothing. You need me to help you close your case."

"I need you to stay clear of this," Ryan says. "Ellen would kill me if I let you —"

"*Ellen* can't walk or keep his eyes open for more than twenty minutes at a time. I think you could take him."

Ryan puts his hands on his hips. "What if you get hurt? Or killed? What then? After everything your family has gone through, you're willing to make them suffer through that, too?"

"They'd do it for me."

Ryan stares at the floor. When he lifts his head again, he looks both willing and able to strangle me where I stand. Have I broken him? That took less time than I thought it would.

"I have to check in at the office," he says. "Stay here and keep an eye on your family. Make sure your mother doesn't go after our suspects."

"Picked up on that, did you?"

"Yeah." He reaches into his back pocket, pulls out a business card, and hands it to me. "I'll be back later, but call me if anything happens that I should know about."

I take the card. Look at that. Ryan is his last name. "Okay."

"Nia, I mean it."

"Relax, Special Agent Ryan. Nobody will murder anybody while you're gone. You have my word."

Ryan glowers at me, then walks away.

Colin and Susannah take the day off from work to keep my mother distracted, leaving me to deal with Craig's impending visit on my own. I wander between bedsides and the waiting room, watching the minutes, then hours, tick by. I don't know where he is, nor whether to be relieved or concerned by his absence.

Neither do I have anyone to ask. No one's saying much. Ryan has yet to reappear. Lew is asleep more often than not, and the rest of my family has nothing to say because they still don't know what to even *think* about any of it.

Dad is particularly quiet. I imagine this news has hit him harder than the others. As bad as it is for us, it must be a million times worse for him. For a while, I sit and watch him. When I can't take the devastation on his face anymore, I reach for his hand.

"Dad," I say.

He pulls away. "Not right now, sweetheart. I just need…" He shakes his head. "I'm pretty tired. Why don't you go sit with Llewellyn for a while?"

"Okay."

"Take your mother's car keys with you."

I smile. It's nice we're all on the same page. "Colin confiscated those a while ago."

"Good." Dad looks at me and sighs. "Love you, kid."

I kiss his cheek. "Love you, too."

Lew's awake when I reach his room, looking in consternation at the television. *General Hospital* is playing.

I sit in a chair to his right. "You a fan?"

"No. This is Ryan's idea of a joke."

"Pretty lame joke," I say. "Ryan's here?"

"I am," Ryan says.

I glance over my shoulder to see him walk into the room, holding a coffee cup. He's showered and shaved since this morning, and changed into a different pair of jeans and flannel shirt. Is his entire wardrobe an endless selection of Levis and plaid flannel? Doesn't the FBI have a dress code? He moves to the other side of the room and leans against the wall. Jonas is nowhere to be seen.

"Leave your Doberman at home?" I ask.

Ryan puts down his coffee cup. "He's in the car."

"I hope you cracked a window. I'd hate to have to report you to the authorities."

"I'm sure you would."

"Settle down, you two," Lew says. "Someone turn that damn show off."

I reach for the remote, watching Ryan out of the corner of my eye. The guy hasn't been here once when the sun's been up. He can't just be here for a visit now. Something's happening, maybe. Or about to happen.

"Parker been by yet?" Ryan asks me.

I switch off the television. "Nope. No visit, no call, no text. I'm starting to feel abandoned."

"Parker?" Lew asks. "Craig Parker?"

Ryan nods. "He's been coming by every day since the shooting to—"

"See if they managed to kill me?" Lew finishes.

Ryan smiles. "Yeah."

What the hell is he smiling about? Does he think this is a joke? I stare at him until Lew groans and shifts in bed.

I look at him. "You okay?"

"Yeah," he says. "No."

"Well, which is it?"

"Would you track down a nurse?" Lew says. "I think I need something for the pain."

I glance at the call button, then look between Lew and Ryan. Their faces don't reveal anything. Ironically, this tells me a lot.

I stand. "Sure. Whatever you need."

I leave the room and turn toward the nurses' station but stop just outside the door. Maybe they won't be smart enough to check.

"Is she gone?" Lew asks a moment later.

Dammit. I stay put and glare at Ryan when he pokes his head out into the hall. He looks left and right, not registering my presence at all.

"She's gone," he says, disappearing back inside.

Wait…what just happened? Did I suddenly turn invisible, or does Ryan actually want me to listen in?

"What is it?" Lew asks.

"They want to use Nia."

"Use Nia to do what?"

Lew's tone catches me off guard. He may be bedridden, but he still sounds capable of killing Ryan and anyone else who believes putting me in danger is a good idea.

"You know what," Ryan says. "She has a relationship with both Parker and Murray. They want to—"

"No. Absolutely not."

"If she could get them to confess, we could end this."

"You want her to get a confession?"

"I want her to provoke those two idiots into saying something they shouldn't."

"No. She doesn't have the training."

"She's an expert at provoking people."

"It's not the same."

"I don't like it any more than you do, but—"

"If that were true, you wouldn't have let this idea get this far."

"She wants to do it."

"No. Figure out another way," Lew snaps. "You're not using the woman I love as bait."

The woman he what now?

"She's a potential witness," Ryan says. "You can't be in love with a witness."

"I know, but I am," Lew responds. "Find another way. I can't—"

I walk away before I hear what he can't do. I don't stop walking until I'm on the train, heading toward home.

The woman he loves. That's me, right? I mean, they weren't talking about anyone else, so it has to be me. Which is crazy. Though…when have Lew and I ever done anything that wasn't crazy? The casual observer might think crazy was just our thing. Our brand.

Not that we have a thing, or should have a thing, because that would also be crazy.

But we do have a thing. An unspoken thing, perhaps, but undeniably a thing. The L-word has been uttered by both of us. Maybe not to each other, but that's probably the least important part. Actions speak louder than words, and right now I need a real action.

I need a confession.

I pull out my phone and call Craig.

"Nia? Where are you?" he says when he answers. "I just got to the hospital and you're not here. No one's here. Is everything all right? Is Morgan—?"

"Yeah. Everything's fine," I say. "I just...I just needed to get out of there for a few hours. Take a real shower. See my dog. That kind of thing."

"So Morgan's okay?"

I look out the window and watch the city pass in a blur. He needs a confession. Otherwise, Josh and Craig will get away with everything. I'll be damned if I let that happen.

"Nia?"

I sigh. "Lew's fine. He woke up."

"He did? That's...That's great. How is he?"

"Well, considering I got kicked out so he could have some secret meeting with his FBI buddies, I guess he's doing all right."

"A meeting? Already? About what?"

"I was eavesdropping behind a closed door, but it sounds like there's some pretty damming evidence stashed in Lew's apartment," I lie. "I don't think you'll have to pretend much longer."

"That's...That's good news."

"I'm surprised you don't already know this. Aren't you working with them?"

"Yeah. I must have missed a call," Craig says. "Listen, I've gotta get down there and see what they want me to do. Get home safe, okay?"

"Thanks," I say. "I will."

I get off at the stop nearest to Lew's apartment and walk around the building to his back door. It's locked, and there's still no conveniently located key under a doormat, but I don't necessarily need a key. Pulling a couple of bobby pins from my hair, I set to work.

Once inside, I switch on the overhead light in the kitchen before walking through the apartment to make sure I'm alone. Everything's as neat as ever, so no one's been by to toss the place yet. I end up on the futon in the living room, drumming my fingers on my thighs.

How long will I have to wait? Probably not too long. It was a pretty crappy lie, but they couldn't risk it being true. Not that I know what to do when they show up. Lew was not wrong when he said—

The front door knob rattles. My head snaps toward the sound. Nope. I won't have to wait long at all.

Shit, this was a bad idea.

Heart pounding, I return to the kitchen. Lew would have had his service revolver on him when he was shot, but that can't have been his only weapon, right? I open the drawer where he stashed a gun the other night and groan quietly when I find it empty. Checking to make sure the front door is still closed, I crouch down, pull out my phone, and call Ryan.

"Nia?" he says. "Why are you calling me? Where are you?"

"Are you with Lew?" I ask.

"Yes."

"Is he awake?"

"Yes."

"Great. I did a stupid thing and now I need his gun," I say in a rush. "Ask him where it is."

"What? Where are you? Hold on."

"Nia?" Lew demands then, his voice distorted by speaker phone. "Where are you?"

"Your apartment. Josh, or Craig, or maybe someone who works for them—I don't actually know who—is outside, trying to get in because I may have told a lie about evidence being hidden here, and thankfully, they're way worse at picking locks than I am, because they're still out there and I'm in here and your gun isn't in the drawer. Where is it?"

Lew is quiet for a moment. "Taped under the kitchen sink."

I open the cupboard doors. "Is it loaded?"

"Do you—?"

"Yes, I know how to use a gun!" I whisper harshly as I crane my neck to see. Oh, thank God, it's there. I remove it, then check that it's loaded. It is.

"Just get out of there, Nia."

I move into the living room and put my back against the wall. "Not until I get a confession."

"Goddammit, Nia. Don't—"

I end the call, open the voice recorder app, and set the phone behind the lamp on the milk crate. The lock gives way, and the door slowly opens.

Josh steps inside, closing the door behind him.

I raise the gun. "Looking for something?"

He's startled, but smiles as he raises his hands. "Did you set me up?"

"Maybe."

"How long have you known?"

"Since the FBI came to my house."

He shakes his head. "You said you believed me."

"Guess you're not the only liar around."

"Guess not." He lowers his hands and moves forward.

"I don't think so," I say. "Stay there."

He stops. "Do you even know how to use that thing?"

I fire off a round just past his head. Josh flinches and ducks as the bullet sinks into the wall behind him. He glances over his shoulder, then looks at me.

"I've logged a lot of hours at the range," I say as the back door opens. Shit, shit, shit. Why didn't I lock it? "Don't try me."

"Damn, Nia. You've never been sexier." Josh looks away as someone approaches from the kitchen. "Hello, Craig."

I keep the gun trained on Josh, but Craig Parker slides into the room, coming in on my right. He's probably carrying, but what the hell should I do about it? What *can* I do about it?

I should not have done this. Stupid, stupid Vinnie.

"Heard a gunshot," Craig says. "Thought I should check it out."

"Nia's in a bit of a snit right now," Josh says.

"Fuck you," I reply.

"Where was that offer when we were dating?"

"Do you want me to shoot you now? Because I can, and I will."

"I don't think so," Josh says. "You didn't feed Craig a story so you could shoot us."

"I wouldn't be too sure about that. I am pretty pissed."

"What do you want, Nia?"

"Answers."

"You think I'm going to tell you anything? You're in bed with the FBI. Literally."

Craig laughs. "Were you screwing the fed, Nia?"

"Jealous?"

"Nah. Angry and bitter has never been my type."

Asshole. Swallowing a growl, I transfer the gun to one hand and haul up my shirt to prove I'm not wearing a wire. "The feds don't know I'm here. They think I went home."

"It's not too late to do that," Josh says. "Put down the gun and go."

"Listen to him," Craig says.

I glance at him. "You're going to shut your damn mouth."

"Thought you wanted me to talk."

"Not you. Him." I nod at Josh. "You're just the errand boy."

Josh grins. "I have nothing to say. If you want answers, you'll have to ask your lover."

I shake my head. "The FBI doesn't know anything. Well, that's not true. They know what you're doing and how you're doing it. They just can't prove it."

"So you're here to prove it for them?"

"I'm here because you shot my father."

"I didn't shoot your dad," Josh says.

"Right. You just set him up—set *them* up—so someone else could do it. Who was it? Him?" I jerk my head toward Craig.

Josh shrugs. "I don't know what you're talking about."

"The hell you don't," I say. "Just tell me why. What do you have to lose by telling me?"

"You're kidding, right?"

"The window's closing. I heard them say it today. Whatever you're doing, you're gonna get away with it."

"Give me a call when that happens," Josh says. "We'll meet for coffee, like exes do. Talk about old times."

"Like that time you shot my father?"

"I didn't shoot your father. Or your boyfriend."

"Yet, they're in the hospital, recovering from multiple gunshot wounds."

"Lots of guns in this city."

"And you know which one did this. You know who pulled that trigger," I say. "Maybe you told them to, maybe you didn't—I don't care. I just want the name. Give me that, and maybe I won't shoot you in the face."

Josh smiles. "You do that, Craig will shoot you."

Yep. Craig's carrying. His service revolver is out, held loosely in his hand and angled toward the floor. I scoff. "With his department-issued weapon? Won't it be hard to explain how that happened?"

"Not as hard as you think," Craig says.

"Right. Because you have a whole flotilla of crooked cops at your command." I look at him. "Maybe you're not the errand boy. Maybe you're the one the feds should be investigating. Josh is the puppet, you're pulling the strings?"

Craig's mouth curls into a crooked smile. "You should stop talking, Nia. You say much more, and we won't be able to let you leave."

"I don't want you to let me leave. I want you to tell me the truth." My mouth is so dry. Where the hell are the feds? "Come on. You know you want to. A little bad guy monologue to prove how smart you are? Because you have been smart. Well, except for telling me you were working with the FBI. That was dumb."

He shrugs. "I didn't figure you would talk to the feds. At least not long enough or politely enough for anything to come out of it."

I need a stronger word than 'asshole.' "Figured wrong."

"Didn't get you anywhere, though." Craig shakes his head. "You should have gone home, Nia."

"You shouldn't have shot my father."

"Couldn't be helped."

Couldn't be helped. This...asshole. This bloody, mother-fucking *asshole*. I point the gun at him.

Outside the living room window, something blue with a hint of yellow catches my eye. An FBI blazer, maybe? Oh God, please let it be an FBI blazer. Multiple blazers. With agents in them.

Craig shows zero concern for the threat I pose. "Patrick wasn't the target, if that makes you feel better. He just got in the way."

Strangely, that does not make me feel better. "He got in the way. Of what? You and a big pile of money?"

He smiles. "People have been killed for a lot less."

I smile, too, as I see more blue. And black. About god-damn time. "Well, it's over now. You're done. No more money for you. Nothing more for you but prison. Hey, remind me, Officer Parker—how do cops do in prison?"

"I'm not going to prison."

"Sure you are. You both are."

Josh laughs. "Give it up, Nia. You're outnumbered."

I shake my head. "Plenty of bullets for you both." Glancing at Craig, I add, "I'd be doing you a favor. You know how the force feels about cops who shoot other cops."

"I don't think you have it in you to shoot me," Josh says, stepping forward.

I fire at the floor at his feet.

He jumps back, then grins. "Missed."

I shoot again, this time hitting him in the shin. "No, I didn't."

He drops, howling in pain. I face Craig to find his weapon up and ready. Any time now, FBI. Any fucking time.

"You should have stayed out of this," Craig says.

Doors burst open then, and chaos erupts. I don't know where to look, what to do. There's a shot, maybe two, maybe more, and I am shoved back against the wall. Pain follows. Lots of pain. What the hell? Someone's screaming—is it me? I can't be sure. I slide to the floor and slump on my side. Parts of me seem to be on fire.

That's probably not good.

"Nia," someone says. "Nia, come on, stay with me. Stay awake."

Ryan kneels at my side, easing me onto my back. Someone else is touching my leg and making it hurt more. Do they have to do that?

"Nia." Ryan pats my cheek. "Come on, Nia. Stay with me."

Am I going somewhere? Where am I going? How am I getting there? I really don't think I can walk right now.

"Nia, come on. Stay awake."

Can't. Too tired. My eyelids are so heavy, I can't keep them open anymore. They slide shut, and I fall into darkness.

42

I CAN'T FEEL MY LEG. Did I lose it somewhere? Is it on a walk-about? No, that's dumb. A leg can't walk by itself. It would have to be on a hop-about instead.

Hop-about. That's funny.

A lazy guffaw rolls through my chest, and I open my eyes. Christ—it's that goddamn ceiling again, all stupid and full of holes. Why am I always looking at this stupid ceiling?

I try to sit up, but only my head moves, and only does so enough to see my leg trapped in some sort of torture-contraption-looking thing.

So I didn't lose it. That's good.

"Hey," Lew says. "Hi."

My head drops—why is it so heavy?—but I look to the right. Lew sits in a wheelchair, one arm in a sling. He extends his unbound arm and takes my hand.

Wait…am I in a hospital bed? How did that happen?

"Hi," he says again. "How are you?"

I am…confused. How did I end up here and Lew there?

"What hap…" I giggle, but it comes out as that same slow chuckle. I sound like I'm auditioning for the role of 'adult' in a *Charlie Brown* cartoon. Wah wah wah wah wah. "What…"

"Painkillers," Lew says. "In your IV."

IV? What IV? My arm is just as heavy as my head, but I lift my hand long enough to catch a glimpse of the magical device. Oh. That IV. "Well…whatever it is, it's swell."

"Yeah," he says. "I'm glad you're not hurting."

I'm not. Seems weird. Or not. How the hell do I know how I'm supposed to feel? I don't even know what happened.

"Do you remember what happened?" Lew asks.

Holy shit—is he a mind reader? No, that's stupid. If he was, he'd already know I don't remember. I shake my head, but I'm not sure it actually moves.

"Do you want to go back to sleep?" he asks next.

Do I? "No. Talk to me. Tell me…"

Lew nods. "You went to my apartment. You told Craig a lie about evidence to get him to go there."

"That was dumb."

"Maybe a little."

Craig. Craig Parker. Good guy. No. Bad guy. Very bad guy. There was something I needed to do. What was it?

"Nia? Are you—?"

"He was going to shoot me," I say. Why did I say that? Was he going to shoot me? "Is that right?"

"That's right."

"Did he…Did he shoot me?"

"Twice."

"In the leg?"

"And abdomen."

Oh. "Am I…Will I—?"

"You're going to be fine."

"That's nice." My eyes close. Craig shot me. In Lew's apartment. Where I…My eyes fly open. "I shot Josh."

"I know."

"In the leg. I shot my boyfriend in the leg."

"Ex-boyfriend, as I heard it."

"Right. I shot my ex-boyfriend in the leg."

"That you did."

"I'm a hero amongst women."

"Not just women."

I laugh, the sound causing me to laugh more. "I'm so stoned."

"I know you are."

I hold up my IV hand. At least I think I do. "What did they put in here?"

"Painkillers, sweets. Really good painkillers."

"Thank 'em for me."

"I will." He squeezes my hand. "Sleep now. We'll talk about the rest later."

"No, no sleep," I say. "Tell me the rest."

"Nia—"

"Tell me the rest."

Lew sighs. "We found your phone."

"We? You were there?"

"The FBI found your phone."

Phone. Why is that... "Oh, phone. I recorded—"

"We know. We heard everything that happened."

"Did it...Did it help?"

"It was enough to scare Josh into confessing."

"Really?" God, my eyelids are heavy. Who knew eyelids could be so damn heavy? "But he didn't...say anything, did he?"

"Apparently, he hasn't watched as much *Law & Order* as you have."

Score one for unemployment. I smile. Even my lips are heavy. "What about Craig?"

Lew's face changes. At least I think it does. It could just be the bendy walls surrounding him making me think so.

I look at the IV. "I think I'm stoned. What did they put in here?"

Lew smiles. "Go to sleep, Nia. I'll be here when you wake up."

I nod, my eyes sliding shut. Maybe I'll take a nap. A power nap. Lew will—

"Wait, no!" I look at him. "You can't be here. You should…You should be in bed. Right? Is that right? Why are you here?"

Lew shrugs. "Sit here or sit there. Doesn't matter."

"It doesn't have anything to do with me?"

"God, no. What makes you think that?"

"Must be the drugs."

"Yeah," he says. "Must be."

I squint at his stupidly perfect face. No one should be that pretty. "You said you loved me."

"You heard that, huh?"

"Did you mean it?"

"Very much so."

"Why?"

"Some things can't be explained."

"That's true," I say. "I think…I think I might love you, too."

"You think?"

"Well, I…don't wanna rush into anything."

He nods. "That's probably for the best."

"I'm really glad I didn't smother you."

Lew's head tilts. "What?"

"Nothing. I'm just…glad."

He laughs. "Me, too, sweets. Me, too." He lifts my hand to his lips. "Sleep now. Please?"

My eyes close. "Okay. But only for a little…"

The next time I wake, Susannah is sitting next to the bed, her forehead wrinkling in concentration as she grades homework. Eventually, she glances up and sees me. It looks like she's been crying. Setting the stack of paper to the side, she gathers herself, then stands.

"This?" She gestures to me. "Not cool. Not okay. Do you understand me? Don't you ever do this again, Lavinia Siobhan Kelly. Do you hear me? *Never* again."

I smile. "Okay, mom."

"If you think I'm mad, wait until your actual mother gets here."

My resulting groan is only partially from the pain. "Why is she mad at me? Doesn't she know I was shot?"

"Why do you think she's mad?"

"Dad was shot, Lew was shot. She's not mad at them."

"Nancy said—and I quote—it's their job to put their lives on the line. It's her daughter's job to be smart enough to avoid those situations."

"I didn't know Craig was gonna shoot me. At least tell me she's more pissed at him than me."

Susannah folds her arms across her chest. "You shouldn't joke about this."

"Sorry."

"It's not funny."

"I know."

"Seriously, Vinnie," she says, her eyes glistening, "don't do anything like this again."

"I don't plan on it." I look around the room. It seems larger than it should be with fewer roommates. Some kind of FBI perk, maybe? "Where is Mom anyway?"

"With your dad. He's having some tests done. She'll stop by to yell at you later."

Oh sure. It's okay if she makes jokes. "Where's Lew? Was he here before, or did I just dream that?"

"Yeah, he was here. The nurses finally managed to drag him back to bed and keep him there." Susannah collapses in her chair. "Your boyfriend kept popping his stitches. They convinced him it was, perhaps, not in his best interest to keep doing so."

Good. "He's not my boyfriend."

"Well, he should be."

"Well, he's not."

"Well, whose fault is that?"

I suppress another groan. "Are you really going to harass me about this right now?"

"Considering you're currently confined to that bed, I can't think of a better time to harass you about this."

"This is so unfair."

"No, what's unfair is how powerless we all were to do anything when the FBI told us what you did."

"This is gonna be a thing now, huh?"

"Yeah."

I sigh. "All right. Proceed."

"You said you loved him, Vinnie."

"I also love waffle fries. Should I be in a relationship with waffle fries?"

"I don't see why not. The three of you could be very happy together."

I laugh, then moan. Damn, that hurt. Apparently, I shouldn't find things funny for a while. "Don't make me laugh."

"Then be serious."

"You first."

"Okay." Susannah leans in, resting her elbows on the mattress. "Brian was the love of your life, and losing him hurt like hell. It makes sense you're reluctant to commit to another cop. Especially one who was recently…injured on the job—"

"Injured on the job? Really?"

"—but you love Lew. Maybe even more than you love waffle fries. So, does it matter what he does for work? You know who he is. You know what he does. Do you love him any less?"

No. God help me, I don't.

"Brian's a part of you—he'll always be a part of you—but he doesn't have to be *all* of you. Not anymore. It's okay to love someone else. Even if that someone is a cop."

Is it, though? If Brian was the love of my life, how could I possibly consider moving on? What does that say about me?

"I know I never met Brian," Susannah continues, "but if he loved you—"

"He did."

"Then he wouldn't want you to be miserable and alone, would he?"

"I'm not alone."

"As fine a companion as Rufus is, it's okay to need something more. Some*one* more."

"Well, I don't need Lew."

"Of course not. You're a hardy New England woman who can kill her own spiders," Susannah says, and I roll my eyes. "Just because you don't need him doesn't mean you can't want him."

"How come you get to make jokes?"

"I didn't put myself in mortal danger."

"Kiss ass." I sigh again. "Even if everything you said was true, it doesn't matter what I need or want. The case is done — or Lew's part in it, anyway. He'll be leaving Boston as soon as they release him."

"What makes you think that?"

"There's nothing to keep him here."

"Right. Because the man who sustained multiple life-threatening gunshot wounds, yet dragged himself out of bed against doctors' orders — thus further endangering himself — just so he could be at your side when you woke up, has absolutely nothing keeping him in Boston."

I close my eyes. "Glad we're on the same page."

"You are so full of shit, Vinnie."

"I think they put in a tube for that."

Susannah snorts. "I'm glad to see there's nothing wrong with your head. Except for what was wrong with it before, of course."

"I'm really feeling the love here. I'm so glad I didn't die so I wouldn't miss out on this."

Susannah doesn't say anything. I open my eyes and look at her. She's crying again. Shit.

"You. Don't. Get. To. Make. Jokes," she says. "You almost *died*, Vinnie, and if they hadn't shot…"

"They who?" I ask. "Shot who?"

Susannah shakes her head. "Forget I said anything."

"No. What happened? What don't I know?"

"You should ask Lew. Or Agent Ryan. He could—"

"I'm asking you. What happened?"

"Vinnie—"

"Tell me."

Susannah takes a deep breath. "Craig. They shot Craig."

"The FBI?"

She shrugs. "I guess. I don't…You have to ask Agent Ryan for the details. He was there; I wasn't. All I know is that they stormed in, or whatever, and Craig fired first, so they…They fired back."

My body is completely numb, and it has nothing to do with whatever drugs are in my IV. "Is he…Did he…"

"He's dead, honey. He died."

Nope. *Now* my body's completely numb. I stare at Susannah. "Get Ryan."

43

My mother arrives first.

She stops in the doorway, her face cycling through emotions. Which one will she land upon? Is she really here to yell at me?

"I'm sorry?" I offer.

That seems to tip her over into annoyance. She steps inside. "You could at least try to say that as though you mean it, Lavinia."

"I do mean it. I just…I didn't know what else to do. I didn't want them to get away with it."

"Well." Mom sits in the chair at my bedside. "They didn't."

I guess not.

My mother's eyes are bright with tears as she rubs my good leg through the blanket. "You don't know the utter terror your father and I felt when that…that man came to tell us what happened."

"What man?"

"Agent…Agent Jonas."

I smile at the bitterness in her tone. "Yeah, I don't like him, either."

"Lavinia."

"Sorry. I forgot I don't get to make jokes. Susannah was very clear on that."

Mom arches an eyebrow.

"Sorry," I say again. "Defense mechanism. Well, you know. You raised me."

"I didn't raise you to be reckless."

"No, you raised me to love my family and to do whatever necessary to protect them."

Mom sighs. "I did do that."

"So, really, this is your fault. If you hadn't—"

"Lavinia."

"Sorry." Shifting, I look at my IV. Did they stop putting drugs in there, or is my mother's disapproving glare more powerful than morphine? "How's Dad?"

"Happy his daughter's still alive."

"That's not what I meant, but good to know."

"We will never *not* love you, Lavinia."

"And you would walk into gunfire for me if you had to," I say. "Why shouldn't I do that for you or Dad?"

"You know why. You are our daughter, and—"

"And you are my mother, and he is my father, and Colin is my brother, and Susannah is my sister. Which makes it a little weird that she's marrying my brother, but—"

"Lavinia."

"We can do this all day—and I do mean that because I literally can't get up and leave—but there's no point to it," I say. "It'll always come back to family, and the fact that the Kellys are just…really fucking stupid when it comes to that."

My mother looks down her nose at me. "Language, Lavinia."

"Sorry. But you know I'm right."

"Be that as it may, I would prefer it if you were to not do this again."

"Me, too."

There's a knock on the door, and my mother and I look up to see Colin and Susannah standing in the doorway, my father in a wheelchair in front of them.

"Is it safe?" Colin asks.

Mom sighs. "Don't be ridiculous."

Colin pushes Dad inside the room. "Is Nia grounded?"

"Until she's eighty," Mom says.

I smile. Good *God*, these people are jerks. Must be why I love them so much.

Colin positions Dad next to Mom, then leans in to kiss my cheek. "Hey, Calamity Jane. Glad you're back."

"Glad to be here," I reply. "Have you —?"

"Rufus is fine. Missing you, but he's fine."

I close my eyes. "Good."

"Lavinia?" Mom asks. "Are you —?"

"I'm fine. Just tired." And full of holes, but it's probably best not to bring that up again.

"Why don't you rest?"

"Not until I talk to Ryan." I open my eyes and look for Susannah. She's standing by the door. "Is he coming?"

She nods. "He'll be here."

"Rest until then," Mom suggests.

Because she'll totally want to wake me when he arrives. I shake my head. "I'm okay. Just...somebody talk about something."

"Talk about what?" Colin asks.

"I don't know. Your wedding."

They oblige. I close my eyes, only opening them when their voices trail off. I don't hear much of what they're saying — flower arrangements and caterers aren't exactly thrilling — but the normalcy is nice. Even if we're having this discussion in a hospital room where two of us are recovering from gunshot wounds.

After a while, there's another knock on the door. Ryan has finally arrived, bringing with him a wheelchair-bound Lew. As they enter, I look at Lew, seeing the man and not the agent.

"You shouldn't be here," I say as Ryan parks him at my side.

"I agree with my daughter," my mother adds. "Llewellyn, you can't—"

"Nancy," Lew interrupts. "I want to be here for this."

Mom stares him down until Dad touches her hand. She glances at him, then nods. "If that's what you want."

Lew smiles at her, but the expression fades when he looks back at me. "Nia—"

"Why didn't you tell me about Craig?"

"You were pretty out of it."

"You still should have told me."

"We would have told you," Ryan says. "That was never going to be a secret."

I look at him. "You shot Craig?"

"We had to do it."

"We? How many of you shot Craig?"

"Nia—"

"Why did you shoot him?"

"Well, he did shoot you."

"That gives you the right to shoot him?"

Am I actually upset by this, or am I just upset, and this is how it's coming out? A glance at Lew suggests he thinks it's the latter. Stupid pitying look. I should have smothered him when I had the chance.

"He also shot at us," Ryan says. "An officer returned fire, and Parker was killed. That wasn't how we wanted it to end, Nia. We wanted to bring them both in."

"You...arrested Josh, though."

Ryan smirks. "It wasn't like he could run away."

Right. That. I run my tongue over my teeth. "Am I in trouble?"

Ryan glances at my mother, who is not the least bit amused. "Not with the FBI."

"I should think not," Mom says. "Given how the FBI put her in danger in the first place."

Ryan bows his head slightly. "Yes, we recruited your daughter, Mrs. Kelly, but we would have handled the situation differently had she allowed us the opportunity."

"You could have told me that," I say.

"You could have given me the chance."

Fair enough. "I didn't plan it, okay? It just happened. I was on the train, and I called Craig, and the lie…just came out." I look at my dad. "I didn't want them to get away with it."

Because of that, Craig is dead. Because of me. Because I told him a lie. Because I told the FBI what I had done, knowing full well they would come after me. If I hadn't…It could have ended differently.

It *should* have.

"Nia," Lew says, "this was not your fault."

I look at him. "How very revisionist of you."

"You didn't make Parker or Murray break the law," Ryan says. "You didn't put them on our radar. You didn't make them go after your father or Llewellyn. You didn't make Parker shoot you, or at us."

I pick at my blanket. "I put him in the room."

"He put himself there," Lew says.

His voice has changed, hardened. Is this what Lew the Fed sounds like, or is this some kind of I-pity-the-fool-who-messes-with-my-girl voice? I'm not sure which possibility freaks me out less.

"What happens now?" Susannah asks. "With the case."

Ryan takes a deep breath and exhales slowly. "Nothing. Your part in this is done."

Done? That can't be right. I look at him. "I won't have to…testify or anything?"

"No. That shouldn't be necessary. One suspect is dead, and the other made a full confession."

That still doesn't sound right. "But—"

"Nia," Lew says. "You're clear of this. You all are. We made sure of it."

"As easy as that?" I ask.

He smiles, but the quality of it is...different. "Nothing about this has been easy."

That's for damn sure. "What did you do?"

"What I had to."

"What does that mean? What did you do?"

Lew looks at me for a moment, then glances back at Ryan. "Give us a minute."

Ryan nods and walks out. My mother stands and motions for Colin and Susannah to follow him.

She pushes my father toward the door. "We'll be in the waiting room if you need us, Lavinia."

They already know, then, and I'm guessing they already know I won't like it. I don't want to complain about being the last person to know things—given how much and for how long I kept secrets from them—but this really sucks.

"What did you do?" I ask Lew when we're alone. "What don't you want to tell me?"

"Nia, I..."

"Is it that bad?"

"I don't know how you'll feel about it."

"Tell me, and let's find out."

Lew reaches for my hand. "What are the odds of you letting this go?"

"You really have to ask? I thought you FBI guys were supposed to be smart."

"When have you ever thought the FBI was smart?"

I decline to answer. "Tell me what you did."

"We made a deal. With Josh."

That...doesn't sound good. I take my hand back. "What kind of deal? The kind that ends with him locked in a cell with a key that miraculously goes missing?"

Lew sighs. "The kind that ends with him entering witness protection."

I stare at Lew for a moment, then shake my head. "I'm sorry—it sounded like you said 'witness protection'."

"I did."

"You meant 'maximum-security prison', didn't you?"

"No."

My chest is tight. It feels like I've been shot again. I look down to ensure I'm not gushing blood.

"Nia," Lew says. "I—"

"He gets away with it? He shoots my dad, he shoots you, and he gets away with it? He just gets to walk away into some other life?"

"Yes."

"Why?" I choke out. "Why would you—?"

"He gave us information."

"Information?"

"Names, places—"

"I know what information is," I snap. "What I don't know is what he possibly could have given you to—"

"He was a stepping stone to something bigger," Lew says. "He gave the FBI the names of his employers, and we'll use that information to go after their employers. That's how it works. They don't care what he did if he can help them take down someone bigger. It's not personal to the Bureau."

My eyes fill with tears. "It was supposed to be personal to *you*."

"I know what I told you, but…" Lew looks away.

"But what?" I ask. "You didn't mean it? You were lying to me?"

"That's the job."

"That's the job?" I echo. "That's what you're going to say to me? That's the fucking job?"

"It is."

"It was your job to lie to me."

"It was my job to protect my cover and close my case. I did that."

"By lying to me."

Lew lifts his head. "Yes. I said and did what I had to in order to get the job done."

"Including lie to me."

"Yes."

"Stop doing that. Stop saying it like it doesn't matter, like I was just this…" I gawk at him. What the hell is happening here? "You said you loved me."

"I know what I said."

"No, you said it…You said it when I wasn't in the room. You didn't know I was—"

"We planned it out ahead of time. I knew you were listening. We thought if I said I loved you, you would get us what we needed."

I shake my head. "No. That's not right. This is…wrong. It's—"

"I'm sorry you were hurt. If there had been a way to avoid it, we would have."

"When I woke up, you said—"

"It wasn't over then," Lew says. "It is now."

I can't stay here. I can't just…*lay* here and listen to this…whatever this is. A dream, maybe. Nightmare. A bad reaction to a painkiller. I don't know. Just something not real. It's not real. It can't be real. I have to go. I have to leave. Taking as deep a breath as possible, I push myself up. The pain is immediate, and I cry out as I fall back against the bed.

"Nia, you need to calm down."

"Ha! You need to—"

"You have a gunshot wound in your abdomen and your leg's in traction. You're not going anywhere, so calm down before you injure something else."

I slump back against the pillows. "Get out! Get out, get out, get out!"

A fresh wave of agony swells in my body. I cover my eyes with my arm. Like it'll keep him from seeing me cry. Like he would even care if I am.

"Nia—"

"Go away. Go disappear into some other life, and leave me alone." I look at him. I don't even recognize him anymore. "I never want to see you again."

Lew nods. "You won't."

44

FOR THE FIRST TIME SINCE we met, Lew keeps his word.

I only see him whenever his picture is aired alongside my father's on the local news. Which, granted, is frequently, given the nature of the story, but my family and I tune in for each broadcast anyway to hear the latest on the cop corruption scandal, as the networks like to call it. First is the seemingly endless parade of suspects being brought in for questioning. Later, we watch coverage of Craig's funeral. *Local officer tied to corruption scandal laid to rest today*, the anchor says, followed by shots of people grieving in a cemetery. It's treated almost as an afterthought. It probably doesn't feel that way to Mandy or Craig's parents, though, and the sight of their tears triggers my own.

"Turn it off," I say, and Colin obliges.

Through all the coverage, my name is never uttered. It's never even hinted at. There's not even so much as a mention of an unnamed witness. It's as if I hadn't been involved at all. I guess Ryan was right. My part—*our* part—in this is done.

The world moves on, leaving us to figure out where the hell we go from here.

Colin and Susannah return to work and planning their June wedding. As soon as he is cleared to return to duty, my father is named the Chief of Police because of his years of impeccable service. The higher-ups had been trying to convince him to take the promotion for a long time, but he always turned them down because he liked where he was. I understand why he accepts it now, and it breaks my heart that it happened that way.

It should have been different. But how many times have I said *that* lately?

Mom hangs out in the hospital with me. We play board games and watch soap operas and game shows while carefully not discussing any elephants in the room. When I'm finally allowed out of bed, we take short shuffling walks up and down the corridor while she hovers worriedly behind me, waiting to catch me if I fall.

But I've done as much of that as I can take. It won't happen again.

I am discharged after the New Year on the condition that I stay at my parents' house until I am stronger and more recovered. I agree on the condition that Rufus be allowed to move in as well, but the truth is I'd agree to just about anything that got me out of that hospital. I never want to see those walls or that ceiling ever again. Even though my mother is well aware of that reality, she graciously accepts my terms, and Rufus and I move back home.

My days are spent between my childhood bedroom, the couch, and exciting walks to the end of the driveway and back—always under the watchful eye of whichever family member drew that day's short straw. For some reason, they don't trust me to follow doctors' orders of rest and recuperation. A wise move on their part, honestly, because I am itching to do something—*anything*—that will take my mind off…everything.

Provided I could find that big of a distraction. For some reason, Sudoku isn't cutting it.

One would think it would be easy. One would think, with all the lies and uncertainty, the last thing I'd want to do is focus incessantly on every moment I shared with Lew. Which it is, but apparently, that doesn't matter because Lew is all that's on my mind.

It seems wrong — *impossible*, even — that someone could lie that well for that long. But maybe that's just more evidence of what a terrible spy I am. Not that I want to be good at it. I don't. Not if this is the cost.

I wonder where he is. What he's doing there. Is he under-cover? Is he alive? His luck could have run out; something could have given him away. He could have a bullet in his brain, for all I know.

And I would never know. No one would think to tell me. There would be no reason why they should. There should be no reason why I'd care.

And yet.

Hours turn into days. Days become weeks. I still have no answers, but life continues anyway, slowly returning to some semblance of normal. Or whatever our new baseline for that is. It may sound dramatic, but shouldn't it be? Will any of us ever be the same? I don't see how.

Rufus and I finally move back to our house in March. I walk through the front door and stop at the unfamiliarity of the space. Strange to think I haven't been here since the day my father and Lew were shot.

The house doesn't look as though it's been abandoned for months. Some people stress eat. My mother stress cleans. Everything is neat and dust-free. The refrigerator has been stocked with actual food to make actual meals. I'm not sure why she felt the need to supply the latter, but it'll probably be suffocating in the most well-meaning of ways.

When the front door slams open, I return to the living room to see Susannah and Colin walk in. With luggage.

"What are you doing here?" I ask.

"I'm moving back in," Susannah announces. "Only until the wedding, though. It'll make the wedding night more special."

There's something I'll never be able to unhear. As Susannah bounces up the stairs, I look at Colin. "She wants to make your wedding night special, or she wants to keep an eye on me?"

Colin shrugs. "She's worried."

"And you're cool with this?"

"Maybe she's not the only one who's worried."

Awesome. "Are Mom and Dad moving in, too?"

"I take it you saw the refrigerator."

"I'm not an invalid."

"No one thinks that," Colin says, and I point toward the kitchen, then the stairs. "I swear no one thinks that. You've just been through a lot. We want to make sure you're okay."

By smothering me? "I *am* okay."

"It's all right if you're not."

"Well, I am. Why isn't that okay?"

"It's perfect," Colin says. "I'm glad you're okay. Now give the rest of us time to get there."

It hardly seems fair that after everything I have to give *them* time. I sigh. "You're doing it again."

"Doing what?"

"Rearranging your entire life to revolve around mine. You did it when Brian died, and I didn't care then—I didn't notice—but I care now. You can't keep doing this."

"Caring about you?"

"You're doing more than that, and you know it."

Colin looks at me, not speaking, not moving until Susannah calls his name. Then he nods and carries the rest of the luggage upstairs. I don't know what the nod means. Does he agree with me? Will he back off? Will he make Susannah and my parents ease up? Or will it be just more of the same?

When my parents arrive for dinner a little while later, I have my answer. We all congregate in the kitchen, the four of them trying too hard to act like everything is normal, while I sit at the table with my chin in my hand.

I am holding them back. All of them. How long will I make them live my life and not theirs?

In an attempt to prove that I am absolutely fine, I throw myself back into a routine. Months are spent alternating between shifts at the shelter, wedding planning, and then the shelter again because I still have no life nor any interest in acquiring one. It works out, though, because I'm at Pine Knolls when a German shepherd named King is surrendered. I fall in love with him immediately, and he remains at the shelter only long enough to confirm that he and Rufus get along. Instead of being a crazy cat lady, I shall be a crazy German shepherd lady.

I am also a model maid of honor, which earns me more than my fair share of suspicious glances from Jacqueline. Apparently, she really expected me to ruin everything, but the only thing I've screwed up is the balance of the head table because I lack a date. Any time the subject is broached, Susannah deftly steers her mother on to some other topic. I don't know how much Susannah told her about my situation—I'm guessing not much—but Jacqueline doesn't seem to suspect that a major contributor to my mood and relationship status is the fact that I'm still too damn distracted by thoughts of Lew.

His number is in my phone, but I can't imagine it's in service anymore. The same goes for the number he gave me when I began my faux informant stint. The urge to call them, just to see, is great, but what would I say if he answered? What would I do if he didn't?

Fear of knowing keeps my phone tucked away in my bag while I focus instead on dress fittings, cake tastings, band auditions, and the bridal shower. Though I am the maid of honor, Jacqueline doesn't trust me to put together a proper soiree. She spearheads the planning, and I carry out her orders. It works because she gets the celebration she wants for her daughter, and I get to be distracted a little longer. I don't know what I'll do after the wedding, but I'm coming closer and closer to finding out.

LOVE & OTHER LIES

On our way home from the bridal shower, Susannah says, "I don't know what you have planned for my bachelorette party, but I'm thinking you, me, and a stack of terrible movies."

"Are you saying that because you're also afraid of my party-planning skills?"

"Aww, honey. You can't be afraid of what doesn't exist." She pats my cheek. "So? You in?"

"That sounds like a pretty lame-ass bachelorette party. Are you sure you wouldn't rather go out somewhere? Hit a strip club? Rob a bank? Kill a male escort and bury his body in the desert?"

"Nope. We've had more than enough excitement in this family. I just want a night alone with my best friend."

"One last movie night?"

Susannah rolls her eyes. "This will not be our last movie night. The only way we're ever going to have one last movie night is whatever we decide to watch right before one of us dies of old age," she says. "You're not getting rid of me, Lavinia Kelly. I just may leave your brother at the altar and run away with you instead, *Mrs. Robinson*-style."

"That's a faulty metaphor. Mrs. Robinson didn't do any running away."

"You know what I mean, you pain in the ass."

I smile. "What should I order for food? Pizza, Chinese, or both?"

"Why waste valuable stomach space with food when it can be filled with alcohol instead?"

That's the roommate I know and love. "The bride's wish is my command."

"Great," Susannah says. "I'll make a list."

303

45

THE WEEKEND BEFORE THE WEDDING, Susannah meets her mother in the city for a spa day. They invite me to go along—well, at least Susannah does—but I opt out. Hot rocks, massages, and Jacqueline is not a combination in which I have any interest.

But as I have nothing else to do, I lounge on the couch with a German shepherd on either side of me, flipping through channels, until my phone rings. I glance at it, my blood turning to ice as 'Craig Parker' flashes on the screen. Obviously, Craig isn't calling me, but who the hell does that leave?

My curiosity gets the best of me, and on the third ring, I accept the call. "Hello?"

"Nia?" a woman asks. "It's Mandy."

Shit.

"I'm sorry for calling you like this…on this phone," she says. "I just…I didn't know if you would answer a call from a number you didn't recognize."

Because calling me from her dead boyfriend's phone was a better idea than leaving a voicemail? Maybe it was. It worked, after all. "What do you need, Mandy?"

"I wondered if…I know I don't have the right to ask you anything, but I wondered if we could talk."

"We are talking."

"I meant not over the phone. Maybe we could meet for coffee? Or whatever you want."

What I want is to go back in time and let this damn call go to voicemail. Why didn't I do that in the first place? Why don't I hang up now?

"Please, Nia? I don't have anyone else to talk to about this. You're the only one—"

"I don't want to talk about what happened."

"I don't want to talk about that, either." She sounds as if she's holding back tears. "Please, Nia?"

Maybe she doesn't know everything that happened. My name was kept out of the news reports; I don't know what she might have heard from other sources. Did Ryan and Jonas give her and the Parkers a debrief after the fact? If so, how much of that discussion involved me? How much involved the actual truth?

"I'll meet you anywhere you want," Mandy says. "Name the time and place, and I'll…I'll be there."

Jesus. I look at the dogs, lazily pawing at one another, and sigh. "There's a coffeehouse called Jitters on Newbury Street. I'll meet you there in an hour."

"Thank you, Nia," Mandy says, and I end the call without saying anything else.

I bring both dogs with me to Jitters. Lacey's working, and after she finishes cooing over King, she prepares my usual order. Taking my latte and bagel, I sit at the corner table to wait.

Mandy arrives a few minutes later, looking dazed and miserable. Did I look that awful when Brian died? I probably looked worse. She at least managed to leave the house on her own. I don't even remember how long it took me to do that. She spots me right away and heads over. The dogs look at her eagerly as she sits, but she ignores them.

"Thanks for meeting me," she says.

I gesture to the counter. "Do you want anything? The lattes are good here."

She shakes her head.

"Why don't you tell me, then, why we're meeting for coffee when you don't actually want any coffee?"

She looks out the window for a long time. I feed the dogs pieces of bagel.

"Your boyfriend died," she says. "Brian, I mean. Not Josh."

My first thought had been Lew. Josh didn't even appear on the radar. "Yes. He died."

"He died in the line of duty."

I tilt my head. "Mandy…Craig didn't—"

"They told us. But he died. So did Brian."

I'm pretty sure I know where she's going with this, but I wait for her to say it.

Finally, she looks at me, fresh tears running down her cheeks. "How do you…" She pulls a napkin from the dispenser on the table and dabs at her nose.

Maybe I won't wait for her to say it. "It sucks. For a long time, it just sucks, and then it sucks some more. There are days when you don't want to get out of bed. Days when you can't get out of bed. It will feel like it'll never get better, that you'll just be this…black hole of depression for the rest of your life."

"What do you do?"

"You get through one hour. Just one hour. And then you get through the next. And then the next."

"That's it?"

I shrug. "That's all there is."

"What if…What if an hour's too much?"

"Then make it through a minute, and then another one. Each time you do, you'll know that you've done it. That you can do it," I say. "That's not what you were hoping to hear, but there's no easy fix. No way to avoid it. You just have to go through it."

"How long does it take?"

"There's no answer for that, Mandy. It takes as long as it takes. There are still days when I miss Brian so much I can't breathe. I don't think that will ever change. But if you're lucky…If you're lucky, you learn to live with it."

"That's what you did?"

"That's what I'm doing." I sip my coffee. "Maybe one day I'll figure it out."

Mandy nods as she shreds her napkin into strips. "I'm sorry for what Craig did to your dad. Patrick's a good man. He didn't deserve that."

"No, he didn't." I probably didn't, either, but if she doesn't know I was there, I shouldn't tell her otherwise.

"I'm glad he's all right."

"Yeah. Me, too."

My tone makes Mandy look me in the eye. She pushes off the table. "Thank you for this. I won't bother you again."

She walks away. A nicer, better person would call her back and reassure her that she's not a bother, but unfortunately for her, my mother is at home. Mandy weaves her way out of the restaurant and onto the street, quickly disappearing into the crowd. I stay to finish my coffee.

"Nia."

I look up to see Ryan standing a respectful distance away. My heart stops. What is he doing here? Is Lew all right?

"Do you mind if I sit?" he asks.

Depends on why he's here. "I don't." I nod to the dogs. "They might."

Ryan's eyes cut to the German shepherds, who watch him with interest. He takes a step back.

"Kidding." I gesture to the empty chair. "All yours."

Ryan keeps his eyes on the dogs as he eases into the seat. "Llewellyn's okay."

My chest relaxes. "I didn't ask."

"You didn't have to. I knew it was on your mind."

He's right, of course, but his certainty is irritating. "Maybe you should be working at a carnival somewhere, with mind-reading skills like those."

"It's always nice to see you, too, Nia."

"What do you want?"

"How are you?"

"Really great." I look around the room for Jonas. "Where's your boyfriend?"

"The office. Should I tell him you say hello?"

"Yeah. Be sure to tell him my mother sends her love, too."

Ryan smiles. "Kelly women don't forgive easily, do they?"

"You could have stopped after 'forgive'. What do you want?"

"Maybe I just wanted to say hello."

"Yet, that's the one thing you haven't said." I lean back. "How'd you find me?"

"You know I'm with the FBI, right?"

"You tracking my phone?"

"Not anymore."

"Following me?"

"You don't really go anywhere."

I arch an eyebrow. "How do you know that? You surveilling me?"

"Not exactly."

"What the hell does that mean?"

"It means Llewellyn asked me to keep an eye out for you."

"For me, or on me?" I ask, and Ryan shrugs. Typical. "And because I…what? Deviated from my routine to get a latte, you decided to stalk me through the streets of Boston to make sure I'm okay?"

"Maybe it wasn't the latte that concerned us. Maybe you weren't the one we were following."

I scoff. "You want me to believe you were following Mandy?"

"Is that so far-fetched?"

"Yes. She wasn't involved in what Craig was doing. If you guys think otherwise, then you're even bigger idiots than I thought."

"We'll make a note of your opinion," Ryan says.

"Please do." I sigh. "What do Mandy and Craig's parents know about what happened? What did you tell them?"

"Only what they needed to know."

I laugh. "What they needed to know and what you think they needed to know are probably two very different things."

"Probably."

"Does Mandy know I was there? Does she know I'm the reason—"

"You're not the reason Craig died," Ryan says. "And no, she doesn't know you were involved—at least not from us. We've kept your name out of it. As promised."

More secrets. Lucky me.

"So," he says then. "How are you really, Nia?"

"Never better."

"You don't have to lie to me."

"I'm not lying."

Ryan studies me. I glare back. Whatever he's searching for, I won't give him the satisfaction of backing down.

"Do you remember the day in Llewellyn's apartment when you confronted Parker and Murray?" he asks after a moment.

"Pretty hard to forget that."

"Do you know what Llewellyn did the moment you hung up on him?"

"Something macho that will piss me off?"

"He tried to go to your rescue."

"So I was right."

"You didn't want him to come after you?"

"I wanted the FBI to do their damn job. Lew should have remembered he'd just had major surgery and couldn't get out of bed."

"He didn't forget, Nia. He didn't care."

"Well, then, he's an idiot."

"Maybe." Ryan sighs. "He didn't want to leave you."

"Which is why you're sitting here, and he isn't."

I look at the street, at the people walking past. Where is Lew now? Whose life is he living? What girl is he cozying up to in order to close a case?

"I don't know where he is," Ryan says.

Shit. He really is a mind reader, isn't he? I rip off two more bagel chunks and feed them to the dogs. "I don't recall asking."

"Can we please stop going around in circles here?"

"Doesn't seem like it."

"Nia—"

"What does it matter? What does any of this matter?" I ask. "Lew left. He's gone, and neither you nor I know where he is. That's how much concern he has for—"

"You told him to go. Rather forcefully, if I remember correctly."

"Eavesdropping outside an open door, were you?"

"Learned from a friend."

"I am *not* your friend."

"You think you invented eavesdropping outside of open doors?"

"I think I'm leaving."

I stand, the dogs springing to attention as I bend to pick up their leashes.

"Do you know why Llewellyn wanted that deal?" Ryan asks.

"Oh yeah. He told me. Information. Names and places, because who gives a shit what Josh did if he can help you take down someone else."

"No. That's why the FBI accepted the deal. Did Llewellyn ever tell you why *he* wanted it?"

I straighten. "Same thing, isn't it? Don't you all want what the Bureau tells you you want?"

"Not always. Will you please sit down?"

"Only if you say something super compelling in the next three seconds."

Ryan glances around the room. "Murray had one last bargaining chip. One Llewellyn wouldn't let the Bureau leave on the table."

"Which was?"

"You."

That'll do it. I sit. "Me."

"Murray threatened to expose you, to give your name to people who would have no problem killing a witness to protect their interests."

My stomach lurches, but I fight to control it. If I throw up, Lacey will be pissed. "So I was, like…what? His Get Out of Jail Free card?"

"Something like that. I think he knew that between your father and Llewellyn, they would protect him if it meant keeping you safe."

That makes sense. Clears up a few things, actually. But it doesn't change anything. At least I don't think it does.

"Nia…whatever you may think of the FBI, we don't like it when someone tries to kill one of our agents," Ryan says. "When that happens, our first instinct isn't to cut a deal with the person responsible."

"Why did you?"

"Llewellyn wanted it. He fought for it, to keep you safe. If he hadn't…If he hadn't, I don't know where you'd be right now."

"What, like, I'd be dead?"

"Like, it was either send Murray to witness protection or send you there," Ryan says. "Yours is the life Llewellyn cared about."

"Why didn't he tell me any of this?"

"You did tell him to leave. Screamed it, really."

"He still could have told me. It wasn't like I could go anywhere," I say. "Tell me the truth. I know that goes against your training, but give it a whirl."

"In addition to the information provided by Murray, the Bureau had one more request before they would agree to the deal," Ryan says. "They wanted Llewellyn to accept a special assignment."

"What kind of assignment?"

"The kind that's above my paygrade." Ryan runs his hand through his hair. "All I know is that as soon as he was cleared to be moved, they transferred him to Washington. I haven't seen or heard from him since."

He really doesn't know where Lew is, does he? I just assumed that was a lie, too. Somehow, the truth deflates me even more. "Then how do you know he's okay?"

"I would have heard if he wasn't."

"Are you sure? Maybe that's above your paygrade, too."

"Yeah. I'm sure."

I look at the table. "Is he…Do you think he's undercover somewhere else now?"

"Probably. He's good at his job, Nia. They weren't about to let him go."

I glance up. "Did he want to go? Did he want to leave the FBI?"

"He didn't want to leave *you*," Ryan says. "I don't know what would have happened, but Llewellyn took their deal because it was the only sure way he had to keep you safe."

"Why didn't he tell me that? Why did he let me think…"

I can't finish the sentence, but do I need to? If Ryan overheard our conversation, then he damn well knows what Lew said.

Ryan rests his elbows on the table. "He thought it would be easier if you hated him."

"Easier? For who?"

"You," Ryan says. Before I can protest, he continues. "You know who he is, Nia. You know what his job entails. He would disappear for weeks or months at a time. You would never know where he was or what he was doing there. You would never know if he was okay. You would never know if any given day would be the day someone knocked on your door to tell you—"

"Stop."

"He didn't want to ask you to live like that."

"So he broke my heart instead?"

"He thought it would be better. A clean break. A fresh start."

As if it had been either of those things. I yank a napkin from the dispenser and wipe away my tears. God damn this man for making me cry. At least he has the good sense to keep his mouth shut while I regain some semblance of control.

"Lew can't have wanted you to tell me this," I say when I'm able. "The Bureau can't have wanted you to tell me this, either."

"No."

"Why did you?"

"I don't know. I hadn't planned on it. I guess..." Ryan sighs. "I guess I don't want you to hate him."

"I don't."

"Nia."

"I don't."

It's true. Life would be easier if I did hate him. *Could* hate him. I hate what he did—no doubt about that—and I certainly hate *this*, but not him. Never him.

"Do you think Josh would have done it?" I ask. "Do you think he would have sent people after me?"

"Yes."

No hesitation. Is Ryan right? It feels like this should be one area—possibly the only area—in which he should be trusted. But maybe only a sucker would believe that. I don't suppose there's any way I'll ever know for sure. Maybe that's a sign I need to walk away from this. All of this.

Starting now.

I sigh. "Okay, then."

"Nia—"

"Look, this has been fun, and thank you for all the deep thoughts, but I have to go." I stand, looking down at Ryan. "Let's *not* do this again sometime."

46

I come home to find my grandfather's toolbox open on the kitchen floor and Colin lying on his back, fiddling with something under the sink. The dogs charge into the space after me, stepping on and over him, in their efforts to determine his identity. Colin grunts and curls inward to protect himself as he sits up.

"I appreciate you calling off your mad beasts," he says, attempting to deflect some enthusiastic face licking.

"Any time." I sit at the table. "Hey, whatcha doing?"

"My blushing bride-to-be said the sink was leaking. I'm fixing it."

"Do you know how to fix it? Do you know how to fix *anything*?"

"I'm not just good with a paint brush."

"Look at you go, Mr. Domesticity."

The dogs finally lose interest, and Colin slides back under the sink. "Well, I will be a married man soon."

"Ah yes, domestic bliss in a broken-down loft in the city."

"At least my sink doesn't leak."

I laugh. "Maybe your in-laws will buy you a house."

"They offered. They find my loft to be one step above a cardboard box."

"Maybe you should tell them about the sink," I say, and Colin throws a crumpled paper towel at me. "Did you turn down their very fine and not-at-all judgmental offer?"

"Of course we did. Neither of us want what they want. We'd rather do things in our own way, in our own time."

"What do you want?"

"Something like this. You know—a normal house, nice neighborhood, good schools."

"Good schools? Oh God. Are you planning to breed?"

"Yes, there's the most horrifying way you could have asked that."

"Not really. I could have said—"

"All right, all right. You can stop there," Colin says. "Yes, we want to have kids. Or a kid, at least. We'll see how that one turns out before we decide on any others."

"I can't believe you're going to be boring married people."

"Yeah, we are." Colin grins. "It's gonna be great."

As he returns to his task, I get up to let the dogs into the backyard. Colin rifles through the toolbox, humming a song I don't recognize. He already is a boring married person, isn't he? It's nice, though. I can't remember the last time I knew what I wanted.

Except maybe I can.

I return to my seat at the table. "You should move here."

"You want us to move in with you?"

"No. I'm saying you and Susannah should live here. You and any future spawn you may have."

Colin snorts. "Very nice. Someday, your niece or nephew will know you referred to them as such."

"I'm sure I'll be the one to tell them so," I say. "Seriously, if this is what you want, you should have it. Gram only left it to me because she thought a family would be living here. Not just me and a pair of mildly neurotic German shepherds."

"Who's to say that's not a family?"

"It is. Just not the kind that needs proximity to good schools," I say. "You should do it. So you're ready whenever the time comes."

"We're not kicking you out of your house for children who don't exist."

"You wouldn't be kicking me out of the house."

"No? Where will you be? The loft of squalor?"

Good question. "I don't know yet."

Colin sits up and wipes his hands on a rag. "You don't know yet? What's going on?"

I shrug. "I need a change. Something big. Dramatic. A real life-changing kind of change."

"Uh-huh. What brought this on?"

"What *hasn't* brought this on?"

"Nia, come on."

I put my elbows on the table and lean in. "I saw Ryan today."

Colin stands. "Agent Ryan?"

"The one and only."

"Where'd you see him?"

"I went to Jitters for coffee, and he showed up."

"Was he following you?" Colin glances out the window. "Is the FBI following you?"

"He says not."

"What did he want? Is Lew all right?"

"So he claims, but Ryan also hasn't seen or heard from Lew since he left the hospital."

"But he knew something or said something about Lew, right?" Colin sits across from me. "I mean, you look like you've been watching abused animal commercials all day and had an extra shot of sadness with your latte. If Agent Ryan interrupted your coffee time with idle chatter, I think I'd be looking at Nuclear Nia instead."

Nuclear Nia. It's not my worst nickname ever. "What do you know about the deal Josh made with the feds?"

"Josh told them about his bosses, and they stuck him in witness protection afterward. Why? Was there something else to it?"

"Josh got that deal because he threatened to give my name to scary people who would murder me in my sleep. Or possibly on the street in the middle of the day. The how wasn't mentioned, but—"

"He did *what*?"

I point at Colin. "You can't tell Mom and Dad about this. They've been freaked out enough. We do *not* need to add to their nightmares."

"But it's okay to add to mine?"

"Hey, you asked."

Colin gawks at me. "Oh my God. I can't…You're being serious with this? You're not just screwing with me?"

Is *he* being serious? "If I was trying to screw with you, I'd tell you…I don't know what I would tell you, but it wouldn't be how my ex-boyfriend was plotting to have me killed."

"Holy shit."

"To put it mildly."

"So…" Colin shakes his head. He needs a full minute before he's able to complete his thought. "You're saying Lew made the deal to protect you?"

"Technically, the FBI made the deal because Lew asked them to."

"To protect you."

"Yeah. But they would only do it if Lew accepted some super secret mission-type thing."

"Which is why he left."

I nod. "Ryan said Lew didn't want to leave me."

"But he did it to keep you safe."

"That's the rumor."

"Shit."

Pretty much. "Hence the pensive sad face."

Colin nods. "Okay. What are you gonna do about it?"

"I wasn't aware there was anything I could do about it."

"You want me to believe the woman who single-handedly cracked an uncrackable FBI case with nothing more than sarcasm can't find a way to do something about this?"

"I also had a gun."

"Nia."

"What? What do you want me to do?"

"What do you want?"

Lew. I shrug. "I don't know."

"I think maybe you do."

"It doesn't make any sense to want that. Him."

Colin laughs. "Since when does love make sense?"

"He lied to me from the moment we met. How am I supposed to trust him?"

"Nia, the man almost got himself killed to keep Dad from dying, then gave up everything he wanted to keep you safe," Colin says. "If that doesn't make a guy trustworthy, I don't know what does."

Could it really be that simple? "You don't care how many lies he told?"

"Maybe this is one of those times when actions should speak louder than words."

"Spoken like a guy who has never had trust issues with a partner."

"Spoken like a guy who just found out his sister's last partner would have had her killed if not for the efforts of the guy who should be her partner."

Well, that just rolls off the tongue, doesn't it? I sigh. "What if there wasn't anything real between us? What if it was just circumstance?"

"What if it wasn't just circumstance?" Colin counters. "Look, no one's gonna push you on this, do what you want, but if you think you want Lew in your life, if you think there might have been something real between you—and, for what it's worth, all of us think there definitely was—then don't you owe it to yourself to find out? What else are you gonna do? Spend the rest of your life wondering?"

"Why not? It's worked out so far."

"Has it, though?"

Nope. Not really.

"Perhaps you make a somewhat valid point," I concede. Colin takes a mock bow. "But maybe I can't get past the lies."

"Perfectly valid."

"Maybe I don't want him back at all."

Colin unsuccessfully hides a smile. "Also perfectly valid."

"Maybe I just want to yell at him."

"Go yell at him, then."

"I don't know where he is."

"Go find him."

"I don't know how."

"You'll figure it out." Colin stands and cleans up the mess he's made. Closing the toolbox, he carries it to the back door. As he steps out, the dogs rush into the kitchen. "Raise some hell, Calamity Jane. See what shakes free."

Raise some hell. I could do that. Of course, some might say it's how I ended up in the hospital with a hole in my gut in the first place. My parents would be more than satisfied if I were never to raise anything even remotely resembling hell ever again.

What would I even do? Go to the J. Edgar Hoover Building and start yelling Lew's name in the lobby? What would that get me besides arrested? Maybe I could take a tour, then slip away unnoticed to access employee records kept in some secret, yet easily found and unprotected government computer. I'd have a better chance if I just knocked on every single door of every single residence in the greater D.C. area.

Or...I could do nothing. I have gotten very good at doing nothing over the last few years. What's a few years more? I'll move on eventually, right?

Right.

I go upstairs to my bedroom and close the door. Opening my top dresser drawer, I shove the clothes aside and remove the ring box from the back.

Oh yeah. I'm so good at moving on.

I sit on the end of my bed and turn the box over in my hands. How would Brian have asked? I hate that I never found out, that I never had the chance to say yes. All that time spent talking about what life would be like, and all that's left are two black boxes.

And me. I'm still here.

I didn't have a choice in what happened before, but I have one now.

I don't want to do nothing anymore.

Setting the ring box aside, I pick up my phone and call Ryan.

"Nia?" he says when he answers. "Why are you calling? Are you—?"

"I need your help."

There's a pause on the other end of the line. A long pause.

"You need my help?" he says finally.

"Yes."

"My help?"

I roll my eyes. "Jesus, Ryan, let's not make a big deal out of this. I'm asking for help, not a kidney."

"Yes, but you're asking for *my* help."

"Never mind. I'll—"

"Nia," he interrupts. "Tell me what you need."

47

THE NEXT MORNING, I CATCH the first available flight to Washington D.C.

I take a taxi to the address Ryan texted me late last night. It belongs to an older but well-maintained brownstone building. My heart is racing as I walk up the granite steps to look at the row of names and the corresponding buzzers. 'Morgan' is listed as Apartment 301.

Here goes.

I press the button, holding it down a little longer than strictly necessary, then wait. No response. Which is perfectly fine. It doesn't mean anything. I check the time on my phone. It's only four o'clock. He's probably still at the office. Undercover FBI agents keep regular business hours, right? Of course, for all I know, he could be working some case in California for the next six months.

But as I need to be back in Boston for a rehearsal dinner in a few days, I really have to hope that's not true.

A pair of women exit the building, the second holding open the door for me. I thank her and slip inside. There's an elevator, but I take the stairs to the third floor to burn off some excess anxiety. It doesn't help.

Apartment 301 is located at the end of the hall. I knock and hit the doorbell a few times. Still no answer. Must not be home. I would think I've been annoying and insistent enough that if someone were inside, they would have come to the door by now.

Which leaves me to wait. I could leave and come back later. I could sit in front of the door and try not looking like a loitering stalker. Or I could break into a federal agent's home. Again.

Option number three, it is.

Glancing side to side to ensure I'm alone, I crouch to examine the lock. Looks pretty normal. Could be deceptively so. Like, some kind of spy trap. Maybe it's an electrified lock designed to keep out enemies and impatient, potentially crazy stalkers who hate waiting in halls.

Only one way to find out.

Opening my bag, I extract the package of completely innocuous bobby pins that were definitely not put there for any dubious and possibly illegal activities. I don't need long to gain entrance. If nothing else, my relationship with Lew has done wonders for my lock-picking skills. Locking the door behind me, I put my bag on the sofa and take in the new space.

Lew's apartment is far nicer than the shithole he had in Boston. Which makes sense, as this is supposed to be his actual home and not just a cover. The living area and kitchen is one open room, more modern than the building's exterior would suggest. It's not huge and lavish, but clean and bright and comfortable. Nicely decorated, too. Did it come this way, or did he do it himself? Maybe his girlfriend did it. No — let's not think like that. There is no girlfriend. The apartment came this way.

It also comes with a pretty decent view of an unfamiliar cityscape. I stand at the sliding glass doors which lead onto a small balcony and look at the Washington Monument lurking in the distance.

God, I hope this was the right thing to do.

I wander through the pristine kitchen next. It doesn't look like anyone has ever cooked anything in here. Maybe no one has. Does Lew cook? I honestly don't know. Maybe the freezer is stuffed full of frozen dinners. Would it be a huge invasion of privacy to look? I already broke into the man's house. Does it matter if I sneak a peek at what's in the fridge? Or should I stick to what's in plain sight and limit my transgression as much as possible?

Could I possibly overthink this anymore?

Shaking my head, I continue on with my self-guided tour. The bathroom has a single toothbrush in the holder on the sink and only men's toiletries in the shower. If there is a girlfriend — which there isn't — she doesn't spend nights here. Yet, anyway.

The bedroom is at the end of the hall and is rather stark and spartan compared to the rest of the apartment, which seems to support my no-girlfriend theory. The full-size bed is so neatly made that I have to question whether *anyone* lives here until I see the framed photograph sitting on top of the dresser in the corner.

It's a candid snapshot of a teenaged Lew and an older woman I assume is his mother. Is this how old he was when he lost her? She has her arm around him, and together they're laughing at something the camera didn't capture. They look so damn happy my heart actually aches. He never had anything this personal on display in Boston.

There's just so much I don't know about him.

What the hell am I doing here?

Leaving the bedroom, I grab my bag and head for the exit, but a key sliding into the lock stops me in my tracks. I glance at the balcony. If only I had the ability to fly away, free climb down walls, or vanish into thin air. As I can't do any of those things, I back up to sit on the arm of the couch.

Nothing to do now but own it.

Lew enters, keys in one hand, a stack of mail in the other. My stomach contracts hard upon seeing him, but he doesn't notice me as he sifts through the envelopes. Should I say something, or wait until he sees me? He'll look up eventually, right? Dropping his keys on a nearby table, he turns to close the door.

"Hi," I blurt, then cringe. Hi? That's what my brain comes up with? Stupid brain.

For a moment, Lew doesn't move. Then the door closes and he sets the mail alongside his keys.

He turns to look at me, his face expressionless. "You really need to stop breaking into my apartment."

"You really need to invest in some tougher locks." I stand. "But don't worry about it. This will be the last time."

"Well, sure. Who wants three felony charges on their record?"

"I'm pretty sure it's only a felony if there's an intent to commit a crime, which there isn't, so this would be a misdemeanor at best. Illegal trespass, maybe. And only my first, because you never charged me with anything the first time. Times."

"*Law & Order*?"

"*Veronica Mars*."

Lew nods. "So long as you have a trustworthy source."

"Probably more so than some."

"What are you doing here, if you're not looking to commit a crime?"

I straighten my posture. "I'm here to yell at you."

"Long way to come just to yell at someone."

"Guess you should have stuck around, then."

"You said you never wanted to see me again."

My hands go to my hips. "And you said you were only using me to close your case. Among other things. *Mean* things, by the way, that were said with the express purpose of upsetting me."

A flash of annoyance crosses Lew's face. "Is there anything Ryan didn't tell you?"

"He didn't tell me what this…special assignment of yours is. Apparently, it's above his paygrade."

"You think it's below yours?"

"I am an assistant director."

"Of an animal shelter. In Boston."

I shrug. "What's your title?"

Lew walks into the kitchen and pulls a Jack Daniel's bottle from the cabinet above the fridge. He sets it on the counter and looks at me. "Would you like a glass?"

I walk toward him. "Only if you put whiskey in it."

"Ice?"

"Sure. While you're at it, maybe you can tell me what the hell you were thinking."

His shoulders sag. "I thought I was making things—"

"What? Better? Easier?" I say. "Well, you didn't. Nothing is better. Nothing is easier."

"I'm sorry I—"

"Oh! You're sorry? Well, that's terrific. Everything's fine now because you're sorry."

Lew's mouth quirks. "You weren't kidding about the yelling."

"Hey, you did this, not me. If I want to yell at you, then you're going to stand there and let me."

"Okay."

"Damn right it's okay!" I slam my palms on the countertop. "How could you *do* that, Lew? You made a choice for both of us without even *discussing* it with me!"

"I didn't think there was a need to—"

"There wasn't a need?" I interrupt. "I said I loved you. At least I think I did. There were *a lot* of drugs in my system that day, but I am, like…eighty-five percent sure I said I loved you and you said it back. You said it back, and you made me believe it, and you didn't think there was a need to discuss you leaving me?"

"No."

"Why? Why would you think—?"

"Because of Brian."

"What does Brian have to do with this? How do you even know about him? Is he in my FBI file?" I pull back. "Oh my God, do I have an FBI file?"

"Your father told me," Lew says. "He thought...He thought there might have been something between us, and he wanted me to understand why it might be hard for you. So he told me how Brian died."

"And you took that information and decided leaving me was the thing to do."

"You don't date cops, Nia. Do you remember telling me that? You don't date cops, and I am the worst kind of cop. I couldn't ask you to live like that."

"You left me so I wouldn't spend day after day and night after night wondering if you were dead in a ditch somewhere. Is that right?" I ask, and Lew nods. "Well, guess what, Special Agent Dumbass, I do that anyway. Every goddamn day. Every goddamn night. Ryan showed up at the coffeehouse, and I about jumped out of my skin because I was sure he was there to tell me you were dead.

"It doesn't matter if I'm there and you're here, and you're this...jerk whose face I want to punch because you're still you, and I'm still in love with you.

"I have tried not to be—I mean, I have really tried—all right, maybe not *really* tried, but effort was made. I tried to figure out what the hell my life was supposed to be without you in it, and that went so well that here I am, in Washington D.C., yelling at you while you're standing there like some big, dumb, stupid guy who thought he was making things better when all he did was make things worse."

"Nia—"

"Shut up! I am not done yelling at you yet," I snap. "You ruined *everything*. Do you know that? Do you even care? It's not like I was issue-free before—I wasn't—but you have made it a million times worse. How am I supposed to trust anyone ever again? Forget all the lies you told—"

"I am not the only one who lied to you."

"No, you're just the one I loved." With that, my anger drains out of me. Shit. I shake my head, suddenly struggling to contain tears. "You did this wrong, Lew. You did it all wrong. Maybe you thought you were doing the right thing, but you didn't even give me a chance. You didn't give *us* a chance."

Lew hangs his head, palms planted on the counter as though entirely dependent upon it to stay upright. "Nia—"

"That's it. That's all I wanted to say." I turn away. "I won't break into your apartment again."

"What would you have said?" Lew asks when my hand touches the doorknob. "If I had told you everything and asked you to come with me…What would you have said?"

I look at him as I open the door. "I guess we'll never know."

48

COLIN AND SUSANNAH ARE MARRIED on a gorgeous Saturday in late June. The weather is so nice, I suspect Jacqueline made a deal with some kind of weather-controlling demon to ensure her daughter's wedding day would be picture perfect.

I whisper my theory into the bride's ear before heading down the aisle to the sounds of Pachelbel's *Canon in D Major*. Colin waits at the other end with the biggest grin I have ever seen on his face. All jokes and sarcasm aside, they really do love each other, and the joy is contagious. Which is nice. I have been lacking in the joy department of late.

The ceremony proceeds without incident and contains just enough fluff to keep Jacqueline from feeling cheated. Vows are sworn and rings are exchanged, sealed by a slightly inappropriate-for-church kiss. Official photos are taken both at the church and the Public Garden before the wedding party arrives at the reception.

Soon, I'm sitting alone at the head table, watching couples dance. I sneak a peek at the clock on the wall. How long do I have to stay to keep my departure from being considered rude? I'm looking longingly at the doors when a tuxedo-clad

Lew arrives. My body immediately goes numb. What is he doing here?

I look away quickly, but I can still feel the moment he steps in my direction. Shit, shit, shit — why is he here? And why does he have to be here when I'm wearing this stupid dress?

He stops at my side. I look at him because it would be awkward not to. More awkward. God, he looks good in formal wear. How is it he looks so damn good in everything?

He gestures to the empty chair on my left. "Is this seat taken?"

I'm in trouble. I swallow. "Does it look like it's taken?"

"No, but I didn't know if maybe you had — "

"No," I interrupt. "There's no one."

Lew angles the chair toward me and sits. Leaning forward, he rests his elbows on his thighs. The look in his eyes is entirely too intense. I pick up my champagne flute to have something else on which to focus.

Because if anything can help this situation, it's alcohol.

"Nia — "

"You seem familiar," I say. This is not why he's here, but I'm not ready to hear the real reason yet. Better to banter until I'm more emotionally stable. Or drunk. "Have we met before?"

He straightens. "Not officially. My name is Llewellyn. Llewellyn Morgan."

Someone kill me now. I gulp champagne. "Llewellyn, huh? That's unusual."

"Apparently, it means my mother didn't like me very much."

God, I am a jerk. "Who told you that?"

"This girl I know. I think you'd like her very much."

"I think you're overestimating my tolerance for the human race."

"I'm really not." Lew takes the glass out of my hand and sets it on the table. "Dance with me?"

I'd like to—at least I think I would—but I'm not sure my legs would cooperate. They seem to be nothing but jelly at the moment.

"I don't know if I can."

Lew glances down. "Complications from your injury?"

More like complications from seeing him in formal wear. But I probably shouldn't admit that. At least not yet.

"I already made it down the aisle without falling over. Dancing might be pushing my luck."

Lew holds out his hand. "I won't let anything happen to you."

Oh boy. If my heart pounds any harder, it will burst out of my chest and smack Lew in the face. The image makes me want to laugh, but I fight to smother any giggles and place my hand in his.

He leads me onto the dance floor and draws me close, his free hand going to my waist. There's a moment where I'm pretty sure I'm having an out-of-body experience before we start moving to the music.

I had forgotten how well Lew dances. Do they teach classes at Quantico? Dance Seduction 101? How To Gain Friends And Influence People Through The Waltz, maybe? Or is it God-given talent, just in case the flawless good looks, blue eyes, and washboard abs weren't enough?

Jesus. If I don't get control of myself, I will be nothing more than a quivering blob of hormones before the song's over. What is wrong with me? Why don't I have any restraint around this man?

"You okay?" he asks.

Nope. Definitely not. I concentrate on the little black buttons on his shirt and certainly not on what's underneath said shirt. "Why are you here?"

"I was invited."

"Were you? Or was that your alter ego?"

"Both. Susannah specifically told me so."

"You talked to Susannah?" I ask. "When?"

"Not long after you left my apartment."

"Did you call her, or did she call you?"

"I called her. I thought it might be rude to crash her wedding."

Susannah knew Lew would be coming today and didn't tell me? I am so filling her car with rice later. "Why did you come?"

"I wanted to see you."

I run my hand along Lew's arm. That goddamn Captain America arm. "Why?"

"I wanted to ask you something."

I look at him. "Lew—"

"Just listen for a minute. Okay?"

I nod. One minute can't hurt. Much. Probably.

"I've never been afraid to be in the field—never—and you have to be fearless in the field. You never know which assignment could be your last," he says. "You never know what could give you away, what could get you killed. It's a dangerous job."

"I know that."

"The people I investigate have patterns and habits and things that can be predicted, and while there are details specific to each case—little things to adjust to—a lot of it is remarkably similar. This case was supposed to be like that. And it was. Except for one thing. One unpredictable thing."

My heart beats harder than ever. "If you're calling me a thing—"

"Just listen, okay?" Lew says. "I went to The Howling Sailor that first night—the night we met—because we thought deals might be happening there. When I arrived, there was one open seat at the bar—between a person I couldn't tell you one single thing about, and you. I wasn't hitting on you that night."

"No, I was just your beard."

"And you performed admirably," Lew agrees. "But the moment I sat next to you, the moment I talked to you…That was the moment this stopped being a typical case. Not because of who your father is, or the jerk you decided to date—"

"Oh, very mature."

"—but because of you. You, this...whirling dervish—"

"Do you even know what that is?"

Lew smiles. "Tasmanian Devil?"

"Maybe you should stop with the metaphors."

"You are a force of nature, Nia, the likes of which I have never seen, and I love you."

My stomach feels like a kaleidoscope of butterflies just took flight. "Which is why you left."

"Which is why I left." His fingers grip my waist. "I had to accept their conditions, Nia. I *had* to. It was the only way to keep you safe, and there is nothing I wouldn't do to keep you safe."

Pretty bold claim. I close my eyes and rest my head against his chest.

"I had to go," he continues. "They wanted me in D.C., and I had to go."

"I know."

"But you were right—I did it wrong."

I straighten to look at him. We stop dancing, but he keeps me close.

"I don't ever want you to think I didn't want you—that I *don't* want you—because nothing is further from the truth."

"Then why—?"

"Because your family, your life, everything—it's all in Boston. I couldn't ask you to give that up."

"So you didn't give me the choice at all."

"Nia—"

"Did you ever think that this...whatever this is between us wasn't real? That it was only the circumstances making it feel that way?"

"No." Lew places his hand on my cheek. "I have spent years pretending to be other people, Nia. I know when something's real."

Good line. *Great* line. I nod. "Then you are really stupid."

Lew's hand falls. "What?"

I step back. "You wasted so much time. Time when we could have been together doing…together-type things. I mean, after the hospital stays and the physical therapy and the whatever, of course, but *months*, Lew. We could have had months when we were happy together instead of miserable alone. At least *I* was miserable. Maybe you weren't, but—"

"I was miserable."

"Then why?" I say. "Yeah, my family, my life, everything has always been in Boston, but maybe that's not what I want anymore."

"Maybe?"

I fold my arms across my chest. "Maybe I want to be with you."

"Maybe I want that, too."

"Maybe?"

Lew smiles. "I'm still an FBI agent."

"I know." My arms drop to my sides. "I will never not like you disappearing off the face of the earth for any length of time, but I think…I think I can accept it."

"Can you?"

"I can try. I *will* try," I say. "I may have to adopt more German shepherds to cope with your absences, but…you like dogs, right?"

"*More* German shepherds?"

"Oh, I adopted another dog. King. His name is King."

"I look forward to meeting him," Lew says, "and any other dogs you bring home."

"I wasn't kidding about that."

"Neither am I. Adopt as many as you want. We'll…I don't know. We'll find you a farm somewhere, and you can adopt every homeless dog out there, if it makes you happy."

"It doesn't matter where we are. *You* will make me happy."

"Will I?"

"Well…if you can stop being so stupid all the time."

Lew laughs as he reels me back in. "I'll do my best."

Is this really happening? I grin like an idiot. "That's all I can ask."

"There is one thing I should tell you, though," Lew says.

My heart falls. So close. We were so goddamn close. I resist the urge to cringe. "What?"

"I'm not an undercover agent anymore."

I blink. My fingers curl around his arms. If I'm hurting him, he doesn't show it. "What? Wh-why?"

"Every newspaper and station in the Greater Boston area splashed my picture all over their front pages, broadcasts, and social media," Lew says. "That kind of thing can diminish a deep undercover agent's usefulness."

"Oh." I have never before been so grateful for social media. "So…no more undercover?"

"I can't guarantee it'll never happen again, but it won't be like before," Lew says. "I'm still an FBI agent, though. I still work whatever cases they assign me. I have no control over that."

"Will you still be in danger?"

"Not nearly as much or as often."

"Well, that's…That's good." The champagne has gone straight to my head. Maybe I should sit. "Just…Why are you only telling me this now?"

"At the risk of you yelling at me some more, I wasn't sure it mattered before. Everything you said was true. I left you behind, I didn't give us a chance…" Lew sighs. "I didn't know if you could forgive that, or if you'd just throw cake in my face when you saw me."

I shake my head. "I never waste good cake."

"Thank God for that." Lew's focus slides briefly to the left, then the right. "We seem to have attracted an audience."

Imagine that. I can feel the eyes on my back but decline to look. "That's what you get for doing this here. You could have waited until—"

"No," Lew says. "I couldn't wait anymore."

That is *so* the right answer. "Okay, then." I place my hands on either side of his face. "Let's make this show worth their while."

I pull him down for a kiss. His arms wrap around me and my hands slip to the back of his neck. Someone whistles—Colin, probably—and my cheeks flush. I laugh, turning and ducking my head, but Lew doesn't let me pull away.

"Come to D.C. with me?" he asks in my ear.

"Yes." I look at him, another stupid grin spreading across my face, and laugh again. "God, yes."

This time, our kiss is met with more cheers and whistles. I ignore everything until someone taps my shoulder. When we break apart, I turn in Lew's arms to look at Susannah, Colin close behind her.

"Hi," she says. "Just thought I would mention that this place does have a very nice coat room, if you'd prefer to take your reunion here somewhere less upstaging to the bride."

"You're the one who invited him," I say.

"Yeah? You're welcome." Susannah smiles at Lew. "It's good to see you, Ellie. Glad you could make it."

Lew kisses the top of my head. "Glad to be here. Thanks for the invite."

We separate, however reluctantly, when my parents join the group. Dad shakes Lew's hand before pulling him in for a hug—a sure sign Colin told him everything he wasn't supposed to. I glance at my brother, eyebrow raised, and he shrugs. As soon as Dad backs away, my mother engulfs Lew in a long hug. He periodically nods so she must be telling him something. Thanking him for saving her wayward daughter, probably. When she finally releases him, she steps back, carefully wiping her eyes.

More Kelly relatives start to drift over, while Susannah's side of the family seems bewildered by what's transpiring on the dance floor. Lew's looking a little overwhelmed, and I hide my amusement behind my hand. He sees it anyway and wades through the growing number of spectators to reach me.

"Something funny?" he asks.

"I warned you," I say. "Save one Kelly, you get endless gratitude. Save two? Well, that's a whole new circle of hell."

"I don't think 'hell' is the right word."

"Double hell?"

"Just the opposite." Lew's smiling as he jerks his head toward the chaos. "You sure you want to leave all this behind?"

"More and more." I shrug. "It's D.C. Not the moon. Nothing's being left behind."

"We're really doing this, then?" Lew asks.

"We're really doing this." I take his hand and tug him off the dance floor. "There's just one thing we need to do first."

"Does it involve the coat room?"

"All right, make that two things."

"Nia," Lew says as we exit the ballroom, "where are we going?"

"The grocery store," I answer. "I need rice. A lot of rice."

About The Author

Comprised of Dr Pepper and peanut butter cups, M.J. Fifield is the natural enemy to every food pyramid ever created. When she isn't hoarding pens, notebooks, and medieval weaponry, she occasionally writes novels. M.J. lives with her family in Florida. Visit her online at mjfifield.com.

www.ingramcontent.com/pod-product-compliance
Lightning Source LLC
Chambersburg PA
CBHW072120250626
47159CB00007B/2513